FORMIDABLE AFFAIRS

A LOVE CHRONICLE

ERNEST K. ANING

FORMIDABLE AFFAIRS

ISBN: 978-1-7324573-2-4

ISBN: 978-1-7324573-3-1 (e-book)

Eighty-one Publishing Group.

Manufactured in the United States of America

Thank You's:
My barely functional laptop for hanging on.
My dedicated team for making this story come to life.
Anyone who's had to put up with me talking about this book for the
past few years.
She's here.

Much love!

By Ernest K. Aning

Formidable Affairs
Can I Be Earnest?

SOUNDTRACK NOTE

Each chapter title is drawn from a song. Readers may choose to listen along or create a playlist to accompany the chapters. The music is not required to enjoy the story, but it exists as a companion to the emotional rhythm of the book.

CONTENTS

Contents

Dedicated to a plethora of influential names and distinctive personality types who have inspired this journey.

1

___

CONFESSIONS

The tranquility of the early morning was delightful. The birds had yet to create a stir, and the neighborhood dogs were silent. Oftentimes, Bryce used the morning stillness to meditate over a freshly brewed cup of coffee. Following a sleepless night, he had already completed a light workout at the fitness center of his complex and knocked out several chapters of Dr. Claud Anderson's *PowerNomics: The National Plan to Empower Black America* before the two-hour drive to Kew Gardens Hills where he'd drop off his stepbrother Omari.

Long drives were usually relaxing except for when it involved traveling to New York City, where his even-keeled attitude was put to the test by the sheer lunacy of drivers. On the bright side, the ride back would allow a long overdue conversation with his best friend Priscilla who possessed the listening abilities of a psychologist. She made a living putting out fires Monday through Friday as a manager for a giant telecommunications company. Little did she know her services were to be called upon on her day off.

Dude, you just spent Valentine's weekend with a married woman. Let that sink in. You're being selfish.

"I hear you."

Do you? I mean think about what I'm saying. You were on a getaway to the Poconos with a married woman, and somehow, you're upset? You've allowed your emotions to get the best of you just as she said you would. Let her take her little family vacation to Disney and get over it.

"P., you're missing the point. She spoke openly during the whole drive there about never being in love with him, not wanting to go to Disney, yada, yada. Meanwhile, she's browsing her phone searching for places we can visit. *Ooh, Papi, let's book a trip here, ooh Papi, let's book a trip there.* Besides that, she's on birth control, so, this whole time we've been..."

You've been what? Dude, don't tell me...

"Okay, I won't."

Are you not wearing a condom?

"You just asked me not to tell you."

I lied. Bryce, seriously...

"So, no, I haven't been... well, in the beginning I was, but..."

But what?

"One night we were fooling around, and the condom disappeared."

Disappeared? Like hocus pocus?

"Yes. Disappeared. I knew something was wrong once the sensation felt too good. I reached for my pants to grab another one. That's when she swatted at my hand saying it was pointless."

Pointless? What?

"I know, I know. She claims I have nothing to worry about. She hasn't had sex with her husband in over a year and says she can count her number of partners on one hand. Believe me, I was uncomfortable. I don't want any problems."

Oh boy.

"You remember Kristen, right?"

Yes.

"She was the only person I've ever had unprotected sex with. So, of course it was a little nerve-wracking."

You guys are a hot mess.

"P., do you honestly think she's trying to get pregnant? I mean, c'mon. There's no way in the world she'd sabotage her life. Come to think of it, the both of you share quite a few things in common."

What we're not gonna do, sir, is compare. Carry on...

"By that I mean she's very calculated. Every minute of her day is broken down into the tiniest of fractions. She's carved out this extraordinary life and isn't about to blow it..."

Sounds to me like that's all she's been doing.

"Clever."

Sorry. I couldn't help myself.

"Like I was saying, she's not gonna give up that lifestyle. She's currently in pursuit of her master's; she loves her job and has made it perfectly clear that she's not looking to leave her marriage. That's my beef."

Aah, so, she wants her cake and to eat it too. Hmm. Okay, so, you've fallen for her, hook, line, and sinker, and it's eating away at you.

"I don't know if I've exactly fallen for her, but why couldn't she focus on her husband? Why is she spending her day texting me and asking that I come over?"

Wait, you're going to her house? Bry...

"Relax. I'm only there when he's out of town, which is usually once or twice a week for work."

What does he do?

"He's a managing director or something. Anyway, she can't leave her daughter home alone, so she hits me up after putting her to bed."

[car horns blaring]

Bryce, what in the world are you doing? Does the thought ever occur that the neighbors are watching? Hello? Are you still there? Don't get quiet now.

"Hold on... in fact, let me call you back. Omari's on the other line."

Omari was in the process of recording his vocals at the in-home studio of John, his rap partner and audio engineering class-mate who went by the rap name "Brixx Dinero." The duo was in the process of touching up their demo and Omari wanted Bryce's opinion on a verse he had begun to write on their earlier drive.

"Bro, try and limit the gun references. You don't live that type of lifestyle."

So, you're basically telling me to rap like KRS-One...

"You say it like it's a bad thing. KRS is a living legend. It's called constructive criticism. You'd better get used to it. I already said you were good, but I want you to understand that words have vibrational power. Don't let your mouth write checks that your butt can't cash. You're talented enough to flip metaphors and punchlines without promoting violence."

Mentorship was a serious job.

Bryce took a hold of the role of big brother immediately after his father, Dale, popped the question to Terri, Omari's mother, several years ago. Though he was cut from a similar cloth as his dad, Bryce, a product of the 1980s and '90s when mobsters and drug dealers were all the rage, understood Omari's attraction to fast living.

When conveying personal life experiences, he spoke Omari's language using the latest slang phrases and idioms. The siblings bonded over sneaker culture, sharing an almost identical Air Jordan collection, but the core of their union was hip hop. Omari was hooked to Bryce's stories of when he formed a three-man group in college known as "Nappy Mobb" or the times he crossed paths with notable rap artists working at an independent record label. Music had the uncanny ability to connect souls.

Their living arrangement came as a surprise, but Omari adjusted well, splitting time between his aunt's home and Bryce's. Listed in a red permanent marker on a whiteboard against his kitchen wall were a set of house rules:

1. Shoes off at the front of the door.
2. No smoking indoors.
3. No unsuspecting company.
4. Wash your own dishes and take out trash.
5. Do not urinate on the toilet seat/bathroom floor.

Bryce maintained an orderly home and wished to keep it that way.

"Bro, I forgot to mention this earlier, stop rinsing out those red plastic cups. There's about four of them sitting in the dish rack. Also, the microwave cover is there for a reason. Use it. The inside of my microwave shouldn't be that filthy. And chill out splattering toothpaste spit particles all over my bathroom mirror."

They spent the next thirty minutes going over which single to push for the group's five-track EP demo. Afterward, Bryce returned to Priscilla's call. She couldn't wait to tear into him some more.

So, let's bring it all the way back. How in the heck are you getting in and out of her house unnoticed?

"There's a back entrance. It's like a basement door which faces the back of the homes across from theirs."

Oh Lord. Have you been in her bedroom? Tell me you haven't.

"Then I'd be lying..."

Bryce.

"What? She showed me around the house."

You know exactly what I mean. Have y'all done anything in there?

He knew the answer to the question, but embarrassment swarmed over him, like dark clouds looming before a summer storm.

Don't tell me the cat has got your tongue. Meow. I'm speaking cat, does that work for you? Hello?

"Listen, it's not as bad as you think. I'm about to cross the Verrazano. I'll be home in another forty-five minutes."

Well, brace yourself. I'm gonna drill you with questions all day tomorrow. You're lucky Val and JuJu are here. Oh, before I forget, you missed JuJu's game this morning. He was raking every pitch.

"I thought the season started next weekend."

Nope, it was today. He had three hits. Isn't that called something?

"It's called a 'good day,'" Bryce snapped.

No, silly. When someone has three hits in a game, isn't there a term for that?

"Well, no. If he would've had four hits, say a single, double, triple, and a home run that's called a cycle. But JuJu's a slacker, so, there's that."

[laughter]

Don't talk about my JuJu like that. And who? A re-cycle?

"A cycle, P. Why do you act like you know absolutely nothing about baseball?"

Well, I only watch when he plays. Cut me some slack, jeez.

"Bye," he replied dejectedly.

The day was still young and unseasonably mild. Bryce's alpine white BMW 535i cruised down Route 9 glistening under the sun as The Whispers played on. He couldn't remember the last time this jam played, but it brought back fond memories of those Saturday afternoons when he and his mother danced freely in the middle of their living room floor. Undeniably, this was her delicate way of saying hello. His opinion grew stronger at the song's completion when the afternoon host proceeded.

Haven't heard that in a while. The Whispers, with "Keep on Lovin' Me." Can't get enough of that feel good music on what has shaped up to be a beautiful afternoon. Speaking of The Whispers, they'll be in town on Mother's Day weekend along with Stephanie Mills. Tickets are on sale...

An empty house was on the horizon with his best friend hosting family and Omari away for a few days. The free time would take getting used to, but without a hot date on the itinerary and Julissa, his "best kept *married* secret," somewhat of an afterthought, it was best to take advantage of some much-needed

R&R. He picked up a few groceries along the way in anticipation of an evening filled with light internet browsing, the sweet sounds of Sade, and a gratifying home-cooked meal.

An adorable elderly couple acknowledged him as he pulled into his driveway. The imagery allowed him a moment to envision replicating a similar stroll with the future Mrs. Taylor. He approached the trunk of his car to retrieve the grocery bags when his neighbor appeared with two enthusiastic young boys on bikes awaiting instructions.

"Wait," she yelled with a pronounced tone. "Three, two, one... go!" The boys proceeded downhill on their bikes while Bryce fought through an enormous sun glare to watch them. The neighbor looked close to average height dressed in a pair of orchid biker shorts and a white hoodie with embroidered letters. Catching his immediate attention, however, was her figure. From his vantage point she was slim up top and bottom heavy. As his good friend Gucci often phrased, "She was thicker than a cold jar of peanut butter."

He spotted the unidentified neighbor from time-to-time, but never quite like this. Preoccupied in thought, he subconsciously undressed the woman, picturing her bent over the hood of one of the parked cars while stroking her from behind. In the same sequence, he thought back to two nights ago when his face was doused in Julissa's juices after she experienced a euphoria of orgasms. Suddenly, the representation of the cute elderly couple vanished into obscurity.

Lizzy, his four-year-old calico, added a faint crackle to her purr stretching from a routine afternoon nap. Bryce placed the groceries onto the kitchen island and opened the house blinds to allow the sunlight to pour in. He rinsed off the fruits and vegetables and peered out the kitchen window while chatting with Gucci.

"So, I tell her to scream into the pillow to keep from waking up her daughter who's in the room next door."

You had her creamin' and screamin'?

"It was complete mayhem. I can't get down with the whole sex thing with kids in the house."

It'll kill your whole drive, like a fucked-up transmission.

He spotted the neighbor walking uphill—this time on his side of the street—with her boys leading the way on their bikes. He rinsed off his hands and proceeded to the coat closet still engaged in the high-spirited conversation.

"I didn't even tell you about ole girl from across the street. She's usually in and out of her car with little to no eye contact. I get the impression she's involved, but dawg, she damn near had me in a comatose earlier."

Word? She's stacked like that?

"Lord have mercy. Stay on the line, I'm gonna put you on mute for a sec."

Don't put me on mute, Playboy, put me on speaker so I can holla.

"What'chu gonna say to her?"

Hey, babygirl, you took my man's breath away, but don't worry, I'll do all the talking from here.

"All right, Billy Dee Williams. Hold on."

Hoping to seize the opportunity, Bryce slid on a pair of Omari's slide sandals—about two sizes too small—thinking he could grab her attention with a neighborly wave. His plan was to act out an imaginary phone conversation as she approached hoping to get a better view of her face. The conspicuous act wouldn't pay off. His efforts were rewarded with a half-hearted smile, as if she were fully prepared for his foolishness.

What more could he have wanted? Did he truly expect her to leave her kids stranded—enter his home, clear off the kitchen island and ride him like a crazed woman on a mechanical bull?

Yes.

The one thing shielding Bryce's ego from the slight blow was his admirable knack for taking the glass half-full approach. Women tend to court when there is interest, and she chose to circle back in front of his home when she could've walked *anywhere* on the complex. Now he was left to wonder if her methodical walk was a tease.

You're using up my weekend minutes, kid. What did she say?

"Weekend minutes? What'chu got, a Nokia phone?"

Time is money, but you messin' with these honeys.

"I've got nothing. She had RBF."

Don't worry about it. You win some, you lose some, but you're still undefeated in these streets. Aye, my hand's been itching all day. Me and the old lady are headed out to A.C. in a couple of hours to try my luck. You should come through. We can catch the games and you can redeem yourself there.

Gucci tried to stay youthful keeping up with the latest fashion trends, but his rhetoric proved otherwise, often sounding like a typecast pimp from the Blaxploitation films of the 1970s.

Reggie "Gucci" Grant was nearly ten years older than Bryce—given the nickname "Gucci" by friends due to his affection for designer clothes and the two Gs in his name matching the Italian brand's fabled logo. The friends met at an old Jersey City office building where he worked as a building maintenance technician. His constant praises of Bryce's array of Avirex leather jackets and their discussions about women led to a rapid brotherhood. Since then, Gucci had become a proud business owner operating a Painting & General Contracting company with his brother Junior.

Ideally, a drive out to Atlantic City would've grabbed Bryce's attention. It seemed like ages since they last hung out. Who could forget that eventful summer evening where cash bets were placed amongst Dale, Gucci, and Junior on who would leave the bowling alley with the highest score. The night was full of trash talk, empty threats, and hurt feelings. However, with Lizzy appearing more clingy than usual, he stuck to his original plan and provided some quality time.

The television remained muted on the NCAA men's basketball tournament while the calming guitar licks from Sade's

"Cherish the Day" filled the room. His furry friend used the time to catch up on some early evening grooming as Bryce proudly shared a few pictures of a smothered chicken and gravy dish on his Facebook page. He was enamored by home-cooked meals starting when his parents sat at the dinner table to discuss their day, and it continued long after when an ex-girlfriend consistently spoiled his taste buds.

He suspected his stomach would loathe and punish him for his breakup with Kristen, a young lady who could've easily carried the Taylor last name. She was amazing in every sense of the word. It was true, sometimes you didn't know a good thing until it was gone.

There are billions of humans on the planet. Why, in my twenties, would I subject myself to one person? In no other area of life are we asked to commit to one thing except for when it involves settling down. I should be able to interact with any woman breathing.

An excerpt from an old journal.

Bryce owned every thought and move he made and refused to classify his sentiments as having "commitment issues." *I don't have commitment issues, I have options, and I am not giving them up to appease anyone.*

Another excerpt read.

He was once young, brash, impassive, and couldn't tell the difference from a tingling butterfly sensation from an upset stomach. In an age where women had become angry and bold, he now wondered if his former submissive southern belle could ever be replaced.

The one-time barefaced Virginia Commonwealth University graduate found himself in a challenging position upon his return to the tristate area. To begin with, he'd rummage through the classified ads of every newspaper in town for an inexpensive apartment closer to lower Manhattan enabling an easier work commute. It was also to avoid an overstay at his father's home who was seriously contemplating a move back south. After a long, tiresome search, Bryce settled for a cheap efficiency in a troubling Northern New Jersey neighborhood fifteen minutes from Manhattan's Financial District. It wasn't exactly Taj Mahal, but it was a start.

Courtesy of his new employer, he was invited to a standing-room-only event headlined by several new music acts—namely, Alicia Keys, who was months away from releasing her debut album. It is where he met Kristen in attendance with one of her best friends. Their interaction got off to a rocky start.

She was full of joy, flailing her arms, dancing madly as the DJ played a few top chart hits before the acts took center stage. Refusing to take a cue from the subdued growing audience, Kristen repeatedly violated his space—igniting his fury. Spilling a drink onto his new two-hundred-dollar designer loafers was the straw that broke the camel's back. Through his experiences, it was always the attractive women who got away with such careless behavior. Not that evening. She needed to be held accountable even if he appeared smitten by her glowing smile, tongue-wagging seductive dance moves, and smooth mahogany skin.

In a surprising turn of events, Kristen showed empathy, helping him wipe his shoes, going as far as to comfortably inter-lock arms as she apologized profusely. Her physical contact was unusual, but nothing compared to the use of the word "sir" through their exchange. A redeeming character trait for their probable tumultuous night. He had gotten used to the term "young man" which produced a sense of inferiority even when used as a term of endearment. How could this beautiful stranger have the wherewithal to address him by the desired proper noun?

Father, what are you up to and why did you send this beautiful woman my way? I know she isn't from around here. Why put her in my path only to have my heart broken? What is it that you want me to see?

His impetuous thoughts were jotted down on a miniature notepad only minutes after the fallout.

It was an unfair assessment, but if anyone could break down the character distinctions between northerner and southerner, it was Bryce. The New York/New Jersey tristate area grew to be his resting place, but during his most impressionable years, he traveled through the southeast long enough to confidently know the difference. Following the event, predictably he picked up Kristen's slight southern accent through a course of conversations at a pizzeria where her girlfriend unexpectedly played third wheel. Amazingly, their connection was instant.

During his struggles with professional setbacks, Kristen took great care of him, opening her one-bedroom apartment as a secondary home when the excitement for his own died. He lacked an awareness of the usual calamities found in low-income housing. The unpredictability of hot water, unruly tenants, or a rapacious landlord who only showed face at the first of the month. Added to his troubles was an unclear career path. The corporate finance major wanted to dip his toe into the music industry before diving headfirst into a dull, conventional profession. Outside of athletics, nothing was more satisfying than music. The revelation sparked a heart-to-heart conversation with his oldest maternal cousin Anton, who in the early '90s worked at a local radio station and stayed in contact with several industry executives.

In the meantime, Bryce relied on his eloquent writing abilities packaging handwritten testimonials along with a shallow résumé to persuade the likes of Def Jam Records and others. His hope was to work in Artist Development. Months passed without traction. Consequently, his written masterpieces went unanswered, likely crumbled and used for a quick game of office H.O.R.S.E. Thanks to the workings of his manager at Tower Records—Bryce's first post-college job where he worked as a supervisor—he landed an internship at a small-time independent label working evenings in their print media & marketing department. In time, the internship turned into a full-time role, and the salary was enough to resign from his primary position. Almost immediately, his relationship with Kristen was tested.

He never expected to become the casualty of a layoff only eight months after the independent record label merger. Then the tragic events of September 11 took place, suppressing city-wide hiring along with a mass exodus of businesses. The vicious cycle led to a high-expected anxiety. He latched on to a temp agency accepting one-day assignments and eventually a mail courier gig dodging the bedlam of yellow cabs on a ten-speed bicycle. With the city at risk and security jobs at an all-time high, he got licensed and worked weekends at an office building minutes from the old Twin Towers. The development caused great shame. A college graduate who triumphantly overcame one of life's greatest challenges—growing up without his mother—had now succumbed to complete career pandemonium.

Kristen's lone plight of leaving the friendly confines of rural Georgia for the belligerent tristate area where, she too, quietly struggled, meant little. As a form of retribution, Bryce often distanced himself using his apartment's rooftop as a retreat to look out at the Manhattan skyline. It is where he talked to his mother in prayer. Coming from a jovial two-parent home, he understood all too well the importance of communication, but still scampered from Kristen like a fleeing toddler. Rather than embrace her unbridled love, he focused on his financial crisis and devised an escape plan after only a year and a half of dating.

As an ultra-competitor, how would he measure up to his peers? The constant badgering of his consciousness nudged him. As a way out of a seemingly pressure-free relationship, Bryce erroneously attacked Kristen's character, falsifying stories and wrongfully accusing her of "thinking" she was better. In this agonizing mental war, he created hypothetical scenarios to stay ahead rather than allow her to naturally react to his sudden decline.

Would she stick with me through adversity? What if she were to come across another man with his affairs in order, would she be easily persuaded to step out on me? What if she didn't want to be tied down in someone else's personal hell?

His insecurities blocked him from mirroring Kristen's love, generosity, and compassion. The one person who would've understood his struggles better than anyone. A woman who exemplified similar qualities of his own mother.

Kristen's landline number was endlessly answered by a taxi dispatch service, her email account deactivated, and her cell phone instantly directed calls to the annoying automated voice mailbox. Punching her name on Facebook produced considerable results, but of the large group of Kristen Davises appearing, her picture was not one of them. The final resort came when he drove to her old apartment in search of a baby blue Honda Civic which she commonly parked at the beginning of the block. Bryce couldn't help but chuckle thinking back on her mini temper tantrums whenever the spot was taken. In retrospect, one could easily accuse him of stalking, but his intentions were pure. He was only looking to make up with a love he carelessly allowed to flee.

Inevitably, they would bump into each other over time because that is how all romantic stories ended, right? Besides, he walked into old acquaintances regularly. Where had she disappeared and why had it become so hard to atone for his actions? All he wanted was to get down on one knee, pour out his soul, and smother her flawless skin with soft kisses. If anyone deserved it, it was her. Sadly, with Kristen's location undetermined, he was now resigned to desperation.

In his inbox was an ancient chain email from Dominique, Kristen's long-time girlfriend. It was his last hope.

To: <Dominique H>
From: <Bryce Taylor>
Subject: (no subject)

Hey Dominique,
Long time, no hear. Hope all is well. Crossing my fingers that this email reaches you. I've tried to contact Kristen, but no luck so far. Is she still at (908) 555-0411? Do you guys still communicate? Would love to chat. Anyway, hope to hear from you soon.
-BAT-

Minutes passed without a bounced email rejection. That was fantastic news.

He wasn't seeking a relationship. The magnitude of hurt was enormous on the other end and there would be a ton of ground to cover. Besides, Bryce adapted quite nicely to the Hugh Heffner lifestyle. Only a miracle could steer him away from that. Reconnecting was about proving his growth with a little "hey, look at me now" mixed in. He was proud of the man he'd become; the man he intended to be during their abbreviated time, and the man she confidently *knew* him as all along when ego besieged him.

2

DAZED AND CONFUSED

A severe head cold and the stress of a hectic morning fogged Bryce's judgment—leading him to recklessly gulp scalding tea. His tongue burned, and his anger soared. To make matters worse, his skull throbbed, and the ingrown hairs along his jaw itched mercilessly, making him question why he'd ever grown this beard. He needed to pull himself together before the day unraveled completely.

He dapped his mouth thinking of ways to address the inflaming itch when suddenly a lightbulb went off. In his desk underneath several coffee-stained documents was a shabby bristle brush. Voilà! A viable backup plan was in order, possibly saving his morning from complete ruination. He pursed his lips to blow off the desk residue and applied soothing strokes against his smooth, dark skin. His weary eyes closed through each motion. The feeling was heavenly. To some, the perception of a man carrying an extra brush could be seen as frivolous—even vain, but it was his readiness for any given situation upstaging the misconception.

His daily workload would prohibit most from stepping away from their desk, but Bryce found ways to circumvent his share of tasks. *If smokers can take unlimited breaks, why couldn't non-smok-*

ers? he often wondered. On his desk was a toy buzzer. When pressed, it resoundingly announced, "break!" like a football team breaking from the huddle. Much to the delight of the chuckling passersby. His subtle approach to interrupting the long day ensured a rejuvenated mind by the time he reached home.

Lunch hour rapidly approached. Thoughts of an unsettled appearance crept in, causing the former student-athlete to quiver. He had many spectators at the job and could not disappoint. He glanced at the "I AM *ONLY* HERE 'TIL I HIT THE LOTTO" banner plastered along the inside of his cubicle before making his way to the restroom, his spare brush in tow.

"Morning. How's it going?" he asked an oncoming woman whose eyebrows furrowed in confusion.

"Good morning. Hey, can I ask you a question?"

"Sure."

"Would you be so kind as to tell me where Alan Kingsley sits?"

"Oh. A.K.? I absolutely can. You're heading in the right direction. This is usually where people get turned around."

"Oh," she cried out.

"Don't worry, I'll make life easier for you. By the way, I'm Bryce. Nice to meet you." He extended his hand.

"Thank you so much," she replied excitedly, taking a hold of it. "Jenna. Nice meeting you."

"Jenna... Barnes?" he asked precariously.

"I am. How'd you know?"

"I was one of your original interviewers."

Jenna, a recent college graduate from the southeast, was the last of several hires set to work in financial services. Leading up to her big interview, Bryce, away on business, became ill upon his return, electing to work remotely in lieu of contaminating the office. This was their long-awaited opportunity to play catch-up.

"It's a pleasure to finally meet you. How's everything?" he asked, making an about-face.

"Aside from feeling like a mouse trapped inside of a maze,

pretty good. Everyone is so welcoming. It's my first time on this side of the floor, so I got a little confused."

"Overwhelming, isn't it? I used to get turned around all the time. Makes you wonder who designed this cockamamie floor plan, right?"

"Seriously. It's as if they were drinking on the job," Jenna giggled.

"I actually know who designed it."

"Wait, you do? Seriously?"

"I do. My father and his team were the hired contractors. They've designed hundreds of office floor plans throughout the city."

"Oh my gosh," she whispered, cuffing her mouth in a display of embarrassment. Her face turned a rose-colored pink. "Are you serious?"

"As serious as a heart attack."

"This is extremely embarrassing. I am terribly sorry."

"It's okay. You didn't know. Just try to be a *little* careful next time," he replied, attempting to hold in laughter. "Hey, I'm only messing with you. You look like you just saw a ghost."

"Oh my gosh," she replied yet again, her skin now beet red. "I was like, 'Welp, guess I should clear my desk.'"

"Stop it. Although, I will admit, the look on your face was priceless."

Jenna took a deep breath. "You know what this reminds me of? It's like the first day at a new school when you're aimlessly walking around scared to death by all the unfamiliar faces, and here comes this big bully looking to make an example outta you."

"Bully? Who, moi?"

"All I need is a 'kick me' sign on my back and I'll be set. Wait, did you..." she paused, glancing behind her shoulder.

"Why didn't I think of that? A 'kick me' sign is hilarious," he snickered.

"That'll just be my luck. Murphy's Law, I'm telling you."

Jenna wiped her hand against her forehead. "I'm a nervous wreck now."

"Don't be. Truthfully, it *is* kinda stuffy in here. Maybe the weather is about to break." Bryce looked at Jenna whose eyes took the shape of a deer in headlights. "What's wrong?" he asked her.

"I'm almost afraid to say it."

"Say what?"

She pressed her lips together before proceeding. "Is fifty degrees considered breaking? I would've brought in some sun block."

"A Debbie Downer on the team. Nice," he said to her delight.

After graciously introducing Jenna to some of the staff, they continued their lighthearted exchange. "Okay, *Debbie*, so, here's the hundred-thousand-dollar question. Discounting our little hiccup, how do you like Hudson Investors so far?"

"I love it. Everyone's so nice."

"I'll check back with you in about a month," he sneered.

"I'd like my hundred-grand... in cash, please."

"Only if you commit to using it for an updated floor plan."

"Not going there."

"So, if you look straight ahead, you'll see glass doors. A.K.'s in the first one to your left. He might be in a meeting, but you can certainly find a couple of seats along the wall and hang out." With Jenna's attention fixed on Alan's office, it allowed Bryce a moment to give her the once-over. His eyes shifted toward her pumpkin-spice colored hair, short A-line dress, and ringless left hand.

"Wow, what an amazing view. I'd never get any work done," she exclaimed, referring to the visibility of bustling Fifth Avenue.

"Oh, before I forget, make sure you call him Alan and not A.K. Give it some time."

"I'm gonna call him A.K. and tell him *you* said so," she quipped. "No, seriously, thank you so much, Bryce."

"Of course. I'm usually drowned in work, but if you ever need a hand just put your 'W' in the air. Kinda like the Batman signal," he instructed, configuring his fingers to form the letter.

"Why a 'W?'"

"I'm over on the west side of the office."

"Oh, I get it. Wesssiiide," she motioned with her hand. "Don't ask me why I just did that. My brother was a huge Tupac fan," she replied to his astonishment.

"Really? We'll have to save that convo for another day."

Jenna was unprepared to bail on their banter. "Do I need to keep one of those life preserver thingies by my desk?"

"I'm sorry?"

"You mentioned being *drowned,* so I figured…"

"Nice. You're gonna fit right in."

He walked away rubbing his mouth to mask an immediate attraction. Jenna's humorous behavior and fashion flair reminded him of his former tenth-grade English teacher Ms. Blake. For a split-second, he hoped to catch Jenna running toward him like a busty *Baywatch* lifeguard, plunging into his waiting arms over a jazzy Kenny G. tune. Instead, she was busy typing on her Blackberry phone.

With Bryce's bladder seconds away from detonating, he scurried off to the men's room. Finally, the moment he'd longed for: a meeting with the mirror. He straightened the collar to his sky-blue Brooks Brothers oxford shirt and brushed his hair like a man determined to eliminate a bevy of lice from his scalp. The precision of his mid-temple fade haircut, courtesy of Omari, was something to be proud of. In fact, he was so impressed by his sibling's wizardry that he practically begged him to enroll in cosmetology school. To no avail. It was Bryce's longest stretch of wearing a low cut since the days of his dad infamously positioning a cereal bowl onto his scalp every other weekend to design the dreaded "bowl cut." Dale Taylor commonly stressed on the importance of a well-groomed man, and his at-home barbershop was a means for bonding following the loss of Bryce's mother.

Bryce swiped away the shine along his forehead, adding brush-strokes to his beard. It was time to wrap up his restroom shenanigans before someone blindly entered, mistaking his grooming routine for narcissism. He rubbed his hand against his jaw in a pretend model pose when suddenly a boisterous voice approached the door.

Can't complain. Blessed and highly favored. Why don't you join us for lunch?

He was unable to discern the mysterious second voice on the other side of the door, but it was clear who was about to invade the men's room. There was no escaping Roy Mitchell's upbeat presence as he entered with his back completely turned.

Roy was repugnant in tone and oftentimes produced insufferable conversation. He was known for making disparaging remarks and would gaze at the outfits of colleagues daringly inquiring about the brand name. His flamboyance caused growing suspicion around the office concerning his sexuality. Yet the professed "ladies' man" continued to put on a front to quiet the existing intuition.

He was notoriously known for befriending those who showed signs of exuberance in a typically stress-filled environment. It was easier to pry into their personal lives once he lured you in: *You stayed home this weekend? Nah, we need to hang out. I'm friends with a few club promoters. Free drinks and thirsty people... you know what I mean?* The latter was his go-to line. Roy was unabashed by his behavior, baiting the unwary with a cunning look. If you fail to mention anything about a significant other within thirty seconds of the conversation, consider yourself single. Surely, his spirited attitude rewarded him with many friends, but Bryce had serious doubts and usually avoided him off company hours.

"Oh, there you are," Roy announced, approaching the sink. "I called your desk."

"I was showing one of the new hires around."

"Who, Pete *Johnston?*" he mocked. "Is it Johnston or Johnson? Seems like a good guy."

"No, the new girl. Jenna."

"Oh, Jenna the Ginger. I met her the other day. She's nice... if you know what I mean." He winked.

"*Jenna the Ginger?* Are we nine?"

"How about the redhead with nice tits, would that suit your fancy?" Roy smirked, slapping Bryce against the chest with a visibly dampen hand. "Yo, I think I've got the same shirt. And since when do you oppose nicknames? We give *everyone* nicknames in this place. Sidebar, can I tell you how much I hate last names like *Johnston?* Why couldn't he simply go by 'Johnson,' you know what I mean?"

Bryce wore an exaggerated simper, brushing his hair once more to detract attention from a delicate subject. "I wonder what's faster—an X-15 fighter jet, a speeding bullet, or the email from HR if somebody overheard this."

"Yeah right. I'm too valuable. This place would turn upside down if they fired me," Roy said, now conversing by the toilet. "Zo's waiting in the lobby. Do you wanna head out or go to the cafeteria?"

"Let's head out. I could use some fresh air. I've got a conference call at two and somehow, I'll need to wrap up a project before the end of day. I'm not staying a minute past five either."

"Loosen up, man. You seem a little unhinged."

"Ehh, just got a lot going on. Plus, I can't seem to shake off this cold."

"Wanna talk about it?"

"Not today, Dr. Phil. You do realize we're talking through a toilet partition with your junk in hand?"

"Hey, gotta secure the investment. Someone may try to kill me for this thing. Besides, 'multi-tasking' is my middle name."

"Not a-hole? You mean I've had it wrong this whole time?"

"Save the jokes for lunch."

Roy had a tiring act of pretending to have all the answers. Furthermore, he managed to find himself involved in every scenario imaginable. If you fell off a cliff and lived to tell the tale, either he miraculously experienced the same or knew someone who did. The tactic worked effectively on the gullible; namely younger women who flocked his desk to flirt and listen to his sensationalized stories. But to most it was hogwash. The last thing Bryce wanted was to give more leverage to someone who unequivocally thought he was God's gift to man.

Ordinarily, the guys traded fashion tips, discussed men's fragrances, or the latest news circulating pop culture, but it was Roy's constant obsession for attention that otherwise clashed with Bryce's calm demeanor. His insecurities were alarming for someone as well respected as him in the workplace. He relied heavily on forceful obnoxious behavior including a timely clamorous sneeze which seemed to only occur when a room was too silent. He openly boasted about the people he knew, places he had gone, and the number of one-night stands he encountered.

What sealed the deal for an unsteady off-the-job friendship was Bryce's genuine belief that Roy lived an alternate lifestyle. He was the only male in Bryce's immediate circle who claimed to like women while still wearing a tongue ring. His judgment was unjust, but Bryce struggled immensely trying to wrap his head around another man mindlessly shifting an object around their mouth. Besides, how would he ever fit in with Bryce's select group of witty alpha-type friends who could detect effeminate mannerisms a mile away? The idea of trying to figure him out became all too convoluted.

A departmental shuffle a few years back saw Roy and his staff move onto another floor opening new opportunities within financial services. This is when he delightedly championed Bryce's name for the newly created role of strategy analyst. With Roy being one of the division's longest tenured and respected financial advisors, his opinions were highly regarded. On top of that, the company was cognizant of the misrepresentation of Black men in prominent positions.

Prior to the recommendation, Bryce grew tired of management singing his praises when the acclamations didn't translate into his day-to-day affairs. His strengths came in the form of communication, identifying business needs, and plan development. It was imperative that he accentuated these skills for mental stimulation alone. Additionally, Bryce's only other goal was to be compensated slightly above market price until a new challenge arises. This is how he gained leverage on the career chessboard. It was business, never personal. He loved his job but didn't vie to sit atop the corporate ladder, hip to the ill-favored politics involved when a person of his stature tried to cement their "I belong" flag onto the enemy's turf. The enemy being corporate bigwigs who didn't look like him. Initially, the lateral move to strategy analyst caused some trepidation. He felt somewhat indebted to Roy—his thought to be work rival. However, without Roy's persistent endorsement, who knows where things would stand.

Following their restroom ribbing, Bryce exchanged a few hellos in passing before taking a quick peek at his watch. It was noon. He grabbed his cell from the inner pocket of his sports jacket and scrolled through the chain of text messages with Julissa.

Her latest picture message showed a time stamp of 11:52 a.m. She was dressed in consummate elegance, sporting a neatly compressed ponytail, semi-rimless specs, and a black blazer overlaying a white halter crop top. The outfit revealed a bit more cleavage than expected, sending him into a feverish state of excitement where he was quickly reminded of their late-night rendezvous. Bryce put on his jacket and approached the elevators fighting a desirable urge to reply. Suddenly, heavy footsteps trailed, like Sasquatch roaming the woods.

"Are those elbow patches?" Roy asked, trying to catch his breath.

"Slow down, O.J.," Bryce replied.

"O.J.? Why'd you say that?"

"Remember those old Hertz commercials where he's running through the airport hurdling over chairs?"

"O.J. couldn't have this much swag if he tried. Hey, I'm feeling that jacket, Smooth. Blue is definitely your color. Is that Hugo Boss?"

"Might be."

He refused to give Roy the satisfaction of knowing that it only took one try to figure it out.

"That pattern looks dope. You've got the whole blue-brown thing going on."

"This-is-what-I-do," Bryce replied, popping his collar.

"There are only two or three people in this entire building with some style. I find it odd how guys are afraid to mix it up. You know me, I'll wear anything, as long as it's designer."

"*Anything*?"

"Yup. What can anyone say to me if my outfit costs more than their rent? Know what I'm sayin'?"

"I can call you a fool."

"Call me whatever you want. Just don't call me broke."

They shared a laugh before entering the elevator when Tom Walters, a slick-haired sliver fox foul-mouth executive, with whom the guys argued amicably, was seen forcefully thumping a box of cigarettes against his palm.

"Hey look, it's Pat Riley," Roy announced enthusiastically. "Going down?"

"What do *you* think, motherfucker?" Tom replied with a gravelly smoker's voice, signaling a fist bump from the guys. "Is it five o'clock yet?"

"Why? You got a hot date?"

"Yeah, I'm picking up your mother. How do I look?" he asked, smoothening his eyebrows with his middle finger.

"Tom might be the only person alive still smoking Kool cigarettes. Where'd you get those from, eBay?" Roy teased.

Tom switched topics abruptly, taking note of the uneasy

appearances of the other passengers. "Can you believe I'm heading to another meeting?"

"This is why they pay you the big bucks."

"I'm already on my fifth goddamn cigarette," he whispered. "They're trying to kill me before retirement."

"We're headed to the shop, need anything?"

"Yeah, pick me up a nice severance package and a diet coke."

The jokesters diverted their attention to the ticker flashing across the digital screen providing coverage of the tragic earthquake and ensuing tsunami slamming Japan. Bryce retrieved his phone. To his surprise, there was another text from Julissa who anxiously awaited his response, hoping to make amends following their recent quarrel. It was unusual to go this long without communicating. Typically, they traded rousing texts like two lovebirds in heat, but he had a point to prove.

At the start of their affair, Julissa vowed he would fall for her like other men from her past. She was right. Bryce's attraction was fierce, but it was shielded in fear of losing out on their friendly bet. Their arrangement was strictly physical, and she belabored the point of having a husband for emotional support if ever a need. All she asked was that Bryce use protection if he wanted to step out. No risk was greater than the one she was taking, and she couldn't afford to have the dapper bachelor living recklessly behind her back. If at any time Bryce felt the task at hand was too much, she advised him to walk away. Her straightforward approach was welcoming, acting as a safeguard for his feelings.

The estranged wife had it all—checking off the boxes to an extensive "things-to-accomplish-before-forty" list. However, through her clear abundant life was a glaring void. Her adventurous sexual appetite was unfulfilled, and a growing apathy intensified her fantasy to have an extramarital affair. The idea of dishonoring her marriage was nothing short of scandalous, but she was a proud, shrewd woman, who marched to the beat of her own drum.

The loving mother was sharp as a tack, but to pull off her wish, she needed a distinct personality type to match her. Someone intellectually sound, trustworthy, discreet, with the ability to set aside emotions. Little did she know the person completing her hunt for a precarious fling would be a man from her past.

Bryce attended Cedar Ridge High School with Julissa but walked on opposite sides of the tracks. He, an academic standout and budding athlete. Julissa, barely staying afloat, whisking away the hearts of boys. Years elapsed before they crossed paths again, when without warning, he received a friend request on Facebook. The request led to an exchange of messaging and picture-gawking lasting most of the day. A day he spent months preparing for— the start of the NFL season where interruptions were usually forbidden.

Julissa Vasquez-Kolowoski

Hey you, remember me?? Class of '95? I was cracking up at your comments on Ted's page yesterday. You're STILL a smart ass. Just wanted to say hi and wish you and your precious 49ers good luck. You guys need it lol.

Their quips were fresh and exciting, lasting through the week. In time, they agreed to a lunch date when it was discovered she lived in Union County, a mere thirty minutes away. She was an open book, and would discuss everything from motherhood, the pursuit of her master's degree, and an unbecoming marriage.

Hours before their seafood restaurant meet up, Bryce casually scrolled through a slew of pictures on Julissa's Facebook page where there was no husband to speak of. Just photos of her prancing around with her daughter. Aside from Julissa's hyphenated last name, the only other time Bryce was reminded of her spouse was when she sipped on a strawberry daiquiri—where resting on the middle finger of her left hand was an exquisite wedding ring. When addressing her husband, Julissa settled for pronouns. To the naked eye, there wasn't much evidence of a happily married woman. Without being too intrusive, Bryce delved into her personal life.

Ugh. Papi, it's complicated. I love him, but clearly, I'm not invested. I mean, why else would I be here sharing mozzarella sticks with a guy I haven't seen since high school?

He could appreciate her honesty.

Over the course of their pow-wow, she expressed concern about being an undesirable single mother after packing on a few pounds. More alarming was her claim of never being *in* love with her husband, pointing out the effects of their contrasts. Julissa was of Puerto Rican descent, while he was a divorced White male, eighteen years her senior. The disparity brought about moments of regret, and she was captivated by the thought of being desired again.

After I left Natalie's father, I was stressed, struggling to keep the weight off. So, now I'm back living with my mother who loves to cook and I'm eating everything. I'm a new mom, I've got stretch marks, I'm breastfeeding, so now my boobs are humongous. My hips are getting wider, I can't fit into my clothes... like, what the heck, man? Not to sound vain, but no one was paying any attention to me. So, I used that time to go back to school and get my bachelor's. Then, of course, when I'm not looking is when I meet him. He's super nice, pero, he's much older than me and kinda nerdy. Oh, and he's completely bald. It looks good on him, but... I don't know. Anyway, he did cute things to get my attention and one day I just gave in. I never thought this would happen. He's a great guy, has a fantastic job, and I absolutely love his daughter, but I'm not physically attracted to him.

She disclosed the most pertinent statement of her story, thereafter.

All I want is to go out once in a while, laugh and have amazing sex. Is that too much to ask for?

~

Thirteenth floor... twelfth floor... eleventh floor.

Bryce became visibly annoyed by the computerized voice inside the elevator. Everyone in the building must have gotten hungry at the same time. The saving grace of a slow-moving elevator ride was Julissa's desperate cry for attention.

She was an absolute pro at leaving a lot to the imagination in her photos, but the latest pictures were scandalous. *Quieres esta?* the text read, followed by two picture messages in its loading stages. He loved when she spoke Spanish to him, and she was awed anytime he showed off his bilingual skills. His heart palpitated as he awaited. He looked up to spot Roy, who was looking down at his phone. A hush crossed the elevator. Finally, a vibrating alert from his phone. Julissa's pictures loaded.

The first was a black-and-white in-shower selfie standing underneath the shower head. Her head was tilted to the back, eyes closed, mouth opened, water dripping down to her sternum. Her nipples were in a euphoric mood. A second picture followed; a mirror selfie, standing with her legs slightly spread. The wet tips of her long dark hair covered her nipples, the shower condensation smeared along the mirror perfectly angled to shield "La Gatita"— the nickname he had given her lady-part. The pics were racy with a splash of art, just as he liked. A text appeared: *Thinking of you.* Blood rushed to his lower region like water flowing through a steep creek. Still, Bryce wouldn't play along as much as it killed him.

"Stay blessed, T-Dub," Roy broadcasted before departing. "I'll make sure to look for that severance package."

Zoë Brooks, Bryce's protégée and work friend, was irritated by the guy's tardiness. "Yo, what the hell? I've been standing here forever. How long is ten minutes in your world? I swear, men have no concept of time."

"Why are you looking at *me?* Smooth was the one in the men's room staring at himself for a half-hour," Roy replied.

"Are we gonna conveniently leave out the part where you were standing at the toilet playing therapist?"

"Eww, who stands at the toilet to pee? Don't you guys have those urinal thingamabobs?"

"Would you rather me sit?" Roy replied, pushing through the glass revolving doors.

"I'm sure it wouldn't be your first time."

"Ooh," Bryce howled. "Get it off your chest, Zo."

It was roasting hour. They hurried through the afternoon rush, landing at their favorite eatery. In front was a small group wearing shamrock glasses and green top hats.

"This place is packed. Why didn't you head over and hold a few seats for us instead of standing in the lobby fluffing your hair?" Roy continued.

"How was I supposed to know we were heading out?" Zoë countered.

"Because I mentioned earlier, 'We'll probably head out.' Duh."

"*Probably.* Where's the confirmation in that word? I'll wait," Zoë fired back. "And at least I have hair. You're completely bald, homeboy."

"By choice. I'd look like one of the Jackson 5 if I went a few days without shaving."

Zoë covered her mouth to intercept her trademark thunderous guffaw. "Well, right now you look like a milk dud."

"Zo, not everyone can afford clown wigs like you," Bryce added.

"Really? Since when do you take his side? At least I don't look like an S-curl model," Zoë fired back, causing Roy's smile to expand as wide as a football field. In an unforeseen move, she forcibly bumped fists with Roy.

"Was that a fist bump *with* sound effects? Do people still do that?"

[hostess greets group]

"Hi there. Table for three?"

Their indecorous behavior acted as a great stress reliever. Zoë's ability to hang out with the guys was praiseworthy to say the least. The Brooklyn College graduate had been working as a contractor with Hudson Investors for the past two years, hoping to latch on permanently. Her diverse background, work ethic, and vibrant attitude astounded Bryce who echoed her name to upper management. Similar to what Roy did for him. As an unofficial member of the team, Zoë continued to display her value, expecting a promotion on the horizon.

"What you got there, Zo?" Roy asked.

"Can I sit down first? My goodness. It's a Reuben."

"Why are you so hostile today? It's Friday Eve. Lighten up."

"Lighten up? What, am I not light enough for you? Are you suggesting I bleach my skin? *Um... Hello? Human Resources? Yes, I'll hold,*" she mocked.

"You guys need a room," Bryce interceded.

"Nah. My mother always said to never trust a forty-year-old man with a barbell tongue ring."

"Were those her actual words?" Bryce instigated.

"Yes. And didn't you just hear what he said? Apparently, my complexion isn't light enough. He has a type."

"Not light enough? You look like the female Bob Ross. Second, I haven't turned forty yet. Third, tell your mom this tongue ring has changed lives," Roy bragged, sticking out his tongue like a dog panting on a hot summer's day. Bryce buried his face into the palm of his hand in utter embarrassment.

"Oh puh-lease. Bryce, make him stop."

"Don't worry, you'll miss me tomorrow. I'm having lunch with my team."

"A.K.A. he's having lunch with Porsha."

"Whatever."

"The jig is up. She used to be at your desk longer than you. What happened?" Zoë inquired. "Suddenly you guys don't speak?"

Roy took a long sip of diet coke from his glass. Beads of sweat formed on his bald head. "Who told you that?"

Bryce maintained his best poker face as he surveyed the scene during their exchange.

Porsha, labeled "Thong Queen" by Roy due to an admittance of owning over one hundred pairs of the preferred undergarment, was quite the character. The middle-aged facilities coordinator caught the eye of many, but she had an eye for sharp, well-assembled younger men.

She was the bourgeoisie type, enchanted by celebrity glitz and glam, longing for a man who could afford her taste. Deep inside her lived a burning desire to become a power couple with a self-made person, though she made it clear how she didn't *need* a man. At times, she came off as a scatterbrain only attracting those looking to seduce her, but Porsha knew how to play the game. Her overzealous flirting habits and lust for attention—including an astonishing tight-fitting wardrobe that often gave the illusion of two basketballs from behind—showed a woman uninterested in settling down. She got a rush putting together outfits and crushing her imaginary competition. It all but explained her connection to Roy. They were like two peas in a pod.

The neighboring employees hit it off long before Bryce's arrival, sending salacious text messages through the day, scheduling mini breaks, and finding remote locations in the building for some quick monkey business. Their sexual escapades stayed a secret until Roy intentionally disclosed information hoping to keep Bryce—the then newbie—in check. It all happened after

Bryce inquired about Porsha's whereabouts amid rumors that she had been terminated.

Nah, she's good. I spoke to her yesterday. She's on medical leave. You know I've been hittin' that, right?

The comment didn't faze Bryce. He was enjoying single life, avoiding the ills of mixing business with pleasure. Over time, Porsha grew tired of Roy's mannerisms, though she wasn't too crazy about composed types who only offered a pleasant smile in passing. That was Bryce. She preferred men on her heels, salivating at the mouth, flagrantly eye-fucking her from across the room. At times, those hard stares activated a palpation in between her legs where she marched off to the restroom to handle personal business. It more than explained her lively at-work mood.

Porsha lived for the chase, but a growing intrigue for Bryce led her to become the hunter. It all went down at the annual holiday party where she uncharacteristically made the first move under the influence of a few apple martinis.

Can I ask you something? Are you afraid of me?
I beg your pardon?
Are you afraid of me? You don't have to be scared. I won't bite.
Afraid? What would give you that impression?
Come on, Bryce, we don't have to play these games anymore. I see how you look at me.

She wasn't exactly his type, but the physical attraction was too intense to ignore. Furthermore, Bryce's ego couldn't be upstaged. She needed to know who 'the boss' was.

After some familiar faces from the office cleared the scene, they followed suit, finding an isolated area down the street to flamingly make out under an array of snowflakes descending from the night sky. When Bryce posed the question of Porsha's evening plans, she brazenly groped him. Her hand was met with a powerful erection sending her vagina into submission. Before long, they were seated side by side on NJ Transit headed to, of all places, his home.

Following their spicy encounter, it was during a moment of

pillow talk where Bryce learned a few things—namely, Roy's preference for gay night clubs, swinger parties, and his kooky in-bed habits.

What's up with you and Roy? You know that I know, right?

He's got such a big fuckin' mouth, I swear. We haven't messed around in months. He talks a good game, but that man can't handle me. Not with that shrimp dick of his. I usually don't deal with his type, but I was single and a sista had needs. He said he had a girl, but that's his problem, not mine. One weekend he invited me to a club. We both got tipsy and... shit happened. But that fool likes his ass to be played with. That's where I draw the line. I may have some freaky tendencies, but that isn't my cup of tea.

After preying on Bryce like a predator in the wild, Porsha expected nothing short of another invite. Maybe even an ongoing tryst where he could become Roy's permanent replacement. Much to her surprise, it didn't happen. A single erotic adventure with a woman of her caliber wasn't enough for most men. But Bryce wasn't like *most* guys. The sex was nothing short of spectacular, but their situation was too delicate. His decision to abolish their involvement had little to do with Porsha or an undocumented "bro code" violation. In fact, it was solely based on protecting his workplace image. Reputation meant everything.

~

"I've been in a relationship for a couple of months now, Zo, that's why you don't see me horsing around anymore," Roy followed.

"With whom? What's her name? Why haven't we seen any pics?" Zoë interrogated.

"What would that prove?"

Bryce was fixated on an unfamiliar face seated alone in a booth. She was of an exotic mix, early twenties with jet black hair, ruby red lipstick, and large hoop earrings. A busy waiter serving a large party blocked his view, directing Bryce's attention back to his grilled chicken and French fry platter.

"Why don't we all hang out tomorrow after work," Roy suggested. "I'm gonna see if a few people on my team are down too. I have a friend who's hosting an event in Tribeca."

"Are you gonna pay for a babysitter to watch AJ in case his dad has to work?" Zoë asked.

"Bring him. He's got a little mustache growing anyway. They'll let him in."

"You're such an ass."

"What about you, Smooth?"

"I have a long day on Saturday. Helping my brother move some stuff out of my place, so it's a hard pass."

"Bro, I said tomorrow. Friday. What does Saturday have to do with anything? And don't you have a three-day weekend coming up?"

Bryce purposely blocked him out, laying eyes once more on the beauty seated in the booth. She took one last bite of her meal before her petite long legged frame drew public attention. She had an obvious sense of style, wearing a black slim fit leather jacket, tight blue jeans, and a pair of black over-the-knee boots. A quick hair flip allowed him a better view of her piercing eyebrows and firm jawline. Sensing his flattering stare, she looked in his direction, threw on a pair of fancy black sunglasses and strutted viciously toward the exit.

"Who's got your eye?" Roy asked, peeking over the booth.

"Good Lord. She was *all* types of fine," Bryce announced, giving a curious look at the exit. "I don't think I've seen her here before."

"Well, it *is* New York City. There's about *ten million* of us here. Didn't you run track back in the day? Go holla at her. Zo, can't you see him leaping over tables trying to catch her?"

"You guys are disgusting."

Bryce removed the grilled chicken from the bun before sinking his teeth into it. "Anyway, the club scene is getting old. Plus, I've been struggling with migraines all week. I'm looking forward to relaxing. Maybe next weekend."

"Excuses, excuses. Yo, you're the only person I know who orders a sandwich but won't eat the bread. You know you can order grilled chicken by itself, right?"

"Am I supposed to take advice from a guy who thinks diet coke has health benefits?"

Zoë burst into laughter, hi-fiving Bryce from across the table. "For real," she agreed. "Diet soda is more toxic."

"What is this, an ambush? Butting into conversations must be a Jersey thing."

"Um, I'm a Brooklyn girl. I lived in Jersey for a year, weirdo," Zoë rolled her eyes. "Yeah, keep sipping your diet soda, mister. Anyway, what time is it? I'm sure it's time to get..."

"Oh boy. Here we go," Bryce groaned.

"What?"

"Don't do it," Roy muffled, struggling to speak with a mouth full of food.

"Do what?" Zoë replied, laughing uncontrollably.

"No James Brown, Zo. I'm begging you."

"Bryce, are you saying you don't wanna... *get on up?*"

"Hell no," Roy cut in. "Sit yo ass down."

The group exited the shop when Roy spotted a pregnant friend standing along a food truck. "Esther... Esther," he hollered. "Let me go rap to her for a few. I'll catch y'all later."

"Notice how he loses the bass in his voice when he speaks to other women?"

"Zo, you have absolutely no filter, and *that's* why we get along."

"Don't get me wrong, Roy's cool, but I wonder about him. He gets so defensive when you ask about Porsha and now suddenly there's a new girlfriend. He shows us pics of everyone *but* the women he claims to be with."

"Let that man live. I'm simply not interested in what he does."

"Neither am I, but why point out every girl you're screwing

then get all worked up when I ask about this alleged girlfriend? It's like he's hiding something."

"He has some weird tendencies, but that's why I keep a healthy distance. What he chooses to do outside of work is his business."

"Now you wanna be all diplomatic? *Um, yes, NYPD, I'd like to report a missing person. Yes, his name is Bryce Taylor, he's about six-two...*"

"Six-four, just saying..."

"Whatever. Yo, I was cracking up when he mentioned we all hang out this weekend. I'm like, 'There's no way you're going.'"

"I'd rather play in traffic."

"Stop being such a hermit crab. You should come out one day just to see how he acts off the job."

"I see this fool every day at lunch. One hour with him is more than enough. Plus, we've done happy hour before."

Bryce's cell vibrated before entering the building lobby.

> La Gatita: Stop ignoring me… come over this evening so we can talk. I'm gonna make dinner. He won't be back til tomorrow night XOXO
>
> Thurs 1:10 p.m.

"Why do you have that silly smile on your face?" Zoë asked, as they awaited a descending elevator to rescue them from the throng of animated employees returning from lunch.

"What?"

"Mm-hmm. You guys are all alike."

"Why do women make blanket statements like that? Have you taken a poll on every guy on Earth?"

"Yes, I have. Thank you. The numbers don't lie."

"I don't have anything to hide. I'm single, enjoying life."

"Mister Kid-Free-Doing-Me. We know."

"And don't you forget it. Sooo, are you hanging out tomorrow?"

"Probably. I've got to double-check with Anthony to see if he's working. It's his weekend to pick up AJ, but sometimes his schedule switches. Did you press eighteen?" Bryce's eyebrow perked.

"No. I thought you did."

"Eighteen, please," Zoë shouted to a boarding passenger. "I still think you should come out tomorrow. It'll be fun. You can bring one of your girlfriends..."

"See, there you go again. Why must you pluralize it? I'm a one-woman man. And why are you announcing my business all through the elevator?"

"I'm whispering."

"Your *whisper* is loud."

"Okay, okay. Has there been any progress with anyone?"

"I've been talking to a few people here and there. Just waiting for the right situation. No rush."

"Well, good luck. What time are you leaving today? I wanna try and catch the five-thirty train."

"Shooting for five... the work on my desk says midnight."

[eighteenth floor]

Bryce and Zoë parted ways. He directed his attention to his cell. Enough time had passed.

Not ignoring you... busy day.

I'll swing by tonight. Just keep me posted.

3

———

PHYSICAL

Bryce used his day off to schedule a visit to the optometrist's office, hoping to find the underlying cause of his condition. His mother had below-average vision, yet he'd mistakenly suspected the deficiency would skip his generation.

At the start of thirty, a combination of blurred vision and migraines hit him like a ton of bricks. He stubbornly withheld this information during annual visits to his personal physician, unwilling to accept his fate. If his vision wasn't impaired, all was considered good in his world. He presumed his current hurdle was caused by the enduring effects of time spent in front of the computer screen, along with the gnawing stresses of life.

"Good morning, I'm here for my nine-thirty appointment."

"Nine-thirty? Your name, Hun?"

"Bryce. Last name, Taylor."

"Hi Bryce. Is this your first time visiting the office?"

"It is."

"Okay, I'll need you to fill out both sides of this form and sign the highlighted lines. When you're done, just attach your dental card onto the clipboard and bring it to me, okay?"

Bryce scoured the room, finding scores of fashionable eyewear taking up an entire wall, before settling next to a cornered table stacked with magazines. Suddenly, he realized his dental card was missing from his wallet. The pacifying sound of the swaying chime bells above the door kept his anxiety in check as he exited the office. Approaching was a wildly grey-haired woman who staggered her way to the entrance. He backpedaled to open the door.

"Such a charming *young man*. Thank you for being so patient."

Ugh.

Technically, she was right, she was more than twice his age but even a full beard with a couple of bristling grays couldn't save him from the aggravating term. He shifted his focus to the misplaced card, irritated by the possibility that it was lost.

Organization was a way of life. The inside of Bryce's home resembled that of a military veteran. His bathroom was nearly spotless, his closet was color-coordinated, his CD and vinyl collection alphabetized by genre, and you could eat off his kitchen floor. His meticulousness earned him the nickname "Mr. Rogers" from some, while women were left dumbfounded—defying the common stereotype that men weren't tidy.

The pungent smell of fertilizer seeping through the windows as landscapers prepped his complex grounds was the reason for a mild case of early morning lightheadedness. Not only did the unsteadiness cause him to misplace his dental card but he would commit a "fashion atrocity" in the process. How else could the designated fashion guru explain his choice to leave the house wearing Adidas track pants with a Nike jacket? Had Omari been present, he would've ribbed him for weeks. As Dale often stated, "Even the great Michael Jordan had an occasional off-night." Fortunately, in Bryce's gym bag was a pair of Nike shorts. Problem solved.

Gym bag!

He reached toward the back seat like he had just received intel on a hidden fortune. Apart from the repulsive stench causing brain fog, there were a set of urgent work emails sidetracking him during an earlier wardrobe swap. There it was—his dental card wedged inside of his short's pockets. The same shorts he originally planned to wear before an early morning chill changed his mind. He returned to the office to find his seat snatched by the same grey-haired woman he previously held the door for.

"Did you find it, Hun?" the receptionist asked.

"I did. Sorry about that. I was in such a hurry to get here," Bryce replied with abundant sarcasm. He observed the office before proceeding to fill out the form.

"Catherine?" a technician asked openly.

"Did she say 'Catherine,' dear?" a plump woman seated across from Bryce asked. He looked up with a state of confusion. "I'm s-s-sorry, I'm hard of h-h-hearing," she added.

"No worries. Ma'am, did you say Catherine?"

"Yes," the technician replied, her eyebrow raised ever so slightly. Are you Cath...?"

"No, no. She's right here," he confirmed.

"Hi, Catherine. Head on over. Are you able to make it?"

"I think s-s-so," she responded, gripping the armrests firmly for added security. Bryce jumped in to assist. "B-b-be right there," she declared.

Bryce thumbed through a Sports Illustrated magazine when suddenly his cell buzzed. His recent efforts to reconnect with Kristen had him hovering over his phone like a teenager. Finally, the moment he'd been waiting for. His long-awaited notification... or so he thought.

H2O: Thx, Big Bro

Mon 9:53 a.m.

It was Omari replying to Bryce's words of affirmation, a regular occurrence to help kick start the troubled sibling's day. Bummer.

Somehow, he had convinced himself that Kristen was somewhere anxiously anticipating his olive branch. He found himself lost in the fantasy of a fairytale, ending where his email to Dominique reached Kristen, who then re-inserted herself into his life all in one swoop. It was only a matter of time. Time being the healer of all wounds. Instead of overanalyzing a legless fantasy he diverted his attention to a game of solitaire.

"Bryce?"

He looked up. Standing before him was an above-average height, fit technician—wearing a top knot, light eyeliner, and a pink and black scrub set clutching a clipboard against her chest. His face lit up with glee. He fumbled to place his phone in his back pocket.

"Good morning," Bryce replied, extending his hand.

"Good morning. I'm Alyssa. I'll be seeing you before Dr. Feinstein."

"Nice to meet you, Alyssa. You guys work fast. No, after you," he insisted, motioning her forward.

"Such a gentleman. Thank you. We *try* to work efficiently—get everyone in and out as best as we can. It's such a beautiful day. Who wants to be stuck in an office," she replied, giggling at her own comment.

"You're right. But you guys make it a lot easier. I don't mind sticking around. You've got a nice little environment here."

"Cozy, right? Makes it a whole lot easier to come to work each day. Okay, so, here we are. You can have a seat right over there. How's your morning going?"

"Not too bad. I'm taking a much-needed day off from work. I can think of a hundred places I'd rather be, but here I am..."

"Aw, that was the sweetest backhanded compliment ever."

Bryce laughed. "Sorry. That didn't come out right. I just meant I'd rather spend time doing something productive than to be told how much my eyes suck."

"Well, hopefully the news isn't too bad, and you can take full advantage of the weather. I love this time of the year. I just pray we have an *actual* spring."

"Seriously. The weather goes from zero to a hundred."

"I know, right? Sheesh."

"I guess it could always be worse."

"For sure…" she paused, offering an extended smile. "Okay, now for the fun part. We're gonna go through a series of tests and you'll be all squared away."

"Tests? Who can I finesse around here for some cheat sheets?"

Had a comedian used this cheesy one-liner, they would've been booed mercifully, riddled with tomatoes, and yanked off the stage with a giant hook like a vaudeville show.

"Too funny. You'll do great. I promise," Alyssa replied.

Bryce had the ability to woo women with laughter. It started young when his charismatic services were called upon while his parents hosted company. He was a conversational smorgasbord, keeping up with current events and watching programs like *Saturday Night Live,* studying the comedic efforts of Eddie Murphy. The idea that humor could emote audience cheer fascinated him and helped to develop a staggering confidence.

Alyssa proceeded with a few health-related questions before the short-list of testing began. Whitesnake's "Is This Love?" played in Bryce's head as he looked on. He was a pro at publicly concealing emotions, but her commanding presence turned him into mush. The world and everything in it were a blur.

"You're doing great. Okay, we're almost done. I'm gonna place this over your left eye and I want you to read the bottom row. Is that okay?"

"Of course. 'N – G – L…,'" he hesitated. "Is that a lowercase 'a' or 'o'?" Let's go with 'a.' 'E – A – M – T'?"

"Awesome!" She followed with rapid claps and a fist bump rewarding his efforts. Her beaming personality was refreshing, but he found her antics over the top. Why was she so excited when the primary doctor was minutes away from sealing his fate? Had he just won an all-inclusive trip to the south of France?

"Well, based on your reaction, I guess it's safe to say I passed the first round. Where's the championship champagne?" he asked. Alyssa proved her worth, signaling a shaken champagne bottle and orchestrating spraying sounds. Bryce stared in awe.

"Hey, not to be intrusive... you know what? Never mind."

"No, please, ask. You wanna know how I became such a goof? Don't worry. I get asked that all the time."

"Not a goof at all. I was just gonna ask, are you originally from New Jersey? You have such great energy. It's unusual to bump into people like you these days."

"Aw, are you trying to make me blush, Bryce?"

"Blush away. I won't tell."

"Yup, I'm a Jersey gal. Born and raised. No one tends to believe me. People think I'm from New York. I've even been asked if I was Mexican..."

"New York? Heck no. Not even close."

"I know, right?"

"Did you say Mexican?"

"Uh-huh. I've been told I look like Selena. Do you remember her?"

"I do. I don't see it, though. I'm getting more Megan Fox."

"Ah, yes. I've gotten that before," Alyssa nodded with approval. "But, yeah, I'm a Jersey girl through and through."

"That's what's up. Listen, don't change for anybody. The world needs more people like you."

Alyssa swiveled her chair to a forty-five-degree angle, clinging to her chest like he'd just grabbed at her heart. "Aw, that is so sweet," she followed, giving him a concentrated stare. Bryce bashfully looked down, observing a glossy costume ring on her index finger.

"I'm serious," he reassured. "You have a great spirit."

His gift of gab had her under minor hypnosis. No one had ever spoken such doting words before. In the meantime, he admired her physique. He had an affinity for women with athletic backgrounds, and she noticeably resembled a real-life action-figure. Think Lara Croft from *Tomb Raider*.

Alyssa jolted out of her spell. "It was so nice talking to you. The doctor will see you in a few minutes, okay?"

"Likewise. Have a great rest of your day."

"You, too. You were wonderful."

"Thanks," he replied, offering a stationary wave.

Parting ways had obviously become a chore.

At the completion of his visit, they waved at one another like school children when crossing paths. Their earlier conversation felt natural, but it was safe to assume Alyssa's act of kindness was just that—an act. A grand scheme concocted by the staff to soften the blow for those on the verge of spending hundreds of dollars on a new set of eyes. In spite of everything, at least she helped eradicate his anxieties concerning an email to an ex-girlfriend drifting along internet space.

~

"We've got a full house," said a jacked-up gym patron who checked-in at the front desk. "I thought I'd have this place to myself."

Bryce chimed in. "This is the New Year's resolution overflow. Give them a few more weeks and it'll be back to normal."

"Either that or everyone decided to call out today," the desk attendant added. "Enjoy your workout, guys."

Bryce loosened up to Stone Temple Pilots' "Plush" in the dark dance fitness room, thinking about life and what could've been. The gym rat maintained a competitive drive even after rupturing his Achilles heel and severely damaging his left shoulder during his playing days at VCU. The demoralizing injuries replayed in his head. In the depths of his heart, he believed he could've made it to the Big Leagues, as did his coaches and a handful of MLB scouts who were often spotted in the crowd.

His sophomore year got off to a thrilling start, leading the Rams in three offensive categories before the injuries cut his playing days short. The aftermath left him with limited power at the plate, a paltry batting average, and a lackluster ending to a one-time promising collegian athletic run. Since then, Bryce exerted himself through Herculean strength and conditioning exercises, holding onto the boyhood dream of playing professionally. Maybe in an amateur league where he'd gain the attention of a Major League club at the *ancient* age of thirty-three. A man could dream.

"What'chu doing in here so early, brotha?" Cortez, his gym buddy asked, peeking through the door.

"I had an early visit to the eye doctor. They're telling me I'm about to look like Steve Urkel," Bryce replied.

"Yeah?" Cortez laughed. *"Anybody got some cheese* ole looking ass. You been bumping into walls?"

"Nah. Just dealing with these silly migraines. What's good on your end?"

"Ain't shit. Just got off work. I'm about to go kick it with the retirees. Ain't no jawns in here 'til the evenings, so, at least I can concentrate," he stressed in his thick Philly drawl.

"The baddies ain't here 'til the weekends. You gotta get here by late morning."

"Naw, it doesn't compare to the evenings. Bitches be in here like it's the club. Just standing around looking cute. Go do a mothafuckin' jumping jack, hoe."

Bryce, on the floor stretching out his hamstrings, laughed hysterically, falling completely onto his back.

"Did you see the game on Saturday?" Cortez asked. "Duke's gonna fuck around and win. I'm telling you."

"Don't jinx it. That's the last thing I need. I got Arizona going all the way in my bracket."

"I'm telling you. Watch. How did they win that game? The fix is in. Another thing, notice how they're suddenly recruiting more street-ballers? Duke ain't never recruit this many niggas with tattoos before."

"Good point."

"Guess they realized they couldn't win anymore with those

White boys with the parted hair. Or those Uncle Tom-looking negroes."

Bryce laughed. "You're ignorant."

"Remember when they had Grant... no, no, not Grant, who's that other Hill? You know, the one who started crying when Laettner hit that shot," Cortez inquired.

"Thomas Hill?"

"Him," Cortez exclaimed.

"Now that I think of it, they had quite a few upscale Black guys. Trajan Langdon, J-Will... Shane Battier. But what's wrong with that?" Bryce questioned.

"All of those boys were soft. Bunch of light-skinned dudes thinking they could hoop."

"Fam, you're the same complexion..."

"That's not the point."

"The only Duke team I liked was the one with Brand and Maggette."

"Brand was okay. Just undersized," Cortez reasoned. "But I couldn't take those earlier Duke teams seriously. How are you putting fear into your opponents with guys named 'Thomas'? I would've terrorized those boys back in my day."

[laughter]

"Switching topics, what'chu about to work on?"

"Shoulders and back," Bryce replied. "Probably do a little cardio afterward. I'm on my comeback trail like MJ, so I've got to get it in."

"Aw shit, you pullin' out the four-five jersey fam?" Cortez mimicked Michael Jordan's patent turnaround fadeaway jump shot. "I'm thinking about doing a little cardio myself."

"When was the last time you saw a treadmill? Walking around looking like the Incredible Negro."

Cortez sucked his teeth. "Actually, I was gonna hit abs first, that's why I came in here to grab one of those yoga balls. Isn't that one over in the corner? Oh, never mind, your ass can't see anyway," he cracked, jogging back to the doorway hugging the inflated ball.

"Look, you're already wheezing. You ain't built for the treadmill life."

The terrifying noise of the blender sent Lizzy running for cover as Bryce prepared a post-workout shake to consume his daily protein intake. He planned to catch up with his semi-retired dad at the local diner. Dale, who worked his mornings as a part-time crossing guard at a local middle-school—after years of operating a profitable pressure washing cleaning business—looked forward to their brunch tete-a-tetes. It broke the monotony of an otherwise predictable afternoon of listening to sports radio.

Bryce took sips of the shake seated on his café-mocha-colored sectional sofa. A display of customized photos flashed on his laptop screen: a beautiful headshot of his mother; the infamous O.J. Simpson white Ford Bronco chase; Bryce standing alongside his dad, grandfather, and uncle at the first ever Million Man March; Cal Ripken Jr. of the Baltimore Orioles circling the field after surpassing Lou Gehrig's consecutive games streak; former San Francisco 49ers wide receiver Terrell Owens standing on the obnoxiously large Cowboys logo at midfield of the old Dallas stadium; the haunting image of Flight 175 crashing into the south tower of the World Trade Center; and finally female adult entertainer Alexis Texas at the eXXXotica expo.

He was searching for the sports memorabilia website where he found a NY Giants Phil Simms throwback jersey. Oddly, the jersey was sold out everywhere except the website, which he foolishly forgot to bookmark. The legendary Giants quarterback was an all-time favorite of Priscilla's, and he wanted to surprise her in time for her birthday.

Bryce skimmed through the search browser history filled with familiar website links and a few questionable ones. He would have to have *another* chat with Omari who he repeatedly cautioned about the litany of viruses attached to pornography sites. Bryce's laptop was the primary source of entertainment, and he didn't want to experience another one crashing on him after his own personal bouts of exploring smut on the web shortly after his breakup with Kristen.

Finally, the link he'd been looking for appeared under *Sunday, December 5, 2010*—the original date he visited the site. Bryce clicked the link to save it to his favorites and immediately typed the name 'Phil Simms' into the search bar.

Low in stock.

Barring pornography links, the browser history displayed visits to a host of webpages about sexually transmitted infections —namely HPV—and blog sites where people openly discussed disease cures. He took a few more sips of his protein shake in an obvious haze. The thought occurred to him that Omari, who was sexually active, was probably better familiarizing himself with the ugliness of sexual diseases plaguing the Black community. If true, his vigilant efforts were commendable. But why such a detailed search? Better yet, why hadn't Omari consulted him for advice?

There wasn't a talking point out of Bryce's reach. He made a concerted effort to self-educate himself beyond school and was painfully forthcoming if you sought his opinion. The browser history wasn't a big deal, but something didn't sit right. Moreover, how would Mrs. Terri react to the news if Omari were inarguably infected? Was it even Bryce's job to tell? He shook off the disturbing thought, shut his laptop, and gulped the rest of his shake before heading upstairs when his cell rang.

"Sup, Pop. I'm about to hop in the shower. Order the pancake deluxe special if you get there before me. Yes, don't worry, it's in the trunk..."

4

—

BAD ROMANCE

Julissa put the finishing touches on a chicken empanada dish for her soon-to-be-arriving famished secret lover. Leading up to tonight's face-off, she allowed her imagination to get the best of her. Bryce was her seven-month long escape from a life of marginal unhappiness, and she envisioned him tasting every sector of her body before thrusting his powerful erection through her walls. The thought sent a cold shiver down her spine as "La Gatita" purred in agitated heat.

～

Her ambivalence toward marriage and a case of vaginal atrophy led her to abstain from sex long before their surreptitious affair. She functioned just fine without it but a week without Bryce's touch caused severe withdrawal. Even Mother Nature couldn't curb her sexual hunger. While on her menstrual cycle, she commonly coaxed him into quick house visits just to perform fellatio. It was through his sexual prowess that her undiscovered side was revealed. He was the only person to make her climax. No longer would she have to imagine what an orgasm felt like. The memory of being suspended in the air against the wet shower wall

—her legs wrapped around his neck—lived in her head forevermore.

Single motherhood was the catalyst for Julissa completing her bachelor's program in behavioral science and securing an amazing job. However, to appease a religious mother who evoked fear at the perils of single parenthood, she begrudgingly accepted her spouse-to-be's hand in marriage. Eight years later, she was in a huff.

She aspired to thrive on her own. With a prosperous career in social work, she could more than afford to pack up her belongings and sprint toward a lifestyle of choice, but she was strategically sound. Marriage to a high six-figure earner who managed their living expenses outweighed the unknown with a flame. Regardless of Bryce's irresistibility, her sole intent was to selfishly maximize their sexual arrangement. Besides, if her husband mercifully got what he wanted out of their marriage—a spicy Latina MILF, as he often described to friends—so would she, as long as Bryce sustained their affair.

The television light illuminated the dark living room as a steady rainfall struck against the windows. Julissa curled up on the loveseat, tugging at her rising boyshorts. She channel-surfed with her cell phone gripped in the other hand.

Papi, come thru the front door when u get here. It'll be unlocked. Her text to Bryce read.

In past visits, she asked that he enter through the basement to secure their privacy and to prevent the front door alarm chime from waking up her daughter. Tonight's anticipation produced an unfamiliar bravery. She tightened her ponytail, rose to her feet, and unlocked the front door when suddenly her phone played a familiar ringtone. *No fuckin' way,* she whispered, racing back to the sofa. She peeked at the microwave clock—7:37 p.m. Her husband's flight was scheduled to depart over an hour ago.

The ill-timed call suggested his senses were tingling. She took a deep breath and placed him on the speakerphone.

"Hey. I was just dozing off. The ringer scared me."

Hey. Sorry. I texted you about an hour and a half ago and there was no response. Figured I'd give you a call.

"You did? I don't see anything."

Yeah, it was a little after six. You know the service at the house is crappy, so it'll probably come through later. No biggie. Anyway, the flight was... [inaudible sound]

"The flight was what?" In a flash, the thought of her evening plans went into flames. "You're coming in choppy. Hello? Hello?"

Can you hear me?

"Barely. You were saying something about the flight and then I lost you."

I was saying the flight was [inaudible sound] ... hello?

"I'm here. All I heard was the flight was..."

Delayed. Can you hear me now?

"Yes. Why was it delayed?"

There was a heavy storm passing. We're boarding now.

She was as happy as a clam. "Really? *Pobrecito.* That sucks. So, what time do you think you'll get there?"

Says we should get to O'Hare around ten our time.

"Ten? Oh yes, they're an hour behind us. So, nine. Okay, that isn't too bad."

Did you take Nattie to your mom?

"I did. She couldn't wait to get there, and I couldn't wait to take her. You have no idea how much of a break I've needed. It's been such a long time."

Two soft knocks appeared at the front door. A tall shadowy figure surfaced, wearing a Baltimore Orioles baseball cap, dark jacket over a white T-shirt, and dark jeans ripped at the knee with an umbrella in hand. Julissa approached him with a sheepish grin, placing her finger on her lip. She grabbed his wet jacket, pointing him in the direction of the kitchen where she followed.

"I'm gonna get my nails and eyebrows done tomorrow morning and pick her up in the afternoon. I need to grab a few more outfits for the trip."

Okay. I've got to touch base with Kelsey's mom to see how far she's come along with packing. We've only got about a week and a half left. Time is flying by. I don't want her waiting 'til the last minute.

Julissa rolled her eyes at the comment as she prepared Bryce's plate.

Oh, sweet...

"What?"

There aren't many people boarding.

"You're in first-class. It shouldn't even matter," she laughed.

Good point. I just don't want any crying kids on here. We've already been inconvenienced.

Bryce observed Julissa's annoyance as she rotated her hand in a hurried motion. Her behavior was cold and insensitive, leaving him to wonder why she continued with the façade. In the meantime, he looked around the kitchen for something to dry his hands.

"All right, well, I'm getting sleepy. I think I'm gonna take a cat nap. Text me when you've landed... better yet, call and leave a voicemail just in case the phone doesn't ring. I'll try to wait up."

Will do. Love you. Hug Nattie for me.

"I will. Safe travel. Have fun."

"Damn, you're cold blooded. You really felt some kinda way, huh?" Bryce questioned.

"Who me? How could you say such cruel, mean things to your mistress?"

"Mistress? I'm not the one married."

"*Bueno,* so then, you're *my* mistress. Wait, *mister*-ress," she joked. "That's what I'm gonna call you from now on."

"*Mister-ress?* That's genius. I should put it on a shirt. You know, we can easily change that title, but you ain't ready for that conversation."

"You'd be in breach of our contract. I'll sue. We had a deal, mister-ress."

"First off, I never signed any paperwork, so, this is all hearsay. Secondly, my love, none of this is permissible in court."

"What would you like to drink, sir?" Julissa deliberately bent over into his crotch while scanning the top shelf of the refrigerator. Bryce caressed her thigh holding firmly onto her waist.

"You honestly think I'm sweatin' you, huh? All because of my feelings about your trip?" He walked toward the living room sofa swamped with guilt, placing himself in the shoes of her husband. This wasn't Bryce's first involvement in an emotionless affair, but he grappled with feelings just as she suspected.

Julissa was unforthcoming about her marriage, only sharing pieces of information when necessary. Since the beginning of their affair, they only shared one extensive conversation and that was on their initial lunch date. If you were to ask her, there wasn't much to discuss.

"Papi, hurry up and eat so you can eat *me*." She smirked, handing over a glass of lemonade. "Listen, the only thing you need to worry about right now is putting your friend right here, *y dentro en mi boca*. Do you know what I just said?"

"You play around too much. Let me reiterate, this isn't about catching feelings. We're simply having a discussion. Let me ask you a question. We've gone from exclusively meeting at my place to sneaking through your basement door and *now* I'm walking through your front door... eating dinner on *your* couch. Don't you think I have the right to know what's going on?"

"*¿Qué carajo?* You're being extra. You're *really* gonna ask questions tonight out of all nights?"

"We've got nothing but time," he laughed. "What's the big deal? You asked me to spend the night. I'm here, so let's have a conversation."

"Obviously, we did the basement thing because Natalie was here. What else do you want me to say?"

"Let's start with this. Why go on the trip if it isn't something you wanna do?"

"Because, *Your Honor,* Natalie is at the age where she'll remember. Plus, his daughter is going as well, and they get along. The trip is for them, not us. He planned it last year. At first, I didn't wanna go. We were having problems, and I thought it was best to let the girls go with his sister and her family. Do you know what else?"

"What?"

"I even suggested he go with his ex-wife and her family if he wanted to go so bad."

"Who would suggest such a thing?"

"I didn't care. They're all cordial. I could take Natalie to Disney by myself, but a part of me would rather her experience a trip like this with kids her age. This was all before you came into the picture."

"Look, I'm just seeking clarity. That's all I'm doing. Remember, in one of our first conversations, you came off like you were checked out of the marriage."

"Okay?"

"Am I making this up?"

"What is wrong with you? I just said OKAY."

"So, what was that look about? You don't remember the drive out to the Poconos where you were talking about booking more trips together?"

"Right. Even then I told you about the possibility of a trip to Florida. That's when you got butt hurt and didn't wanna speak."

"Can I finish? So, the whole ride you're explaining how complicated your situation is, how he's never home, how you're not really in love..."

"Okay, I don't see the point."

"You keep cutting me off..."

"*¡Mira!* Because you're not saying anything. He's only home about sixty percent of the time and he usually sleeps in the basement because of his insomnia. He spends the other time traveling for work. I told you before, it's his home. He bought it after his divorce. He was the only one living here. Natalie and I moved in after we got married. His daughter visits, but she lives with her mother. He asked if I wanted him to sell the house. I said no, let's stay here. He takes care of the expenses, and it has allowed me to pursue my masters. Happy now?"

"So, you've got a Sugar Daddy."

"If that's what you wanna call him. If that makes you happy. *Dàmelo*," she mouthed, pointing to his plate.

"It's a joke. Why are you getting so defensive?"

"Yo, why do you do this? Why come over to have an intervention about my life? All I ever asked is that you don't mess with another bitch while with me... or to at least wear a condom. Other than that, I don't ask you anything. *Nada.*"

"That's fair."

"Like, why are you so worried about my situation if I'm not giving any thought to it? That just means you've caught feelings."

"I've never made it a secret that I'm attracted to you."

"I'm not talking about attraction. You've caught feelings. F-e-e-l-i-n-g-s..."

"You can spell? That bachelor's degree is *finally* paying off, huh?"

"Finally? I'm about to get my master's, what about you, mister?"

"Here you go with this master's stuff. I'm doing quite well but thank you for your concern. All right, so, last question. Where will you guys sleep?"

"What do you mean?"

"Where will the two of you sleep on this trip?"

"Aah, is that what this is about? You're *really* paranoid."

"Simple question. Considering everything you've told me; will you share a bed, yes, or no?"

"*¡Dios Mio!* Natalie and I will share a bed and he'll be on the floor, the balcony, or in the hallway, I dunno," she replied angrily.

It was the first time Bryce recalled a visible light in the living room during the handful of visits to her home. He stretched his arms out against the sofa to observe the dining area. Catching his eye were various wall paintings and a portrait of Julissa, two girls, and an older gentleman who resembled actor Michael Keaton. One big happy family, or so it seemed. In an impoverished attempt at playing detective, he desperately wanted to peel back the layers of a mystifying situation. In his eyes, she was cheating herself out of a life of normalcy trying to compartmentalize feelings for two men.

Their affair had become exasperating. Bryce grew tired of sneaking around, parking his car out of the eyeshot of neighbors, and camouflaging his feelings while she obtained everything she wanted. He had enough of being groped by the genitals or grinded against for a rise. Deep inside was a ravenous craving for love. The art of kissing was his forte and he ignorantly believed he could take away her unhappiness if only she allowed him. He placed Julissa in a bearhug hoping to reduce the tension.

"Stop," she yelled light-heartedly. "Hit the dining room light, please."

"So, you're gonna wash dishes tonight, out of all nights? Really?" He turned his cap backwards, advancing to the nape of her neck, and performed light kisses to her notable sweet spot. Julissa begrudgingly tilted her head, unable to resist his touch. Standing face to face, she brought him closer to her five-foot-seven frame, wrapping her arms around his neck. Bryce moved in on her lips. This was the moment he'd been waiting for. Unfortunately, it wouldn't happen tonight. Julissa knew how to separate fornication from romance, shifting her face to exhibit the side of her neck. Bryce sampled it again, gripping her soft backside in one motion. She released a gentle moan leaping into his arms as they wobbled along the kitchen floor.

"Hit the light, Papi."

Bryce threw her onto the sofa with unusual vigor, setting himself in between her propped legs. He removed her tank top and immediately sucked her perky nipples with exuberance, licking in circular motions. Tender bites and gentle blows were mixed in to soften the sting.

"Take this off," she implored, discarding his baseball cap.

"Let your hair down," he whispered back. The appearance of long hair—even in darkness—was aesthetically pleasing.

She scooched up, anticipating his next move, tugging at his penis through his pants as he stripped to his boxer briefs. Bryce held onto a fistful of Julissa's hair and backed her into the armrest of the sofa arriving at her exposed neckline. He applied more tasteful licks and off the wall suggestive talk. She sank lower into the sofa, craftily wrapping her legs around him. Moisture beaded his tip. The sensation of his manhood pressed against her vulva was outright orgasmic.

He moved his hips forward, doing his best to break free of the hold. His warm breath swept across her skin. Finally, he escaped, pulled down her shorts and tantalized with more licks around her abdomen. He tugged at her nipple with one hand and inserted two fingers deep into her secreted hollowness with the other. Moving at a moderate pace, he shifted his hands to her anxious mouth where she received a taste of her own juices. "I bet you taste as good as you smell," he murmured, before burying his face in between her legs. Julissa's moans heightened while Julia Roberts and Richard Gere frolicked on the television screen.

Bryce awakened from a snooze on the king-size bed with Julissa's hand pressed firmly against his bare chest. Lying motionless, he listened attentively to her breathing patterns through the heavy raindrops thumping against the windowsill. She appeared flat on her stomach, her face sunken deep into the pillow, untroubled by the disturbance outside. Following an evening at an indescribable high, it was a wonder if she was still alive.

Bryce's tired eyes combed the room in search of the digital clock on the dresser until it registered, he wasn't in his bedroom.

He reached down to the floor to find his cell. It was 4:12 a.m. Staring at the ceiling fan and pondering the next course of action, he wanted to leave before sunrise, freshen up at home, and connect with Priscilla for her nephew's ten o'clock game. In the blink of an eye, Julissa showed signs of life. She repositioned her right leg over his and impulsively shifted her hand downward to massage his genitals.

"What time is it, Papi?" she muttered.

"A little past four. I'm about to get ready."

With her trip to Disney less than a week away and a visit from Mother Nature scheduled upon her return, they were looking at weeks before another arousing experience. She latched onto his excitement, motioning upward and descending swiftly. "*Dame*," she whispered in Spanish. Bryce removed the bed sheet to the exposure of her plump behind radiating through the blackened room. She placed her body a few inches to the center of the bed where he transferred his weight on top of her back before inserting himself. He clasped her wrists, and together, they closed their eyes.

5

———

WORKING FOR THE WEEKEND

"You're gonna call me Uncle Sam by the end of the night," Gucci uttered to Lorenzo "Fish" Gill, Bryce's childhood friend, who made a rare Friday appearance for a high-stakes' night of bowling. The car sales manager and married father of three was the only other high school classmate Bryce regularly communicated with. Lorenzo usually spends Friday evenings watching Disney movies with his daughters or catching a slate of basketball games, depending on the time of year. Miraculously, the guys talked him into hanging out during the start of the NBA playoffs.

Their friendship spanned two decades, meeting in homeroom as freshmen at Cedar Ridge High School. Bryce served as Lorenzo's best man at his beach destination wedding to his high school sweetheart Daija and was named godfather to their children thereafter. Lorenzo, "the voice of reason" as friends called him, was strongly against Bryce's involvement with Julissa. Though he vaguely remembered her, he continued to urge him to maintain a healthy distance from a potentially ugly situation.

"I'm just getting warmed up, brotha. You know I show out when the spotlight's on," Lorenzo announced, attending to his wrist.

"You look rusty as hell. There's a thousand-dollar pot on the line and you're over here bowling gutter balls. Look at the little cartoon character on the screen, even *he's* embarrassed. Playboy, I think it might be past Fish's curfew. Where's Dale's spry ass? We need some competition."

Gucci's brother returned with a plate of chicken fingers, fries, and a cup of soda hanging onto his teeth by a thread.

"Junior, can you believe Fish just bowled a gutter?"

"You're kidding," he replied, shaking his head in disgust.

"Easy money tonight, baby."

"Well, when you think about it, where else but Aerial Lanes can you make a quick stack without getting arrested?"

"How Don King says it? *Only* in America," Gucci answered, laughing at Lorenzo's horrendous display.

Bryce interrupted their little gang up. "Relax. It's the best of three series. Y'all got us the first game. If you fools think I'm gonna hand over my hard-earned money *that* easily, you've got another thing coming."

"Aye, y'all got two options—call on God or quit," Junior blurted.

"Fish, go and grab my wrist brace from the trunk," Bryce declared, tossing his car keys in hopes of curing Lorenzo's woes.

"Oh shit, not the wrist brace," Gucci barked, wiggling his fingers with imaginary fear. "Junior gave y'all two options and you think a wrist brace is gonna save y'all? Aye Junior, they can't be serious."

"We can end this early if y'all ain't ready to play," Junior added in an impassive tone. "I just walked by some fine ass ladies over in the other lane."

"Fish been changing shitty diapers for so long he forgot how to bowl and now Playboy thinks a wrist brace is gonna save them. Nah, I'm not gonna let you go out like this. What's Dale's number?"

Gucci should have known better. Good-natured ribbing had an adverse effect on Bryce going back to when he traded jabs with older kids on the playground. As his father always told him: "If you want the center stage, you'd better perform."

All right, ladies and gentlemen, we're gonna take it back to 1976. Here is ABBA with "Dancing Queen," the recorded deep-voiced DJ followed.

Bryce powdered his hands, creating a light smog. He wiped his personalized multi-colored marble ball with a cloth. He was laser focused on the pins as the guys stared in suspense. Suddenly, silence.

"Bong," he yelled with jubilation.

"Let's go," Lorenzo screamed, high-fiving Bryce with tremendous force. A stunned family in the next lane looked on. It was Bryce's third consecutive strike. Lane number twenty-four was alive and well.

"Oh, *now* y'all wanna get loud?" Junior questioned. "We're still up. What's all the fuss about?"

"Since y'all like pointing at screens, look at that S.O.B. now. The turkey's doing the running man on y'all."

"Talk your shit, Playboy," Gucci voiced. "That's what I like to hear. I *knew* you still had it in you."

"It never left. Next time I'mma bowl left-handed on y'all. Don't forget, I'm ambidextrous."

"What did he just say?" a puzzled Junior asked.

"I don't know. Some shit about Abercrombie & Fitch."

Gucci, dressed in an all-blue velour sweatsuit, looked up at the scores before calmly approaching the floor.

Gucci: 67 - J.R.: 73

Fish: 39 - B.A.T.: 90

The left-hander aligned himself along the left side of the lane and promptly maneuvered his traditional toothpick along his mouth. He offered up more figurative language before his next bowl.

"I'm 'bout to put y'all on game. Heroes don't always wear capes. Aye, Junior, tell 'em what they wear."

Junior waited until his brother released the ball and in a piercing voice yelled out, "Gucci!"

Gucci hit his familiar pose, standing with his arm rested in the air, his left leg wrapped over the right as the group watched the ball spin toward the center of the pins.

"C'mon... damn," he mouthed, clapping his hands with force.

"Pick up that spare, big bro. Two pins. Light work. We do this in our sleep."

After the fifth frame, the group took a quick interval. The series was tied at one game apiece led by Lorenzo's amazing comeback. Junior ran off to grab a few drinks while Lorenzo checked on his wife and kids. Meanwhile, Gucci, within earshot of Bryce, chatted up a couple of young ladies with another classic one-liner.

"You remind me of the twenty-one letters of the alphabet..."

Twenty-one? Aren't there twenty-six?

"Oh, my bad, you're right. I forgot the U - R - A - Q - T..."

Bryce stood alongside his car, folding three crisp one-hundred-dollar bills and four fifties into his wallet. He hummed along to the high-pitched tunes of "Night Fever" pumping through the exterior speakers of the bowling alley. Lorenzo approached him, clutching onto the wrist brace like an heirloom.

"That S.O.B. was a life saver, wasn't it? You need to go home and tell the girls how their god daddy saved their daddy," Bryce announced to Lorenzo's amusement.

"Damn, Denver is about to get swept by OKC. Those boys came to play tonight," he reported, reading playoff updates on his phone. "Anyway, good lookin' out, dawg. My wrist is screaming. I was trying to hide it the whole time."

"No problem. I usually keep it in the trunk. My pop swears by it."

"Dale the Destroyer needs assistance?"

"Yessir. Ever since he beat me a few months back. He'll bowl with his buddies without it, but every time *we* meet up, he's like, 'Where's the brace, is it in the trunk?'"

"I couldn't tell you the last time I bowled a one-sixty. Does this mothafucka have magical powers?" Lorenzo asked, staring at the brace with astonishment.

"I can't call it, but you left the bowling alley five-hundred dollars richer. Maybe there's something to it. Oh, here come these fools now. Yo Guc, why are you walking with a limp? Pockets feeling lighter?"

"Sometimes you've gotta eat shit and like it. What can I say?"

"Y'all wanna run this back?" Junior suggested. "Put your money where your mouth is."

"Shut yo ass up," Lorenzo fired back. "It's damn near midnight. Y'all talked shit all night long. Y'all can dish it, but can't take it?"

"Fish, I know you ain't talking. How many gutters did you bowl? We almost had to put bumpers up for your punk ass."

"How was I supposed to see with that glow-in-the-dark bullshit?"

"Y'all hear this dude? We *all* bowled with the lights out."

Gucci barged in. "Switching subjects, y'all see all the ass in there? How was anyone supposed to concentrate? I might be five hundred dollars lighter but at least I walked away with a couple of numbers."

"He bagged two numbers in a velour suit," Bryce responded to the group's amusement. "That's when you know life ain't fair."

"Don't hate the player, hate the game."

"Well, the game's rigged."

[laughter]

"You know what we need to do? Let's start planning a guys' trip for later in the year. I'm serious," Gucci replied.

Bryce added, "We've talked about this a million times before. Nothing ever surfaces." The crew paused to admire three attractive young ladies chuckling amongst themselves.

"Y'all ladies have a good night," Gucci said.

"Thank you. You too."

"Aye, I bet y'all look pretty when y'all wake up. Am I lying?" They were amused by his words of flattery but continued pacing through the parking lot in search of their vehicle. "There's four of us and three of y'all. The night's still young," he continued.

"It's almost twelve," one girl yelled.

"Okay, Cinderella, what about your friends?"

"We're good but thank you."

"That's why you can't walk in heels, you ole knock kneed bitch," he mumbled, causing the guys to burst into laughter.

"Why'd you whisper the last part?" Bryce asked, grinning from ear to ear. "Say it with your chest."

"Fuck them."

"I've always wanted to hit up the Dominican Republic," Junior continued. "I've heard some wild stories about the girls down there. My boy was telling me something about how they grab you as you walk by. I can't remember the name of the spot, but he goes every year."

Gucci countered. "A bitch better not grab me. I'm from the hood, she might get grabbed back, nahmean? Yo, where do they do Hedonism at?"

"Jamaica," Bryce replied. "Why? You wanna walk around with your nuts out?"

"Y'all ain't ready for that type of spectacle."

"You know what I truly miss? Freaknik. Back when Atlanta wasn't mainstream. Fish, what year were we at Piedmont?"

"Had to be '96. Right before the Summer Olympics."

"Didn't you say you went to school in Virginia?" Junior asked Bryce. "There are enough baddies out there. Alexandria is fuckin' loaded."

"True, but I've got fam all over VA. That was a regular destination for me."

Lorenzo continued. "Personally, I thought Daytona and Myrtle Beach were better than ATL. Freaknik was at its peak around '93, '94. We *just* missed it."

"Daytona was nuts. That's when I brought my boy Dan. Dude ain't ever see that many buns in his life. The sistas were on him like white on rice. Fish, what was the name of the Nigerian dude from your school? It's at the tip of my tongue..."

"Who, Emmanuel?"

"Emmanuel, that's it. Yo, this cat Emmanuel got drunk—made out with a chick and threw up on her. I still remember the look on her face."

"That was crazy," Lorenzo replied. "She was horrified. I think I still have footage of Daytona. Remember that big ass camcorder I brought down there?"

[laughter]

"He lives in Houston now," Lorenzo followed. He's a doctor. Big house, married with kids, the whole nine yards. We haven't spoken in years but follow each other on Facebook."

"Another African doctor? You can't make this shit up. They shoot for the stars and land on the mothafuckin' moon, don't they?" Gucci blurted. "When's the last time you saw an African bus driver?"

"This guy is a total nut job," Bryce proclaimed. "Anyway, how do y'all feel about Miami or Vegas?"

"Vegas is poppin'."

"Fish, your married ass can't go anywhere," Junior snapped. "Go sit your 'happy wife, happy life' ass down somewhere. We ain't changing shitty diapers on a guys' trip."

"I've been out there quite a few times. I've got comps too."

"Can you go *now*? That's the question. Look, y'all, he's tensing up. The thought of having that conversation with his wife made his entire body clench up. Now he's holding his wrist. This man is hilarious."

"This fool's just mad cuz I'm counting his money with the same bad wrist," Lorenzo retorted, dabbing his thumb against his tongue while flipping fictitious money. "One hundred, two hundred, two fiddy..."

Gucci chimed in. "Fish, you know there are four rings to

marriage: The engagement ring, the wedding ring, the boxing ring, and the suffer-ring." The group erupted into uproarious laughter. "Seriously fellas, we need to narrow it down. I just wanna go where the ladies are."

A night out with the guys was a means of catharsis for Bryce after a week of working radically to mitigate Julissa's absence. It was the final night of her seven-day trip, and their lack of communication ate him up. Upon his arrival at the bowling alley, he'd check his phone periodically. Not one "hello" or "I miss you" text. Julissa was in the safe care of her husband. If only the thought could translate through his stubbornness.

After the guys' departure, Bryce sat alone in his car, skimming through a wave of notifications from women complimenting his profile on a dating site. A person of interest who he exchanged messages with leading up to Julissa's trip left a riveting comment.

New message from: Vonn-with-the-wind
Hey handsome, sorry for taking so long to get back to you. Busy week.
Yes, we should absolutely get together soon.
Call me: (718) 555-0281. Maybe this weekend?

The weekend was lined up. Bryce had already committed to attending the International Auto Show at the Javits Center with Priscilla on Saturday, and following Sunday's church service, there was a gym visit in store and a lunch date with an acquaintance. Instead of blindsiding his new interest with an unexpected late phone call, he opted for a quick text announcing who he was. Within minutes, she replied.

They spent half of the call lauding one another. Bryce satirized her seductive voice while she repeatedly gushed over his titillating pictures. A stimulating discussion ensued on Astrology, the demands of their jobs, and several key bullet points found on their respective profile pages. Yvonne, as she would soon be revealed, pressed him on the accuracy of his "not married" claim, having grown tired of meeting men who secretly lived double lives. She found Bryce to be someone of refreshing candor, and they entertained each other with captivating stories through the night.

~

It was Sunday afternoon. Bryce exited the gym, placed an oversized hood over his head and approached his pre-heated car. A wintry mix fell from the overcast sky. He gazed through the blurred windshield, wondering when spring would officially come out of hiding. The see-saw weather trend had tirelessly run its course.

He retrieved his phone from the glove compartment—he'd been using his iPod during the workout—only to find a string of notifications and a voicemail.

Where are you, mister? Call me when you get a moment. Oh, in case you ain't know, I'm baaack. Eww, did you hear my voice crackle? I need some tea. That was terrible. Anyway, bah.

Bryce smirked at Julissa's wacky humor. It was one of many traits he grew to admire, but it was clear she was oblivious to his feelings. It didn't even cross her mind that they hadn't spoken since her departure. He weighed calling back to emphatically voice his displeasure but that was senseless. Instead, he sent a text.

[Julissa's distinct ringtone]

"What's up?"

Eww. Is that how you greet your pretend girlfriend? I give you all this love and that's what I get back? I'm not one of your homeboys.

"What's up, Mrs. Kolowoski? How was your trip, my dear? Did you have a good time?"

Dear? What am I, an old lady? I want you to say, "Hey, baby, I missed you. I'm so happy to hear your voice and I'm thrilled to know that you're safe."

"You are *seriously* buggin.' I'll ask you one more time. How was your trip? It's a simple question."

With Bryce's routine morning fasting complete, he pulled into a burger & shake drive-thru for a light snack before his lunch date. Julissa shared details about her vacation, specifically news of the sleeping arrangement with her husband and a slight hiccup involving her daughter.

We had the most fun at Universal Studios, but Natalie's period came on our third day there.

"Wait, how old is she again?"

Eleven. She's been complaining about her stomach for a while now, but they were all false calls. I don't know. I feel like I should've been more prepared. So, unfortunately, we couldn't do the water park that day, which sucked donkey balls. Overall, she had a blast. She was like, "Mommy, can we move to Florida?"

"Is that someone snoring in the background?"

[soft giggle] That's her. We had a late flight, and the girls stayed up 'til God knows when. She's being extra clingy today. I let her tag along since he had to drop off his daughter. She wants to help me cook tonight, so I'm letting her pick out the food.

"Cool. Well, I don't wanna take up too much of your time. Send me some pics. I'm sure you took a million selfies."

Is that your way of rushing me off the phone? Anyway, I was thinking, for our next meeting, we need to have wild, drunken sex. Deal?

"You're so random."

You love my randomness...

She wasn't lying.

The wintry mix converted to a light dusting. Bryce pulled into his development—to the display of a courageous young man entertaining his friends by laying topless on the patchy front lawn grass, creating a snow angel. Things got interesting as he circled the corner leading to the front of his house.

He recognized the alluring neighbor walking leisurely from her mailbox unit, exhibiting a grim expression flickering through the mail. She sported a tightly wrapped multi-colored head scarf, denim jacket, and loose grey sweatpants which failed to hide her hips. While trying to process her entire frame, he struggled to concentrate on the rearview camera backing into his driveway. On his mind was the neighbor's most recent spurn, and her child-bearing hips, but it was vital that he give her a dose of her own medicine. He grabbed his belongings and made a quick dash to the front door as if she didn't exist.

"I see you're always on the go."

He peered over his shoulder, trying to ascertain who the comment was directed at. There she was, sneering in his direction with a hand placed on her waist. Bryce offered a smile, motioning with his finger to allow him a minute to unload the items in the foyer before he made a swift about-face.

6

———

BACK AND FORTH

Who needs friends with a circle like mine?
When you look-up the word 'real,' guess whose pic you'll find?
I keep the chrome at the waist—chrome, chrome, at the
waistline...
Push your wig back more than Bron, Bron's hairline...

-H2O

Anticipation grew for the rap duo's compelling five-track demo. Omari and Brixx nodded their heads in unison, awaiting the arrival of their crew. They traded a blunt cigarette back and forth like a game of hot potato, staring through a cloud of marijuana smoke. A heavy bassline track played on.

"I still think you should switch 'look up' with 'search," Brixx suggested. "When you *look up* the word real, guess whose pic you'll find? When you *search* the word real, guess whose pic you'll find?"

"Nah... it feels like I'm stretching it out. *Look up* flows better," Omari expressed during the playback. "You see, right there.

Imagine if I would've said 'search.' Push comes to shove, we can always add an ad-lib, but I think it's fine just the way it is."

Omari's eyes wandered around the stush basement studio, seeking validation from Brixx's trusted sidekick and weed supplier, Rashad, who was setting up an incredibly expensive camera on a tripod to record their studio session.

"Personally, I like 'look up,'" the spotty beard hanger-on advised. "But that LeBron line goes hard." Omari approved, acknowledging Rashad with a hand slap.

Under the advice of Brixx's stepfather, it was critical for their long-term success to document each studio session. Inserting behind-the-scenes footage to an already electrifying portfolio could catapult their movement and separate the group from the rest of the pack. Meanwhile, Brixx continued playing the verse.

> **Brixx:** I'm the hood's favorite, wait til y'all get a whiff of me...
> **H2O:** We're giving rappers the boot, like the map of Italy
> **Brixx:** Gangsta 1-0-1, that's the class we in...
> **H2O:** Fuck around, our guns dump like Kardashian's

"Oh, y'all doing the back-and-forth thing like Jada and Styles? When did y'all record this?"

"A few months ago," Omari replied. "We're basically done. We have two solos—one where I rhyme the hook and another where Brixx does the same. Then we have the storytelling track with the whole team called "Unthinkable.""

"I think I heard that one. Is it the one with Harmony singing?"

"Yeah."

"Yo, Harmony got a man?" Rashad asked.

"Bro, relax. That's my little sis," Brixx replied.

"You ain't answer the question. Y'all ain't blood related," he countered, ducking a ballpoint pen fired at his head.

"Then there's the back and forth joint you just heard called

"Back 2 Back," Omari concluded, jugging down his third bottle of water. "We're just stuck on what the fifth song should be."

"Four tracks might be enough. Have y'all decided on a group name?"

"T.S.U. is the entire squad," Brixx stated.

"T.S.U.?"

"Tri-state Unit," Brixx replied. "That's me, O., Harmony, Don-Pro... well, he's Don-P now, and Ford. Me and O.'s two-man group is a combination of our names. I'm 'Brixx Dinero,' he's 'H2O'... so, we've been messing with the name 'CashFlow.'"

"CashFlow? I like that."

Omari broke in, "Either CashFlow or B-2-O."

"B-2-O?"

"Yeah, it's kinda like Brixx is handing me the mic," he demonstrated. "It can also be used as a drug reference like a brick to an ounce."

"Aah, gives y'all a little street appeal."

"Yup. But the name is too close to B2K and with my name being similar to Omarion, it wouldn't be a good look..."

"Word. Nobody would take y'all seriously. Two *rappers* talking about street life doing choreographed B2K dance moves is wild," Rashad joked. "I got a name for y'all. How about B.O., cuz it's musty as fuck in here."

"It ain't start smelling 'til your bum ass walked in with those dirty socks," Brixx retaliated, taking a pull of the blunt. "O., look at the bottom of his socks—looks like he's been stomping in mud all day."

"That's because of your dirty ass floor," Rashad hurled back.

"O., you wanna wear the airbrushed tees for the video or stick with the black tees?"

"Let's do the airbrush tees," Omari replied, scratching at his midsection. "Let's wait 'til the sun sets and then we can get some B-Roll footage wearing black with the gold chains. That visual will be dope."

"True."

"I'm ready for this cypher. What time is the rest of the team supposed to arrive?"

"Should be on their way. Let me hit up Ford."

Omari excused himself to the bathroom, triggered by a prickly sting in his urethra. He hurtled past Zeus—Brixx's pit bull Rottweiler mix—leading upstairs to the discovery of a yellowish-white discharge which he suspected was his body's way of flushing excess fluids after a recent sexual encounter.

Omari once resented his virgin status in the world of young people occupied in feckless behavior. At seventeen when his boys shared tantalizing stories, he too wanted to join the fray dishing out fabricated tales of how he'd become the generation's next great adult entertainer. In truth, he was at home loafing around on his gaming system. It wasn't until he officially lost his virginity that change precipitated.

He was coerced by a few imprudent friends to ditch condoms in favor of the withdrawal method after complaining about his inability to ejaculate. The subtle savor of a woman's womb sent him over the edge. Through the heat of the moment, many of these impressionable women gave into his plea. This would include Shauna, his dubious on-and-off ex-flame, who he reconciled with at a New Year's Eve gathering.

It was only after experiencing a brief irritation to his genitals that he conducted a search on STD's. However, without any notable symptoms, Omari put all worries behind. He didn't realize the infection had already begun its silent course—steadily spreading through his bloodstream since exposure. Through further examination, not only was the color of the secretion off-putting but so was the slight skin rash on the tip of his penis. The rash didn't cause any pain, but it was easy to gloss over as it masked his skin tone. Clearly, something had gone awry. He flushed the toilet and sat along the edge of the tub, doubled in pain with a flurry of thoughts. Who could his transferrer have been?

In Omari's personal game of Russian roulette, there were only a few suspected names to mull over. The question wasn't whether he was exposed, but *which* virus was he exposed to? He reached down into his shorts to conduct another search, becoming numb to the findings of more off-colored matter.

[loud dog barking]

"Zeus, go!" Brixx instructed his overprotective mutt, who grew anxious by the front door commotion. His monstrous, startling barks echoed through the walls.

"Hold on. Yo, O., you all right?" Brixx shouted from behind the locked door, where a rowdy group congregated. "Are you taking a shit?"

"I'm good... just reciting my rhymes. Gimme a sec," he yelled over the running faucet water.

"You're reciting rhymes taking a shit?"

Omari unlocked the bathroom door to Brixx's surprise. "My bad. The team's here. They said they've got some fire for you."

"Fire? For whom??"

You. Fuck you mean? someone answered back.

"Y'all ever witness a murder on camera?" Omari asked.

What did he say?

"Have y'all ever witnessed a murder on camera?" Brixx repeated.

No. Why?

"Tell them they're about to," Omari ensured.

"Ooh, he said y'all punk asses 'bout to," Brixx stirred up, slapping Omari's wet hand. "What the? Why are your hands so damp? You whacking off?" he asked, wiping his hand alongside his camouflage shorts.

[laughter]

"You and these lame ass jokes. I'm coming down now. Grab me another water."

Omari stood before the mirror in complete outrage as he loosened his black du-rag. The longer he stared, the angrier he got. It was at that moment he wanted to lash out on his biological father —a man who selfishly found the idea of raising his own children trivial. Still, there was no one to blame for his personal blunders but himself. To snap out of a commanding trance, he splashed cold water onto his face. The droplets fell slowly from beneath his brown eyes onto his pencil thin mustache. Inside of his pockets were two Cubic Zirconia diamond stud earrings that he placed in each ear before wrapping the du-rag over his head.

The rowdy group sang along to a song they planned to shoot a video for later in the day. When Omari's verse played, he listened intently from the bathroom mumbling the words:

I'm on the edge, man, I swear it could get ugly
Bullets'll have you shielding your face like you're doing the Dougie
H-2-O, homie, I don't deal with the fakes
Fuck with my bread, get your body spread—Land O' Lakes...
Arms in Manhattan, legs out in Staten
Head in the BX, they're handing your family Kleenex
Hop over to Teaneck, dump the rest
I'm on the I-9-5 bumpin' Red and Meth...

Brixx declared his personal verse the best at the song's conclusion. Taking exception, Omari rushed to the basement.

"I knew your ass would come down after that," Brixx shouted.

Rashad set the main camera to face the glowing graffiti-laced wall serving as the backdrop while the group flipped a coin, determining order placement for the cypher. Don-P set things off. Omari followed and then Brixx. Ford was given the assignment to record each member's performance with his fancy new iPhone. He'd go on last. Their respective acts would be combined into one whole video and eventually uploaded to their growing YouTube channel.

"That last cypher we put up got one thousand and twenty-three views," Brixx whispered to Omari, who appeared withdrawn, standing with his arms folded. "You heard? O.?"

"Yo."

"Bro, you good?"

"Yeah. I was thinking about which verse I wanted to spit. I might just freestyle through the first round."

Omari wasn't "good" at all. Not by a long shot. He was busy wondering what had gone wrong with his body. He grabbed his rhyme notebook from the inside of his duffle bag and shuffled through the pages until he found a verse fit for the classic DJ Premier track playing in the background.

~~Never been a shook one, but I'm always second guessing~~
~~Life gave me answers, but I've still got questions~~
My life is real, no other way to define it
Dad was a deadbeat, to help Mom I grinded
Now anger haunts me, time after time
Got me feeling like Cyndi Lauper, rhyme after rhyme
All the shit I've been through messed with my mental
Y'all keep talkin' 'potential' while I'm loading up my pistol...Tri-
State's most wanted, been official since day one
Got that flava for ya ear and I'm feeling like Ty-son...
You know it's on if u see me with gun in hand
Desert Eagle got you coming out the pocket like Cunningham

7

HAPPY FEELIN'S

Following church service, Dale directed his attention to some light spring cleaning in his garage-turned-man-cave, taking advantage of the mild temperature. The vivacious, graybeard homeowner busted into a light sweat vacuuming his sofa and area rugs, swapping out an oversized Washington Redskins throw blanket as he mumbled the melodies of Maze and Frankie Beverly's "Happy Feelin's." He attended to a half-smoked Nicaraguan cigar, helping himself to another pull. The flavor-scented smoke encompassed the air. Meanwhile, actor Peter Falk coincidentally raised a cigar over his head at the same time. Dale, an avid crime drama viewer, never missed an opportunity to watch *Columbo* even if he owned the complete series on a collection of DVDs. He walked toward the cul-de-sac to greet an arriving Bryce.

"Pop, when are you gonna upgrade this ugly license plate," Bryce asked, referring to his father's powder blue New Jersey tags reading "TALRMDE" on his sleek black Mercedes-Benz C300. They performed their personalized handshake and a half-hug before Dale threw lightning- quick jabs to Bryce's outer bicep. Mrs. Terri, who was inside completing a little purging of her own, came out the front door.

"I got your beautiful Mother's Day card. Thank you." She offered Bryce a welcoming hug then handed two bulky garbage bags for him to load into the trunk of her luxury SUV. Mrs. Terri planned to run a few errands, which included a stop at the thrift store. It would give way to some much-needed father and son time.

Their last interaction was at brunch a couple of months ago, where they spent the rest of the afternoon bowling. However, when together for long stretches of the day, you never knew how their conversations could sway. At times, their witticisms were ear-splitting, other times they sat in complete silence to the enjoyment of a televised game. Bryce had often been told he looked like his mother, but he mirrored Dale's personality traits from soup to nuts. Watching both father and son engrossed in a heated discussion using duplicated body language and mannerisms was quite the show.

Dale Robinson Taylor—nicknamed "Jackie" due to his father's allegiance to Brooklyn Dodgers legend Jackie Robinson—took fatherhood by the horns. A realization dawned on a snowy February morning as he and Candace—Bryce's mother—listened to the rhythmic heartbeat of their unborn child during the ultrasound. In the months that followed, Dale whispered to his son through Candace's abdomen or applied headphones to her stomach, playing comforting tunes of his favorite soul tracks to calm Bryce's overpowering kicks. His actions jump-started a father-son connection lasting to this day. In fact, Dale credited himself for Bryce's musical discernment. However, part of his act was caused by a whit of guilt for the role he played in derailing Candace's dreams.

Under no circumstances would Dale have expected to submit to Candace, a dazzling undergraduate, following their introduction at the University of Maryland, College Park, in the fall of 1970. She was easily the most beautiful woman he'd ever seen.

Despite their grade difference, they gave love a chance, discussing their passions and coveted living areas. After graduating in the winter of 1972, Dale favored suburban DC for its proximity to a new civil service job while Candace, still enrolled, aspired to perform on Broadway and would attend a performing arts school in New York City.

When she received her bachelor's degree in fine arts, she waited a year before heading north. It was in the summer of 1975 when Candace moved in with her maternal aunt, uncle, and their son Anton, inside their lavish Harlem brownstone. Dale and Candace traded hand-written letters and polaroid pictures until their relationship cooled off. Just when it felt like they had gone their separate ways, she re-emerged with a heart-felt letter projecting her love and fears of living in the big city.

The news of David Berkowitz, better known as the Son of Sam, and his acts of violent crimes against women was an immediate cause of concern. Though Candace wouldn't fit the description of the crazed serial killer's intended targets, it wouldn't stop the recurring panic attacks as she traveled about. While Berkowitz terrorized New Yorkers, the striving thespian made frequent long-distance calls to Dale and her parents, expressing loneliness and deep regret. She was only alone in theory, yet the horrifying news generated continuous worry. Her parents persistently pleaded that she rely on faith while shelling out for the performing arts school.

Meanwhile, Dale had other plans—hopping aboard Amtrak every other weekend for the three-hour ride into Penn Station on a quest to protect his love.

To prove their reunion was destiny, Dale eventually quit his job and made a permanent move to New York City at the height of Berkowitz's strikes. By virtue of Candace's hotshot Jewish uncle, they found a spacious one-bedroom apartment on West 143rd Street and Convent Avenue. Candace's uncle and aunt afforded their rent until they could withstand it. As their love unfurled so would an outcome forecasted a mile away.

Candace announced her pregnancy months after settling into their new digs. The news sent shockwaves back home. Her traditional Christian parents were apoplectic with rage and falsely accused all parties of engineering the event. The expectant couple were damned to eternal purgatory for conceiving a child in sin. They applied for their marriage license to eliminate the existing doubt of their love, with hopes to exchange vows before the delivery due date. Candace's ill-disposed parents thought little of the act and in protest of their nuptials, refused to show up to the Justice of Peace.

Bryce was introduced to the world on August 28, 1977, at St. Luke's Roosevelt hospital a month after the infamous New York City Blackout. New York is where the young family remained through some of its bleakest moments in history. Dale oversaw a couple of boutique shops while Candace played homemaker, sending their son off to school. A rash of arsons impacting one of Dale's businesses and the Bernhard Goetz subway shooting reignited Candace's almost faded fears. The event to spark an abrupt move, however, was the stabbing of an aspiring actress found dead on her apartment rooftop after the woman returned from a Broadway play. Candace couldn't escape the thought of how easily she could have fallen victim to the heinous offense as news circulated nationwide.

Back in Maryland, they settled for a modest single-family ranch home in Prince George's County. Candace worked as a

Performing Arts middle school teacher with an impulse for theatre. Unfortunately, time was running out and it wasn't the industry's harsh take on age that factored. After she recaptured a love for the arts, Candace was diagnosed with pancreatic cancer, a genetically-passed illness which compromised the health of her mother. Encouraged by a leading cancer care hospital based in New York City, the family loaded their Mercury Grand Marquis and uprooted to New Jersey for a closer commute. Dale's title of husband was of great significance, but nothing compared to "hero" if he could exert himself to find every resource available to save his wife.

Mournfully, the doctors were unable to eradicate the malignancy, ending Candace's courageous battle just shy of her thirty-ninth birthday. Dale poured his eyes out at her bedside, gripping her hand, giving thanks to God for allowing her into his life. In his final words, he promised to protect their son just as she would. Surely his efforts were lauded from above.

Dale's knack for playing hero renewed following the death of his father. For the first time in six decades, his mother lived alone in his childhood home in Suffolk, Virginia, and a move back to the Old Dominion state appeared imminent. During this time, Bryce grappled to untangle the imposing web of finding employment and an apartment. He encouraged Bryce to join him to help run a box-trucking business if his struggles continued. As the widower planted the seeds for a return south, without notice, Terri, an attractive, middle-aged woman serving as a weekend church usher, acted.

Terri was enamored by Dale's likability and dapperness, regularly addressing him with complimentary talk upon arrival. She presumed his infectious smile, and succinct replies were an act of shyness. In truth, there wasn't a timid bone in his body. His precipitous behavior was caused by an increased awareness of public presumption and a lasting state of mourning. These were dismal times for the usual upbeat optimist.

On a blistering cold Sunday following service, Terri extended to him an invitation to join several members of the congregation at a midweek gathering, where they served hot meals, offered uplifting words, and mingled through church-related activities. Thanks to Terri's modest approach, Dale became a regular attendee and received a sneak peek at her amazing culinary skills.

A decision to remarry wouldn't come easy. In the pool of women to cross his path, where many were considered unworthy of carrying the illustrious Taylor last name, there was something especially different about her. Terri was a loving Christian woman who would provide support and comfort to an emotionally battered man. That said, Dale couldn't escape a feeling of guilt. How would Bryce react watching him move on with another woman? Would he feel a sense of betrayal?

When Candace was laid to rest, Dale remained quiet, secluded, and dedicated to his job. He dated sparingly when Bryce was away at college, but it took an astonishing six years from Candace's burial before Dale fraternized with anyone. His celibacy streak heedlessly ended with an upscale escort. The decision caused him a bit of remorse, raising the inevitable question of "how soon is too soon" following the death of a loved one. Through a bit of self-justification, he chalked up the sexual encounter as an emotionless attachment and subsequently began a new streak. There was no bringing his ex-wife back, and loneliness inflicted an unhealed wound.

As time evolved, Terri's companionship was increasingly desired. Dale sought Bryce's blessing. Trust and respect were at the epicenter of their bond. Bryce approved their pending relationship, going a step further during a tear-jerking speech at their wedding, where he personally thanked Terri for resuscitating his father. At this point in life, all Bryce wished for was his dad's happiness while he was still alive.

To most, the wise decision for Dale would've been to joyfully ride off into the sunset like the end scenes of a Western. Why add more to an already amazing story? A Black man from southeastern Virginia who went unscathed living through the social unrest of the civil rights movement, becoming the first member of his family to graduate college. Furthermore, he works fervently to grab a hold of the American Dream and turns into a surviving spouse who perseveres by sending his only child off to college. The story wrote itself. However, he allowed a moment of vulnerability to facilitate his greatest gamble. As his love for Terri developed, so would his fearless efforts with a mammoth undertaking that involved raising another man's child.

Terri was left with the parental responsibility of Omari Harris, whose father drifted about procreating with multiple women. As the pungent taste of single parenthood and animosity steered her in the direction of faith, Dale was set on becoming a shining example of a male figure. Omari was almost similar in age to Bryce when Dale took over as his sole guardian, but the results were enormously different.

Omari egregiously disowned the same blueprint Bryce once grasped tighter than an infant, holding onto their mother's finger. By seventeen, he became a full-time irritant. The powerless teen was defenseless against the inducing urges of peer pressure and the penetrating bullet of an absentee father. Even Dale's domineering presence wouldn't do the trick.

Omari narrowly escaped high school and quit community college midway through his first-year, frothing at the mouth of a world of lawlessness ahead. Instead of higher learning, he spent his days getting high, applying his unique barbering skills as a means for cash, while sneakily selling marijuana from the house to support an elaborate sneaker collection. For Dale, coming home became a chore. He was unhinged at the sight of unruly young men walking in and out, loitering on the front of his property. Their opposing views on life were too vast to ever work harmoniously. The turmoil fostered a trip down a slippery road where Dale wondered if designating himself stepparent to a malcontent was worth the trouble. Terri's advertised 'packaged deal' looked more like unwanted baggage.

He loved his new wife dearly, but his joy for their union dissipated as her son continuously sabotaged it. She pleaded for patience, claiming the Lord's timing would prevail in such unsettling matters, but his patience had run thin. More so after learning of Omari's shady dealings from their home. Dale called for an urgent family sit-down, unable to watch Terri expunge his errors any longer. There would be no more helping hand for a young adult in need of a life preserver. With their marriage in jeopardy, it was either the uncivil sloth changed his ways or left.

Terri conceded following her husband's lead, proving scripture would be triumphal at their house. More Black families needed happy endings, and it was Bryce who came to the rescue. No challenge was too great for the unflappable mentor who was confident in his abilities to rehabilitate his troubled sibling.

"BAT, hand me that crate, I'm gonna stack those records in the corner."

"You've got some classics in here. How come I've never seen these?" Bryce asked, thumbing through the collection of pristine vinyl records sitting neatly in Dale's garage.

"I don't know. They were in the basement of the old house. You know, in the back of the closet where I used to keep my old boxing VHS tapes."

"The closet next to the shelf of trophies?"

[cigar burning sound]

"Yes," Dale replied, his eyes following a thick cloud of smoke.

"Yarbrough & Peoples? Chicago? Con Funk Shun? You haven't even opened these."

"Take the Chicago record. I have their Greatest Hits CD somewhere. Yarbrough & Peoples was your mother's. Take that one too. We used to buy duplicates. I had this whole plan where

I'd stash the unopened records hoping they'd be worth a damn, and we could cash out. They had all of us going. Can you believe that?"

"Just like my baseball cards. What am I supposed to do with all of them? I've got thousands sitting in a storage unit."

"Don't get rid of those cards unless you wanna square up," Dale voiced, shuffling his feet in a boxer pose.

"Okay, Muhammad Ali. You swear you can take me down."

"Don't get it twisted. Just cuz you're in the gym don't mean jack squat. Card collecting is a Taylor tradition, BAT. Pop-Pop is probably doing backflips in his grave at the bare thought of this conversation. Me and your Uncle Gibby still have Pop-Pop's coin collection, and I started collecting sports memorabilia before you were born. You can pass everything down to your kids when the time comes."

"I guess the tradition might just end with me," he joked. "Um, why is this song *still* playing? Is this the Puff Daddy remix?"

"Oh, now you wanna act all funky about my music? This is timeless, my boy. We used to play this..."

"*Every time I started crying...* you've told this story a thousand times."

"Good. Here's to one-thousand and one. Now you wanna sit up here and talk smack. Aye, Terri," Dale signaled to his wife, who exited the house fully prepared to run errands. "You hear this guy?"

"What are y'all fussing about now?" she asked, clutching her Louis Vuitton purse.

"He's talking about how long this song is. This *same* song used to stop him from crying when he was a baby. I'd run over to the stereo and turn it on as soon as he got fussy. His eyes would go like this," he mocked, bugging his eyes in a state of shock. "And just like that those crocodile tears disappeared."

"You hear this guy? Be real, how often have you heard this story? You know 'Happy Feelin's' ain't thirty minutes long. What time did I get here? Wasn't it a little after one?"

"Something like that."

"It's a quarter to two. What happened to the other songs on the playlist?"

"This song ain't been on for no half-hour."

"I'm not getting into this," Terri chuckled. She kissed Dale before hugging Bryce goodbye. "I just finished seasoning the steaks. They're wrapped up inside of the Frigidaire, and the potatoes are in the pot on a low boil. Were you making any vegetables?"

"I'm thinking potato salad might be enough to go with the steaks. Do y'all have a taste for anything in particular?"

"I thought you were making burgers," Bryce said.

"Well, I'll be... I did tell you that. Good thing we left the patties in the fridge. I can throw a couple on the grill."

"All right, well, surprise me. Let me head over to this thrift shop. You two play nicely."

Dale removed his Redskins floppy cap to towel dry a perspiring bald head. Meanwhile, Bryce shifted his cap backwards. "Son, I'm trying to tell you, wait 'til you have kids. You're gonna remember every detail. Trust me when I tell you."

"Lizzy doesn't play nice with others, so I don't know how that's gonna work."

"What'chu got going on underneath your cap?" he asked, noticing Bryce's unusual hair growth.

"I'm just growing out my curls. I couldn't get Omari to come by the house, so I started growing it out. He shaped me up this morning though."

"Oh, he's over there today? You could've just come over here and let me clip your hair."

"No thanks, Edward Scissorhands."

"I wonder if his mother knows he's here. Turn around, let me see what he did." Bryce faced the opposite direction, allowing a better view. "I like how he blended the fade into your beard. You know, I just don't understand that boy. All this talent and he'd rather run the streets."

"He works at the car rental place near the airport. His boy John hooked him up. Have you met him?"

"I couldn't tell you. That boy had all types of people in and out of my house," Dale replied with a look of despair, which quickly turned to anger.

"Look at that bulging vein in your forehead. Stop getting all worked up. That thing is gonna burst one day. Anyway, John is his classmate at the music institute. His family lives about twenty minutes from the airport. Omari stays at his house most of the time."

"Wait, he quit school? Again?"

"No, he's still there. He had better be. I just made a payment for next semester."

"You know I have no other way of knowing. He doesn't speak to me or his mother."

"His class meets three times a week, and from there he heads to work. I told him he needed to stay busy and get his money together."

"Which airport are they next to, JFK?"

"LaGuardia."

"Oh. Well, it's a start. I try not to waste my energy asking about that boy anymore. No, I take that lie back. I asked Terri this morning before church if he reached out."

"What did she say?"

"She claimed he must've forgotten. How the heck can you forget Mother's Day with all these commercials popping up? You don't treat your mother like that."

Bryce shook his head in obvious disappointment. "Well, the day's still young. I'll have a chat with him when I get a moment."

"That boy put us through a lot, BAT, and I just don't like the way he treats her."

"I'll be honest, he's been on point since I've had him. It's only every now and then where I have to remind him of a few things, but nothing indecent."

"You get that patience gene from your mother. Ain't no way I was gonna continue putting up with him."

"Maybe. I just remember being lost and confused around that age. For some reason, it wasn't until senior year when Mom's death hit me like a ton of bricks. On the day we were packing my stuff to drive to VA for school I remember wanting to share that moment with her and couldn't. Then, I went through those painful injuries. No offense, but I didn't want your tough love. I wanted to be coddled and have my back rubbed," Bryce snickered. "She wasn't here to do that. I watched my dream fade away and went through semi-depression. I just played it off well. When I moved back up here, it felt like my life was in shambles. I couldn't figure out what to do."

"BAT, give yourself more credit. You were never as hard-headed as that boy."

"That's because I didn't wanna fail. You and Mom did well for yourselves. Uncle Gibby and Aunt Paige too. I was next in line."

"See? And that's the difference. Your priorities were in place. You were observant, you asked questions, you had tremendous drive. These kids today don't give a damn about that. They want everything handed to them. Listen, I commend you for taking on the big brother role. You ain't have to do that. I married a woman with a problem child, not you. That's on me. But I can look myself in the mirror and confidently say I gave it my all."

"It had to be the generational gap hindering the relationship because he doesn't challenge me at all. I'm a little closer in age so maybe that has something to do with it. I see his potential; I'm just trying to get him to tap into it."

Bryce helped his father clean by dusting the wall of iconic portraits. He stared at a framed photo of the hordes of people gathered in solidarity at the Washington Monument for the Million Man March rally. The picture was unlike the one saved on his laptop, but it brought back memories of his first year of college, where Dale encouraged him to play hooky and join the other generation of Taylor men in witnessing history.

He moved onto his father's favorite section—a shrine, of all things Washington Redskins, where an autographed Doug Williams jersey was displayed in a glass frame case. Williams would make a splash, becoming the first Black quarterback to win a Super Bowl and be named its Most Valuable Player, but Bryce was equally impressed by his father's own accolades. In a world where the masses were indoctrinated to falsely idolize celebrities, Dale "Jackie" Robinson Taylor was unquestionably his hero.

"BAT, this right here is the sign of a quality cigar. You see this?" Dale sat in his lawn chair, examining the long ash. They watched it fall to the pavement, disintegrating into light dust.

Dale's fear of a back flare-up put the thought of completing the remaining cleaning tasks on hold. He hadn't fully recovered from the aching ailment which derived from a minor car accident years ago. But he kept in phenomenal shape, dedicated to core muscle workouts and daily two-mile jogs. With Bryce's helping hand readily available, there wouldn't be a need to go the extra mile this afternoon.

He thought back to an earlier conversation where Bryce outwardly brushed off the idea of starting a family. His son's fastidious ways and impulse to control his own narrative prevented fatherhood thoughts. Bryce was infatuated by his flourishing career and the liberation outside of it. If someone sensational were to cross his path, then perhaps he would entertain the thought. At this rate, pigs had a better chance at flying. The continuance of the Taylor last name was of the utmost importance for Dale, an uncle of four girls. He desperately wanted to expand his family with Candace until pregnancy complications marred them. Now, at sixty-two years old, the ship had sailed long ago.

~

The burning smell of charcoal met Bryce's nostrils as he finished seasoning the burger patties inside the kitchen. He followed the trail of smoke to the backyard, joining his father, who was chomping at the bit to pick his brain.

"Let me ask you a question," Dale said. This was the exact way he posed a question whenever Bryce was about to receive a lecture. "You seriously don't want kids? Not even one? You ain't getting any younger."

"Lizzy's a certified Taylor. Just look at her name: *Liz Taylor*. She's a throwback. You should appreciate that."

"Quit playing. We need to keep the legacy going. All your cousins on this side of the family are girls. What are the chances they'll all keep our last name? I don't know why you and that Kristen girl couldn't make it work. Y'all would've made some beautiful kids. I'd like some grandkids while I'm still active."

"Pop, let me have fun while I can. I like what dating offers. I get to learn about the different personality types out here and still have my peace and solitude. If the right one comes along, I'd be down to explore something, but I'm not gonna just settle and have kids with anyone. Why would I sabotage my life like that?"

"You're not looking in the right places, BAT. There's plenty of single ladies out here who would snatch up a fella like you. I see them all the time."

It all sounded good, but Bryce's life was non-negotiable. "Oh, speaking of Kristen, did I tell you I reached out to her?"

Dale's eyes widened in wonder. This was the news he'd long waited for.

"Say what now? What did she say? Are y'all getting back together?"

"Dad, take it easy. I reached out to one of her girlfriends a couple of months ago. I don't know if they're still in communication, but I took a stab at it. I haven't heard anything yet."

"Well, at least you tried. Don't lose hope. She'll come back around. How long has it been since you've last spoken?"

"I don't know. We stopped talking around the time you and Terri met. Maybe before then."

"And you ain't been in a relationship since?"

"I dated *many* people after her, I just never announced it. And hold up Mister *Six-Year-*Celibate. I *know* you ain't talking."

"Look, I'm not trying to push your back in. I trust that you know what you're doing. I just want you to find happiness at the end of the day." Bryce nearly choked on a cranberry drink as he eagerly waited to refute the comment.

"Why do people assume having kids equates to happiness?"

"You're not listening, BAT..."

"You *just* said..."

Before he could finish his sentence, Dale cut in like a manic New York City driver. "Not the kid aspect, BAT, but finding your soulmate. There's someone out here for everyone. Let me tell you something, your mother was God sent. Neither of us were looking for the other. When we met, we formed this incredible bond. Grandma Shirley and Pop-Pop took her in as their own. She was their first daughter-in-law. Everyone loved her, and we loved each other enough to bring you into this world. It's the family dynamic that I want you to experience overall." Dale opened the sliding door leading into the kitchen with hopes of continuing their conversation over running water—a terrible habit—causing Bryce to miss his enthralling soliloquy. When he returned, Bryce leaped out of his seat to assist his old man with carrying the tray of steaks. Despite their differences concerning his love life, he honored his father enough to show common courtesy.

"Thanks. Like I was saying, it's more about the connection that I'm highlighting. Even with Terri, we've been married, what, almost five years? I've known her for eight. I can honestly say I married my best friend. She filled in several voids and I'm thankful for her."

"Okay, so why didn't y'all have kids?"

"Well, for one, she had her tubes tied. Two, I was already in my fifties, and three, what have I always told you?"

Puzzled, Bryce raised his pronounced bushy eyebrows like Dwayne "The Rock" Johnson, searching through his expansive memory bank for all the sound advice given to him.

"I can't think of anything…"

"Try not to have a child with anyone in an already-made family. If the woman has one child, say, a teenager, that isn't too bad. But don't pursue anyone with multiple children."

"Wishful thinking, no? How do you escape women without children these days, especially in my age group?"

"Hold on, let me finish. The other issue is someday that same woman or one of the children will accuse you of showing favoritism toward the child y'all share together. I'm not telling you anything I wouldn't tell my own daughter. All I am saying is *try* and stay away from the single parent thing. It's not a popular opinion but I'm not in the business of being politically correct. That's not something I want for my son. There are plenty of single, childless women out here looking for men like you, so why not pursue them?"

"What if the woman with kids checks off all the boxes? Why hold her children against her?"

"Shit…"

Not known for his vulgarity, Dale allowed his emotions to get the best of him. "You messed around and made me say a cuss word. Forgive me. Now my blood pressure is up."

[Bryce laughs hysterically]

"How is that my fault?"

"Listen, she can check off every box under the sun, but if she ain't check off the 'no children' box, I wouldn't touch her with a ten-foot pole. I ain't mean to cuss. I'm just passionate about this stuff. Date whomever you want. I'm only talking about marriage. When you're ready to settle down, it shouldn't be with *anyone*. Make it count. Start your own bloodline with a woman without kids. You don't want the headache of dealing with a child who isn't yours. I'm living proof. Again, I'm not saying this applies to everyone. There are exceptions to every rule. I just want you to be mindful of it."

"Shouldn't I get credit for taking my time then?"

"Well, you've got a point."

"Pop, this all sounds like buyer's remorse," Bryce conjectured. "Let me turn it around on *you*. If you had to do it over, would you?"

Dale appeared deep in thought. It was so silent Bryce fabricated a quick yawn for the sake of sound.

"Aye, when did you start putting onions inside of the patties? I've never seen that done before."

"Was that your way of deflecting from the question?"

"What was your question?"

"Oh, now you wanna play 'old man?' I asked, would you have married Terri if you had to do it over? I hope your silence isn't indicative of you wanting to hop into the dating scene."

"Man, y'all youngins ain't no match for me. Consider yourself lucky. I'd be snatching these honeys in my sleep if I was still active. No one even believes I'm sixty-two."

"You ain't bagging anyone saying *honeys*. Not in those hideous Steve Harvey suits. You're better off staying married."

"How do you think I got Terri? In those same doggone suits. Ask her, she'll tell you. Listen, I'm happy. Was I in love with the idea of marrying a single mother? No. But I thought I could help that boy out. There wasn't a need for me to jump into a relationship and have another child after you'd already finished college. That's *another* eighteen years. Besides, I would've been comparing everyone to your mom had I done that. So, I took my time."

"I get that. I'm asking if you have buyer's remorse now."

"No. Terri fits me. It's the boy I don't particularly like. That's what I'm telling you. Don't put yourself through that. We don't get a 'practice life.' There's no need to complicate the one we have. We won't be here forever. Time is too valuable to waste on nonsense."

8

—

AROUND THE WAY GIRL

A noticeable commonality between Priscilla and Bryce was their somber faces when they met at a buzzing call center in Jersey City's redeveloped Business District. Neither had an awareness of the other's problems, but it was a dismal period in both their lives.

The self-critical Rutgers University graduate struggled to make sense of how she landed a dead-end job. The demanding years and accrued student loan debt for a psychology degree only to find herself seated next to dozens of people wearing headsets didn't sit right. Yet she was behooved to manage her financial obligations.

Priscilla's rambunctious arriving class of new hires walked onto the floor, following their strenuous six-week training course, clueless of the emotional stress ahead. When the group was formally introduced to the staff, Bryce, already a few months in as a temp worker, was spotted with his face buried deep into his palm as an irate caller chewed him out. Understandably, he was in the wrong headspace to offer an acceptable welcome. When acknowledging the group, he instantly noted Priscilla's uninviting appearance.

A fortuitous seating arrangement placed the pending friends

close enough for her to get a whiff of his collection of soft-scented colognes, but they were limited to swift salutations and eye contact only. At lunch was where many of the temporary workers congregated to chat about family and the events leading to their arrival at the new multi-million-dollar glass tower. However, Priscilla grew weary of the repetitious trend and eventually branched off on her own. At times, she sat alone bearing a noticeable scowl, listening to her MP3 player or walking along a nearby jogging trail overseeing New York Harbor.

Typically, a woman of her stature would have set him ablaze. She was highly attractive, wearing a basic wardrobe that emphasized her cleavage and love for gold necklaces. But it was Priscilla's mystique and aloof persona that preoccupied him. *Smile through the pain, no matter what life throws your way*—lasting words from his mother, a term that changed his perspective on life. It was too soon, but he hoped to share these encouraging words with Priscilla one day.

They developed a *je ne sais quoi* through matching gazes of distress following inbound calls from blood-thirsty customers, but Priscilla refused to extend herself any further. This was new grounds for Bryce, having been accustomed to the modest of personalities overexerting themselves to be around him. It was a one-sided game of psychological warfare, trying to crack a presumed introvert. The challenge excited him.

Their friendship cultivated during a team-building luncheon, where they discovered their similar New York City roots, neighboring New Jersey townships, and shared love for football and films. Astoundingly, behind Priscilla's deadpan expressions was a parallel logical mind and twisted sense of humor. Before long, they would lean on each other as personal therapists, offering dating tips among other life affairs. She gradually learned about his feelings toward Kristen, and he learned about her prior relationship, alcoholic father, and her love for family—her nephew, Julian, in particular. The pair hit it off nicely with each other's closest friends as well. However, Bryce couldn't allow a sleeping dog to lie. In time, he incited a singular conversation about the possibilities of a hint of an attraction. She admitted to finding him "interesting," adding that it was her thirsty friends he needed to be concerned about. Thankfully, the discussion wouldn't drive a wedge between their sibling-like fellowship.

Priscilla's booming sound system signaled her arrival at Bryce's townhouse. Lizzy trotted to the front door with her tail curled, anticipating a long overdue massage from her one-time cat sitter.

"Hi, Mama, c'mere... ooh, look at you... so cute, ooh, you miss Mommy's awesome rubs, don't you? Daddy doesn't rub you like this. I know you hate his hard callous hands. You like Mommy's soft moisturized hands, don't you?" she announced in her best baby voice.

Priscilla was originally planning to keep Lizzy after her sister's cat gave birth to a litter. That is, until Bryce hounded her on the idea of becoming a pet parent. It happened when he accompanied her to the veterinarian to drop off Melo, her lovable eighty-pound German Shepherd. She imagined he was better off with a self-sufficient animal. One who fit his on-the-go lifestyle. As a surprise for Bryce's thirtieth birthday, Priscilla arrived at his doorstep unpredictably with canned food, toys, and a precious unnamed kitten inside of a carrier.

"I lotion my hands all the time," Bryce replied.

"This chick is such an attention whore. Like father, like daughter."

Bryce welcomed her with a half hug and side cheek air kiss. "You just got here and already talking smack," he replied, snatching a DVD from her hand.

"I love you too."

"Whatever. Did you watch it?"

"Huh?" She smirked.

"Dude, you had *one* job."

"I'm kidding. I got halfway through it and then I passed out. I figured we could watch it later or even tomorrow if I'm not hungover."

"How'd you feel about Shia LaBeouf?"

"He's absolutely gorgeous."

Bryce gave her a penetrating stare before continuing. "Yo, what is your deal? You know I wasn't talking about his looks."

"Oh, you meant his acting? It was good, but Gordon Gekko is my boy. He single-handedly stole the show. Those one-liners cracked me up."

"Michael Douglas is the goat, bar none. *Bulls make money, bears make money, pigs get slaughtered,* he quoted. It doesn't top the first *Wall St.*, but I thought it was good. What were you listening to when you pulled up?" Bryce asked abruptly, pouring fresh water into Lizzy's dispenser. "That bass could wake up the dead."

"'Teflon Don' stays on repeat. I can't help myself."
"Rick Ross? I should've known. The plates in my cabinet were rattling. I'm sure my neighbors hate you."

Priscilla stood in the powder room mirror adjusting her collective thin gold chains, combing through her straight jet-black hair. It was her birthday weekend, and they were heading out for an early breakfast. Ahead was a busy day, which included a surprise pop-up visit to an entertainment center to celebrate her nephew Julian's sports-themed ninth birthday.

"You know, I was thinking, it sucks sharing a birthday with JuJu. Today should be all about me."

"Your birthday was yesterday though, so technically, you're raining on *his* parade."

"Yeah, but I was born first. Nobody told my sister to get knocked up in the month she did. I can assure you it was done purposely."

"And you say that I've got issues?" he laughed.
"I've got to try and fit him in before I go out tonight, and you know he's not gonna want me to leave early."

"What time does the party start?"

"It's from two to five. Then I've got to rush back home, shower, and meet the girls."

"Where at?"

"In the city. They wanna try out this restaurant in Chelsea. We might go to a club after that. I don't know. But I'm gonna be exhausted."

"I think if you leave Julian's party an hour early, you'll be good on timing."

"*You?*" she asked precariously. "Don't try to get out of going. If I can't get out, neither can you."

"I'd rather have a root canal than be surrounded by screaming kids for three hours."

"You can't renege, homie. You've already promised. Plus, they have a batting cage."

"Cute. Trying to sell me on a batting cage," he chuckled. "Yo, wait 'til I tell you about my date last night. Whoever came up with the phrase 'third time's the charm' is a straight up liar."

Priscilla stifled a laugh. "Oh gosh. Which one was this?"

"The Tiffani chick I texted you about the other night."

"The one who went to Montclair?"

"Kean."

"Aah, good ole Kean. Did I tell you I almost went there? I can't wait to hear this."

"Brace yourself. Who's driving, me or you?"

"Um... I'll drive to the diner if you drive to JuJu's party," she bargained.

"Isn't that backwards? If I'm the one treating, shouldn't I drive?"

"Um... no. If you drive to the party, you can be my excuse to leave early."

"So, you're basically using me?"

"Yes, but in a loving way."

"Whatever. Do you want your gift before we go?"

Priscilla pondered the thought, resting her elbow on the banister, resembling the famous 'Thinker' sculpture.

"Dude, it's not rocket science."

"I'm thinking."

"I can see that," he exclaimed. "Try not to think too hard." Bryce dragged her by the hand while holding onto the gift bag with the other. Meanwhile, Priscilla bullishly maintained the pose through the door.

"Lizzy, get your father, he's being mean to me."

"Stop playing around. You know the diner is gonna be jam-packed." Bryce held back to take an extended look into the tinted passenger window of Priscilla's full-sized SUV. The opportunity for a customary dig was too good to pass up.

"Where is your booster seat?"

"Ha-ha, very funny."

"How can you see through the rearview mirror? Of all the cars made for short people, why do y'all insist on driving monster trucks?"

"Do I look like the diminutive spokesperson? Wait. Don't answer that."

"Where should I put this?"

"Oh, give that to me." She motioned for her nephew's gift. "I'll put it in the backseat. Like I was saying, I can't speak for everyone else, but for me, it's a sense of comfort. I like being above ground. You *know* I can whip this bad boy around with ease. Why would you even question me?"

"Wouldn't you get more comfort in a compact car? I've watched you sit up from your seat just to back into a spot. That doesn't look like comfort to me."

"You're full of jokes today," she applauded exuberantly. "Let's take this show on the road and make some cash money. *Cash Money records taking ova for the nine-nine and the two thousands.* Yo, I'm about to bump that right now. Say I won't."

"No, because I know you *will*."

"Look inside the armrest for a gold CD with white lettering.

It should say 'Southern Jams.' Speaking of compact cars, do you remember the tiny car I sat in at the car show? They were calling it a Smart Car or something. I *really* wanna get that. Can you imagine driving that thing around?"

"You mean the circus clown car? You can absolutely pull that off."

"Was that a dig?"

A lane closure created light road congestion on the short drive to the diner. It allowed Bryce a moment to break down the events of his fiasco of a date until Priscilla's sister Valerie interrupted with a last-minute request.

"Why can't *you* pick up Mommy?"

Because I'm getting the kids ready, and Moe is running errands for the party. Stop being so difficult.

"I'm not being difficult. You never even asked if I was busy. You just assumed I was sitting around."

Priscilla pointed out a bumper sticker to Bryce on the vehicle ahead reading: *Gas, Grass, or Ass. Nobody rides for free.*

"Tell Val I said hello," Bryce whispered.

Priscilla held up her index finger. "B., do you hear this nonsense? She wants me to stop everything I'm doing to pick up my mom. Bryce says hi."

Hey Bryce. Tell your girl to stop being an ass.

"Not while she's driving. She can barely see above the steering wheel." Priscilla nudged him with a sharp elbow. "I'll let her know once we're all nice and parked."

"How am I being an ass? Listen, we're at the diner. Let me think about it. I have things to do today too, you know."

"Take the next jughandle," Bryce instructed.

"Right here? I have such a love-hate relationship with this state, I swear. The diner is literally right *there*. What is so criminal about making a left turn? Why can't we just be normal like other states? It's insane."

Girl, at least we don't have to pump our own gas. Can you imagine that?

"Pumping gas is a piece of cake."

Not for me. They pay people for that.

"I've changed my own oil plenty. I've had to change my tires too. I love that type of stuff. Anyway, we're here. Call you when we're done... and don't take that as me picking up Mommy either."

Whatever. Bye.

As expected, the diner was stuffed to the gills. Bryce looked through the passenger window for an open parking spot while Priscilla waited patiently for a group of coaches and little leaguers to pass by.

"Are you guys leaving?" she yelled out of the window.

"Yes."

Bryce's stomach growled like a guard dog. After a long wait, it was time to chow down. He cut up multiple pieces of pancake, added it to an already cut sausage link, and jammed it into his mouth, almost colliding with his pearly white teeth. In her best prosecutor rendition, Priscilla cross-examined him on the events of last night.

"So, what was her reaction when you asked the waiter to split the bill?"

"She had a smirk on her face. It was as if she knew I was annoyed. Ask me if I care."

"Did you care?" Priscilla asked facetiously. Bryce chewed his food methodically, wearing a blank stare. "The energy wasn't there. I wasn't feeling her vibe. It was like pulling teeth just to have a conversation. Like I said, *she's* the one who hit me up out of the blue asking that we start fresh. I was minding my business. Out of sight, out of mind."

"Wow. So, before last night, when was the last time you saw her?"

"I don't know. Six months ago?"

"She ghosted you for six months. Hmm... that would've been around, what, November? Cuddle season. Oh yeah, one of her exes came back into the pic for sure. He wanted his boo-thang back, and she was probably conflicted." Priscilla doused packets of sugar into her coffee mug before proceeding. "You were the new guy, and she had a history with the ex. Don't quote me, but something tells me that was the case. What was her energy like on the first date?"

"Dope. We met up for lunch at an outdoor cafe. Lots of eye contact, friendly conversation, light flirting. From there, we gave each other a long hug and went our separate ways. On the second date, we chilled at the bowling alley. I thought we were clicking—we even shared food."

"Shared like eating from the same plate or shared like *Lady and the Tramp* spaghetti scene?"

"I literally fed the girl chicken fingers straight from my hand. I even bit the chicken afterward as a way of letting her know that I was interested," Bryce laughed.

"Eww. Gross."

"I'm kidding."

He wasn't.

"She was eating it all seductively too," Bryce demonstrated with his tongue.

"Don't ever do that in public again," Priscilla laughed out.

"She could've been a little tipsy, but in my head, I'm thinking 'Oh, yeah, I'm definitely in the door.' What woman allows another man to feed them if there isn't any interest?"

"You've got a point. So, what happened next?"

"It was late. I walked her to the car. We gave each other another long hug. I thought about going in for a kiss. She was giving me these provocative bedroom eyes throughout the evening as if she wanted to do something, but I played it cool."

"Let me stop you right there LL *Not* Cool J. That was your mistake right there. You should've kissed her. She's allowing you to feed her. That was the first sign of interest. Well, the first sign was going on a *second* date. The hand feeding was your other clue. Hello, is anybody there?" She pointed at his brain.

"Nah, P. You had to be there. She gave mixed signals all night.

At times she seemed loose, other times she regressed. If I go in for the kill and she rejects me, now I look like the thirsty one. I don't have time for that. Either we're gonna do this or not. I'm used to women taking charge."

"She was playing it safe. I'm sure she thought you were uninterested once you didn't kiss her. Girls don't take rejection well either."

"But can you see how I was stuck between a rock and a hard place? If I make the move, now I suddenly become the typical guy she adamantly spoke out against. She stressed the importance of taking things slowly. So much so that I second-guessed hugging her on the first date."

"Okay. Understandable. Now what?"

"So, after the bowling date, we spoke sporadically through the weeks, but you could feel the shift. The intrigue wasn't the same. Every now and then, I'd go back to the dating site and notice she was on there. It shows when the user last logged in. I don't know if she was looking for a different type of dude or whether she was responding to messages. Now that I think of it, I do remember her mentioning something about an ex texting her, but she seemed annoyed by him."

"Yup. He's the culprit. That's why she disappeared."

"You might be right. Circling back to last night, after dinner she invites me to her apartment for wine."

"Wine? Did she really wanna have drinks after that dud of a date? What is wrong with this chick?"

"The hell if I knew. We had to go back to her place anyway to get my car. She offered to drive to the restaurant since we were in her neck of the woods, so I sat back and let her do her thing. Again, this whole thing was her idea. I'm thinking she needed something to get her juices flowing. I wasn't expecting sex..."

"Yes, you were."

"Okay, well, maybe. Either that or we could fool around. Truthfully, I wanted to kiss her. She had nice lips."

"Hmm, now I'm totally confused. *I know this date blows*

chunks, but come upstairs and have some wine with me," she mocked.

"That's what I'm saying. When we left the restaurant, it looked like we were both ready to bail. The last thing I'm thinking about is continuing the evening. You should've seen my face."

"I need another cup of coffee," Priscilla informed, drawing the attention of their server. Bryce continued. "We're upstairs now, she pours the wine, turns on the TV and promptly sits on the couch—directly across from me. It was about as far as those kitchen doors," he pointed.

"Uh-uh. No way."

"That's the exact face I made, like, 'You're *really* gonna sit across from me?' So, I was thinking of a good excuse to leave. Something like, 'It's getting late, I need to feed my goldfish.' I had to get outta there."

Priscilla's eyes watered as they usually did whenever she fought back laughter. "I've got to feed my goldfish. Really? Hey, did it ever occur to you that she was shy? There's no way she would've invited you into her home if there wasn't interest. You should've made the first move."

"At this point, I don't even care. She can take her sweet time with somebody else."

Priscilla removed her attorney cap to don that of a rabid sports fan. She was psyched about the recent NFL draft and the Giants' first-round draft pick. A switch to the topic of football created the perfect segue for Bryce to present her birthday gift.

"I'm just happy we got 'The Prince,'" she joyously announced, referring to cornerback Prince Amukamara. "He solidifies our DB's. The NFC East is wide open. I can almost feel a shift."

"My pops said the same thing. He's still in disbelief about the Redskins not improving. I'm equally annoyed with the Niners. We had a chance to take Andy Dalton in the second round and..."

"The Bengals snatched him," she interjected.

"Didn't see that one coming. I thought Dalton was a better

option than this Kaepernick guy. I'm not sure why we needed another run-first, short-passing QB. Alex Smith already does enough of that. I'd much rather build around a pocket passer. Hey, at least we have Harbaugh as coach. I'll take the good with the bad."

They continued to josh around when Bryce handed her the gift bag. He took out his phone to record the impending melodramatic display.

"Since we're on the topic of football, here. Happy Birthday, chump."

"Ooh, for me?" Priscilla inquired spiritedly.

"Don't be a weirdo."

She closed her eyes and reached into the bag for clues. "Hmm... mesh material. This is either a type of clothing or... no, no, it's a blanket." The suspense was unbearable. She opened her eyes and shuffled through the wrapping paper. To her surprise, there was a home edition New York Giants Phil Simms throwback jersey. She let out a monstrous shriek, as if she spotted a multi-legged critter feasting on her French toast dish. "I'm wearing it right now," she declared. Priscilla panicked. Her sweatshirt was entangled with her hair and jewelry as she struggled to pull it off.

"Does *America's Funniest Home Videos* still air? I think we've got something," Bryce added.

She called on Bryce's immediate assistance to shield her from wandering eyes who could catch a glimpse of her plunging tank top underneath.

"How does it look?"

"Looks damn good," he confirmed. "Thank goodness I didn't get you a small. Your girls would've busted through the seams."

"Shut up," she snapped, backhanding his chest ahead of their warm embrace. "Thank you, brother from another."

The ride home went smoother, albeit a bit longer, after Bryce suggested taking the back roads. With a couple of hours to spare before her nephew's gathering, Bryce contemplated swapping outfits for something more agreeable. He looked over at Priscilla, who was in sheer bliss, wearing her new Giants jersey, singing along to a bass thumping Rick Ross track. Her light brown skin absorbed the late morning sun as she made a smooth one-handed left turn into his development. They nodded their heads in accordance with the beat before she pulled into her familiar parking spot. To her left was an idle Dodge Chrysler with two children running at full speed toward the back seat. Bryce tried to identify the driver of the Chrysler through the tinted window to no avail but standing on the passenger side was the attractive neighbor. She waved off the silver sedan and stalled in an obvious probing of Priscilla's vehicle. Bryce adjusted his sunglasses before exiting.

"What up, Tasha?" He waved from the opposite side of the street.

"Oh, hey Bryce. I wasn't expecting you to come out. Isn't that your car in the driveway?"

"It is but I'm being chauffeured today."

"What a friend *he* is, right? He's getting chauffeured on *my* birthday," Priscilla blurted out, standing to his side.

"Her birthday was yesterday. Don't let her fool you."

They continued their light-hearted conversation over Tasha's side of the street, where Bryce looked to introduce them. The neighbor stood on a grassy patch in flip-flops with a noticeable fresh pedicure and tight blue jeans. Her face had an unusual glow.

"P., this is Tasha. Tasha, this is my good friend, Priscilla."

"Nice to meet you," Tasha replied. "Did he say 'P'? Do you prefer that?"

"Oh, that's his nickname for me. I have quite a few nicknames, but Priscilla is fine."

"That's just something I do," Bryce added. "I don't think anyone in my circle gets called by their government name."

"That's interesting. Well, since we're all standing here, can I say something?" Tasha's swift attempt to switch topics produced a look of concern. Priscilla removed her sunglasses while Bryce clutched onto his Cuban link chain.

"Can I tell y'all how cute y'all look together?"

"Well, you *just* did," Priscilla exclaimed, producing a nervous laughter. "We get that all the time. But thank you."

"Phew. I was about to say, *I-am-not-the-father*," Bryce added, mocking the widely popular phrase often heard on *The Maury Show*.

"You're so silly. Seriously, y'all do," she replied. "Remember when you asked me why I wouldn't speak much, and I told you it was because I didn't want any problems?"

"Yeah P., she was giving your boy the cold shoulder. I'd wave hello and she'd look the other way."

"No, I wouldn't. I'd wave back," she giggled, directing her attention to Priscilla. "The thing was, I'd see your truck often, so I figured the two of you were a thing. I didn't want any problems."

Priscilla's left eyebrow perked high enough to escape her face. "Really?"

"Yes. I was like, um, no, not gonna happen. Some nights I'd leave for work to see the sight of a different car in his driveway. I wasn't sure who was who. Not that it was any of my business either, but we live directly across the street from one another…"

"Right, so it's hard to miss," Priscilla said.

"Exactly."

"I get it. I used to tell him to stop inviting so many people over. He's a Virgo, you'll have to forgive him."

"A Virgo who's *single* and enjoys hosting, so, there's that."

"*¡Càllate!*"

"Now she wants to bust out the Spanish. I can't get her to speak it any other time."

"You guys are too funny. Priscilla, are you Hispanic?"

"My mom's Puerto Rican, my dad is Black, and I was born in New York… so, I guess that makes me…" she hesitated.

"American?" Bryce chimed in.

"Well, yeah, but I was going with Nuyorican."

"Nuyorican?" Tasha asked. "I've never heard of that."

"It's a city thing. Don't mind her."

"The crazy part is that my sister and I lived with my mom, but surprisingly we never spoke much Spanish if at all."

"Oh, wow," Tasha paused. "So, did you guys meet in New York? I don't hear an accent from either of you."

"We met in Jersey... Jersey City, to be exact," Bryce cut in. "Story for another day. But I only lived in New York until about the second grade."

"And I moved from the city when I was three. I guess you can say New York is one of many things we have in common."

"That's so cool. Well, like I told him, I wasn't trying to be a bitch or anything, I just figured you two were involved. That, or he was a popular guy. I try to stay drama-free."

Bryce and Priscilla made eye contact as if one knew what the other was thinking. He stayed quiet while she assured his prying neighbor there was nothing more to their friendship. "We're good friends. He's a free bird. Free to roam and do whatever he pleases. That's my bro. Another reason I'm always here is because he *hates* going to my house."

"Not true."

"It is so."

"But it's not."

"I have an eighty-pound German Shepherd who he adores..."

"You do? What's his name?"

"Melo. That's my baby but he sheds everywhere, and Mister Neat-Freak usually has a fit."

"Well, that part is true. But don't act like you don't enjoy coming over for my food."

Tasha gave him a deep stare. "You can cook? Is that where those good smells come from?"

"I do my thing from time to time."

"He's a *great* cook. I'll give him that. I'm trying to get him to create a recipe book."

"Okay, I like the sound of that. I make the same boring meals. I have a couple of picky eaters at home. I'll have to try one of your specialties one of these days."

"You know where to find me."

"I do," Tasha smirked. "Well, I'll let you guys get on with your day. It was nice meeting you."

"Nice to have met you, too," Priscilla waved, joining Bryce as they crossed the street. He commended her efforts for selling his culinary artistry, sensing it was a clear passageway into his neighbor's pants.

"You know I've got your back. Dude, did you see the drool coming from the corner of her mouth? I wanted to give her a bib so badly."

"Nah, I missed it. My mind was in the gutter," Bryce replied, unlocking the front door.

"So was hers. She was taking off your clothes in plain sight."

"You think so?"

"I know so."

9

——

DRUNKEN LOVE

"I wanna fuck Senator Booker in one of those large board rooms with the big desk," Julissa declared. It was official; the peach-flavored Ciroc vodka had kicked in. She rose from the sofa and walked toward the kitchen to pour another glass. When she peered over her shoulder, Bryce was seen shaking his head mercilessly.

"What?" she asked. "I do. He could get it."

"Would you have this same energy if he were Republican?"

"Maybe not. You have nothing to worry about, though. He looks like he might be boring, so, you'll have to do for now."

She had such a subtle way of putting things.

Bryce scrolled through his cable provider's extensive music selection, hoping to set the mood. "Ooh, leave it right there," Julissa demanded, placing the empty glass onto the kitchen bar. She pulled up her T-shirt, tying a knot to the side which exposed her fuchsia lace boyshorts. He watched from afar as she swayed her hips to the Latin dance track. The prospect of sleeping with another man's wife after only hours of confessing his devotion to the Lord did not sit well with him, but he was instantly charged.

According to Julissa, she and her husband were marginally separated now, but would occupy the same living space until further notice. He was visiting family in Cape Cod for Memorial Day weekend, creating the perfect opportunity for her escape. The liquor may have contributed to her spilling the beans—it was the most straightforward she had ever been about their marriage. Her agenda for the evening was to get intoxicated and give Bryce the ride of his life. As harmonious as the thought was, Bryce found himself agitated by their promiscuity.

"Papi, this is more of a Dominican thing. *Ven aquì*, let me show you." Julissa's neck tilted—her flowing hair hid the name 'Garcia' plastered on the white oversized 49ers T-shirt he'd given her to wear. She pressed against her thighs, bit down on her cherry red lips, and performed a seductive booty roll with a glazed look in her eye. Her hips swayed from left to right, morphing into a Bachata dance. Bryce tried to avert his attention from her little performance, however, the more the buzz set in, the more she increasingly looked like a five-course meal. He sat up to adjust himself from an obvious arousal. His hunger expanded. It was true, the merry adulterer longed for the touch of a state senator, but the masculine hands of her bare-chested paramour would suffice. She tugged at Bryce's arm, asking that he join her on the kitchen floor.

"Put your arm around the middle of my back," she ordered. "Now rest your leg in between mine and move your hips. No. Like this, Papi. Yes. Now, when I cut this way, just follow me. Keep moving your hips."

They were standing nose to nose, staring deep into each other's eyes like two flunkies auditioning for *Dancing with the Stars.* Undoubtedly, a good dancing display was one of the pathways to the Puerto Rican beauty's heart, but Bryce was ready to engage in the wild kinky drunken sex as she so eloquently proposed the night before. Time was slipping away.

"I like your hair this way," she uttered inscrutably, running her fingers through his new do. "Don't cut it."

Bryce lifted Julissa onto the kitchen countertop. She shrieked as her bottom grazed the cold marble surface. With her leg arched, she inched back against the wall, predicting his next move. Bryce peeled her shorts with reckless abandon and pressed against her fresh Brazilian wax where his hand was met with light moisture. He advanced his dribbling mouth to her sweet spot, flicking his tongue, adding gentle sucks. She bit down on her bottom lip, fighting the urge not to release an ear-piercing moan. Marc Anthony's "Ahora Quien" sounded in the background.

"*Si justo ahí,* Papi. Don't stop." Bryce eased up, to Julissa's dismay, pressing his finger along her mouth. She fought back tears, bothered by his hasty finish.

"What the entire fuck? Like, who does that?" she whined.

She despised being finessed, however, she was up against a mastermind. A true student of the female anatomy. It was part of why she was hooked on Bryce in the first place. What she perceived to be a callous act was all by design.

The idea of enticing his partner before the big contest gave Bryce an unspeakable rush. He gained a sense of control, watching a woman's body slither whenever he pulled out the ole giveth-taketh away move from his arsenal. It was a learning tool used to measure their tendencies and motions, likes, and dislikes. His unselfishness set him apart from the rest of the pack. Women from past encounters found themselves randomly daydreaming about him, even with many of them involved in new relation-ships. It wasn't unusual to receive a "Hey sexy" text from someone he hadn't spoken to in years. Bryce was a showman—the bedroom was his grand stage, and if tonight were to be the last hurrah, it needed to be the performance of a lifetime.

Sex on the kitchen countertop was a first. Julissa quivered wildly, digging her nails deep into his shoulders after an explosive orgasm. Bryce pulled her toward him with defiance, lifting her near-lifeless body up the stairs. Her arms were secured around his broad back, their genitalia still clamped together. She looked him in the eye in a state of bliss, wondering what their unbridled get-together would offer next.

"Hurry up, Macho Man," she teased, holding on for dear life as he struggled to turn the bedroom doorknob. "I'm not that heavy. I'm only a hundred and forty-five pounds." The setback gave rise to a quick chuckle. He attempted to remove himself from her warmth, placing her body on the plaid-patterned comforter set on his queen-size bed.

"Let go, so I can close the door," he ordered.

"Make me," she dared, showing amazing leg strength as "La Gatita" wailed for another round. He'd gotten out of her tight squeeze to close the door, where Lizzy was prancing through the hallway. When he turned around, Julissa was on all fours bouncing her backside at the edge of the bed like a video vixen. Bryce cunningly placed himself behind, and in one fell swoop, gave her bottom a ringing smack. Julissa asked for another. Her widened grin resembled that of the Grinch. She reached for his decorative pillows and lowered her back to preserve a fascinating arch form. Bryce hopped onto the bed, scooching her up by the abdomen. With a fist full of hair, he tugged her head back far enough to look her in the eye.

"Are you ready?" he asked. Julissa added a slight jiggle, which was either code for "yes" or she was highly amused by her twerking abilities. Finally, she responded.

"Fuck me, Papi."

Their flesh collided. He thrusted in a rhythmic motion—his gold chain bounced off his lightly haired chest. The idea of being in an imaginary competition with a state lawmaker fired him up... as did the name "Kyle" tattooed on her lower back. He'd seen the name plenty, but oddly, it struck a chord this afternoon.

Julissa was years removed from Kyle—Natalie's biological father—a prospering business owner and happily married man, but as struggling young parents, she found herself baffled by his entrepreneurial spirit, ceaselessly questioning his preference for menial jobs with a reputable college degree and new mouth to feed.

A flexible work schedule enabled Kyle to earn a real estate license and build his business from the ground up, yet his career path's uncertainty became a source of her irritation. Their present-day relationship was very middle-of-the-road, but Bryce imagined he must have been important for his name to appear in such an intimate spot. One could only imagine the type of psychological damage it had on her husband.

As Julissa's lustful sounds echoed in the room, Bryce's mind became clouded. There were too many questions and not enough answers. Rather than lose himself in a moment of twisted fantasy, he thought back to his father's hitting words of not overcomplicating life. Even Gucci put forward an encouraging reminder about the dating game: *She's not yours—it's just your turn.* The wordsmith's empowering declaration played over in his head.

Bryce indisputably understood the game. This wasn't his first rodeo, but Julissa was right, he had absolutely fallen for her. The inability to sweep his dancing partner off her feet during an illicit romance was unheard of. By now, someone would've tried to coerce him into a relationship. What a hapless feeling.

If by chance Julissa's separation led to a divorce, where would that leave him? How could he build a relationship with a woman who wished to fornicate with a politician? That wasn't the liquor talking. She was forthright and definitively believed she had a chance with the New Jersey state senator. At heart, Bryce wanted to become someone's priority. He had a spontaneous impulse to fall in love, and for the first time, his feelings for Julissa wavered. She made him feel less desirable, like he wasn't good enough. On the contrary, *she* wasn't good enough for him.

You're allowing your emotions to get the best of you, just like she said you would.

I wanna fuck Senator Booker in one of those large board rooms with the big desk.

We don't get a practice life; there's no need to complicate the one we have. We won't be here forever. Time is too valuable to waste on nonsense.

The expressions rang in his head like church bells. Suddenly, Julissa surprised him with an announcement.

"*¡Ay que rico!* I'm comin', Papi."

Bryce tightened his grip around her waistline. His arousal expanded and his heartbeat went amuck. She pleaded with him to finish the marathon through each pounding thrust. "Come, Papi... come for me." The melodic sounds of amplified moans, heavy panting and cries to God filled the bedroom. At last, they erupted together. Bryce's drained body collapsed onto her lower back as they crashed violently onto the bed. He gathered enough energy to place soft kisses on Julissa's perspiring neck. She laid flat with her arms stretched. Her face looked like the cat that ate the canary.

10

SHOOK ONES

As a teenager, Bryce struggled to contain his emotions on the days leading up to his mother's death anniversary. Memorial Day weekend—a time of honoring and remembering those who lost their lives serving in the armed forces. The unofficial start of beach season for others. Dale used to schedule road trips down the South-Atlantic coast as a distraction from the transpiring gloom, where they visited family or caught an Orioles game if the team was in town. Tomorrow marked twenty years since Candace's untimely demise. Where had the time gone? Thankfully, the lasting effects of his mother's passing didn't spill into adulthood, though some would argue that he continued to create a diversion following Julissa's recent visit.

∾

Today's weather forecast brought about clear blue skies, following a dreary week where the sun played peek-a-boo with the clouds. Adding to Bryce's joyous mood was the exhilarating sunset on the ride home. It was as if Mother Nature had a point to prove. Upon his arrival at the Park & Ride, he wrapped up a sexually charged texting exchange with Yvonne and turned his attention toward the twilight sky, tapping into his inner paparazzo, snapping away pictures of tonight's featured star to add to a collection of breath-taking sunsets on his phone.

Thursday evening gym visits were rare, but after enduring winter's chill, sometimes spring's warmth called for extended time outdoors to thaw. He acknowledged the usual suspects upon his entrance. The unsavory smell of sweat and rubber seized the room. No matter the time of day, they were there, the *same* faces. How was this even possible?

He changed from his work clothes, lifting his black tank top to the display of a toned stomach. Despite the horrendous lighting in the men's locker room, he never found a mirror he didn't like. The mirror selfie made for a great fourth picture to his dating profile and became one of many saved to his phone as he documented his lean-out process. The former two-sport stud always had an aversion to abdominal workouts even after sustaining a defining six-pack through college. It took time to convince friends and teammates that he never executed a sit-up. Not once.

After a decade-long bulk-up, Bryce's sole purpose on his current fitness journey was to stay fit and reignite his love for competition. Even if the competition was with himself. Competition generated a sensation which only sex could provide. *Good* sex. Even a well-earned raise. He wanted to assess his physical limits, having gone from a slender 175 pound collegiate into a 210-pound Rock of Gibraltar. Yet despite his obsession with the body, he couldn't make sense of the worldly appeal for a six-pack. It didn't qualify as proof of strength, just eye candy for women to salivate to. Not that he needed one; women were captivated by him without it. Okay, so, *maybe* he wasn't Tyson Beckford, but if you were to ask Bryce, Tyson Beckford wasn't *him:* tall, dark, handsome, educated, physically fit, and single, crossing off boxes like a game of tic-tac-toe. He peered into the mirror at the count of two measly abdominal muscles. Different from his one-time sculpt stomach, but progress, nonetheless. Four more to go, to add to an already mesomorph build. The allure of a new challenge.

Challenge accepted.

~

The evening was abuzz as shoppers flooded Jamaica Avenue, hoping to get an early start on the bargained sizzling hot fashions for the upcoming summer. Omari and Brixx took to the streets with their videographer Rashad, his younger brother Cory, and Harmony, after wrapping up a video shoot inside of her apartment stairwell. In a show of unity, the group members wore matching custom black-and-white T.S.U. hats and retro Air Jordan sneakers. Harmony wore a black scarf over her signature honey-colored box braids with the letters T.S.U. written in cursive. Their attire attracted plenty of spectators.

Without any local buzz, the group's aura screamed of superstars. All they had was a growing YouTube channel and the conviction that they were the hottest thing since sliced bread. Harmony led them through a slew of pedestrians, using rapid hand movements, performing lyrics to her featured song as the guys lurked in the background. She drew the eyes of male admirers with her heavy lip gloss, midriff top, and Florence Griffith Joyner-like nails. It was surreal to watch men fawn over her and carelessly disrupt the flow of the video.

Queens, New York, the city's largest borough by size, the birthplace of a list of hip hop's most prestigious figures, and where some of the most beautiful women in the city roamed, is where Omari primarily rested. It was closer to work, and it was Bryce who once shared how some of the world's most renowned artists started out cohabiting with fellow band members when honing their craft.

Aunt Ramona's Co-Op City high rise in the Bronx didn't present the same liberties as rooming with Brixx. Coupled with that was the chance of bumping into his biological father—Ramona's brother—this time of year. For now, Omari's immediate future existed inside of his friend's carpeted basement surrounded by music, good company, and enough weed to make Willie Nelson jealous. The stars were aligned if he was ready to ditch a life of incertitude and become the next hip hop phenomenon. *If,* being the operative word. The only obstacle standing in his way was an unspecified health matter.

Rashad backtracked along the sidewalk as the crew approached a row of bootleggers, who shouted the names of the latest pirated music and film over a reverberating ambulance siren. The small-time swindlers used aggressive selling points to attract business—impervious to the plummeting disc sales in the ever-growing digital age. Meanwhile, Harmony moved out of the camera shot to make way for CashFlow, who prepared to deliver their verse. Cory boosted the sound of the portable speaker, helping the guys stay coordinated with the track. This was vital. Nothing irked them more than watching playbacks during final edits, where it looked like dialogue from an old Bruce Lee film.

"We should record a scene on the subway," Omari said.

"Yo, I was thinking the same thing," Brixx answered. "The subway or the park."

"The subway is gonna be busy at this time and the park might be closed," Rashad cautioned.

"I just thought we could splice up 'Mony's two scenes and do the same with our video."

"I'm down with whatever. Let's just try and knock this out in one take. The battery is getting low, and I'm starving," Rashad added.

"Ayo, I'm Brixx, the one-take king," he confidently announced with his signature raspy voice. "O., do you hear this dude?"

Omari smirked, admiring a group of girls in skinny jeans. "I'm with Rashad. My stomach's been growling for twenty minutes."

"'Mony, you hungry?" Brixx asked Harmony.

"No, I'm good. Wait, are those the True-Blue Cements in my size?" she asked, referring to the window display of the upcoming Air Jordan sneaker release. "Can we go inside while y'all go find something to eat?"

"Those joints are fire," Brixx added.

"Yo, what are we doing?" Rashad inquired, visibly annoyed. "Is someone gonna pull the trigger?"

"All right, bet, let's go grab something. Brixx, I'll text you our location and y'all just meet us there or we can meet at a neutral spot," Omari bargained. Cory handed him his phone, which he immediately placed on its holster before the trio walked in the opposite direction. They were strolling through the neighborhood, hoping to narrow their food choices, when Rashad came to a screeching halt.

"You good?" Omari asked him with a look of befuddlement.

"Yeah, I'm just tired of carrying this shit," he replied, unzipping his bookbag before approaching the crowded intersection.

> We're at Mickey D's across the street from the Cineplex on Parsons.

Rashad and his brother shared a ten-piece McNuggets meal with extra sweet & sour sauce to go with several items off the Dollar menu. Omari ordered a mouthwatering Quarter Pounder with cheese loading up on what was arguably the Golden Arches' best food item: French fries. He took a picture of the artery-clogging dinner, hoping to get a rise from Bryce who was sure to blow a gasket.

> Brixx: Alright, cool. Harmony copped the J's.
> We're over at the Sprint store.
>
> Thurs 7:14 p.m.

The guys raved at the earlier footage in between bites, in particular Harmony's staircase scene, noting her flair for the camera. Omari delved into future video ideas and business groundwork as he set up to put the world on notice.

"We've got to get this merch poppin'. How much do you think a permit would cost if we wanted to set up shop at a street fair this summer?"

"That's a good question. I know there's an application process involved. You probably couldn't sell anything legally until receiving notice," Rashad replied.

"Nah, I disagree. Do you honestly think those bootleggers took the legal route? Just imagine how much bread they're making selling *illegally*."

"True. That's exactly why they start running when the Boys pull up."

"Let me see how much the application costs. I'll just shoot my bro a text. He'll know."

Omari helped Rashad jam the fancy equipment back inside of his bookbag before making a beeline for the exit. The guys were replenished and ready to film their last shot of the evening. They turned the corner where cars flowed through the traffic lights with the omission of a Ford model, which suddenly pulled up slowly in front of a clothing store on the same block. Omari spotted three passengers stuffed like canned sardines with the headlights off. Most noticeable was a fair-skinned woman seated in the passenger seat, who gave him a bone-chilling stare. If this was a crime ravaged community and not a commercially dense one, it would've been safe to assume they were being targeted for a mugging. Omari remained vigilant. Just when he was set to text Brixx of their whereabouts, a shadowy figure emerged, causing him to whiplash.

"Good evening, gentlemen. Do you have ID on you?" a Latino man with a wheatish complexion and ridiculously over-sized clothes asked. Cory, the youngest of the bunch, froze, calling out to Rashad who continued walking.

"ID for what? We're just walking," Omari replied.

His alertness elevated. This was a set up if he had ever seen one. He thought about making a break for it when out of the corner of his eye, he noticed a badge hanging off the mysterious man's hip.

"What the fuck we do?" Rashad asked, walking toward the gentleman.

"Sir, watch the language," said a piping voice surfacing from behind a tall White male in a backwards baseball cap. It was the same woman with the cold stare who sat in the passenger seat. Her hands rested calmly at the center of her waistband.

"Watch our language for what?"

Omari chimed in, "You're asking for ID, and we've done nothing wrong. You haven't even identified yourselves."

Their outrageous wardrobes all but hinted at undercover officers. Rashad forcefully handed the tall gentleman his driver's license.

"These mothafuckas are trippin'. Just give them your shit, O. Don't say nothin' else." Omari dug inside his wallet to retrieve his driver's permit and Audio Institute ID.

"Sir, ID?" the woman asked Cory before Rashad cut in, "He doesn't have an ID, he's only in eighth grade..."

The Latino officer continued. "Men, the reason we're stopping you is because we've gotten calls about recent robberies in the area. Unfortunately, the two of you fit the description of the suspects involved."

"The description? What's the description? Everyone out here looks like us," Rashad blurted. "Y'all buggin'."

"Sir," the tall gentleman replied before the female officer interrupted. She ordered Rashad against the wall and asked that he remove his bookbag before completing a frisk. "Open your bag, sir."

"For what? That's *my* equipment, *ma'am*," he taunted. "I bought this with my own money. I make videos."

The Latino officer addressed Omari. "Sir, you have a New Jersey residence. Can I ask what you're doing in Queens?"

Omari lashed out. "Fuck you mean why am I in Queens? How am I supposed to respond to that? Y'all stopped us for no reason and now you wanna know why I'm visiting friends?"

The officer handed him his IDs. "Sir, I asked a simple question. Not once have I raised my voice."

"But why should I tell you my reason for visiting friends? That's none of your business."

"Sir, that's all you had to say. Face the wall. Spread your arms and legs." The officer assured him all would be fine if he complied, but his word of appeasement didn't matter. Omari was humiliated. His heart raced at top speed, trying to make sense of it all. "I don't understand why you're singling us out. We were minding our business and yet you made us feel like criminals. That shit don't make sense."

"Sir, we're just doing our jobs," the officer replied, continuing the frisk.

The officers advised they leave the area at once to avoid another bout of mistaken identity. Their unsolicited advice was like pouring salt on a wound. The guys walked away from the scene visibly disturbed—Cory especially—a straight-A student whose eyes welled up with tears. Rashad went on a profanity-laced tirade while Omari gathered his thoughts. It was his introduction to being stopped and frisked, and he regretted not collecting the officer's name or badge number. Everything happened so fast. Though tempers flared, he was relieved emotions had not boiled over, but why was it so easy for their rights to be violated? He looked at his phone where a text from Brixx appeared.

Brixx: Yo, where y'all at??

Thurs 8:42 p.m.

~

Bryce concluded a thirty-minute workout on the StairMaster and removed his earbuds to towel dry his dripping face. Cortez was spot-on. The StairMaster was the machine from hell. He wrapped up his workout adding a quick bicep exercise and a set of pushups. In and out in under an hour as planned. It was a quarter to nine, too late to prepare dinner, but how glorious would it be to go home to a warm plate of food with a loved one sitting across from him. He needed to send Kristen one more SOS until the thought occurred: "Pain is temporary, Pride is forever"—a quote from an unknown source. It had been three months without a response from Dominique. Perhaps not returning his message *was* the message.

He offered a wave goodbye to the friendly juice bar clerk as he sipped on tonight's dinner—a strawberry-flavored protein shake. Enroute to the locker room, a long dark-haired woman approached him, walking with her head down. There weren't many people who could shake his composure, but she immediately caught his attention. The gym wasn't the ideal place to play Prince Charming even if it had become the latest hotspot for attention-deprived women. Still, as a show of common courtesy, he greeted anyone who made eye contact. As his mother used to say, "kindness comes at no cost." All he needed was for this beauty to look his way.

To no surprise, he already scouted every inch of her body from the white cropped tank top down to the cherry-brown tights and matching Nikes. A physically fit color-coordinated woman. When she lifted her head, he noticed a cute pair of glasses. He had a thing for women in frames. She looked like she could teach a class of kindergarteners and fight crime at the same time—an intellectual badass. A woman unknowingly after his own heart.

"Have a good evening," he uttered, motioning a slight wave. It would've been criminal had he not said anything. She removed her earbuds.

"I'm sorry?"

"I was just saying have a good evening."

"Oh. You, too." She smiled.

There was something about the knockout grabbing at him, but he couldn't put a finger on it. His brain went in motion, thinking of a creative way to keep her stalled.

"Hey, sorry to hold you up. You look awfully familiar."

"Really?"

"Big time. Did you go to Cedar Ridge High?"

She combed her fingers through her hair as they squinted at one another.

"No."

"I never forget a pretty face. Maybe it was in the city or at the Park & Ride."

The intense cross-examination would have made Perry Mason proud.

"Aw..." She blushed. "No, I haven't worked in the city in quite some time. I usually drive to work."

"Sorry to be intrusive."

"No, no, you're fine. I'm equally intrigued," she chuckled softly.

"Did you happen to work in midtown when you worked in the city?"

"No. Battery Park, but again, that was ages ago."

Bryce paid close attention to her voice but was captured by her eyebrows. They were as thick as his, but long and perfectly shaped like someone carved them with a switchblade. Moreover, her arms were nicely toned and moderately vascular. Her stomach muscles put him to shame. She scooted out of the pathway of an approaching mother and daughter, who stared a hole into them.

"You know, come to think of it, you kinda look familiar too," she replied to his amazement. Bryce reached into his pocket to pause a still in-play iPod.

"This is crazy. Could we have seen each other *here?* I'm drawing a blank."

"Maybe. But I've only started coming here recently. Um... this might sound like a silly question, but have you gotten your eyes checked lately? I work at an optometrist office. Could it have been there?"

It was essential that he figured out the mystery woman before she connected the dots. Bryce's curiosity charged. Did they blindly stumble across each other at his eye appointment?

"Is it Bruce... Bret?" she asked, snapping her fingers. "It's something with a 'B.'" She was getting warm. Who was she? He flashed back to the appointment day. As far as he could remember, only two women addressed him by name, and the person standing before him looked about twenty years younger than the front desk receptionist.

"Wait, Alyssa?"

"Yes? And you're... wait... isn't it, Bruce?"

"Close. It's Bryce. Although I'm sure I can pass for Bruce," he said sarcastically.

"Bryce. Oh my gosh. I'm so sorry. I was so close. How are you?" she asked, folding her hands in front of her chest.

"I'm great now. Small world, isn't it?"

"I know. Nice to see you."

"Likewise. No disrespect, but you don't look anything like the person at the office. Didn't you have an updo the last time? I don't remember the glasses either."

"Yes, yes," she excitedly repeated. "You remembered. I'm about as blind as a bat. I go back and forth between contacts and glasses. As for my hair, I know it's a mess."

"No, it looks great down."

"Thank you. The updo is my go-to look for work. It's much easier to maintain. At the gym I'm usually all about the baseball cap or a messy bun," she chuckled. "I took it down in the locker room. Anyway, that's my 'I'm in the zone leave me alone' look. This is so funny. Oh my gosh. How are your new glasses?"

"I don't think you were there on the day I picked them up, but I'm getting used to them. I was a bit light-headed at first."

"Yeah, most patients new to glasses tend to have that problem," she interrupted.

"I've heard. I was thinking eh... this isn't gonna work. But it's gotten much better. Hey, were you headed out?"

"Yes. Were you?"

"I am. Just need to grab my stuff from the locker room."

"Okay, I'll wait up."

Bryce was as jubilant as a child on Christmas morning. He rushed inside to wipe down his perspiring face, rinse off his hands and take hold of his gym bag where on his phone were two notable picture messages. The first, from Gucci, of a shapely woman in a fitted dress with the caption reading: *Thicker than a cold jar of peanut butter.* The other, Omari's high-calorie dinner monstrosity.

Alyssa was seen staring to her right, running her fingers through her hair as Bryce exited. She looked like a million bucks even when slightly rumpled. They conversed in front of the gym's main entrance, discussing fitness goals, their preferred workout playlists, and the unnerving event spearheading her swift gym relocation. The most unusual part of their hour-long exchange was Bryce's neglect in asking for her phone number. Since entering the land of online dating, his interfacing skills had noticeably declined, and he kicked himself for the missed opportunity. For now, the only thing he could do was play the waiting game and hope to see her again.

11

———

INTO THE GROOVE

Hudson Investors's middle management received company-wide training in blurring the lines between their professional careers and personal lives. This could explain the decreasing volume of visitors lollygagging at Roy's cubicle and others. Porsha, however, found a loophole. What else could explain her back-to-back stints at Bryce's desk? By all accounts, she was giving him a taste in a roundabout way of what he was missing, or she could sense another woman barging in on his orbit. She would've still been showing off birthday pictures of a curve-hugging outfit with spiked studded Christian Louboutin heels if it weren't for Bryce's upcoming call with a major client.

We were given some inefficiencies in our lending process and... correct... that's correct. As you can imagine, from a company perspective, it has become a bit cumbersome. I feel like we were splitting hairs. Precisely. Here's the silver lining, I was able to identify some of the problems and come up with a proposal which we can circle back to later this afternoon. Oh, absolutely. And let me thank you for being so patient on the matter.

Ugh! Okay. Sounds good. Talk to you then.

Break!

Bryce's Monday moods were upbeat unlike the rest of the

office, who were often overheard counting down the hours until Friday. Following his most recent tie-in with Alyssa, it more than explained the obvious pep in his step. He leaned back in his chair and tossed a stress ball in the air like taking a game-winning shot. Next, he added the client's paperwork to a manilla folder and responded to Zoë on the company's new message chat.

Zoë Brooks to Bryce Taylor: How's it going? Umm... I need helpppp!!

Bryce Taylor to Zoë Brooks: The call went better than expected. Haha I'll swing by in five mins.

Zoë needed a second set of eyes on a clean-up project she had been working on. At least the intermission would prevent a frequent visitor from popping up and allow him a chance to spread a little positive cheer through the office. First, he made a pit stop to the men's room where he was instantly met with an unpleasant smell. Bryce was certain it was the same offender who had a resistance toward using his own bathroom before his work arrival. That or an incorrigible stomach that only sensed his presence. He held his breath and counted to thirty as a distraction before storming out with speed unseen since Coach Woods named him captain of the Cougars track and field team.

"Sup, lady?"

"Thank you in advance, kind sir. Eww, what's wrong with your face?"

"I don't know, what's wrong with it?"

"Why's your lip curled like Elvis?"

Bryce paused. "Cuz I'm all shook up."

"That, sir, was super corny."

"Was my facial expression *that* noticeable?"

"Um... big time."

"There's some dude in the men's room. I don't know who it is and what he eats, but he seems to set up shop whenever I make a quick stop there. I didn't even wash my hands." Bryce shook his head in disappointment. "Can I use your hand sanitizer?"

"That's hilarious. How do you know it's the same person?" she asked, handing Bryce a near-empty bottle of hand sanitizer.

"I mean, he wears the same shoes every day. That couldn't be me. No one would ever find out I was the one responsible for the atrocities in there. I'd be flushing the toilet every five seconds with my feet in the air."

Zoë's chuckle nearly turned into a full eruption; her face turned a blush red. "Maybe he doesn't care."

"Captain Obvious."

"You don't wanna know what goes on in the women's restroom, homie. Trust me. I've got horror stories for days. We've got y'all beat."

"I love a competition. It can't be *that* bad, can it?"

"Wanna bet? I promise you'd never look at some of us the same again."

"Yikes. Never mind. Anyway, what'chu got?"

"So, I was going batshit crazy over here. How can I find the process gaps screen, and exactly where on the system do I set up account analysis?"

Bryce took control of Zoë's mouse. "Let me take a look."

"Ooh, what type of cologne is that?"

"This? I'm surprised you can still smell it after that restroom experience. Um... Bleu de Chanel."

"That smells fantabulous. Anthony refuses to wear cologne. He's always complaining about the prices," Zoë replied, reaching in her purse for a breath mint.

"Is that a new one?"

"What?"

"*Fantabulous.*"

"I've always used that."

"Oh, wait, it's the *other* made-up word."

"'Wonderiffic?'"

"That's it."

"Fantabulous is an actual word, sir."

"So is 'conversate.' Doesn't mean we should use it."

"Um, no it's not…"

"It is so. Look it up. Wait, let's not get sidetracked."

"I was just saying how Anthony won't spend money on cologne. He buys body sprays."

"What? Like Axe?"

"Yes."

"Ugh. No thanks."

"I hate it too."

"To each their own. He's got a point about the prices though. Certain brands are incredibly expensive. I usually buy a bunch of my favorites in travel sizes and spend top dollar on a large fancy brand. Or, better yet, I'll butter someone up around the holidays and let them come out of *their* pocket."

The death stare given by Zoë was one for the ages.

"I'm kidding, Zo. Sheesh."

He wasn't.

"Oh, cuz I was about to say. What a douche move. Speaking of douches, have you seen your boy yet?" she asked Bryce.

"Who?"

"Who's the only douche we hang out with?"

"Roy?" he asked, with a befuddled look. "No, why?"

"Oh my gosh, he cut off his goatee. He's clean shaven now. I saw him walking through the office with two other guys. They looked to be headed to a meeting."

"You know what they say, right?"

"What?"

"Never trust a White man with a mustache or a Black man without one," he whispered. Zoë's eyes popped out of her head at the comment. She immediately covered her mouth with one hand, adding the other for added protection.

"Zo, don't. It's too early."

"That is freakin' hilarious."

"It's true."

"I wanna laugh and you won't let me. That's not fair."

"If your laugh didn't set off fire alarms, we'd be cool. Anyway, I can't find the process gaps screen at all. I wonder if... oh, I know what it is. They haven't given you access yet because of the confidentiality restrictions when you were a temp. That should be an easy fix since you're permanent now. Let me see if I can get a hold of IT."

Bryce and the rest of the work crew were planning to celebrate Zoë's recent promotion in the coming weeks after she accepted the company's full-time offer. However, her decision wouldn't come easily. The diligent employee held onto a pinch of resentment toward management when they ignored their own ninety-day direct-hire promise set during the initial interview. With that, she refused to capitulate into the fickle world of Finance, promising to take a lucrative offer relative to her degree if something materialized. Yet a move out of Hudson Investors wasn't exactly fitting. Though Zoë's patience had reached its peak, she was already knee-deep in the company's culture, having formed relationships with key staff members. Following the corporation's recent annual profit achievements, as a new hire, she was on the receiving end of a prodigious salary increase and bonus, warranting her decision to stick around.

"I'm gonna browse around Lord & Taylor for lunch. Wanna tag along?" she asked.

"Ugh... I'm supposed to meet some of the guys from Wealth and Management and Accounting. We're doing a final roster count and going over the shirt sizes for the softball league."

"Why hasn't anyone asked if I wanted to play?"

It was a rhetorical question, one which made him uncomfortable. Bryce knew exactly the reason but found himself tongue-tied. It all stemmed from Zoë's prior employment status as a temp worker. They weren't seen as equals with the company. He looked around hopelessly before formulating a response.

"Who even knew you liked softball? This is the first I'm hearing about this."

"That's not the point," she replied.

"I'm almost positive there'll be several open spots as the weeks go by. You know everyone won't be able to commit for the long haul."

"Okay, Tonya Harding."

"Tonya Harding? That was more Kristi Yamaguchi," he replied, fetching a fist bump. "Come on, Zo, I'm not skating around the question. Don't be mad at *me,* I wasn't in charge of setting up the league. I'm guessing they were only looking to include full-time staff this year. We had some temps play a few years back, and the next thing you know they were let go."

"I didn't even know about the league last year. Why do jobs treat temps like red-headed stepchildren? Who cares if we're not *officially* with the group," she mimicked. "Some of us are equally important. Most of the company is fueled by the hard work of temps."

"I would agree. Hey, look, I was a temp a few times, so, you're preaching to the choir. Besides, it's a moot point now. You've got a fancy name plate on your desk, a 'welcome to the team' banner... flowers... you're *very* welcome, by the way. Your health benefits should've already kicked in, you've got vacation time out the you-know-what... a sweet bonus... what are we *really* talking about here?"

"Don't try to paint this rosy picture. When does the league start?"

"In two weeks. I'll know for sure today."

"And where are the games played?"

"That's one of the topics being discussed at lunch. I'm thinking Central Park. That's the most convenient location. Plus, we played there last year. Seriously, if you're down, I'll ask. It's us, Wealth and Management, Asset Management, some of the guys in IT, Accounting... Compliance... Customer Service..."

"Sounds like fun. I'm intrigued."

"Yeah, it's a fun time. Last year I was in and out because of my shoulder, but I'm hoping to redeem myself. Oh, and we played on Wednesdays. I think it'll be the same this year."

"Why Wednesday?" she asked, gripping an imaginary baseball bat with her hands adjusted the wrong way. The visual was internally cringe-inducing for Bryce.

"Just to break up the work week. Can you believe some people wanted to play on Friday? I was like, 'Uh, no thanks.' I don't wanna see any of these jokers past five. Anyway, let me get going. I have another call in a few... aye, look who it is." From the corner of his eye, Bryce spotted Aadesh leaving the workspace of another employee. Aadesh was one of the youngest members of IT and a big-time Yankees fan who constantly teased Bryce during baseball season. He also had a major crush on Zoë.

"Sup, bud-dy," Aadesh teased, expressing a bashful wave at Zoë.

"Aadesh, are you playing softball again this year?"

"Of course. But first can we address the elephant in the room? Why are you guys still in last place?"

"We're only six and a half out. It's early. We've got the A's tonight. What do I always say? One series at a time. Hey, while you're here, can you look at this? We're trying to add the process gaps screen. Does Zoë have to put in a ticket or is this a quick fix?"

"Hmm... something like this should be expedited by management. Oh, well, you have authority, so it can easily be done. I'll try to get it taken care of ASAP. Not for you though, for Zoë *only*."

"That was Derek Jeter smooth." Bryce winked. "I've got to run. Chat with you folks later."

12

—

JOY & PAIN

There was no sign of Tasha's mint-colored chevy cobalt in her driveway, and now was as good a time as any to see if he still had the magic touch. Bryce had autonomy to speak to whomever he pleased, but how well would it have been received by Tasha if she had found him conversing with the tempting mail carrier, just hours before their scheduled movie date? On top of that, he needed to recuperate after bungling his chance with Alyssa.

Bryce had seen the fast-moving mail carrier several times before, however, their first and only encounter was an unmitigated disaster. It all happened on a mild autumn afternoon, a little less than a year ago, when he elected to work from home. Through his kitchen window, he noticed a woman in a pair of fitted uniformed shorts reaching over in a confined area of the mail truck. Undoubtedly, she was hard at work, minding her own business, but he had a skewed way of thinking. Without giving it much thought, he placed his sandwich down, muted the conference call, and boldly walked over to the cluster mailbox unit to receive the mail in hand. Unfortunately, his plan fell short as he embarrassingly closed in on her with a full skincare face mask. Bryce never forgot the look in her eye, a coy smile where she folded her lips to restrain herself from laughter. She would further insinuate how close she was from setting his eyes on fire with a bottle of mace.

A couple of valuable lessons were discovered that afternoon:

1. Don't chase. Attract.
2. Always conduct a mirror check before exiting the house.

~

"Long time no see," he waved, disposing of a large trash bag into the garbage can.

"I know. They have me on a different route now."

"Oh. I thought I may have scared you away."

"Never that. Just cuz you see a pretty bitch in uniform doesn't mean I won't throw down. You're lucky you didn't get your ass beat that day." The brazen woman chuckled, noticeably pursing her lips. Through their continued small talk, he learned her name and how long she worked for the postal service. Nothing impressed him more than the discovery that her natural butt-length hair never got in the way of performing the arduous job.

"You're at eight twenty-six, right?" Joy asked of his house number.

"Impressive."

"I thought I saw a package for you somewhere." She sorted through a bunch of plastic wrappings. "Here it is." Bryce looked down reading the name 'Omari Harris', who made his way back to New Jersey only days ago in time for the delivery.

"Thank you. One of these days I'm gonna get you to smile and this time, it won't be because I made a fool of myself."

Joy pressed her lips together before responding. "I don't just wake up and smile at everyone. It's not that type of party. You'll have to give me a good reason to."

She continued to shield her face through their powwow. Bryce wondered if he had lost his touch. It was possible that she was trying not to tip her hand.

"That sounds like a challenge. Let me take you out one time," he courageously suggested. "Your cheekbones will thank me later, I promise."

Eye contact was pivotal on his personal three-step 'rules of engagement' list, yet Joy refused to look at him. "Take me out where? I don't know you." She batted her eyelash extensions, looking over a handful of envelopes. "You could be some type of nut."

"Well, *get* to know me. Think about it, what can I honestly do? You know where I live, the type of car I drive, you've got my government name... you can *actually* see my face today... it'll be easy to describe me to the police." He had a point, and she nearly cracked a smile after realizing the gaffe.

"What does that mean? There are plenty of weirdos in nice areas with nice cars. I see them all the time."

"Find out if I'm a weirdo. Unless, of course, you're involved. I don't wanna overstep."

"You don't think coming out in a full-face mask automatically qualifies you as weird?"

"You got me. I don't even have a good comeback. Was that all the mail for today?"

Joy walked over to the truck. The sound of ripped paper caught Bryce's attention. She returned with a random promotional mailing with the ripped paper which included her phone number posted on top.

"Are you seeing anyone? I don't like messy."

"I'm as single as a dollar bill," he smirked.

"You're so corny," she laughed. "Here, let's see if you know what to do with this. Bye."

It wasn't often that he bumped into women who intentionally avoided his handsome features. Their exchange was only supposed to be a test. Admittedly, it left him puzzled.

[hair clipper sound]

"O., you've got a package."

Omari requested time off from work and unexpectedly arrived at Bryce's house mid-week, spooked by the recent event with the undercover officers. He wouldn't open up about his unforeseen visit, hoping to avoid a pending lecture, but Bryce, a sharp-witted reader of body language, was too observant to turn a blind eye.

The final straw that something was amiss came when Omari fired questions about the pursuit of legal representation. The more he spoke the more he revealed. Eventually, the conversation advanced to health concerns though he withheld the particulars. It wasn't an easy conversation but as his condition declined so did his confidence. He agreed to visit a walk-in clinic first thing on Monday to find the underlying cause of what was robbing him of finding joy.

[hair clipper sound]

"O.," Bryce repeated.

"You called me?" Omari yelled from the top of the stairs.

"Yes. You have a package."

The moment arrived. With an unreadable face, Omari strolled down the steps to retrieve what he hoped to be the cure for his current symptoms.

"I need you to shape me up when you're done," Bryce insisted. "Aye, those waves are spinning, my boy. I had no idea. You're usually always wearing a du-rag."

"I've been wolfing my hair for the past month. I'm gonna try and get the seven-twenties," Omari replied.

"I thought about that after I first cut my hair from locs. The only person I ever saw pull it off was Raekwon from Wu-Tang."

"Really?"

"Yes. Most of the cats my age rocked three-sixties or had the waves on top with the fade going around. I should've tried it."

"I'm feeling the curly blow-out though. That's a good look on you," Omari complimented.

"That's what the ladies tell me. I might keep it around for the summer, but I'll need you to stay on top of it."

"I got you. You about to head out?"

"I might get the car washed, why?"

"I was gonna ask if you can grab me something to eat."

"There's plenty of food in the house."

"Yeah, but I don't want a *turkey* burger," Omari teased.

"It's a cheat day for me, so I wouldn't mind a little junk food. What do you want?"

"I don't know. I was thinking pizza."

"Be specific. You know I'll call up Domino's. If you think your life is in shambles now, just wait."

"Oh, hell nah. What's the name of that place over by the strip mall..."

"Giovanni's?"

"I think that's it."

"That's in the same direction that I was headed. You still do the pineapple-onion thing?"

"Um, nah... let me get sausage and green peppers."

"All right. I'll just get a whole pie and tell them half-cheese-half-sausage and green peppers. I'm not getting soda, so don't ask. Oh, I know what I meant to tell you. I need you and Brixx to get your stuff together pronto."

"Stuff like what?"

"Your music. I'm talking to someone who works in broad-casting."

Omari's eyes glimmered. Finally, some good news. Bryce continued. "She used to work for BET. Says she stays connected with a few execs in the industry and has a promoter friend who arranges open mics around the city. I told her about y'all."

"What did she say?"

"Nothing really. Well, she did ask where she could find your music. I told her about the demo."

"Why you ain't tell her about our YouTube page?" Omari inquired, his voice cracking like a pubescent boy.

"Aw, my bad. I completely forgot. It's not too late. Just send me the link and I'll forward it to her," Bryce replied, busting out his infrequently worn OG Air Jordan 1s. "She travels a lot for work, so we haven't connected yet. I just wanted to plant the seed in her head."

With Bryce running errands, there was ample time for Omari to test out the items in the package. The new findings to his genitals had him so wired that he made an impulse purchase, getting himself a non-FDA-approved topical medicine from a sketchy website. He entered the powder room to remove two miniature tubes with green lettering. His eyes brushed over the fine print of the instructions, overlooking obvious typos in search of the estimated healing time:

Eight to twelve weeks.

In bold lettering was the caution label—**Warning: Product will burn.** He was hopeless, but it would have to do. He pulled his shorts down, applied the white menthol-scented substance across the tip of his index finger and onto several evolving warts. Within seconds, his eyes watered up in pain from the burning sensation. Life was gratuitously unfair.

"I'll drive. Don't mind my car. It's a little junky."

"A little?" Bryce replied, entering the passenger side.

"Shut up. That's what happens when you have kids."

"I'm just bustin' your chops. It's not too bad."

"Can you fit?"

"Oh, we'll find out soon enough, won't we?" He smirked, raising his eyebrows like Groucho Marx.

"Get in the car so we can go, please." Tasha replied, peeling off like a woman in a hurry to catch movie trailers.

Their energy was collaborative from the start. Only a few months ago, Bryce was crafting ways to get his seductive neighbor to break free of her shell, and now he was in her passenger seat.

This was one of many intricate details of the dating experience he cherished and why there wouldn't be a sense of urgency to settle down.

Consumed with work, school, and motherly duties following a ho-hum relationship of almost two years, Tasha was ready to unleash. She wore a touch of make-up, gold hoop earrings, a yellow tank top, and blue jeans that looked painted on by the stroke of a Picasso brush. Catching Bryce's immediate attention was her choice of foundation. She donned red lipstick with a shade of blue eye shadow, complimenting her flawless brown skin —a combination unseen since his mother modeled a similar look in the '80s.

They left the concession stand holding onto their preferred snacks—Bryce a large, buttered popcorn, Tasha bearing enough sweets to open her own candy shop. *Hangover 2* had already been on the big screen for a month, yet the air-conditioned theater was filled. They were left with the unpopular choice of settling for the lower front row.

She appeared frisky, insisting on Bryce's instant thigh rubs to keep warm while sitting snug underneath her denim jacket. Other times, she was frolicsome, cracking jokes through each scene. There were plenty of laughs to go around, but none greater than an eye-opening segment involving actress Yasmin Lee, whose amusing one-liner nearly made Tasha fall out of her seat. Back on the home front, they goofed off like two adolescents. Her boys were away, and she offered an invitation inside which he respectfully declined, citing Omari's emotional state. Turning down the request wasn't easy.

Their night ended without any hiccups, unless you were to include those inconsequential bothersome phone calls from her boys, or Tasha's startling unladylike releases of phlegm onto the pavement. They openly hugged before Bryce added a hit of comic relief, standing inches from her door.

"Be careful getting home."

~

MONDAY MORNING

The thought of confessing to a physician how he'd senselessly sabotaged his own body was humiliating. That said, nothing demoralized Omari more than when the same physician inserted a Q-tip the size of a pencil into his urethral opening. The swift pain was torturous, and he was left frazzled. Afterward, Omari sat in the waiting area with Bryce. His body was as numb as a polar bear plunge participant. The physician had come across similar cases, but he was affected by the pain in the young patient's eyes.

Deep within, Omari knew the verdict: Guilty of the act of stupidity. The only question was whether his sentence was a mild reprimand or life imprisonment. He stared ahead to the release of short breaths through chapped lips, muttering to himself incomprehensibly. A minute passed without blinking his eyes, then another. Suddenly, he rocked back and forth like a crazed person plotting a big payback, as Bryce tried effortlessly to talk him off the ledge. Omari fiddled with his phone, contemplating another call to Shauna, the person suspected of transferring the infection. She had unexpectedly fallen off the face of the earth. How convenient.

Omari was alone in thought, the surrounding sounds incoherent. At last, he responded to Bryce's question of whether he slept with others.

"Yes, but I wore protection."

It didn't matter. His current irritation was passable through skin contact, leaving more victims stripped of their innocence. Guilty by association.

The car ride home was radio-silent. Folded in Omari's hand was the medical document which sealed his fate. He stared out the passenger window, watching a flock of birds fly symmetrically. Being a bird didn't sound so bad. Maybe in another lifetime. In the interim, one infection was confirmed, another was found, and he was burning mad. The only thing left was to heal and ask for forgiveness from the victims. They didn't deserve this. It was the moral thing to do. Then again, perhaps it was too soon. Shauna hadn't touched base with him. He could selfishly do the same.

13

——

CHEERS 2 U

There were a myriad of adjectives to best describe Bryce. At the workplace, he was coolheaded. However, if a gum-flapping colleague uttered the phrase "Happy Fri-yay" one more time, his top was about to blow. Yes, it was Friday. That reality had been established sixteen hours ago. In fact, Saturday was much closer, considering the time of day. In any event, it was payday—the main reason to be exuberant. The other: Zoë's long-awaited gathering at a midtown rooftop bar to celebrate her recent promotion.

Roy knew of all the hot spots around the city, and it selfishly awarded Bryce fresh ideas for future dating experiences. He outgrew the nightclub scene after spending a chunk of his twenties in and out of some of the city's most notorious locations. The goal now was something simple, a more relaxing place that could supply the same number of visually pleasing people. According to Roy, the rooftop bar provided a soothing ambiance of music and food with a direct view of the Empire State Building.

Enjoy your weekend. See ya Monday.

Bryce offered a friendly wave back to his colleague, but their baseless assumption bugged him. What made this person confidently believe that either of them would be back on Monday?

What if he were to miraculously hit the lotto as the banner at his cubicle suggested or had an epiphany and shockingly quit his job? Worse, what if he were to get run over by a yellow cab on his way to Zoë's celebration? Sure, some of the developments were improbable, but that wasn't the point. Their robotic replies exposed the effects of a dateless work system, which for generations enslaved and influenced the minds of millions. Bryce couldn't wait to get home and research the person who engineered one of the greatest deceptions known to man: The 40-hour work week. It was truly a "Happy Fri-yay" after all.

"Don't be in such a rush to leave," Porsha warned, sneaking up to his cubicle. She followed with a warm stroke to his jawline.

"Don't do that. Why are you starting trouble at five o'clock?"

"What did I do?" she questioned bashfully. "No one even saw me."

"I'm not talking about *that* type of trouble. You know exactly what I mean."

"Oh, please. You're still scared of me."

"Are you coming to the rooftop bar?"

"I don't know. Zoë and I don't really communicate like that, so, probably not. I'm working late anyway. Come to think of it, I should go. You remember the last time we all went out," she winked, hinting at the infamous Christmas party gathering.

He stood up from his desk. "How can I forget? We'll only be there for a couple of hours if you change your mind."

"I'll see. Don't get your hopes up though." Porsha courageously helped herself to a free genital pat down.

"Any plans for the weekend?" At a moment's notice, Porsha's eyes shifted to Bryce's crotch. She added a hard bite to her bottom lip before looking him in the eye.

"Never mind..."

"Exactly, cuz you already *know* what I'm thinking."

Porsha was right, she and Zoë didn't speak much. There could've been a bit of jealousy involved. Zoë was the shiny new toy, the apple of the eye to everyone from lobby security to high-profile executives. Not to mention a good part of her day was spent around Bryce, something Porsha craved.

Now mildly aroused—thanks to Porsha's flirtatious ways, in his view was Zoë, seen heading in their direction. He immediately flagged her down as a precautionary measure to prevent Porsha from doing anything inflammatory.

"Hey, lady, ready to go?"

"Yes, sir. Hey, Porsha. I like your shoes."

"Congrats on the promotion," she replied, ignoring the praise.

"Thank you."

"Well, let me get going. Y'all have a wonderful time."

"Are you not coming?" Zoë asked.

"No, girl. I'm here 'til seven," she announced, strutting away nonchalantly. "Bryce said y'all were only staying a couple of hours. I've been there plenty of times. You'll love it."

There wasn't a plausible explanation for his sexy co-worker to take the long route back to her department, but Porsha loved to torture him with cruel and unusual punishments. Almost a quarter of the way down she glanced back with a sultry look in her eye in an ongoing play of mind games. Bryce tried his best to ignore it.

"I like the French braid look on you."

"Thanks. Yo, what's that girl's freakin' deal?"

"I don't know. Pay her no mind." Bryce used the opportunity to check Porsha out, but she was already out of view.

"She's trying to provoke me. I swear. I've been nothing but nice to her."

"She's petty. Don't let it get to you."

"See, and this is why I don't have a lot of female friends. I don't have time for pettiness."

"I hear you. Switching subjects, do you wanna walk to the bar?"

"Walk? Isn't it further downtown?"

"I think Roy said it's on the corner of 27th Street."

"Dude, that's almost twenty blocks from here."

"So what? You act like we've never taken long walks before."

"Not *twenty* blocks, Mister I've-got-to-get-my-steps-in." The comment gave rise to a quick laugh.

"It's twenty *New York City* blocks, Zo. That's a breeze. You're wearing flats too. Hey, if you wanna take the subway, we can. Just remember, it's warm outside and we're in rush hour. Not the best combo."

"Well, at least it'll be air-conditioned."

"You'd better hope so. How's Roy getting there?"

"He already left with a group from his department. They took a cab."

Jenna Barnes, who joined them for the evening, turned out to be the difference maker, suggesting they ride the subway halfway there. Exiting at 34th Street-Herald Square station was a wise decision. It shortened their walking distance to the chic penthouse bar and saved them from experiencing a major service delay had they remained.

[EDM playing in the background]

"About damn time." Roy stood up to greet the guys, holding a cocktail with a lemon slice resting comfortably on top. "I was starting to think you were gonna stand us up at your own celebration," he continued. "Jenna, welcome, glad you can join us. Smooth, long time no see. Always a pleasure."

"He's already doing too much," Zoë whispered, squeezing next to Bryce. "And he's wearing a thumb ring."

"And you wonder why I don't hang out with him," Bryce cautioned.

Seated at the table were two faintly familiar faces who Roy formally introduced. "Guys, this is Mandy Cervelli and Steven Wang, they work with me in Revenue Management."

[affectionate greetings]

A comforting breeze moved along the rooftop. Zoë, who was cold intolerant, rolled down the sleeves to her white button-up shirt, sipping a raspberry mojito. Meanwhile, Roy was just warming up. He removed his seersucker jacket and prepared to do what he did best. Bloviate.

"There's this one guy in our department, I'm not gonna say his name. Steven, you know exactly who I'm talking about." Steven nodded manically, smirking at Roy's expected joke. "He's always seeking date confirmation with a calendar right on his desk. *Is today the twenty-first?*"

"Don't forget the time too," Steven added.

"Yes. Dude, there's a wall clock right there."

Steven continued, "Not only is there a wall clock, but who doesn't have a cell phone?"

"Right?"

"Or he could always peek at the bottom right corner of the computer monitor," Mandy included.

"Exactly," Roy continued. "The prehistoric days of watching the sun shift through the sky as a time barometer are long gone. As a manager, I've got to be professional, but what the heck is wrong with this guy?"

"Is he an older gentleman?" Jenna inquired.

"No. He's gotta be, what, late-forties, early fifties?"

"Well, that's ancient to me. I'm in my twenties," she chuckled.

"Me too, girl, "Zoë endorsed.

Bryce sampled a virgin citrus mocktail before chiming in. "He's probably looking to make conversation. I can't think of any other reason. It's funny you should mention pet peeves. There's one lady who comes to our side. I think she's from the mailroom. She loves saying 'Happy Fri-yay' so, now, she has everyone saying it."

"Toni," Zoë burst out.

"You have no idea how much that annoys me. I'm saying to myself, 'Why is this middle-aged woman trying to sound hip?' I don't even think 'the cool people' use that term."

Steven barged in. "The slogan TGIF must be too '90s for her."

"Zo, did you say her name is Toni? Tall, petite woman with glasses... red hair?" Roy inquired.

"Uh, I don't remember seeing glasses, but the red hair, yes."

"I think I know who you're talking about."

"Hey, leave us gingers alone," Jenna playfully instructed to the laughter of the table.

"You know I've been meaning to ask you, is that word considered derogatory?" Roy questioned.

"Wait, do I look like the authoritative figure for redheads?"

[group laughter]

"No, but you're the only one I know."

"I mean, I guess it all depends on context. Personally, I don't have a problem with it, but I know people who are uber sensitive to things like that."

"Got it. Bryce and I had a conversation once on whether the word was proper."

"Uh, Bryce, was this like a meeting or something? Why didn't you clue me in? I could've been the honorary guest speaker," she continued.

"Here's another thing..." Roy resumed.

"You're just full of pet peeves today, aren't you?" Mandy asked.

"Somebody snatch the fruity drink out of his hand," Steven cut in.

"I'm not drunk... yet. But what's with people hanging up sweaters? Smooth, we've had this chat before."

"We have."

"Wait, wait, that's the second time you've referred to him as Smooth. The suspense is killing me. What's the story behind the name?" Mandy asked.

"We have plenty of time to get into that," Bryce smiled. "Please, allow the Hudson Investors's fashion guru time to finish his gripping story."

"So, hear me out. I've been wanting to get this off my chest for some time now. I'm noticing guys at work are hanging their sweaters in the closet instead of folding them into a drawer. Wait 'til sweater season arrives, you'll see. There are people walking around with hanger-shoulders."

"No more drinks for you, bud." Steven joked.

Roy tugged at the tips of his shoulders to demonstrate. "It looks like they're wearing shoulder pads. Don't tell me none of you have seen this."

Zoë teasingly rolled her eyes at Jenna before murmuring a stern warning. "So, when he starts playing with his tongue ring, it means he's getting nervous."

Bryce stood up to capture the surrounding pink cirrus clouds and Empire State Building view.

"That view is out of this world, isn't it?" Mandy expressed.

"Okay, so I know I'm a newbie and, like, I probably shouldn't say a whole lot..." Jenna offered.

"This is a judgment-free zone, please, pet-peeve away," Steven advised.

"Yes, girl, we're off the clock," Zoë added. "I'm calling next. We're not gonna let Roy bore us to death with his rants."

"Yeah, the floor is yours," Roy replied. "Just make sure Dick ain't around."

"Who's...?"

"Jenna, don't," Zoë warned. "Ignore him and his childish behavior."

"You don't know Dick?" he followed. Jenna frightfully looked around the table for help. She was met by Zoë's repulsive face and Mandy's look of puzzlement. Steven's eyes filled with water—his face was red as a tomato. Bryce was unobservant, having grown impatient with the waiter. Finally, he responded to Roy's ambiguous question.

"Hey Jenna, don't listen to this guy. He's referring to the CEO."

Zoë joined in. "Yes. He wanted to hear you say, 'I know Dick.'"

"Not *I know*, I was waiting for her to say *who's* Dick? These guys are such party poopers," Roy surrendered. "So, Jenna, Dick Savage is the CEO. For some godforsaken reason, he prefers to be called Dick with that last name. He's got to be pulling our leg."

"Our *third* leg..." Steven cut in before a dark-haired woman at the table behind them turned around.

"Hiyo!" Roy replied.

"I'm sorry," Zoë cut in. "Did we agree to meet up at a rooftop bar or a boy's locker room?"

"Take a peek at his signature line the next time we get a company email. He puts Dick in quotations," Roy air quoted.

Steven's face still showed the effects of tittered laughter. "*He puts Dick in quotations.* I can go so many places with that."

"Please don't," Mandy alerted. "For the love of God."

"I won't. Let me just add this little disclaimer. I don't know how many times you'll run into Dick since he only stops by twice a year..."

"Yeah, Dick can be stingy..." Roy followed. Zoë squirmed deep into her chair.

"By the way, you don't wanna refer to him as Richard. Not even Rich," Steven carried on. "He'll kindly ask if you call him by his nickname. I kid you not."

"What if I called him Mr. Savage? Better yet, why don't I just call out sick whenever he announces his visit," Jenna offered.

"What's the matter, Dick made you sick?"

"Roy!" the group howled.

"Saved by the Dell," Bryce joked, referring to Aadesh's arrival, much to the delight of Steven, who appreciated a good pun. "Thank you for saving us from a litany of penis jokes. Please, take a seat."

"Wait, let me sit over here. No offense, Bryce, but your Orioles losing streak might be contagious. What did I miss?"

"You don't wanna know."

The cheerful bunch laughed away, joining the throngs of jolly people gathered at the fancy venue. Their fun-filled evening was topped off by an impressive menu. Bryce gobbled down a delicious garden salad, and thanks to Jenna's persistent pleas, he tried hummus for the first time.

"Guys, if I may," Bryce presented. "Zo, I know how much you hate this type of stuff... which is why I felt inclined to do it in the first place."

[group laughter]

"I promise I'll keep it short and sweet."

"Smooth, are you about to do what I think? *Is he about to propose?*" Roy whispered to Steven.

"I'm gonna need everyone to look at Roy and say, 'shut up, fool,' on the count of three. One..."

"Shut up fool," Zoë yelled prematurely.

"In all seriousness, I'd like to prepare a toast for your recent achievements. You've been nothing short of amazing during your time with us, and I am truly honored to have you as a colleague and friend. Congrats on a well-deserved promotion and what is sure to be a promising future ahead."

[cheers]

The rest of their shindig included a collection of topics from the best television sitcoms of all time to their whereabouts on 9/11. Also inserted was a subject matter gaining a ton of mainstream coverage—the approaching end of the Mayan calendar. However, the night wouldn't end without several surprises. Overtaking Bryce's order-to-go of the likeable spreading dip was the emergence of the Vice President of Hudson Investors. She recognized Bryce from his feature on an investment magazine subtitled "rising stars" and alarmingly sat at the table behind them. Despite that, the crowning moment was Roy throwing caution to the wind. He admitted to Bryce and Zoë of his current romance with Suzanna—the attractive Dominican office custodian, who was rumored to be sleeping with the head of building security. It wasn't the "coming out party" they expected, but it certainly gave light to the meaning of a drunk tongue speaks a sober mind.

14

AMERICA THE BEAUTIFUL

Father, I ask that you grant me strength, health, and protection
during my workout.
I ask that you continue to shield me from any approaching danger
and allow each of us to reach our destinations safely.
In Jesus name I pray, Amen.

Silent prayer was as much a part of Bryce's daily routine as breathing. It is what kept him afloat in a world filled with lunatics and unexpected activity. Before exiting his car, he looked through the windshield with great concentration at the person ahead. The aches and pains from yesterday's rigorous company softball game had suddenly vanished. He never doubted the healing powers of his Lord and Savior, but this rapid recovery, albeit temporary, had little to do with Him.

It was Thursday, the last day of June. Summer was in full swing, but Bryce remained frozen in the driver's seat. His heartbeat fluttered, his body desensitized to perpetual soreness. He recognized the individual exiting a crystal blue Mazda CX-5. She wore a drop-shoulder gym top with Metallica written on the front, dark tights, and red sneakers. He grabbed his gym bag and rushed off, calling out to her. She spotted the direction of his baritone voice and looked his way with a twinkle in her eye. His incongruous behavior was unusual. There was something about her that provoked a string of emotions. She could light up a room and shift his mood with no trouble. As he drew near, he wasted little time reaching for a half-hug, showering her with words of flattery from their last encounter—the first Thursday of the month. This was too good to be true.

They went about their workouts separately and agreed to reconnect near the locker rooms in an hour. His eyes wandered the floor, petrified at losing her amidst the crowd. Alyssa was seen anxiously exploring the gym as well. There was an unexplainable interconnection brewing between them. That or she was engulfed with paranoia, still haunted by the creepy old man at her previous gym—the driving force to why she would become a member at Bryce's gym.

It was 7:58 p.m.—an hour since they last stumbled upon each other. He finished his final leg workout, nodding to U2's "Pride (In the Name of Love)". His gaze swept the gym; no sign of Alyssa. *Did she absentmindedly bail on our agreement?* He wondered. On the surface, Bryce appeared calm, but there was no fighting the feeling that he had been duped. How could this kindred spirit be so cold and heartless?

He started his walk of shame to the men's locker room where groups of people lined up against the machines, laughing amongst themselves. The longer it took to get there the louder the laughs grew. He couldn't help but feel like the biggest punchline. Alyssa's unexpected disappearance is part of what discouraged him from settling down. There was no sense in trusting modern women whose attitudes frighteningly mirrored men. A lightbulb went off in his head. Bryce had accepted his fate and vowed to remain single from this day forward. It didn't matter if a collection of his favorite women morphed into one. No one would smash his heart into a thousand pieces ever again.

Dispelling his morbid mood was the quiet noise of a harp playing in his head as he rounded the corner. Finally, he was at peace with his decision, when suddenly, the glorious harp sound switched to a violent record scratch. His ill-advised angst, all for naught. Standing next to the locker room as confirmed was Alyssa.

"You waited," he announced.

Calling him a good actor would be just.

She proved to be a woman of her word. Again, the onus was on him. Yet another overreaction—an ongoing theme from the Kristen days and it almost cost him.

He struggled to formulate a sentence outside of their usual gym talk. He genuinely cared about Alyssa's healthy eating habits and how she sculpted her body, but he was just as eager to pry into her personal life.

W.W.R.D. What would Roy do?

"By the way, I don't need to use the locker room. I only worked on my legs. Barely broke a sweat."

"Really? I was drenched. I needed to wipe myself down. There was no way I was gonna let you catch me like that," she laughed. Bryce took mental notes. She was focused on her appearance around *him*. Interesting.

"I'm sure you looked fine." Awkward silence followed. The worst possible thing for a conversationalist. He held the door for Alyssa—proving chivalry was still alive and well. Emerging on her face was a grin as wide as the horizon.

"Aw, thanks. I'm not used to people holding doors anymore."

"Really?"

"Really. This might sound weird, but if I'm walking behind someone, I'll purposely slow down just to avoid the disappointment of having a door slammed in my face," Alyssa laughed.

"I get it. Well, get used to it..."

If Mandy wanted to know how I earned the nickname Smooth, that was confirmation right there, he thought.

"Oh, you're gonna slam doors in my face too?" Alyssa questioned.

"No, no, I meant get used to doors being held."

"I'm just messing around. I knew what you meant."

"A woman with a sense of humor, who lifts. Am I dreaming? Whoops, did I say that out loud?"

"A woman with a sense of humor who lifts *and* does more pullups than you. Remember you mentioned that last time?"

Sweet, a reference to the last interaction. "Right. I forgot about that. Anyway, pardon my old-fashioned ways. That's just something I'm unwilling to change. I'd like to think my parents raised me well."

"That's so awesome. Well, looks to me like they've done a wonderful job."

Their mutual attraction was supported by Alyssa's lasting gazes, which he later speculated were caused by the gym towel lint on his forehead. Unlike Joy, the mail carrier, Alyssa successfully checked off two steps on his 'rules of engagement' list: *eye contact and sense of humor.* The final test—*stimulating conversation*—was sure to be a breeze.

Bryce was attentive to the widespread belief that a man's only goal in life is to get into the panties of a woman. That was partially true. However, he would need to show another side of himself to keep Alyssa's cynicism low.

Over the years, he learned that most women despised the cocky, obsessional sex-crazed man. That wasn't who he was—at least not publicly. Sex with Alyssa was the furthest thing from his mind. But with the allure of her beauty and bubbly personality, how could anyone blame a guy for leading with the wrong head? He genuinely wanted to become acquainted and worked arduously to earn his share of points.

"So, are you a true Metallica fan or are you one of those people who wear trendy rock shirts and never listen to their music?"

Alyssa gasped at the question, swooping her dark hair from one side to the other. "Are you seriously gonna insult me like that? I'm offended."

"Sorry. Sometimes I let that type of stuff get to me," he offered, half-heartedly. "I'm sort of a music enthusiast."

"Don't be. I get it. I listen to a bit of everything. Right now, I'm obsessed with this group called Train. Have you heard of them?"

"I haven't."

"They're like a mix of Pop, Rock, and Country. Alternative Rock is my fave, though. That and anything '90s."

"Music to my ears..."

"Oh my God, I love puns."

Bryce let out a forced laugh. "Anyway, I don't wanna hold you up..."

"No, not at all. You're fine."

She's receptive to the idea of extending the conversation.

"Cool. I just wanted to be mindful of the time. Wasn't sure if you had to rush home."

"You're good... today is my Friday. Four-day weekend. Woot-woot." She raised both hands with uniformity. It was the first time Bryce witnessed anyone 'raising the roof' since President Bill Clinton was fornicating with a White House intern.

"Really? I'm jealous. Do you have plans for the holiday weekend?"

"I do. I'm heading down the shore tomorrow with my mom... well my mom, sister, and her fiancé. We have a beach home out there. I'm super excited just to pig out and get some sun."

No mention of a husband or children. Time to make a move.

"Ah, beach life. I love it. I could use a tan myself."

"You're kidding, right? You have such amazing skin. It's one of the first things I noticed."

"Thank you. Hey, not to make things awkward, but..."

"I friggin' *love* awkward. Lay it on me."

"Okay, so, how comfortable are you exchanging numbers? Too soon?"

"Yeah, absolutely. Not soon at all."

"Since you mentioned going to the beach, I was thinking just in case I never see you again."

"What do you mean?"

"You know Jaws tends to pop up and eat people around this time of year."

"Bryce, don't say that. That *would* be my luck."

"You've got to pardon my nerd. I'm a movie buff. There are certain films I only watch during the season they were released..." He paused. "That's my number calling you now."

"Got it. Saving it to my contacts. It's so funny you should say that. I do the same thing. So, I'm guessing you've seen *Die Hard*, right?"

"Of course."

"When do you watch it?"

"Ooh. Trick question..."

"Trick question? That's an easy one."

"Is it? When was it released, summer of '88?"

"Yeah, but it's a Christmas movie."

"Eh..."

"Eh? Bryce, please don't tell me..."

An early morning downpour put a damper on church plans. Rain had an odd way of altering things and making him lazy. Instead, Bryce decided to whip up a massive breakfast, and conduct some light household chores, in between catching baseball highlights from the night before. The constant movement functioned as a deterrent to keeping his mind off a whirlwind of recent activity.

Unmistakably, things were looking up. There was the ongoing weekly softball league, he removed himself from Julissa's duplicitous life, and excitement grew for an upcoming trip to visit a childhood friend. However, in private, he worried deeply about the long-term psychological effects of Omari, who hadn't replied to his texts since the clinic visit. He agreed not to share the disturbing news but couldn't escape the image of his sibling's pupils dilating on the ride home. It was as if his soul was being snatched away, and he feared Omari might inflict harm on himself. Rather than harbor these feelings, Bryce wanted to have an off-the-record conversation with Dale about it.

A generic text alert sounded through the violent crash of rain. Bryce's immediate contacts had specific tones, resulting in a mystery. He hoped it was Alyssa but didn't expect her to initiate conversation so soon. Yvonne was the other thought, after she treated him to a late-night course of provocative selfies and videos from her South Beach hotel room, but she was likely in bed, still hungover.

> Sexy Neighbor: Good morning. Is it supposed to rain all day?
>
> Sun 10:44 a.m.

It was Tasha. If giving people nicknames were a business, Bryce would be the handsome face of a corporate giant.

> I don't think so.

> Sexy Neighbor: Ok. Good.
>
> I'm about to pick up the boys from the sleepover.
>
> Are you still coming to the BBQ?
>
> Sun 10:45 a.m.

> Um, yes, I'm still down.

> Sexy Neighbor: Are you dressed?
>
> Sun 10:46 a.m.

> What if I'm not?

Sexy Neighbor: Then I'm gonna fight u…

I was gonna stop by before I left.

Sun 10:46 a.m.

Ok, well, in that case, I'm butt-booty-naked.

Sexy Neighbor: LOL Stop playing.

Sun 10:47 a.m.

Come by. I'm just cleaning up.

Sexy Neighbor: OMW

Sun 10:50 a.m.

If he would've known about her pain in the neck boys tagging along, he would've connected with Lorenzo's family for their annual July Fourth cookout instead. At least he could've gotten more exposure to a life he desired and a chance to see his mild-mannered godchildren. But Tasha was too irresistible to pass up. As he moved closer to copulating, all he could think about was the things he wanted to do to her body.

[doorbell ring]

"It's open," he yelled from the top of the stairs.

"Mmm, it smells good," she announced, placing her umbrella in the corner rack.

"Welcome to B-Hop. We've got pancakes, cheesy eggs, and bacon. Care for some?"

"Is the bacon pork?"

"Is there any other way to eat bacon?"

"Eww, I don't do pig."

"Your loss. You know what's weird? I'll buy pork, but I won't keep red meat in the house."

"What? He-Man doesn't eat beef?"

"Not much. Only if I'm at a restaurant or if someone is grilling it. But I won't buy it. My step-bro usually has a fit."

"You're weird."

"Says the person wearing a bonnet over a headscarf and flip-flops in the rain." Bryce received a stinging blow to the arm following the comment.

"I just got a doobie wrap yesterday, thank you. I'm not trying to mess up my hair."

It was Tasha's second visit to his home, the last being a quick walk-through of the first floor when she wanted to compare household appliances. She moved into the development shortly after the houses were constructed, long before an abundance of newer models with top tier equipment were built.

"Not that it's a problem, but what made you wanna come by in this crazy weather?"

"I don't know. I was just sitting around bored. Why? Were you expecting company?"

"No."

"You have a brand-new dishwasher too? I didn't see that last time."

"Man, I don't even touch that thing. I wash dishes by hand."

"So, answer my question."

"I did, and then you asked another one."

"Oh, I didn't hear you. So, are you expecting company? I don't wanna interrupt whatever you got going on."

"Here we go." He rolled his eyes. "And what could be going on?"

Tasha offered a snarky reply. "I don't know. You tell me."

"There's nothing to tell. I'm doing laundry, 'bout to vacuum and then hop in the shower..."

"Wait, can I see your bathroom first?"

"Sure. Upstairs, first door to your right."

Tasha walked upstairs, unaware of Bryce's inward eye. He watched her peach-shaped bottom gobble her panties through a pair of translucent gray biker shorts. It was a struggle not to say anything inappropriate. Especially on the Lord's Day.

"Let me get the light for you."

She stood comfortably in front of the wide sink mirror while he transferred a load of clothes from the washing machine to the dryer. "We have the same cherrywood vanities, but your bathroom looks a lot different than mine. I like your wall paintings too," she replied, adjusting her rising shorts. "Nice job, youngin'."

"We're *only* four years apart. Relax."

"Was this shower head already installed?"

"No. I bought that. I wanted the rainfall effect," he laughed. "If I could add a shower bench I'd be set."

"I like it. I need to get one. I'll have to come over and take a shower one of these days," she engagingly replied, sticking out her tongue. He finished showing the upstairs layout before they headed downstairs. Tasha sat at the kitchen island; the same spot he pictured her sprawled out a few months ago.

"Do you care for anything to drink? Water? Juice?"

"I'm good. Thank you. I guess I'll go and get my babies now. I should be back in a half-hour."

"Okay, cool."

She emitted a yawn walking toward the door. "I don't know why I'm so tired. Anyway, I'm thinking we can leave around one. Do you think you'll be ready?"

"One is fine. I'll be dressed long before then. Um, are you wearing those shorts?"

It would've killed him had he not asked.

Tasha came to a complete standstill, causing their bodies to collide. Bryce wrapped one arm around her waistline. There wasn't a doubt she felt his fervor.

"Why would you stop in front of me like that?"

"Did anybody tell you to walk on my heels?" she replied, punching his arm. "And no, I'm not wearing these shorts, thank you. But if I did?"

"I was just asking."

~

The barbeque was great, minus the blistering sun and swarms of mosquitoes feasting on Bryce like *The Last Supper,* and the ride home ended the same way it began—more whining from her sons about the other's lack of sharing a gaming device, let alone more of Tasha playing "Iron" Mike Tyson to his tender arm. He was formally introduced to Tasha's relatives as a "friend," yet their interaction was indicative of more—according to her chirpy aunt who observed plenty of physical touch and flirting.

His ears still rang hours later, due to Tasha's boisterous yells to her sons who were often spotted playing too aggressively with other children, but overall, the day showed promise. He learned of Tasha's foster care upbringing and the reason her oldest son's father is sitting in a state prison. The chilling announcement wasn't an attempt to play on his emotions—nor would it hinder his ever-growing friendship with her. She made it perfectly clear she wasn't looking for anyone to play stepparent. At this juncture, Bryce's *only* concern was her overbearing masculine energy and short fuse. Something he'd have to get over as he inched closer to bedding her.

[Def Leppard "Hysteria" playing in background]

He rinsed off the day and unwound with a glass of red wine, awaiting Tasha's queue. Tonight called for a little one-on-one time as they planned to watch a mixture of comedy specials once the boys were asleep. In the meantime, he channel surfed, landing on *Jaws 2.* On a dime, he thought of Alyssa.

[generic text chime]

> Sexy Neighbor: Are you still up?

> Sun 9:00 p.m.

Lizzy stared Bryce down, applying short-pitched meows, trying to determine his movements for the evening. In time, the lovable pet found her answer. Within minutes, he was laid out on the couch snoring away, too worn out to put on a show with two condoms stuffed inside of his short's pockets. Sadly, the night with Tasha remained a mystery, as Lizzy kneaded Bryce's lap in preparation to snuggle.

~

MONDAY, JULY 4

Bryce awakened to the brightness of the living room ceiling light, television glare, and a chain of 'hello?' text messages from Tasha. He felt bad standing her up, but he was zapped after yesterday's affairs. Today, Priscilla would accompany him to Dale and Terri's for some tasty food and a chance to hang out with their friends, but first, he needed to get something off his chest. It was a few minutes past seven and Dale was an early riser.

Morning, Son...
"What's up, Pop? Why do you sound out of breath?"
Do I? Oh, I was in the garage shuffling through some old tapes. I can't seem to find the Great American Bash video.
"It ain't *truly* July Fourth unless you've pulled out one of those wrestling tapes, huh? Which year?"
Uh, the one we went to when Flair wrassled Luger.
"Oh, Bash '88. By the way, can I borrow that? I'm gonna take it to Dan's."
Just as long as you bring it back.
"Bring it back? You haven't even found it yet."
Right. So how do you know you'll be able to borrow it?
"Fair."
What time were you getting here?
"Early. I've got to pick up Priscilla."
Isn't she closer to me?
"Yes, but her truck is in the shop. I keep telling her to stop messing with these American cars."
Is she still driving that Denali?
"Chevy Tahoe. You're thinking about Fish."
Oh...

"Her truck rides well, but she was complaining about a ticking sound. Anyway, do you have a few minutes?"

Well, we've been on the phone for at least five...

"I wanna share something about Omari but you've got to make sure Terri's not around."

You're not about to start my day off with any foolishness, are you? I just came in from my jog. I don't want my blood pressure to go up.

"Pop."

BAT...

"I'm being serious."

Okay, okay. Let me go inside and see where she is.

Surprisingly, Dale showed compassion when informed of Omari's condition, but it wouldn't be a Dale-conversation without a Bible quote found in Galatians 6:7-9. Furthermore, he encouraged him to continue counseling Omari while keeping a keen eye for signs of depression. When dealing with life complexities, one of Omari's gifts was writing poetry. Bryce had previously begged him to endorse this inconspicuous side, seeing it as a useful coping mechanism to inspire others. Now was the perfect time for Omari to take him up on the advice.

[generic text chime]

> Sexy Neighbor: Good morning sleepyhead.
> Stop by before you leave.
>
> Mon 11:11 a.m.

Bryce raced across the street and was instantly met by Tasha's smugness. She stood in the doorway, wearing an oversized fluorescent green shirt and turquoise biker shorts, like she had just left the set of an MC Hammer music video.

"Come inside for a sec."

His nose was met by the satisfying aroma of a hearty breakfast and lavender air freshener. Suddenly, rumbling footsteps generated overhead.

"Stop running," Tasha yelled.

"Hi, Mr. Bryce," her sons shouted from the top step.

"Hey, fellas."

"Stop being so nosey. Go back to your room and play."

"Leave them alone."

"They're so hardheaded. Anyway, I made breakfast. I wasn't sure if you'd eaten yet."

Bryce stood with his mouth agape. "Yo, I feel really special right now."

"Shut up. I didn't necessarily make it for *you* but there's extra if you'd like."

"You *really* know how to make a man feel good... said no one."

"Whatever." She smirked. "Do you eat sausage? I think it has a blend of pork and beef."

"I thought you didn't eat pork?"

"Did I say the sausages were for me?"

"No, but you bought them."

"Oh my God. They're for the kids, dum-dum."

"Sorry. Sheesh. Why are you so tense?"

"Nobody's tense..."

"I can help you with that if only you'd let me."

He sat at the round kitchen table to a plate of scrambled eggs, grits, and sausage, watching Tasha wipe off the kitchen counter. His mind was hijacked with guilt. The audacity to eat in this woman's home and not share the same passion for advancing their friendship.

She had undoubtedly grown on him. What better way to a man's heart than through his stomach? However, for a serious relationship to develop, Bryce sought mental stimulation, good food, and great sex. In that order. Tasha's cantankerous ways didn't give their association much of a chance. In other respects, even if the sex turned out to be immaculate, she was still the mother of two young children who shared different fathers.

Self-aware men know what they want; it is only the needy types who settle.

She took his plate and directed him through the lower level of the house to examine the degraded areas. Soon after, they were standing outside of the door where he thanked her for the meal, promising to make up for lost time.

"You'd better. You know I start my new hours soon," she replied.

He leaned in for a parting hug, trying everything in his will to avoid brushing her robust bottom. That mission failed the moment she tiptoed into his arms. It was as soft as a marshmallow pillow. Typically, they would avoid public displays of affection, but not today, as an unfamiliar face wearing dark sunglasses issued a scandalous stare from a distance.

"Hey, Mr. T, long time no see," Priscilla greeted Dale in her best rapping voice. "Ooh, did you hear those bars?"

"I know you ain't come over here wearing a Giants shirt," Dale disapproved. "This is Redskins country."

"But we're in New Jersey..."

"That's not the point. Don't make me send your butt home," he laughed. "Aye, when are you and BAT getting married?" Bryce was within earshot gathering disposable tableware from his back seat.

"This guy wants me to marry *everyone.*"

"I mean, how long y'all wanna keep up this friend façade?"

Priscilla cracked up before countering. "I don't know. Isn't incest illegal?"

"Y'all ain't related. We need some grandkids around here. The last time I brought this up to him, he told me I'd better get used to the damn cat."

Priscilla fought through tears of laughter. "That's our baby. Be nice to Lizzy."

"I'll be nice and dead by the time my grandchild arrives."

"How long have we been friends, B.?"

"About seven years…"

"That's a damn shame," Dale cut in, sorting through a crate of VHS tapes. "And neither of y'all have the seven-year itch?"

"It doesn't work that way with friendships," Bryce added. "Oh, you found it. Perfect."

"Priscilla, you wanna see Bryce when he was younger? Maybe y'all can show *Dizzy* some of the footage."

"He called her Dizzy. I just can't," Priscilla cried out.

Dale, a dedicated wrestling fan of the old territory days, inserted the NWA Great American Bash '88 tape into the VCR/DVD combination player. This was the same event where he'd once sat front row at the Baltimore Arena, flanked by two wide-eyed eleven-year-old wrestling junkies for the pay-per-view extravaganza.

"Is that you with the bowl-cut fade? Aw, you were so cute."

"*Were?* You see how she just past-tensed me, Pop? And you want us to get married?"

Terri peeked into the garage, holding a baking pan of seasoned drumsticks. "I thought I heard another voice in here. How are you, Priscilla, long time no see?"

The Fourth of July cookout had a nice turnout of accomplished bourgeoisie couples arriving in luxury vehicles with bad dye jobs, oversized clothing, and designer purses. The laughs were never-ending, and the soul music was an overall vibe. The neighbors must have been tired of hearing "Everybody Loves the Sunshine" by Roy Ayers Ubiquity as the song replayed for what seemed like hours.

Priscilla finally caved in and tried one of Dale's cigars, joining his flock of friends with Bryce in one section of the backyard while Terri wined and dined the wives. Coming as a major surprise was Alyssa's 'Happy 4th' text—seen as unprecedented within Bryce's circle of friends. It was comparable to receiving a 'Happy Earth Day' greeting. *Who would send such a thing?* That said, the acknowledgement was huge. Alyssa's pleasant text included a picture of the crashing Atlantic Ocean waves with her outstretched arm holding what appeared to be an Amaretto Sour, making for a great follow-up question in their ensuing conversation.

~

[cell phone vibration]

Sexy Neighbor: I'm putting the boys to bed early tonight. Tomorrow is their first day of camp. Come over when you're ready.

Mon 6:05 p.m.

Bryce showered, added a spritz of cologne, and put on his most provocative T-shirt, grabbing the same condoms from the night before. He retrieved *Eddie Murphy Raw* from the spinning media rack to include with the other DVDs in hand.

[light door knock]

Tasha poked her head through the door crack and smiled. If only she did more of that, it would unarguably add to her appeal. "The man, the legend?" she asked, reading the words on his shirt. "That's bold. Where'd you find that?"

"At a vendor stand on Times Square... and before you say anything slick, yes, it still applies no matter where you point the arrows," Bryce joked, closing the door behind him.

"I wasn't gonna say anything."

"Yeah right," he replied, licking his lips tentatively.

"Anyway... I like your glasses."

"Why are you blushing?" he replied. "I *know* you're dying to say something smart. Go 'head, say it."

Tasha examined the DVDs. "Oh, please. Ain't nobody blushing. You just *want* me to say something. What did you bring? Ooh okay. Don't judge me, but I've never seen *Raw*. I've seen

Bigger and Blacker plenty... hmm... *You So Crazy*... let's watch this one," she replied, snatching away the 1994 Martin Lawrence stand-up comedy. "We still have time before the fireworks."

The remaining sunlight poured into the living room before nightfall set in. They shared a bowl of grapes, howling at Lawrence's performance, when her buzzkill kids pointlessly ran downstairs a fourth time. Fortunately, bedtime was on the horizon. Enough was enough.

"Goodnight. Don't make me say it again," Tasha yelled from the bottom of the steps after hearing the boys rumbling above the ceiling. Bryce eyed the time, 8:38 p.m. One hour to spare before the upcoming Macy's Fireworks Spectacular. She turned off the kitchen light. The house was in total darkness, setting the scene. Chris Rock's *Bigger and Blacker* was the next choice despite her earlier confession of having never seen *Eddie Murphy's Raw*. Strange. She stretched across the couch this time, resting her head comfortably on his lap.

"Lift your head for a sec. You're lying on *the legend,*" Bryce cautioned.

"What? I don't feel anything."

"Ooh, low blow. You don't wanna start cracking jokes. I'll finish you like a game of *Mortal Kombat*."

"Shut up."

He understood the assignment about five minutes into the DVD. Tasha had no intention of watching the comedy. It is why she decided to play something she'd already seen. She was itching to create fireworks of her own.

"So, you're just gonna keep staring at me? Keep playin'," he dared. They traded a few more jests. Tasha wouldn't back down. Finally, their anxious lips met head-on. He opened his eyes for confirmation. It was really happening. The euphonious kissing sounds blended nicely with the noisy central air unit in case her kids were eavesdropping.

Tasha's lips were soft as velvet. She held firmly onto Bryce's neck, tugging at his bottom lip. He pulled away and repositioned himself. The pain from leaning downward became unbearable. She straddled him thereafter. Their lips touched, and their tongues rammed, jockeying for position. It was long ago since he last participated in such a heated make out session, and he proved to be no match for Tasha's overpowering tongue.

[cell phone notification chime]

"Must be one of your hoes," she whispered, addressing the resounding alerts trumping the thunderous audience laughter. Tasha continued to outline the surface of his mouth with her tongue. Her warm cotton-candied breath activated the hair on his face.

"And which one would that be?" Bryce asked, gripping a handful of her rump.

"I don't know. You tell me."

"That's your favorite line. I'm not playing that game."

"It's probably the one in the blue Hyundai." That was a dig at Julissa, who Tasha may have witnessed a time or two leaving his home. "You ain't giving a man that type of ringtone."

Tasha's seductive eyes sparked another long kiss. "Hold on, let me make sure these kids are asleep." She hopped off and adjusted the strap to her tank top. Meantime, Bryce could barely move. *If this is how first base felt, the home run would be unparalleled,* he thought. When she returned, she switched the channel to the fireworks display, pulled her sweatpants up by the thighs, and hopped back on him for another ride.

Thousands of people rejoiced in celebration of America's independence as a splash of colors lit up the blackened New York City sky. They took a breather to browse the ceremony, but the spontaneity of their red-hot evening reigned supreme. Before long, they were both asleep with Tasha laying comfortably across his lap. Bryce jumped out of his catnap to the familiar voices of the eleven o'clock local news, signaling the end to an entertaining weekend.

"Hey..."

"Huh?" Tasha muttered.

"I'm gonna head out. I've got work in the morning," he replied, stroking his hand against her jawline. She gave out an exaggerated stretch before walking him to the foyer where they shared another kiss.

"Be careful getting home," she teased.

"Don't steal my line."

"To be continued, I guess. Maybe tomorrow night?"

Bryce grabbed a hold of Tasha's chin, as she moved in anticipating another kiss. Instead, he placed his finger on her nose and playfully ran it down her lips at a snail's pace.

"Maybe," he replied, walking out nonchalantly.

She closed the door behind him, mildly turned on by the gesture.

15

———

THE BOYS OF SUMMER

A July weekend with the Orioles playing at home called for a drive down Interstate 95. Bryce put the pedal to the metal, nodding his head to some of his favorite tunes, until the insufferable DMV traffic clogged the lanes. Maryland was still home. It was where he lived as a child for five years, made repeated trips as a teenager, and now back for his annual summer visit to Camden Yards with Dan, his childhood pal.

The long-time friends met in Mrs. Forsythe's third-grade class at Beacon Heights Elementary with hip hop, wrestling, and their beloved Baltimore Orioles at the core of their friendship. Dan of Irish Catholic descent remarkably embraced Black culture at a time when people of his background trembled at the thought. He could recite "Eric B. is President" word for word and imitate D.C. Scorpio's dance moves from the "Stone Cold Hustler" music video flawlessly. Moreover, the blue-eyed classmate took a liking to women of color—particularly Lisa Bonet. His infatuation escalated after joining Bryce and friends at Daytona Beach for Spring Break '97. Now, married to a beautiful woman of Black and Korean descent, Dan was the perfect mind to pick on how to handle the undertaking of an interracial relationship.

Bryce had only been romantically linked to Black or Latina

women. *Even* in the suburbs where they were awfully outnumbered. He didn't have a preference per se, just playing the hand he was dealt. He listened to Bryan Adams's "Summer of '69" thinking back to Ashlyn Scott, a blonde bombshell Hilary Duff lookalike who audaciously hooked up with him in college through the soaring racial tension set off by the O.J. Simpson trial. Interestingly, a relationship never surfaced. Since then, he attached himself to a heap of dating sites where White women were hot on his trail. The types who were often shunned by their White male counterparts for their glaring second-class behavior and body type. If he were to mingle with anyone outside of the normal, the person had to fit the bill—no exceptions. Alyssa, who he learned was of Italian and Lebanese mix, appeared to be the closest thing yet.

[Dan's custom ringtone]

"Aye, brotha."

[proper voice answers]

Yes, Good morning, my name is Gary Smith, and I am calling on behalf of Dan Ferris for the Glen Burnie Charitable Fundraising Program. Am I speaking with Bryce Taylor?

"Fam, *Gary Smith?* I may have fallen for it had you chosen a better name."

Damn, I had a whole speech prepared too. Where you at? I was trying to see if I had enough time. Yo, is that "Sittin' on Chrome" playing in the background?

"You already know. I've got to listen to this joint uninterrupted though, so I'm running it back after we hang up."

[laughter]

Oh, my bad. That beat still knocks too.

"Hold on, let me put my earpiece in..."

We absolutely destroyed that tape back in the day. The first thing that comes to mind is that drive to Daytona.

"Yes... in my '91 Nissan Max with the twelve-inch JL audio subs."

Didn't you have the Rocksford Fosgate in the trunk?

"Good memory, brotha."

Where has the time gone? We've got to bump a few joints later for old times' sake.

"Of course."

How long before you get here? Amina wanted to pick up some groceries.

"Oh, you have plenty of time. I haven't even reached Delaware yet. I can shoot you a text once I cross into Maryland."

Okay, that works. What you wanna do for lunch?

"It's a cheat day so probably something out of the ordinary."

As long as it ain't seafood.

"You still don't mess with seafood?"

Heck no. I don't eat crab in Maryland, I don't eat lobster in Maine.

Bryce laughed. "We'll figure something out. Before I let you go, did you ever set up the VCR in the basement?"

Yessir, and we finally connected all the old gaming systems. Wait 'til you see the setup. Why, what's up?

"Perfect. I'll show you when I get there. Also, I need to pick your brain later if you don't mind. You and Amina. Lots of stuff going on. Nothing crazy, I just need some advice."

Already. You know we got you.

"All right. Go do the married thing. I'll hit you back."

Bet. Safe travel.

Most of the men in Bryce's life were married, but it was a non-issue for the time being. There was no sense in trying to fit a square peg into a round hole with the current cast of meagerness in his world. He was fine with being the unofficial spokesperson for men in their thirties, who weren't checking off honey-do lists or placing car seats in the backseat of the family car. Comparatively, he couldn't picture resting such an item on his peanut butter colored leather interior anyway.

He arrived at Dan and Amina's colonial style townhome after nearly three hours of singing along to the best of the '80s and '90s, now nodding viciously to Black Moon's "How Many MCs" as he parked in the guest spot. Ahead was Dan, his heavily tattooed friend, sporting brown aviator sunglasses, an amazing Hipster red beard with a white Orioles throwback jersey, and camo cargo shorts.

"D., what up?" Bryce announced from the driver's window. He exited the car to embrace his friend while Amina waited at the top step holding Daisy, the couple's Yorkshire Terrier. "Is this supposed to be the stairway to heaven? Nobody thought about adding an escalator on the side?" Bryce teased, counting each step to their front door before sharing a hug with Amina.

The happy newlyweds closed on their three-story home— 1400 square feet with two bedrooms and two bathrooms—back in March and were in the latter stages of unpacking. The guest room where Bryce stayed was painted in Orioles' orange, decorated with cultural wall art and a towering potted plant. A sleeper sofa, seventy-inch television console for their flat screen, and a spacious closet designated for Dan's whopping sneaker collection filled the room. Bryce toured the rest of the house, which included a back deck overlooking an area of trees and a bedroom walk-in closet larger than a Manhattan studio apartment. As expected, this is where Amina proudly helped herself. Their basement is where the fun began.

On the wall leading down the stairway was an Orioles 1983 World Series Champions banner and a large canvas photo of the old Memorial Stadium. It is where Dan's father, a one-time season ticket holder, took him to watch Eddie Murray, the switch-hitting Orioles legend, crush balls into the bleachers. Around the corner was a mounted neon-lit display of the phrase "Dan Cave" lined with framed movie posters, DVDs, toy collectables, comic books, and an arcade machine favorite, *Street Fighter II*. Bryce savored the impressive display, growing inspired by his friends' momentous achievements.

With time to spare, they cruised around in Dan's silver Volkswagen CC Sport, wandering through the well-to-do neighborhood before the last place Orioles battled the AL Central leading Cleveland Indians.

"You should come back out here," Dan declared. "We're only eleven miles from the ballpark. I can put a word in for you at the DOT and you'll get an interview the next day. I promise you." It wasn't a terrible idea, except the cost of homes and state taxes were extraordinarily high. No different than New Jersey, a state that would tax the sun if it could. If Bryce ever moved, it needed to be somewhere he got the most bang for his buck.

They settled for lunch at a popular grill restaurant less than a mile away from the house. Bryce pigged out on Fish & Chips with a side of Old Bay tartar sauce, apropos of his return to the Old Line State.

"We're moving at a moderate pace and all, it's just those two inescapable factors," he continued, expressing concern about Tasha.

"Those are *major* factors, bruh, let alone y'alls proximity. Too close for my blood. That's just me though."

"Don't make her fall in love if you can't love her," Amina interrupted.

"Good point," Bryce conceded.

"I can't get over the constant spitting part," Dan laughed. "Does she scratch her groin too?"

Bryce's phone was unusually quiet. He searched for the cause, finding that it was still powered down after giving it a quick charge at the house. There was a text from Alyssa sent over an hour ago.

> I Think I Might Wife Her: Hey. I went to the gym by my house today and guess who I saw...
>
> Sat 2:33 p.m.
>
> Sorry. Just now seeing this. Was it the guy with the Bozo the Clown haircut??

> BTW, in MD with friends. About to head over to the game. We can still text.

He felt bad about his tardy reply but couldn't wipe away his electrified look as he scrolled through their text thread. "So, *this* is my dilemma and who I wanted to pick your brain about."

"Okay, Wonder Woman." Dan nodded, observing a recent picture of Alyssa's sculpted back muscles. "Is she a powerlifter?"

"Not even. She says she played soccer in high school and participated in a community softball league once or twice."

Amina grabbed his phone. "Oh, wow. Let me get my ass to the gym."

"For the record, I've never dated a White woman, and this is why my brain's been a bit cluttered."

"For what it's worth neither have I," Dan laughed.

"Something clicked the moment I laid eyes on her. I don't know, there was a strange connection like we'd met before. Something feels right. She's quirky, we have a similar sense of humor and come to find out she's a member at my gym."

"This sounds like some ole soulmate shit. I can dig it."

"I don't know about soulmates, but it's weird."

"Do you have a picture of her face?" Amina asked, readjusting her tan Orioles baseball cap.

"Um, not yet... just her golden retriever. Oh, and the dinner she prepared the other day."

"Booooring," Amina announced.

"I know, right? By now I'd usually have pictures of someone playing with themselves."

"We're in the age of selfies and BBM poses. Women love the camera. I'm surprised you haven't gotten at least an ass shot."

"BBM poses?" Amina questioned.

"Hun, I know absolutely nothing about this stuff. I read it online. I don't even own a BlackBerry," Dan cautioned.

[laughter from Bryce]

"There's another girl I talk to. She sent a video of her deep throating a dildo," Bryce shrugged. "Haven't even met her yet, but that's the stuff you get used to."

"Oh my gosh." Amina's mouth dropped. "These women are triflin.'"

Dan cut in. "You can kinda see her butt crack in the pic."

"I'm surprised she even showed *this* much skin, but we were discussing fitness goals. She works with the public so I'm sure she wants to keep things professional."

"What does she do?" Dan and Amina asked.

[server approaches table]

"How's everything over here, you guys all right?" The delightful pimple-faced server asked the group.

"Yes, we're fine. Thanks." They replied in unison. Bryce continued. "She's a tech at an optometrist office. Speaking of which, maybe I can find a pic on their website." He typed in Alyssa's office, finding a crisp photo of the staff. "Here's a little something. I don't know if you can see her face clearly. Let me zoom in. That's her at the very end."

"My gosh she's pretty," Amina declared. "Her eyebrows are perfect. What's her background?"

"She was born in New Jersey. Her mom is half Italian and Lebanese. We were chatting about food one day and I mentioned trying hummus for the first time. She had this crazy grin on her face. I'm like, 'What's wrong?' She tells me carrots and hummus are all she ate as a child. That's when she mentioned her background."

"This almost feels like a rom-com straight off the Hallmark channel," Amina announced. "I'm about to cry."

"I'm really diggin' her, but at the same token, I like Tasha. With Alyssa, I just find myself tiptoeing. Most of our conversations are about fitness. I'm trying not to do or say too much. It's a change of pace from what I'm used to."

"That's normal," Dan replied. "Baby steps. At least she's reciprocating."

Amina added. "Yes, if she wasn't interested, I don't think she'd initiate. We usually won't."

"Right. We've only been texting for a couple of weeks now, and she's the one who usually texts first. She isn't as accessible during the workday, so I try not to bother her. One time it took hours for her to get back to me. I was like, 'Damn, I just got friend zoned,'" he laughed. "She was apologetic, but it kinda threw me off."

"Friend zone isn't necessarily a bad thing," Amina countered. "Dan and I dated as friends for about a year."

"I was impatient as fuck," Dan revealed. "I'm like, 'Oh, it's cuz I'm White, ain't it?'"

"Babe, it had nothing to do with that. I thought you were extremely attractive, but I was just getting out of an ugly relationship."

"I know. I'm just playing... *no, I'm not,*" he whispered to Bryce.

"And that's the thing, when she mentioned her background, I was like, 'Nope, there's no way I'm gonna crack through this door.' It's extremely rare to find an Italian chick mixing it up with a Black dude. *Especially* in Jersey. If so, it's with some biracial looking guy."

"Like Tiger Woods?" Dan laughed.

"Facts. Tiger, Drake, Boris Kodjoe. Those types. I'm guessing they're safer," Bryce air quoted.

"But there lies the challenge," Amina pointed out.

"And *that's* my middle name."

"Think about it this way. No matter what, she still exchanged numbers. You're already in the door," Dan replied.

"Maybe she felt bad."

"Nah, I know you. Ain't no way you'd press the issue to *even* get to that point. Besides, if she had a dude, she would've happily told you. You know women love to share that part. It's like a badge of honor."

"Don't be too sure about that. Especially these days," Amina noted.

"Hun, we're all about spreading positive energy and cheer to our good friend."

"She's speaking facts though," Bryce replied. "I've experienced my fair share of women in relationships who still wanted to kick it."

"Go O's!" A random spectator concentrating on the group saluted, inciting cheer.

"By the way, I didn't bring the tickets," Dan advised. "They're on the living room table."

"That's cool. I wanted to switch out of this shirt anyway. I was sweating like a pig on the drive, foolishly trying to take in the summer air."

"It's supposed to be hot and muggy around gametime."

"So, let me ask you guys this, how do you handle getting stared at by other people?"

"We really don't have that problem out here. Interracial couples are a dime a dozen."

"Yeah, seriously, and who cares what people think?" Amina filled in emphatically.

"You know what we should do? Let's walk along the harbor before the game," Dan suggested. "Nothing but pasty White guys and Black women."

Dan's announcement was encouraging, but Bryce's mind was already close to being made up. "That's the thing, 'Mina, I really *don't* care, but for some reason I'm trying to predict the future. Like, how would I manage a dirty look? I'm not even talking about from White dudes, but from the sistas."

"Who cares what *anyone* thinks. Love doesn't have a color," Amina stressed.

"You're right. Let me preface what I'm about to say next. I mean absolutely no disrespect by this comment, but usually when I meet someone, it immediately leads to sex. I'm talking right out the gate. And for the record, it isn't me who's pushing it," he added, putting his hands up in a surrender pose. "Maybe we'll have one or two stimulating conversations that same week, arrange to meet up and the rest is history. Or *sometimes* by date two, if they wanna feel you out and prove they're not easy," he eye-rolled. "The point is, we talk about what we're looking for from the onset and get right to it."

"Understood. There are no misunderstandings that way," Dan responded.

"Precisely. I don't have to worry about taking romantic strolls in the park or anything like that. I'm either going to her place or she's coming to mine. Public perception is out the window. I've dealt with a couple of White women in the past. The most recent one..." Bryce paused, snapping his fingers to remember her name. "Erica—I think that was her name. She said she was *looking for friends.* That's usually code for 'I want my back blown out.'"

[laughter erupts]

"I'm dead serious."

"Oh, I believe you," Dan said.

"All the encounters were in-house. Come to think of it, I probably should've kept her around a little longer. She wasn't bad at all. But she wanted to swing by the house five days a week."

"Oh, she was trying to drain your balls."

"Babe, stop," Amina cut in, cracking up.

"I was seriously about to ask her to go Dutch on the mortgage. That was too much for my blood. Story for another day. Anyway, I didn't care about her ethnicity because it was irrelevant."

"Y'all just got straight to business," Dan affirmed.

"That's it. With Alyssa, I can truly see us hanging out and doing couple-like things. There's an excitement I get just from being around her. Sex doesn't even cross my mind. Well, it does, but not off rip."

"Have you ever thought about public perception during the short periods you've been with her?"

"Not at all. We're completely tapped into the conversation in our own little world. By the way, kudos on your follow up questions, my guy," Bryce replied, hand-clapping Dan. "A young Walter Cronkite over here."

"I think you've got your answer."

"I think y'all should give it a try. You can bring her out here next year when you start house hunting." Amina winked. "I know you mentioned she played softball sparingly, but does she watch baseball? Maybe we can double-date."

"I haven't even gotten that far."

At the house, Bryce switched into his orange Cal Ripken Jr. throwback edition jersey, hoping it would lead to another Orioles victory. They were undefeated since he started wearing it to the games. He removed the *Great American Bash '88* VHS tape from his overnight bag to Dan's amusement. Amina was left awestruck, watching her spouse cheer along with their wrestling favorites.

"You guys look so cute and innocent."

"My friend Priscilla had the same reaction. You remember her, right?"

Amina repeated the name trying to connect the dots. "Was she the one you brought to the wedding?"

"Yes."

"Oh my gosh, how is she?"

"She's great. In fact, we were on the phone on the way out here. I forgot to tell y'all she said hi."

"She was super cool."

"Dawg, I can't believe your dad still has this. I need a copy."

"He's got a whole library of wrestling tapes. He went out and bought a VHS to DVD converter. Now he wants me to convert everything as a backup. I'm like, dude, some of the actual DVDs are online for sale. Just buy them."

"True. Doesn't Vince McMahon own the entire wrestling library?"

"And that's the reason he wants me to convert the tapes. Most of the DVDs are under the WWE imprint. He still hates Vince for buying up the competition. Just the other day he was like, 'I'm not giving that man another penny.'"

"Can't say that I blame him. We've always been WCW guys. Yo, last week made fifteen years since Hogan joined Hall & Nash."

"Yup. 'Bash at the Beach.' I called you immediately after it happened. You could look at Hogan's face and tell he was about to turn heel. When's the last time you ever saw him march out to the ring like that?"

"I remember. The next thing you know he's leg-dropping Macho," Dan laughed. "He was the only WWF wrestler I ever liked. His death still hurts, man."

"Wait, Macho Man died? Wasn't that the guy in the Slim Jim commercials?" Amina asked.

"Ooh yeah!" Dan replied, imitating the legendary wrestler's signature catchphrase.

Michael Brantley, the Indians' young outfielder, hit a scorching line drive foul ball over the first base line. It was the third plate appearance of the evening for the Indians' leadoff batter, yet Bryce continued to rave about his polished swing.

"He's taking some nice cuts tonight. I get the feeling he might hit one out."

"His swing reminds me of John Olerud's."

[Peanuts! Peanuts here!]

The Orioles catcher jogged to the mound to ensure he and the pitcher were on the same page for the next sequence of pitches.

"I can see Brantley winning a batting title if he can stay on the field."

"For sure. There was a conversation going on Twitter asking who from the list of players could bat four hundred. It was Miggy, Big Papi, Joey Votto, José Reyes... I forgot the last guy."

"Brantley wasn't on there?"

"Nah, probably because he's only in his second or third year. The other guys are more established."

"Those other dudes strike out too much, and Reyes doesn't take enough pitches. It would have to be someone who's patient at the plate. If I were a betting man, I'd say Miggy."

"I think Miggy has a better shot at winning a triple crown, no?"

"Good point. Honestly, if Wade Boggs or Tony Gwynn couldn't eclipse the record, I can't see how any of these other guys can. Those dudes were the epitome of hitting."

"Gwynn was raking during the '94 strike season. I think he would've done it."

"I *still* get upset thinking about that season," Bryce paused.
[sound of bat striking baseball]
[crowd jeers]
"Unbelievable," Dan muffled.

"What I tell you? He *just* missed it," Bryce replied, referring to Brantley's one out, two-run double to right field, tying the game at two. Amina was the only person in section twenty to rise to her feet as she voiced her displeasure. Dan adjusted his official score card.

"I don't know why we do it to ourselves. It's the same crap every season."

"It's only the sixth. We've got plenty of time. I'll give it to Simon; he's pitched better than I expected."

"Dawg, I have PTSD after we lost the first twenty-one games to start the '88 season. That was twenty-three years ago. No eleven-year-old should ever experience anything like that. It nearly destroyed my childhood."

"Yeah, it's been tough."

"At that point, I was only coming to the games to catch home run balls, usually by the other team." Dan chuckled.

"I'm surprised I didn't grow up to be a Yankees fan. I was still living in New York when I first got into baseball."

"Didn't you say your dad hated the Yankees?"

"Still does. But he was a huge Reggie Jackson fan. He watched them just to see his at bats. I only gravitated toward Rip when we moved out here after my coaches were trying to groom me to play shortstop. That, along with you always calling first dibs on Murray when we played in the yard."

[Amina laughs]

"I'm serious. He'd be Murray and I'd have to play the balding White guy. I was like, 'Something is totally wrong with this picture.'"

[laughter]

"Was he balding back then?" Dan asked.

"I can't remember."

"Murray was my guy. The fact that he's Black didn't even register. Remember I used to wear the helmet over the cap like him?"

"Yup. It's all good though. Rip turned out to be one of my favorite players. I was gonna wear number eight because of him, but it was taken so I grabbed twenty-four."

"Twenty-four? For Rickey Henderson?"

"No. Rickey was my guy though. But when you multiply two and four you get Rip's number eight, and it was my way of honoring Jackie Robinson once you reverse the numbers, so it all worked out."

"I never put two and two together. That was clever."

[fans applauding]

"See what I mean? No one takes pitches anymore. They killed their own rally," Bryce complained.

"The Indians could've busted the game wide open. Well, at least we've got the top of the order coming up."

[cell phone vibrating]

I Think I Might Wife Her: Hope you're having a great time :)

Sat 8:32 p.m.

"So, back to Alyssa while we have a moment."

"Shoot."

"Hold on, let's answer this trivia question. I've got to redeem myself."

[Maroon 5 "Moves Like Jagger" playing in background]

"God, I hate this song," Dan blared.

"Me and you both."

Who was the first player to hit a home run onto Eutaw St.?

A. *Cal Ripken Jr.*
B. *Mickey Tettleton*
C. *Brady Anderson*
D. *Sam Horn*

"It's B. Final answer. Babe, who do you think it is?"

"A?"

"Nah, I don't think it was Rip," Bryce voiced. "He usually pulled the ball to left field. Eutaw is over by the warehouse in right. I'm thinking it had to be a left-handed power hitter. Maybe Brady in the season he hit fifty?"

"Camden Yards opened in '92 though," Dan advised. "Brady started hitting for power in '96. I'm almost sure it wasn't him. Sorry, Babe, I don't think it was Cal either. Did Horn play on the '92 team?"

"He did. Left-handed bat with some pop, but they're not asking for the year. It's who was the first to do it. The home run didn't necessarily have to occur in '92."

"Hmm... I'm sticking with Tettleton. That batting stance screamed power. I remember all the hype that came afterward when they measured the home run."

"It's tricky. All these guys played with us, but Tettleton and Horn had the shortest stints. That stands out to me. Now I'm thinking it might be one of them."

"I don't think Tettleton played with us when it happened," Dan countered.

The guys could talk baseball all night long. Bryce took a moment to snap a picture of the field in response to Alyssa, while fans shouted random answers watching the scoreboard with anticipation.

We're having a blast. Sitting a few rows behind first base. How's your Saturday going?

[crowd roars]

"Pay up," Dan pointed at the scoreboard. "What did I tell y'all?"

Answer: B - Mickey Tettleton of the Detroit Tigers on 4/20/1992 off Orioles pitcher Ben McDonald.

"My guy doesn't miss. A real-life baseball encyclopedia. Dang, I thought I had that one. Anyway, back to my own trivia question. This is for both of you. What were your biggest fears going into dating each other? Amina, you go first."

"Biggest fear? Um... he was totally hip hopped out."

"Still am," Dan interrupted.

"No, it was different. You used to do the sideways cap thing with earrings. Everything was baggy. Lots of slang. You used to speak with your hands... I was like, 'What in the Slim Shady is this?'"

"You ain't hit her with the du-rag, D.? You know, he was the first White guy I ever saw with waves."

[laughter]

"Seriously. We hung out once, this was years back, of course, but some of the girls thought he was Jon B. We just ran with it."

Dan gripped the top of his low fade. "Yeah, no one could tell me shit at the time. Even though I had red hair and looked nothing like him. 'Mina used to think I was an extra on *The Wire*."

"That's not true. One thing I will say is you were the sweetest guy in the world, and you had a little style. He didn't wear those cheap kiosk gas station sunglasses like a lot of White guys wear. Everything about him was smooth."

"Like a baby's bottom," Dan added.

"What about you, D.?"

"I thought she was gonna be super conceited considering her modeling background. Oh, and mad conservative..."

"Why, because I'm part Asian?"

"That's exactly the reason. But nah, she's the total opposite. Probably more rebellious than I am. Look at the tat sleeve on her arm," Dan joked. "Anyway, to echo off her earlier point, I think this time next year you and ole girl will be out here house hunting and we'll be double dating. Just don't overthink things. What's that saying? Que Sera, Sera?"

16

——

DREAMS & VISIONS

The bathroom was semi-dark, lit by two scented candles on the edge of the sink, one of which waned over time. On the fringe and fading fast, symbolism of Omari's young life. He sent another call to voicemail as he soaked inside his aunt's bathtub, attempting to drown away his problems. Heavy tears crashed into the suds; his wailing sobs deadened by Jay-Z's "Diamond is Forever" instrumental playing from the portable speaker. He pressed his head against the wall, closed his eyes and hummed along to the elevating bassline through short sniffles.

There was a continuous, mild shock even months after discovering his first symptom. How could he ever pull himself together when he was reminded of his error every time nature called? Though the ointment from the janky website seared the surface of his skin—hiding the visible evidence—the infections remained.

His younger cousins thumped into the walls, chasing one another outside of the bathroom.

Omari!

One cousin screamed his name for rescue. It was Omari in need of saving. He concocted words in his head, murmuring to the looped beat, trusting something good could come out of a gloomy situation.

Had dreams, had visions, made a couple of bad decisions...

He ran more hot water to take away the chill of the bath. The bathroom was his sanctuary, the only place besides his rap note-book that brought solace. It was here that he learned how to cut his own hair and conjure up some of his best writing material. Where he celebrated his looks without preconceived notions and pointed out his palpable imperfections. All he needed was a miniature refrigerator for those late-night snack cravings and he was set.

Omari hadn't eaten much since his troubles. He was naturally lean, but the noticeable weight loss in his face did catch Aunt Ramona's sharp eye. He needed to do a better job screening his food aversion if he wanted to keep his private life a secret.

Had dreams, had visions, made a couple of bad decisions
Bounced back, spit raps, tried to stay out of prison....

His extended trip to the Bronx took everyone by surprise, including his aunt who welcomed his extra set of eyes for her mischievous kids. He was unmoved by the serenity of Brixx's Queens single-family row home neighborhood and desired the gritty environment of his old stomping grounds. The sounds of random gunfire and loud music helped to create more street-influenced content—at least that is what his mouth said. In truth, he went home to soul-search, seek Shauna, and acquire protection—but not the kind that could've cleared him of this calamity in the first place. He wasn't on anyone's hit list unless you measured Shauna's actions as intentional. Even then, there wasn't enough proof to accuse her. Yet, the more hurdles Omari faced, the more he wanted to embrace his violent rap alter ego whilst his only brush with the law came from a body-search.

Since the unwarranted frisking, his paranoia had increased. There was a case of being in the wrong place at the wrong time when he and Brixx inadvertently walked into a late-night crossfire after leaving a party in South Jamaica, Queens. He also witnessed a robbery attempt within a short distance from a Bronx subway station. All too close for comfort. Obtaining an illegal firearm was as easy as pie. He knew of the right people to talk to. The problem was finding a place to store it. He couldn't consciously leave it at his aunt's apartment, not with his younger cousins roaming around. Brixx's home was too risky, and all hell would break loose if Bryce ever laid eyes on a weapon at his bachelor pad.

Had dreams, had visions, made a couple of bad decisions
Bounced back, spit raps, tried to stay out of prison
Did that, young and Black, but I'm still displeased...

Life was only beginning and not at the expiration point, as the test results led him to believe. This is why it was important to find another voice other than Bryce who could mollify him.

Aunt Ramona was no stranger to bedlam, raising three kids on her own, one of which she had given birth to at seventeen. The youth worker was fully capable of rallying the troops, but her approach was far too aggressive for his current delicate state. There was his elderly grandmother whom he loved dearly but wouldn't have the courage to burden, and lastly, Mom, whose tender love and care would probably do the trick. The only parent to truly take the job of parenting seriously. However, Terri's decision to side with Dale continued to fuel a slow burn.

He yearned for his biological father whom he hadn't seen in seven summers. Their last interaction was a fly-by-night "Ayo" shout and wave as Omari played basketball at a nearby playground with friends. Prior to that was fifth grade, where he popped up at Terri's then-Bronx home with a bag of school supplies months after the school year began. It was unwise to underestimate a father-son bond no matter how infrequently they communicated.

The presence of a male authoritative figure has always been paramount in fostering a child. Omar was the first man he knew, and Omari was a chip off the old block. A heart-to-heart wouldn't eliminate the years of disgruntlement, but it could provide closure during these bleak times.

Had dreams, had visions, made a couple of bad decisions
Bounced back, spit raps, tried to stay out of prison
Did that, young and Black, but I'm still displeased
Cuz I slipped up, no rubber, stuck with a disease...

"Ugh... I can't say that. What rhymes with displeased?" he asked himself. The wordplay for the looped beat would expose his truth if he didn't alter the lyrics. He thought about using fictional characters to share the dejecting detail of his confessions. Brixx and the others would be uninformed and impressed by the range. Consulting Bryce was the next option, but that conversation could easily go left since they hadn't spoken in weeks.

"Hold on, girl, let me check on my nephew... O., you all right?" his aunt yelled through the door, placing her phone call on hold. "That's a mighty long bath, boy."

"I'm good, just thinking," Omari replied, sucking up mucus.

"All right, I'm going in the room. Don't have me wake up in the middle of the night to find your ass sleeping in the tub," she laughed.

"I'm about to get out."

An hour-long bath might've been a stretch—it wasn't going to wash away the problem, but it did enable a clear mind. It was late in the evening, enough time to grab a bite and catch a few loitering friends. That would be his alibi. Admittedly, he wanted to investigate Shauna's disappearance. They texted every so often until she backed out entirely. Something didn't sit right. Shauna only lived across town in a middle-of-the-road neighborhood where she rented the top floor of a duplex house owned by her uncle. There was always the possibility she was unavailable, but what was one more gamble? He grabbed his Yankees cap and arranged a cab service for pickup in search of answers. Did she know of the disease ahead of time? If so, why didn't she inform him?

"Where are you going?" his oldest cousin asked, resting the PlayStation controller on the bed.

"I'll be back."

"Can you grab me a bag of Cheez-Doodles?"

"Okay. Auntie, I'll be back," he informed, poking his head through her bedroom door. She acknowledged him with a head nod while babbling on.

The leather seats of the livery cab produced a squawking sound when he shifted. The car smelled of fresh lemons. He attempted to complete the rap verse in his head over the constant dispatch chirps playing over the radio transmission.

"Morris Park, Papa?" the driver verified with a thick Spanish accent.

"Yeah."

Finally, a few minutes of silence.

Had dreams, had visions, made a couple of bad decisions
Bounced back, spit raps, tried to stay out of prison
Did that, young and Black, still not pleased
I slipped up, now I'm on my hands and my knees
Lord, forgive me, please, for I have sinned...

He looked out the window to the familiar neighboring streets, wondering if his father would pop up through the crowd. It wasn't inconceivable. Even at Omar's age, there was something about hanging out on the block, cat-calling half-naked women and mixing up with neighborhood friends that never got old. A tiger doesn't change its stripes.

Word on the street was Omar resided in Rhode Island while others mentioned he was as far away as Kissimmee, Florida, but one thing was certain, he'd always find time to visit the city during the summer. For Omari's sake, he was unable to track his father down during the drive, now arriving at his destination. He asked the peppy livery cab driver if he could stick around, hoping to take the same cab back home in case Shauna wasn't present. Such a request was usually rejected with other passengers awaiting pick-up. Besides, his request had all the makings of a robbery attempt—where a suspect enters and exits a building leaving with valuable possessions and using the cab driver as the getaway driver while being held at gunpoint. There was no true way of knowing a passenger's intentions. Thankfully, Omari's calm, quiet demeanor during the ride wouldn't give the driver cause for concern. He alerted dispatch of the proposal.

"O-kay, boss, five minny," he warned Omari.

A dim light glowed through the main window of the top floor of Shauna's home. There was hope after all. He called her from the car expecting to see movement through the window. No such luck. Two rings preceded before her voicemail sounded. Instead of the automated voice, it was her own personal recording:

Hey y'all.
This number will no longer be active by the end of the month, but I'll still be checking in for messages. Anyway, your girl is making a few changes as I continue to grow. If you don't receive a call back, then I'm afraid you're one of the changes. No hard feelings.
Have a blessed day.

A multitude of descriptive colorful words traveled through Omari's head. He sat stationary in the back seat. His face was expressionless, his eyes slightly red from his flowing tears from earlier. If looks could kill, Shauna would be six feet under.

"Papa, you go or no?"

"I'm going now."

"O-kay, five minny. Remember."

For a summer evening, the neighborhood was unusually

quiet. He stepped out of the cab, checked his surroundings, and made his way to the front entrance where a sign appeared.

Broken Doorbell.

"Shauna... Ayo, Shauna," he yelled from the side of the house.

His previous appearance came on Valentine's Day where they linked up at City Island for seafood and disturbingly slept together on the tail end of her period. The only time he used a contraceptive. Over the past year of their unidentified arrangement, Shauna gave up the goods without a serious discussion of their future. It was beyond her to sleep around without establishing a label. She craved a relationship, and the options were plentiful, yet she couldn't resist Omari's appeal. He wanted to be with her but enjoyed sleeping around. A relationship would get in the way of his pursuit of a record deal, and they cut ties.

"Shauna!"

"You *no* knock?" the driver asked, signaling with his fist.

"Nah, I don't want the..." Before he could finish the sentence, a short-armed heavy-set male with a thick goatee marched to the door.

"Who are you looking for?" he asked, breathing heavily.

"Oh, my bad. I was trying to see if my girl was home. I tried calling but..."

"That's *your* girl? You don't look like the guy who was..." The gentleman got sidetracked by his spouse.

"*El esta buscando a su novia,*" he alerted her.

"*No, no, ella se fue hace horas,*" she replied. "*He estado en casa con las niñas.*"

"My wife said she left hours ago. She's been at home with our kids this whole time so she would know."

"My fault. I saw the light on upstairs and thought she was home."

"I wasn't gonna say anything at first. I thought maybe you had the wrong house, but my kids are trying to sleep."

"My bad, big man. I thought a hard knock would be worse."

"I get what you're saying, but that would've been better than yelling. Just a little advice, try not to show up to someone's home at this hour screaming their name. If you did it during the day, cool, but there are a lot of families over here."

"I get that. I already said my bad. How many times do you want me to apologize? Like, what the fuck?"

"Watch your tone. We're having a conversation."

"Watch my tone? Who the fuck you talkin' to? I don't know you."

"Listen, if you're gonna be rude and disrespectful, then you should leave. Leave or I'll call the cops."

"Call the fuckin' cops, you punk ass bitch. Is that supposed to scare me?"

[taxi driver frantically honks horn]

"What did you say to me? Yo, I will crush you. Get off my property."

[wife speaking in Spanish trying to calm husband]

"Your property? This ain't your shit. Yo, get out of my face. I'm not gonna tell you again. Back the fuck up or I'mma fuck your fat ass up... in front of your wife."

"Listen, kid, don't show your face around here again. I promise I'll hurt you."

"Suck my dick."

"Oh yeah? Try me. I swear on my kids life I'll squash your bitch ass."

"Nigga, I dare you. Wassup?"

The driver rapidly honked his horn, tapping his wrist, reminding Omari that time had vastly exceeded. "Five minny. You no pay," he yelled.

The shouting match concluded. Omari tossed a twenty-dollar bill into the passenger window of the cab, paying the driver for the initial route. "Just go," he ordered the driver, who heatedly sped off, cursing in Spanish. Several spectators gathered around. Angered, Omari walked off. His emotions had gotten the best of him, and he needed to cool off.

He elected to walk through the unfamiliar neighborhood, still stewing over the neighbor's threatening remarks. A warm breeze transported scraps of garbage along the ground as he paced along. Anxiety grew with each passing car. The idea of owning a weapon intensified. He scrolled through his contacts seeking out names of people who could turn his plan into a reality, coincidentally ending up on Shauna's name. He was boggled by her voice message. *No way was that meant for me, was it?* He pondered. It just didn't make any sense. Maybe it was for the "other guy" the neighbor alluded to. *Who is this guy? Was he the one who infected Shauna?* Desperate, Omari dialed her number one last time leaving a detailed message.

Sunday evenings usually called for Bryce to cozy up to an enjoyable book ahead of work. His latest read, *The Allies of Humanity,* would wait until morning. He laid on Tasha's sofa for their routine after-dark get-together. His lust pressed against the inner parts of her thigh—their mouths dripped with joy in what was another French kiss clinic. Tonight, it brought about a distinct zeal with the kids sound asleep.

They had yet to have the conversation about sex. She was only a year removed from a two-year relationship and hadn't been intimate since leaving her ex, and Bryce just hit the two-month period without a release of his own. Bachelor torment. The coupling act of kissing was exciting, but it brought about an urge. Perhaps a conversation was unnecessary on logic alone. She was undoubtedly one of the sexiest women he'd ever been linked to.

He moved away from her warm lips, onto her thyroid gland, and down to her chest, applying soft licks. His tongue was covered with body soap and a subtle perfume. With each lick, he drew closer to removing Tasha's clothes. He could feel it in his bones. She spoke to him in a hushed tone as he tasted her skin. If penetration weren't in the plans, he could serve her in other ways.

When it came to foreplay, Bryce was undefeated, like the '72 Dolphins.

"What are you doing?" she murmured, as he attempted to pull off her biker shorts. He motioned forward, licking his lips inches from her ear.

"Let me work."

She turned her head and extended her tongue toward his mouth, where they shared another long kiss. He caressed her breast through the tank top—her happy nipples met the middle of his palms. She gripped his neck and sucked on his tongue like a baby to a pacifier. Bryce thrust steadily in between her legs, signaling his readiness. By now, the question of whether he brought protection should have already been probed. Instead, she wanted to overindulge in sucking faces. He awaited the signal until he could no longer stand it. His appetite was unmerciful.

"What'chu wanna do?"

"What'chu mean?"

"Are you ready?"

"Ready for what?" she asked, seemingly puzzled.

"Oh, is that what we're doing?"

"What am I doing?" Tasha asked cluelessly.

"How long do you wanna kiss? You *do* know how dangerous this is, right?"

"Dangerous?" she chortled. "How?"

He placed her hand on his crotch. "*This* dangerous. I can clock someone over the head with that."

Tasha laughed. "Oh my God. Shut up."

"No pressure, just thought you wanted to take advantage of the opportunity."

"We *are*. The kids are sound asleep."

"You know what I'm saying. I'm only bringing it up since you're about to switch to overnights."

"I'm only filling in 'til the fall."

"Right, so how often do you think we're gonna have opportunities like tonight?"

"So now kissing me is a problem?" she asked. Her face was contorted with irritation.

"I didn't say that. I'm just gauging the situation. It's getting late and I have work in the morning. The opportunity is there."

"Can you, like, shut up? You're killing the vibe, man. Just nap over here."

This wasn't the response he wanted. A summer filled with house visits, temptation, and explosive erections—without action—wasn't going to cut it. Bryce participated in Tasha's lip-lock fest for a few minutes before calling it a night. She could detect his attitude before exiting.

"You mad?"

"Nah, I'm cool," he replied, trying to tuck away the frustration.

"Whatever."

"Seriously. I'm not trippin'. This is different, that's all. I usually don't get this intimate without it leading to something. I'm starting to feel things I haven't felt in a while."

"There's nothing wrong with taking things slow. Besides, we could've kept going."

Either Tasha didn't get it, or she was playing dumb. Standing between them was more than just his erection but a lack of communication concerning their long-term desires. How long were two consenting adults supposed to partake in a smooch fest at their level of attraction? They needed to get on the same page. Bryce accommodated her request for one last kiss, leaving his eyes open like the first time... except now, he was plotting his next move.

17

—

THE SIGN

t was August, the dog days of summer. The cicadas were out in droves, calling and responding to each other across tree-tops, eager to mate before the cool weather arrived. Bryce sat comfortably in Priscilla's backyard, chatting on the phone with Gucci, while Melo rested his head on his lap bidding for more rubs. Priscilla returned with a tall glass of iced tea and a bag of popcorn.

"Thanks. Gucci says what's up."

"Hey, Gucci..."

"I'll put him on speaker."

"Hey, Gucci," she repeated.

What's up, babygirl? I see Playboy got you working overtime in the heat. You are too pretty for all that.

"It's cool. He promised to let me take him to the club for his birthday if I pampered him for a day."

Oh, you bribed her, Playboy? That's some foul shit.

[group laughter]

When's your birthday again?

"The twenty-eighth. She's doing a wonderful job so far. Let's see how long it lasts."

"When are you coming out here, Guc? We haven't bowled in forever."

It's been too damn hot... I've only been at work or the casino, where it's cool. Maybe when this heatwave goes away. You know, when you look good, you play good.

"Here we go. Sounds like excuses," Priscilla replied. "So basically, you're still in hiding from the last time I whipped that tail, huh?"

[delayed silence]

"Brotha, she just called you scared. What says you?" Bryce asked.

Nah. I'm from the hood. I ain't ever scared.

"Were you ever scared as a child?" Priscilla questioned.

Nope.

"What about scary movies or Halloween?"

Nah. The only thing scary about Halloween is the rent is due the next day.

[heavy laughter]

"I can't with him. All right, Guc, I'll let y'all finish up. It was nice talking to you."

All right. I'll be out there soon. I'll let Playboy know.

"Yeah, brotha, you're *only* in Montclair. That's less than an hour away. You act like we live in Timbuktu. Truthfully, we should all link up at Lorenzo's soon and raid his fridge."

"B., come get me when you're done," Priscilla whispered.

Shit, that's an even longer drive. I'm down. Just let me know. Finish telling me about ole girl from across the street...

"So, to make a long story short, she basically told me she wants to refrain from sex until we've established ourselves as a couple. She's not wrong for that, I'm just annoyed because we never addressed this prior."

Right. Y'all were just kickin' it.

"That's what I thought, except her idea of kickin' it is slightly different than what I envisioned. Now I'm hot and bothered. I mean, I understand where *maybe* she felt we were heading in a different direction. We've hung out like a couple. I'm around her kids often, so it has a feel of something more. I should've been more upfront about my needs."

True, but take this as a sign. If she ain't putting out now and you don't see a relationship happening, is it even worth waiting around? You know my slogan. Shit or get off the pot.

[Bryce makes inaudible sound]

"I've gotta find a way to smash though. That thang softer than Charmin."

[laughter]

Them cheeks got you waking up in cold sweats.

"She's the true definition of slim-thick. I need to just go ahead and make it official."

Why? Just to hit it then break up?

"Basically. *It ain't you, baby, it's me,*" Bryce continued. Gucci laughed on the other end.

Don't hit her with that. She might Lorena Bobbitt you.

"I've got to do something…"

Look on the bright side, at least you still got the married chick. She's the real MVP. Chick been breaking you off for a year. My kinda gal.

"Not quite a year yet. Man, I ain't even tell you…"

Tell me what? Come on, Playboy. Don't tell me you folded like an omelet…

"Yo…"

Oh, hell nah. I'm not trying to hear it. You ain't ready for the Big Leagues. What's shorty's number?

"Why? Does your girl suddenly like girls?"

No. My girl is straight like six o'clock, but she might have to make an exception if she truly loves me.

"How long do you think we were supposed to keep up our little charade? She's married."

For as long as your joint still works. Fuck you talkin' about? I'm living vicariously through you, and here you are letting me down.

You got a fine ass married chick hitting you off and you're blowing it.

"Ehh, I think I'm just ready to hang up the jersey. I've been running through these women for nearly a decade. The next situation has to be favorable, that's all."

You ain't missing out on a mothafuckin' thing with this relationship stuff. Take it from me. If you wanna trade places, let me know. What other options do you have? One is married, the other ain't giving up the cooch...

"There's a couple more... actually digging this White girl at my gym."

White, Black, Green, don't matter, as long as that box is pink. If it ain't, then wrap yo shit up like a mummy and pray to Jesus.

"Nah, a box that ain't pink is non-negotiable. Ain't no wrapping going on. I'll tell a chick fast 'have a nice day'."

Stay single, Playboy. You don't want these relationship problems. Not with the type of women out there these days.

～

[Priscilla sings along to Amy Winehouse's "You Know I'm No Good"]

"I'm still crushed. She was so young."

"I know. What a shame. I didn't listen to her music much, but I can see why her sound was popular."

"Val called me all hysterical on the day she passed away. I was like, 'Dude, what's your deal?' When she told me what happened, we both sobbed like babies."

[cell phone vibrating]

I Think I Might Wife Her: This was my tire flip workout earlier. I had my sis record it. It was SUPER hot out. My body is gonna hate me tomorrow. Should've gone to the Shore instead :)

Sat 4:18 p.m.

Bryce showed Priscilla his phone.

"Really?" she replied unamused.

"What?"

"Her contact name. I'll give you an 'A' for effort. So, *this* is my Super Woman friend you've been talking about. Is she flipping a tire across a field? What in the world?"

"That's her. She might be stronger than me."

"You guys are gonna have a bunch of athletic roided-up babies."

Bryce gave her a death stare.

"So, here's the thing, she's mad chill. I get the idea she's single. I haven't asked because I don't wanna make things weird. Just going with the flow for now. She's texted me as late as eleven... so I'm using that as my indicator."

"Or you can just ask if she's single like a normal person would. Problem solved."

"Who's at the wheel of this car? Me or you?"

"Yeah, but you're driving a lemon with the check engine light on and squeaky rotors. I'm trying to save you before the car breaks down," Priscilla snapped. Bryce wasn't at all amused.

"Anyway, aside from fitness, we seem to have a few things in common."

"Like?"

"She's adventurous, we enjoy some of the same music, and she played sports in school. Oh, and no kids..."

"Woo-hoo! Team-No-Kids."

"Exactly. She has a really great sense of humor, too. She's even caught on to a few of my Michael Scott references."

"She watches *The Office?* Oh, she's an absolute keeper. I'm guessing there's a 'but' somewhere..."

"She's got a nice one of those, too."

"God help me. Let me know when you're done playing around."

"Okay, I'm done. The 'but' part is... I've never dated a White girl."

"What's the problem?"

"Not really a problem, I'm just afraid... like, what if she dances like a deer on ice?"

[Priscilla laughs]

"I'm serious. What's the girl's name from the "Dancing in the Dark" video? You know the one I'm talking about... the one who was on *Friends.*"

"Who, Courtney Cox?"

"That's her. What if she dances like that?"

"Who cares how she dances. Why would that even matter if you aren't clubbing anymore? And quit snappin' on my girl."

"You haven't even met her yet."

"I'm talking about Courtney Cox."

"Oh."

"Well, there's only one way to find out. Why don't you invite her to the club for your birthday?"

"Invite? I'm not even sure if *I'm* going."

"Oh, you're going all right."

"You haven't even kept your end of the promise. You call this pampering? Where's dinner?"

"Um, excuse me, sir. Dinner? Do you help pay the mortgage around here? There's only one man who can make those types of demands—come and give mommy some love," Priscilla cooed Melo.

[aggressive dog bark]

"Oh, that's how you wanna act?"

Bryce laughed. "Good boy."

"Don't bite the hand that feeds you, chump. You're gonna

wanna take a walk later and I'm gonna say no. Now go sit over there," she scolded him.

Beast…

"Let's go inside. These mosquitoes are tearing me up," Priscilla swatted at her bare leg.

"They've been loving me all summer long. Guess I've still got it."

"Make sure the screen door is shut, please," Priscilla commanded.

I Think I Might Wife Her: Thx. Guess what?
Just found out I'm gonna see Train in a couple
of weeks!

Sat 4:32 p.m.

Nice. Where are they performing?

I Think I Might Wife Her: Susquehanna Bank.
Maroon 5 is supposed to be the featured
attraction – Ugh lol But I'm super excited.

Sat 4:35 p.m.

"Phew. Nice and cool," Priscilla announced, relieved to be back inside. "I meant to ask, how's Omari doing?"

"I suppose he's breathing. We haven't spoken much. In fact, he should be off work now."

"I'm sure it's been tough on him. Poor guy."

"Remember, P., that's between me and you."

"I know. I wouldn't say anything. Is he still in school?"

"He'd better be. He's got less than a year left, and he's been going hard with the music. Those are his only outlets."

"Good. I was hoping we could check out one of those clubs with open mics where they do Spoken Word. That'll be a wonderful way for him to get recognized."

"Right. I know someone who used to work at BET who said the same thing. She gave honest feedback when I gave her their YouTube page."

"Well, that's promising. I'm really hoping things can turn around. He's a good guy. When is he coming down? We should take him somewhere."

"That's a good question. I'll shoot him a text."

~

[Omari retrieves phone]

> Big Bro: When u get a chance, read Jeremiah 31:25 and Proverbs 3:5-6. Some of my favorite scriptures when I'm feeling down. Also, Priscilla was asking about u. Wants to know when ur coming out here. I need a cut too. Hold ya head, lil bro.
>
> Sat 4:44 p.m.

"Turn the volume up," Omari instructed Brixx, placing his cell back inside the car cup holder.

[song plays]

H2O: *Back on my B.S*

Brixx: *Yes*

H2O: *The proof is in the pudding, Jell-o*

Brixx: *Smooth like Melo*

H2O: *Hel-lo to those who doubt me, rushing to judgment: Drago-Rocky...*

[Brixx pauses music]

"What'chu doing?" Omari asked.

"Yo, rushing... *Russian*... Drago, Rocky. They rushed to judgment thinking Rocky would lose."

"You *just* figured that out?"

[Brixx presses play]

Brixx: *Beat the odds, cocky—even with a little rust*

H2O: *Eyes on the currency, they say 'In CashFlow We Trust'*
Brixx: *It's that time of the month...*
H2O: *You in some deep shit*
Brixx: *If you ready to die...*
H2O: *We're on our BIG shit...*
Brixx: *Do you dirty*
H2O: *Cut you off mid sen-tence*
Brixx: *I don't mess with a bitch*
H2O: *If she ain't worth ten cents*
Brixx: *Dimes*
H2O: *Time out waiting for hand-offs*
Brixx: *I'm on my grizzly in my city—Zach Randolph*
H2O: *You and your man's soft...*
[Omari turns volume down]

"That looks like that fat mothafucka's wife right there."

"You think he's home?"

"I don't know, but I would shoot his shit up if I saw him."

"You wildin'. Shoot him with what, your fingers? Pow, pow." Brixx playfully gestured, unaware of Omari's shiny new toy inside his backpack. "Yo, call Shauna and ask what time she'll be here. Didn't she say she gets off at three-thirty?"

"Yeah, but it's about a forty-five-minute train ride."

"It's past five o'clock."

[Omari dials Shauna on speakerphone]

"Damn, straight to voicemail," Brixx replied.

"Maybe she's still in the tunnel or stuck at work."

"Where does she work?"

"Not far from Madison Square Garden."

"Oh. I was gonna say we can pick her up but never mind, I ain't driving into Manhattan."

"Give her a few minutes. You really think she'd ask me to meet her at the house and not show up?"

"I don't put anything past these chicks. What do y'all have to talk about in person anyway? We could be recording right now."

~

TUESDAY, AUGUST 23

[Protestor shouts over megaphone]

It's the end times. Repent. Trust Jesus. Today was simply a warning. Don't be fooled. These are the last days. Jesus saves...

Pete Johnston joined Bryce and Zoë as they crossed Sixth Avenue to a sea of worried faces. An earthquake, measuring 5.8 on the Richter scale, struck the east coast shortly after lunch, and the city had an eerie feel reminiscent of the days following the September 11 attacks. The quake—centered in Virginia—was considered a walk in the park compared to Japan's devastating 9.0 five months before. Still, a tremor of its magnitude on this side of the map was unusual. With the recent natural disasters happening in succession, maybe there was something to the preacher's prophetic words.

"The first time I felt my chair shake, I immediately looked behind me, thinking it was you," Zoë expressed to Bryce. "Then, I was like, 'Where'd he go?'"

"I'm not that nimble anymore."

[group laughter]

"I thought maybe the building was about to collapse when my chair shook the second time," she continued.

"That's exactly what I thought," Pete chimed in. "I was having lunch at my desk holding the sandwich to my mouth. The next thing you know..."

"You should've seen A.K.," Bryce added. "He looked at me in horror. You know he keeps a telescope in his office, so we took turns looking down at the street level. It's crazy because everyone was looking upward."

"Yup, probably looking for Jesus," Zoë announced.

"I don't know, but the whole Judgment Day thing has gained a lot of traction."

"Doesn't the Mayan calendar end on December 21?" Pete asked.

"Wait, December 21 of this year? That's AJ's birthday."

"Next year," Bryce informed. "We talked about it at the rooftop bar."

"Did we?"

"Briefly. They're saying next year, but the date has changed many times."

"No way. So, like, what's supposed to happen?"

"Watch the movie *2012,*" Pete advised.

"Wait, there's a movie about Judgment Day?"

Pete laughs, "Where have you been?"

"In another world, apparently," she answered.

"Zo, relax. No one truly knows when that day will arrive. I have the movie at home if you wanna borrow it. Wasn't that great in my opinion."

"I loved it," Pete exclaimed.

Zoë shooed away a group of pigeons with her foot. "You know, thinking back to earlier, none of it felt real. Even when they told us to evacuate the building, it just felt like one big school fire drill. Now I'm completely annoyed."

[lively conversations nearby]

"Take a deep breath. Everything will be fine. See, we made it to Port Authority in one piece."

"All right guys, see you all tomorrow."

"Later, Pete."

"You think *I like* walking? Did you know Pete walks all the way to the Upper West Side?" Bryce informed Zoë.

"Really?"

"Yup. I think he lives around Beacon Theatre. That's a little past 72nd Street. He told me he's not paying MTA a dime."

"He does seem like the type who would bike in to work."

"Do you want me to wait with you until your train arrives? I don't mind catching the next bus."

"I'll be alright, just feeling a bit overwhelmed," Zoë replied.

"I get it. I'm sure it's gonna be talked about all through the bus ride, so I can forget about reading. All right, well, be safe. We'll do it again tomorrow... unless, of course, Judgment Day strikes... *den-den-dennnnn.*"

"Weirdo."

"I'll make sure to bring in the DVD."

18

——

WILD NIGHT

After years of circumventing the club scene, Bryce agreed to step out of his comfort zone to celebrate his birthday. He grabbed his gold eyeglasses and a handful of peppermints, hurrying through the door. Like a flash, Tasha crossed his mind. Her home was dark, blinds shut, and the car long gone on what was night three of a ten-hour shift. The start of their sizzling summer was now a cool flame.

Bryce started his car and notified Priscilla of his ETA.

[Cherrelle and Alexander O'Neal's "Saturday Love" playing in the background]

P-Nut: Ok. Celeste just got here.

Sat 9:14 p.m.

Bryce lowered the rear windows, creating a cross mix between the cool evening breeze and the air conditioner. He drove through the dark back roads until Route 9 appeared with all its glare. In a few hours, he'd celebrate turning thirty-four, hoping for better birthday results than last year.

He could remember like it was yesterday: an erotic evening with Jennifer—an attractive woman he met online—went terribly wrong. She laughed nervously trying to make sense of why his bed sheets resembled something off the ID Channel. Her menstrual cycle was still weeks away. She teased him about his equipment below being the probable cause. It was more than what she was used to. No way could that have been the reason. Nevertheless, Bryce was too bothered by the bloody massacre to acknowledge the compliment. Spending the wee hours of thirty-three washing bed sheets wasn't on the itinerary. Thank goodness, the condom stayed in place. Even so, he was a bundle of nerves until his test results came back negative. He never shamed her for the accident, but they wouldn't hook up again.

The exterior of Priscilla's 1980s model two-story house looked as though it could use the handiwork of a notable HGTV host. She was twenty-six at the time of purchase—her first ever property bought dirt-cheap a few years before the housing crash of 2008. Regardless of its condition, Priscilla wore the home-owner title proudly.

I'm here.

P-Nut: Coming.

Sat 9:32 p.m.

He opened the passenger rear door for Celeste, Priscilla's voluptuous life-of-the-party friend from college, who emerged first.

Celeste was an inviting brassy woman with enough spice to set off a wildfire. She was the overturned vehicle in a two-car collision, someone who craned necks, leaving a trail of men with their tongues wagging. She wore a plush-colored backless crop top with a matching short set and heels. In an alternate universe, Bryce would've hooked up with her long ago.

[Celeste sings Beenie Man's "Sim Simma"]

"Hey, sexy birthday boy in the Bima."

"*Que lo que Preciosa.*"

"*No mucha.* Chillin'..."

[cheek kiss embrace]

At present, there wasn't anything to keep them apart. In fact, Priscilla briefed them years back on the possibilities of a mutual attraction. However, due to their serial dater parallelism, they remained amiable.

"Why are you trying to outshine me on *my* birthday? Lookin' all fine..."

"Thank you. You know I had to do it big. But look at you. Dayummm..."

"Stop it."

"I know, right? Let me calm down. Priscilla will be out in a minute."

"So, basically, we'll be waiting another *fifteen* minutes..."

"Exactly."

"Do you wanna sit behind me or her? You know I might crush those legs."

"Ooh, dirty talk. I like that," she laughed. "I can sit behind her. *¡Mira!* I like the white pants on you. Don't get too carried away tonight. Me and Priscilla will smack a bitch."

"You are hilarious. You know I had to get one more wear in before Labor Day."

"Oh please, do people actually follow that rule?"

"I was being facetious."

Playing dress up wasn't Priscilla's thing. She could attract attention by simply wearing sweatpants and a baseball cap, allowing her to fit in comfortably with the guys while keeping others at a loss. However, when it came down to stepping out for an occasion, she could turn the biggest cynic into a believer.

"Let's go, fancy," Bryce shouted at Priscilla, who surprisingly emerged just under the fifteen-minute mark. "Aye, don't turn off the porch light. Let me see your outfit."

"Don't get used to this heel stuff. You know I'll throw on a pair of Air Force Ones lickety-split."

"No, you won't," Celeste challenged.

"Don't test me. Come to think of it, I should grab my flats just in case."

"Let him see. Just spin around," Celeste instructed.

"Okay, okay."

"Nice. Looking good," Bryce said. "Um, so, didn't you say the line at this place wraps around the corner?"

"I did."

"Well, if you wanna get there before eleven, your flats will have to wait."

"Don't worry about the time. My flats are at the door."

A light mist materialized, persuading Priscilla to turn around to check on her windows. The about-face caused Bryce to raise an eyebrow. She wore a black ruched top with a black high slit skirt. Her jet-black hair was styled in a silk press. Through the years, Bryce only saw pictures of his best friend dolled up, now he was up close and personal. She looked stunning.

"Where did *that* come from?"

"What?"

"*That.*" He pointed.

"My butt?"

Celeste, seated in the back with the door open, made a request.

"Twerk it, mama."

"No-no, there will be no public twerking. I'm a model citizen, thank you."

Celeste egged her on. "Twerk it, mama, twerk it, twerk it, mama, twerk it. Or drop it low, bitch. Do something."

"Okay, okay." Priscilla held onto the bottom of her skirt, dipped to the pavement, and gave them a quick show, stunning Bryce.

"There, happy now?"

"Let me find out you've been living a double life," Bryce jested, closing the passenger door behind her. "Too bad I don't have any singles on me."

"Ooh, you've got the whole Crockett and Tubbs thing going on. An open shirt with white pants... I like it."

"Right, girl? We were just having that conversation." Bryce looked at Celeste through the rearview mirror. "I'm always wardrobe-ready. Y'all know that. And I stole the unfasten button look directly from P.'s playbook."

"That is so true," Celeste replied. "You know Priscilla will put on a button-up shirt and leave about four buttons open."

"Who, me?"

"Yes, bitch. You."

Priscilla read off the club's street address as Bryce inserted the information into the GPS.

"Now it says we're gonna get there *past* eleven. You rushed me out the door only to be the tardy one."

"We'll be fine. Don't you trust me?" Priscilla winked.

"Trick question. Okay, I'm feeling a bit generous tonight so I'm leaving it up to y'all to play DJ. What do you wanna listen to?"

The car went silent.

"I'm gonna slam y'all with '80s music if I don't get an answer in eight seconds."

"Eww, why so aggressive?" Priscilla asked.

"And why eight seconds? That's so random," Celeste replied.

"I know, right?"

"Seven, six, five..."

"Hey, I like '80s music," Priscilla yelled.

"Me too, but only if it's Freestyle."

"Spoken like a true Latina," Bryce replied.

"Boricua... Dominicana," Celeste happily proclaimed in a melodic tone, highlighting her nationality.

"You're in luck."

The hour-long drive brought about a mix of topics, notably

the approaching hurricane expected to slam the Northeast, the recent earthquake, and Bryce's plans to board a Party Yacht Cruise for his thirty-fifth birthday. Through the drive, Priscilla released several inessential giggles, prompting him to question whether she had been drinking beforehand. It was unusual behavior. Priscilla was the same person who wouldn't crack a smile if the bottom of her feet were tickled in a room filled with laughing gas.

They exited the Holland Tunnel en route to 14th Street. Celeste finished singing the last thirty seconds of The Cover Girls's "Show Me" while Priscilla touched up her makeup in the overhead visor.

[Priscilla's cell phone rings]

"Hey girl, I was just about to call you."

"These garage prices are outrageous," Bryce announced. "I'm gonna circle the block. There's gotta be a spot somewhere."

"Good luck," Celeste followed.

"Yaris, hold on. Uh, Bryce, are you seriously gonna make us walk in the rain?"

"It's only drizzling. We would have to walk whether I parked in a garage or not."

"Dude, just park in the garage. I'll pay."

"Uh, no. There are hidden gems all around here. Please, allow the 'P' in your name to stand for 'patience' for once. Thanks."

Bryce scoured the buzzing Chelsea neighborhood as Priscilla wrapped up her call. "Okay, Yaris and her dude just got there. They said the line is bananas."

"Did they drive?" Celeste followed.

"No, they took a cab down."

"See? And this is why I always tell you to trust the process," Bryce confidently expressed after finding a parking spot.

"Uh, aren't those project buildings?" Priscilla asked.

"Are you trying to get us killed, birthday boy?"

"Relax. We're not even in the hood. It's the West Village."

"So, what?" the girls yelled collectively.

"Bryce, no. I don't feel comfortable here."

He continued the parking search, finding a spot on a quiet historic cobblestone block lined with million-dollar homes, minutes from the nightclub. On that very same street was a cheaply priced parking garage.

Only in New York.

The drizzle let up. They walked along Eighth Avenue, where Priscilla made a request.

"Promise me you won't get mad."

"What, did you forget something? It's already eleven twenty-five."

Priscilla clutched her purse. "I didn't forget anything."

"Celeste, what is your girl talking about?"

"Don't ask me. I have no idea," she replied, remaining tight-lipped.

"Just promise me you won't get mad."

"Dude, what are you getting at?"

[Alice Deejay "Better off Alone" booming from the club]

The scene outside resembled that of the old Studio 54, with crowds of people dressed to impress, waiting to get selected. Priscilla cheerfully hugged Yaris and her boyfriend before they were introduced to the others. Bryce stared dejectedly at the sweeping line, their chances of entering the club dwindling by the minute. The last thing he wanted was to search for another location and lose his well-earned parking space. He directed the group to follow him toward the end of the line. Oddly, no one budged.

"Yo, the line is back this way. Celeste, can you get P.'s attention?"

Celeste turned to him momentarily but continued conversing with Yaris. Meanwhile, Priscilla was having a jolly old time with a gentleman in a suit and a beefy bouncer who looked like he could rip a phonebook in half. She reached into her purse and handed over a piece of paper with her driver's license. The gentleman in the suit thumbed through a legal pad. Finally, Bryce was motioned over.

"What's going on?"

"You guys are good," the host declared. Bryce glared at Priscilla, whose face was seconds from exploding. He eyed Celeste next.

"*Waa? ¿Que paso?* I didn't do *ennnything.*"

"Yo, what exactly is going on?"

In time, Priscilla gave in. "So, remember I asked that you not be upset?"

"Yes."

"By the way, you never did promise."

"Never make a promise you can't keep," the host interrupted, causing laughter.

"Exactly. She's never listened to Dru Hill."

"Remember a few months back at JuJu's party when I asked to use your phone?"

"Uh, yes. When your battery died..."

"Right."

"Okay..."

"I lied."

"So, your phone *didn't* die."

"No. I knew you listed your co-workers by full name, and I specifically remembered we had a conversation about a guy named Roy. You said he had the hookup, etcetera..."

"Nice try. Still not buying it."

"Wait, it gets better. So, I saved his number and sent him a text asking if he could secretly help me arrange something for you. This was after we talked about how much fun you had at the rooftop bar."

Bryce was visibly annoyed by Priscilla's admission. "When did you reach out?"

"Right around the time you drove down to Maryland."

"Girl, look, you've pissed him off twenty minutes before his birthday," Celeste warned.

"Dude, what did you want me to do? I was scrambling, trying to figure out something. I thought about the rooftop bar, but you'd already gone there. I was even thinking about getting tickets to the U.S. Open."

Bryce took a deep breath. "Roy can't hold water. He would've told me about it long ago."

"B., he was super cool. He told me to reach out before your birthday and he'd have everything taken care of."

The host interjected, showing Bryce a list of RSVP names. As a show of proof, he pointed down to "Quintana", Priscilla's last name. Next to it were the letters "P.S." with the numbers seven through ten in parentheses.

"Okay, I'm sure there's thousands of Priscilla Quintanas."
[laughter]

"Come and get me when you guys figure out what you're doing," the host notified. "I've got to help this other group."

"What does the P.S. stand for?" Bryce asked.

"Promoter's Special," the bouncer replied. "Meaning the promoter okayed the RSVP entry. There's no cover charge. Open bar. Nobody pays a dime tonight."

"Woo-hoo!" Celeste cheered.

"What about the seven through ten?"

"That's the expected party size."

Bryce performed a head count. "There's five of us."

"Luiz from my job is running late," Priscilla informed.

"That makes six. Celeste, I *know* you knew about this. That's what all the giggling in the car was about."

"Who, me?" she replied, flashing an insincere smile.

"I gave them a range of seven to ten in case there were any late additions," Priscilla added.

Is that the birthday boy? A distinct voice questioned from afar. Bryce cocked his head to one side. It was Zoë along with Anthony, her son's father.

"Zo? You can't be serious," he replied with amusement, embracing the couple. "Don't tell me you were in on this too."

"Guilty. Yo, I almost gave it away at lunch the other day. Roy kicked my shin so hard it left a bruise," she confessed.

"Aw man, this is crazy. I'm speechless."

[Priscilla greets Zoë]

"So, you and Priscilla have already met."

"Not formally, just through text," they replied.

"Milk Dud has a stomach virus. I don't think he's gonna make it tonight," Zoë informed.

The thought of one of his best friends conspiring with a long-standing rival didn't sit well, but having pulled this off under his nose was quite impressive. They called a truce before the host led them into the two-floor building.

Inside was a king-size chandelier, glowing amber lights, and roaring dance music. Curved booth seating and leather sofas bordered the dance floor. A DJ booth enclosed with purple velvet rope sat directly across the cocktail lounge.

"I'm assuming this is the first level?" Priscilla asked the host.

"Yes. Upstairs is hip hop only. Looks like you agreed to the first level, which is where they play a mixture of songs. Personally, I think that was the better choice."

A diverse crowd danced to Sean Paul's "Like Glue." The women were plentiful. Some grooved in bunches, others stood in pairs, waiting to be schmoozed by the dapper men at hand. Bryce wasted little time hitting the floor, sandwiched in between Priscilla and Celeste. Yaris and her boyfriend followed. Taking in the atmosphere were Zoë and Anthony, who ordered drinks.

"What time do they close?" Bryce asked over the jacked-up speakers.

"The confirmation email showed four in the morning."

"Do you all wanna stick around 'til then?"

"It's up to you, birthday boy. As long as my feet can hold up, I'll be good," Celeste said.

"Let's play it by ear then."

～

AUGUST 28 - 1:07 A.M.

[DJ interrupts music]

Let's give a shout-out to all my Virgos. Where y'all at? Make some noise...

[sweeping cheers]

[air horn sound]

The DJ went through a small list of names celebrating birthdays in between songs.

Fat shout to Bryce a.k.a. Smooth. Where are you, homie? Salute.

Bryce's personal section cheered along.

"You gave them my birthday?"

"No," Priscilla shouted.

[DJ Khaled "All I Do Is Win" plays in the background]

"Under no circumstances will I dance to a DJ Khaled song. Y'all go ahead. I'm gonna sit this one out," Bryce declared.

"Need more tequila anyway," Priscilla admitted.

"Let's do shots, girl," Celeste replied. "Come, birthday boy."

"Nah. I've got to be the responsible one tonight. The car can't drive itself."

"Just one drink... it should wear off by the time we leave."

"Guys, are you doing shots?" Bryce asked the others, who mingled in the VIP. Zoë and Yaris rushed to join the ladies while Bryce picked up a conversation with the guys. He checked his phone. There was a "Happy Birthday" text from Tasha sent at exactly midnight. As he started to reply, easing through the crowd making their grand entrance was the club connoisseur himself.

"Smooth," he shouted. "Happy Birthday, my man." Bryce rose to his feet, giving Roy a firm handclasp and a quick one-armed hug in a rare show of brotherhood. "Thanks, brotha. I really appreciate this. I mean that. It means a lot."

"No doubt. It just sucks that it took your birthday to *finally* come out and chill."

"I get it. You know if it were up to me, I would've found

another way to celebrate. This was all Priscilla's doing. I'm still in shock. I've got to commend y'all."

"Did the DJ shout you out?"

"Oh, that was *you*? I should've known once he called me 'Smooth.'"

[shared laughter]

"Did they let out confetti?"

"Nah."

"No? Confetti was supposed to drop from the ceiling."

"Maybe there's a shortage."

"What up, Anthony," Roy exchanged greetings with Zoë's partner.

Bryce continued, "Let me introduce you to the others. This is Priscilla's co-worker Luiz and... I'm sorry, brotha, what was your name again?"

"Daniel."

"Sorry about that. Roy, this is Daniel, Yaris's boyfriend. She's over there with Priscilla. Daniel, this is my guy, Roy."

"Nice to meet you, fellas," Roy replied. "Daniel, you look familiar. Where do I know you from?"

"Heyyy Milk Dud, you made it," Zoë acknowledged Roy.

"I'm only here for a few minutes. Just wanted to poke my head in and make sure everything went smoothly." Roy waved to a few club employees in passing.

"Is this Roy?" Priscilla asked Bryce.

"Don't try to pretend you don't know him."

"This is my first time *actually* seeing his face, dum-dum." Priscilla and Roy shook hands. "Wait, are you getting ready to leave? You just got here."

"I know. I've had a stomach bug all weekend. I was just telling Zoë how bad I felt, but I wanted to check in with you all."

"Oh, that sucks. How far is your travel?"

"I'm only about twenty minutes away. I live in Harlem."

"Well, at least have a drink with us before you go."

"Yeah, Milk Dud, have a drink... or two or three," Zoë replied hysterically.

"Smooth, you see Zo's trying to kill me?"

Locking eyes with Bryce the entire time was a slim, brown-skinned woman, sipping a drink with friends in the next section. She had sexy, suggestive eyes and wouldn't look away when he returned the favor. Bold.

[Rihanna's "Don't Stop the Music" plays in the background]

Roy was long gone but his pop-up wasn't the only surprise of the eventful evening. A drunken Priscilla dragged Bryce onto the crammed dance floor and encouraged Celeste, who was all merry, to join in. Together they danced suggestively to the R&B sensation's hit record.

"We should have a threesome," Priscilla expressed.

"Birthday boy, what did she say?"

"She said, 'Help me, I'm drunk.'"

"No, I didn't. I said we should have a threesome. Come on, it'll be fun."

"Are you serious, girl? Where and when?"

"Celeste, don't listen to her. That's the brown liquor talking."

"I'm super, super serious. I've never had one. You?"

"I plead the fifth, girl..."

"Hear me out, B., I've thought logically about this. You're like the only guy I trust. I know you're responsible... well, I know with me you'd be, and it wouldn't get in the way of our friendship. Celeste, we've known each other for years, and I know you and Bryce are both attracted to each other. We're all single, so why not?"

Bryce appeared irritated. "Priscilla, chill out."

"Why are you calling me by my first name?" she slurred.

"Yeah, girl, I know that's not what you want. I'm not saying that I'm completely against the idea, but what if someone catches feelings?"

"We won't, though. Especially not the two of you."

"Hey, I resent that," Bryce replied.

"We're all strong-willed, that's why it'll work. What's one time? If it doesn't work out, so be it. We all go back to being friends."

"I can't lie, birthday boy. She's got me thinking..."

"What, that she's a total nut job? I would agree. Please don't entertain her."

"See? At least Celeste understands..."

"That's because I'm the *only* sober one here. Listen, I don't care if it's a one-time thing or how good it sounds, it's not happening."

"I can respect that," Celeste said. "There aren't many guys willing to turn down two bad bitches."

"I'm not *most* guys though. For the record, it doesn't mean I don't find y'all attractive. I've expressed my attraction to Priscilla in the past, but we're far removed from that. And the only thing keeping *you* and *me* from kickin' it is our mutual friendship or else..."

"We'd be fuckin' like rabbits?" Celeste attempted to finish his sentence.

Bryce offered a charming wink at Celeste as confirmation.

"I'mma keep it a buck with you, birthday boy, I could *definitely* see us hanging out. Consider yourself lucky."

"See? He knows it could work. He's just being difficult," Priscilla interrupted.

"Priscilla, stop. You know better than anyone that I don't run from a challenge, but I've got to draw the hard line in the sand. I'm not sleeping with my sis and her friend."

Bryce left the women to dance to themselves. Before long, they were joined by Luiz and a spiffy gentleman in hanging suspenders who pressed up against Celeste. Bryce walked toward their VIP section, retaining mixed feelings about Priscilla's daring proposal. Without delay, someone gripped his wrist.

"You wanna dance?"

The woman's voice was entrancing, her touch gentle. It

took a moment before he could look past her risqué outfit—a crisscross cutout halter top exposing plenty of cleavage and stomach. She sipped through a straw gazing at him lasciviously.

"Say it again, the music is too loud," Bryce asked, pulling her closer.

"I asked if you wanted to dance." Her smile was one of dominance as she grew impatient.

Asking her to repeat herself bought him enough time to think. Who was she, where did she come from, and did Roy have a hand in this?

"Why are you playing games?"

"I'm not, love..."

"I know you heard me the first time. I'm not gonna ask you again."

"Why the attitude though?"

"I don't have an attitude," she smiled contemptuously.

"Is that how you talk to someone on their birthday? What if I'm hard of hearing?"

"Happy birthday. Don't act like we weren't looking at each other earlier."

"Thank you. And I don't know what you're talking about. I was minding my business."

"Well, I wasn't. I was checking you out. I like your whole getup. My friend was telling me to come say something to you before another bitch did, so..."

"I appreciate your boldness. How do you know I'm not here with my girl?"

She sucked her teeth. "If you were, then why look back at me?"

"People look at each other."

"Not like *that*. You were looking at me like a plate of food. Like, you hadn't eaten in days."

"Maybe I grew an appetite," he replied, faintly licking his lips in anticipation.

"Oh, is that right? By the way, I'm not drunk or anything," she confirmed, pulling down the side of her rising skirt.

"Not even a little?"

She took another sip from the glass. "I could be a bit buzzed, but I'm good."

"Why'd you give me that disclaimer?"

"Because my approach can come off too strong. I tend to go after the things I want."

"Your approach is fine, love. Can I tell you something?"

"Say it again. I couldn't hear you."

"I asked if I could tell you something..."

"Let me guess... you *do* have a girl?"

"Nah."

"Don't tell me you're gay. I mean that respectfully..."

"Chill out."

"What then?" she giggled.

"I like your locs. You're stunningly beautiful, but I'm sure you get that all the time."

"Aw, thank you."

"I've also been staring at your braces this whole time, hoping you wouldn't catch me in your mouth," he laughed. "I've got a thing for the loc/braces combo."

"For real?" she laughed bashfully. "Let me find out you got a little game."

"No game. Just facts. God really took his time with you," he charmed her.

"Okay, fly guy," she beamed. "I appreciated it. Thank you."

"What's your name?"

"Jazmin. And you?"

"Bryce."

[Drake's "Fancy" playing in the background]

He whispered playful words in her ear as she ground against him on the dance floor. The exchange continued until she walked over to her section, grabbed her purse, and informed friends of her return. Bryce was seen instructing his personal server until he and Jazmin walked inconspicuously toward the main entrance. He shared a lively conversation with the bouncer, who observed Jazmin texting aggressively a few feet away. Their chat ended with a fist bump, sealing the deal for Bryce's temporary exit.

"Okay, you're good on re-entry," he explained to Jazmin as they left the club walking under a fine rain.

"How far did you park?"

"Not far." He grabbed her by the hand as they hurried along.

19

—

ALIVE AND KICKING

The potency of summer resurfaced two weeks after Hurricane Irene soaked the entire Mid-Atlantic. Bryce and Priscilla were gathered at Lorenzo's, inviting four-bedroom Ocean County home for food, laughs, and the start of the NFL season.

"I started at Old Bridge in the fall of ninety-five," Priscilla explained to Daija as they conversed in the kitchen. "Wow, so you came in right after we graduated. No wonder we never crossed paths." It was their first time meeting, and they hit it off, sharing stories of former teachers and the reason Daija bolted from a stressful corporate role to become a real estate agent.

The home was incredible, from the spacious backyard to the purple and gold basketball court dedicated to Lorenzo's darling Los Angeles Lakers. It is where he stood with Bryce, decked out in full Dallas Cowboys attire. Meanwhile, Bryce, in true nostalgic form, wore a red and white Deion Sanders 49ers throwback jersey. They spoke regularly on the phone, but their conflicting lifestyles kept them from hanging out. It was a miracle they saw each other twice in under six months while only living twenty miles apart. Lorenzo was a true family man. He and Daija were legitimate best friends, the epitome of a happy marriage.

Bryce shared his phone, attempting to explain his recent squabble with Tasha.

> Sexy Neighbor: I don't know. Maybe it's me, but it seems like ever since I started the new shift you've pulled away.
>
> Sun 12:35 p.m.

Lorenzo's face reeked of disapproval, knowing full well of the type of woman Bryce desired. The idea that his friend was involved with another already-made family went through him like a knife. He did, however, praise Tasha for her commendable act of setting boundaries.

"She sounds like a good woman, and I applaud her for not giving up the cookie so easily. At least she's making you work for it. Think about it, what if she just gave it up after the first date and got pregnant? Now there's three kids in the equation. Have y'all ever had that discussion?"

"Nah, we haven't even gotten that far. She can't get pregnant through kissing."

"You mentioned her sons having different fathers, right?"

"Yes. One is locked up."

"Nah, bruh. No kitty-cat is worth putting yourself in a scenario like that. Especially someone of your stature. I could see if she only had one child. Not two."

"You sound like Dale."

"I'm just saying if y'all were to get into a thriving relationship —say one leading to marriage—then the sting of a pregnancy wouldn't be *as* bad with one child in the pic. Not two."

"Fam, why are you focused on me knocking her up? When have I ever been *that* reckless?"

"Cuz the way you described her, she might be fertile as hell," Lorenzo laughed. "You just never know with some of these women. They'll tell you beforehand that they don't want kids until the pregnancy test comes back positive. You've got to think of all the possible scenarios. Some of them will switch up at the drop of a dime. If I'm being completely honest, I think the cons of this situation with Tasha outweigh the pros by a landslide."

"Really?"

"One thousand percent. I'd tell you to avoid sex altogether... at least until the right one comes along... but then I remembered who I was dealing with."

[laughter]

"Bro, whatever you do, don't waste your time trying to commit to her for the sake of smashing. Another thing, are you still messing with ole girl from Cedar?"

"Julissa? Nah, I moved on. Wasn't worth the headache. Gucci had a conniption when I told him."

"Tell Guc to shut his ass up. He wants to be twenty-one so bad."

"You can tell him. He's on the way with Junior."

"How long has he been with his girl?"

"I'd say at least ten years now."

Lorenzo's daughters circled around to the side of the house. "Uncle Bryce, can you play with us?"

"Daddy and Uncle Bryce are talking. Go play. Tell Mommy to bring the baby to me."

"In a little while, girls, okay?" Bryce offered. The girls rushed off to advise their mother of Lorenzo's request.

"What were you saying again?" Lorenzo asked.

"We were talking about Julissa. That whole situation was a wake-up call. Don't get me wrong, I wouldn't have dealt with her if I didn't want to, but dealing with her was a blessing. It allowed me to unveil my true feelings."

"Feelings for what?"

"That I'm ready for a commitment."

"Get the fuck outta here. You ain't fooling me."

"Nah, I'm serious," Bryce laughed. "Looking back, I'm thankful she rejected my advances. I was falling for her. The alternative could've destroyed her entire marriage and I'm not here to do that. She played the game accordingly. This falls on me."

"So, what do you do now?"

"Just sit back. The dots will connect when the right one comes along. When you know, you know."

"True. Listen, look how long I've been with Daija—even with our little sabbatical through college."

"Right. You wanted to be together."

"I did. She was doing the sorority thing, and I was out here cuttin' up," Lorenzo laughed. "I let her do her thing, but I knew she was the one. We identified what we wanted early on, and the rest was history."

"That leads me to another thing. Remember Kristen?"

Lorenzo dribbled a basketball against the asphalt, repeating her name. "It doesn't ring a bell. Wait, is that the customer service rep?"

"The who?"

"The rep you hollered at over the phone and hopped on a plane to see."

"Oh, you're talking about Kerri. The girl in Texas who helped with my cell phone bill," Bryce chuckled.

"Yeah. Her. I still don't know how you pulled off getting her number on a recorded line. Did she ever get in trouble for that?"

[Bryce laughs]

"Maybe. I was the one doing all the talking. I ended up falling for her accent and then I started hinting at how I needed to visit Texas. She was egging me on but in a cagy way. Next thing you know, she's texting me her personal number while we're on the call."

"These women are just as bad as us," he laughed.

"I know. She was gorgeous, though. That was my first long-distance situation. But, no, that's not Kristen."

"Kristen... Kristen. Is that the dancer?"

"Don't say *dancer* like she was swinging from a pole. She majored in kinesiology & dance."

"You know what I mean. That's the one you took to the WNBA game."

"Your memory is sharp, my boy."

"Now I remember. It *must've* been love if you were willing to sit through that shit show for two hours. I'm a basketball junkie and I couldn't even do that. What ever happened to her?"

"I honestly couldn't tell you. I wanted to be with her, but if you can remember I was going through a chain of events and decided to put the relationship on hold. I didn't wanna burden myself."

"Nah, man, that's when you find out if they're a true ride or die," Lorenzo added.

"I get it. I wasn't thinking that way at twenty-four."

"I wonder what she's up to."

"I reached out to her girlfriend six months ago, hoping to get some feedback. Crickets." Bryce informed him.

"Damn."

"It's all good. I took a stab in the dark. I can't expect a person of her caliber to sit around forever. I'd put out an APV if I didn't have my sights set on someone else at the moment."

"You're out here living, brotha. You know better than anyone how vast the options are. Just choose wisely. Everything will fall into place soon."

[Lorenzo's oldest daughter returns]

"Daddy, Mommy said she's about to feed her."

"Okay."

Lorenzo was right, things were going exceptionally well in Bryce's personal life. Never had he felt more alive. But after many years on the dating market, he was ready to fill that missing piece to his puzzle. In the meantime, he replied to Tasha's text.

What do u mean by "pulled away?"

I told u the other day I wouldn't be home.
We've communicated almost every day.

[Gucci pulls up with Junior in their company work van]

"Get that junk away from the front of my house," Lorenzo yelled. "You're lowering my property value."

"We ain't even put this bitch in park and you're already talking shit," Gucci retorted.

"Damn right. 'RL Painting,' what's the 'RL' stand for, 'real lame'?" Lorenzo replied, referencing the brothers' logo plastered on the side. The letters represented their first names used as an acronym for their painting and general contracting business. "I've got time today. Y'all on *my* turf."

Back inside, Bryce showed Priscilla his football picks for the early games.

"You picked against my Giants?"

"Had to. Look at the spread, how could I not? You know I quietly pull for the 'Skins just for my dad's sake."

[doorbell ringing]

"The pizza's here," Daija announced.

[text notification]

> Sexy Neighbor: I'm not talking about today. I meant in general. IDK. Like I said, maybe it's me, but it's like your whole attitude has changed.
>
> Sun 1:11 p.m.

"Playboy, what time do the Niners play?" Gucci asked.

"Four o'clock. What's up?"

"Since we're all here, we might as well discuss this trip for the end of the year."

"Can it wait 'til halftime? I've still got money going on these early games."

Indifferent to the flurry of activity, Gucci had other plans. "Well, I'm gonna step outside then."

"What trip?" Priscilla asked.

"We were thinking about taking a guys' trip at the end of the year."

[text notification]

> Sexy Neighbor: Hello?? Why is it taking you
> so long to reply?
>
> Sun 1:21 p.m.

Tasha had a fair gripe concerning Bryce's recent behavior. He excused himself to give her a call with their texting tiff becoming unbearable.

"This chick is buggin' out."

"Who?" Gucci asked, sparking a cigarette next to his van.

"The neighbor."

"Oh, word? What'chu 'bout to do?"

"Call her. She's doing too much. If I don't respond in time, she starts accusing me of playing games."

"Well, you know I don't care about football. I'm only here to eat and talk shit. Let me talk to her. I'll set her straight."

"Man, I got it."

"Never trust a big butt and a smile, Playboy. New Edition warned us."

"You mean Bell Biv DeVoe."

"Same shit. She has kids, right?"

"Two boys."

"Damn. What is with you and these MILFs? You're the true definition of a mother fucker."

[laughter]

"Well, this mother ain't putting out."

"You had it good with the married one. I can't recall any disagreements."

"We had our share. Here's the part you're missing, Guc, we were breaking every moral code in the book. I'm not a home-wrecker. There's a big difference if she was only *seeing* another guy and wanted to kick it on the side. I've been in those scenarios plenty. But she's married. Time to move on. We had our fun."

"You're better than me. I'd still be clappin' those cheeks. Yo, here's an honest question, why don't marriage licenses have expiration dates—you know, like a driver's license?"

"Is that a real question?"

"Hell yeah. What's with this *'til death do us part* bullshit? People should have the option to renew after a few years. Better that than an ugly, drawn-out divorce."

"Has anyone told you your mind works differently?"

The brainy idea to block Julissa was to help disassociate himself emotionally, however Gucci's constant chatter triggered him to unblock her. He located the 'blocked messages' folder on his phone and proceeded to read a set of messages—one of which Julissa inquires on his availability and whether his silence meant the end of their romantic involvement. It was Julissa who once told him to desist from the affair if the role became too much, and so, he acquiesced.

Her last text was a picture message sent on August 28, his birthday. He zoomed in, running his eyes over a consent form from an abortion clinic. Her personal signature and that of the physician appeared. Underneath the picture was a jaw-dropping caption:

> La Gatita: Happy Birthday, and you're welcome...
>
> Sun 8:12 p.m.

"What's up?" Gucci asked, taking a pull from his cigarette. "I thought you were gonna call the neighbor." Bryce handed him the phone. "Who is La... how the hell do you pronounce this? Ga-ti-ta? What the fuck is that?"

"That's the married one. Zoom in on that last pic."

Gucci's eyes widened in shock as he read on. "Oh snap. You

knocked that up, Playboy? Mannn, your pull-out game *weak* like seven days. You mean to tell me I was about to become an uncle?"

Bryce sighed, wearing a confused look. "She's been on birth control, and I've always pulled out despite that. I have no idea what happened. We haven't communicated in months."

"How y'all go from breaking each other off every damn week to not speaking? You ain't telling me the full story, dawg. There must've been a disagreement."

"Nah. I just blocked her as a way to move on."

"So, you went from giving her D to not giving an F. They need to send yo ass to detention."

"That's a bar. I like that one. I'll ask my lil bro if he can feature you on one of his songs."

"You've got that super sperm. What'chu put in those protein shakes?"

"That ain't it. Maybe she wasn't on the pill. Or it could've been her fertile week. Who knows. But she wouldn't have taken a chance like that. Not without telling me."

"You never know, kid."

"Dang. Now when I think about it, I definitely didn't pull out."

"Aaah damn, Playboy. Like I've always said, sex without a condom is like using a phone without a case. If everything goes smoothly, great. One false move and it'll cost a lot of money. She did you a solid. She's a real one."

Julissa's whimsical text wouldn't help Bryce's sense of guilt. He would've never intentionally left her stranded to make such a rash decision with her body had he known otherwise. Bryce wasn't heartless, he was only trying to think with his heart less. Now he felt obligated to reach out, offer a sincere apology, and assist in any way that he could.

20

——

A SONG FOR MAMA

calming breeze whisked across the grassy gravesite as Bryce placed sunflowers on his mother's grave. It was a faithful deed executed annually on her birthday. Interrupting his train of thought was a honeybee gliding overhead, drawn to the high-quality nectar and his sweet-scented cologne. He never experienced a bee sting, but the threat reminded him of a time in summer camp when a ring of spider bites left him in a panic state. It was Mom who came to the rescue and assured him everything would be all right.

Today would've marked Candace's fifty-ninth birthday, had life only granted her a little more time. Death didn't have an age, but to be taken away from the world so young seemed unjust. Still her memory lived on. There was the beautiful headshot portrait on his laptop, the pocket-sized photo of them at his first Little League game tucked in the mirror crease of his bedroom dresser, and lastly, a picture hanging on his living room wall in her full element performing on stage. The latter often became an instant conversation starter when in the presence of company.

Candace's job as a mom wasn't done—even twenty years later. Bryce believed she continued to watch over him like a hawk. Those with a firm foundation of faith would support the claim. At times, he could hear the softness of her voice in his head or detect signs of her closeness. He desperately wanted to look her in the eye and speak candidly about life's peaks and valleys, learn her thoughts on interracial dating, and ask questions on how to cope with his own fears and insecurities. It was understood Dale was a stellar single parent who overcompensated on many levels, but Bryce hankered after his mother's listening ear.

He remembered late spring of 1991 like it was yesterday, his father rising early each morning glued to the news before visiting Candace at the hospital. As the end of the school year had neared, Bryce was allowed to make regular visits before class. Candace's eyes sparkled, teasing Bryce about his noisy windbreaker outfits, which she often heard from down the hall. They'd make a second trip in the evenings when she was usually asleep or just waking up from a nap. To be by her bedside, if only to hold her hand, was rewarding.

The heartbreaking news of Candace's passing happened as Bryce was taking a makeup exam. A hallway monitor alerted Mr. Bogart, his math teacher, of Dale's sudden arrival at the school. Bryce gathered his belongings unaware of the event and casually walked to the principal's office. If this had anything to do with his mom, he was sure she'd pull through. She always did.

Candace, a zesty sports fan, was denied an opportunity to watch her son thrive athletically. Bryce once dug a hole deep into the hollow ground of her headstone, burying a first-place medal from state relays, to include her with his triumphs. It was added with his first-ever home run ball from junior varsity. The baseball was eventually given to Dale for display; however, the gold medal remained almost twenty years later. That would be their little secret. When it came to her son's sports participation, she was as vocal as any male family member, and it was only after her health deteriorated that she started to miss games.

A normal routine when visiting the gravesite was to read Psalm 23, her favorite prayer, which was taught to him at an early age. He fell to one knee, wiping away the grit from her headstone, laying his right hand against her name.

Candace Nicole Taylor
September 12, 1952 – June 3, 1991

The Lord is my shepherd; I shall not want.
He maketh me to lie down in green pastures: he leadeth me beside
the still waters.
He restoreth my soul: he leadeth me in the paths of righteousness for
his name's sake.
Yea, though I walk through the valley of the shadow of death, I will
fear no evil: for thou art with me; thy rod and thy staff they
comfort me.
Thou preparest a table before me in the presence of mine enemies:
Thou anointest my head with oil; my cup runneth over.
Surely goodness and mercy shall follow me all the days of my life:
and I will dwell in the house of the Lord forever.

Bryce fought back tears, wondering how his mother would fare in today's social climate. He imagined her expressive reactions to some of the major stories hitting the news circuits. The advancement of technology or the unshakable race wars. The influence of pop culture and social media. The athletic achievements of the Williams sisters, or the unthinkable, a man of color winning a presidential election. It was 1984 when his family witnessed Jesse Jackson's presidential campaign. That was monumental, but would she have bawled her eyes out during President Obama's victory speech like others? The complexities of the unknown ate him up inside.

He thought back to his pre-adolescent years when he observed the pain in his mother's eyes as she thumbed through a scarce family photo album. Candace's voice would often crack when pointing out Bryce's grandparents, who only saw him through photos before their own deaths. His only communication with his mother's side of the family came through Anton and his parents—Candace's aunt and uncle. It was Dale who had shared the traumatic story of why Bryce's maternal grandparents never took an interest in their newly formed family.

Candace hadn't deserved the unfair treatment. She was the type of person to hold you while you cried and stay awake just to make sure you were okay, even if she was breaking inside. A natural giver who didn't have a bad bone in her body. Even so, she'd call on those around her to read Matthew 6:14-15—a scripture connected to forgiveness. That was the type of person she was.

As the afternoon sun crossed the clear blue sky, Bryce bounced around a few ideas to honor her memory. The thought of tattooing one of her many words of wisdom crossed his mind, but he wasn't sold on the idea of inking his body. Eventually, the flesh would dissipate. This goodwill gesture needed to be cemented somewhere forever. He wanted to start a new tradition, perhaps donating to a nonprofit in the fight against cancer. Or with the help of his church create a charitable event for those battling a similar illness. Another idea was to support a cause near and dear to his mother's heart—something involving theater.

He wiped away tears behind his Ray-Ban sunglasses while a large family grieved in the distance. He rose to his feet; his bones snapped like a twig breaking off a tree. He looked to the sky where an ear-shattering airplane engine sounded foreseeably preparing for landing at nearby Newark Liberty International Airport. Time was never a factor on days like this, but he asked his mom for thirty more minutes just to brief her on the ongoings of his personal life. The thought of her hurrying him along as she often would whenever he produced useless chatter—especially during her favorite TV shows—made him smile. Surely, she wouldn't want to hear a long-winded story about his adventures, not while she was occupied in one of her own. Somewhere in Utopia.

"All right, Ma, I'll make it short and sweet," he began.

Bryce sat reclined underneath a shade of trees; a white

butterfly fluttered nearby. The car windows were down, and a late-summer breeze circulated. He hadn't eaten all day and didn't have a sense of urgency to grab lunch. All he wanted was to sit immobile with his mother by his side. Acknowledging her birthday was significant, however, today was about stillness, listening closely for her word and recharging. He gave one last look to her headstone and the massive oak tree some short yards away. Suddenly his eyes welled.

He hadn't cried this much since his thirteen-year-old traveling team lost to a powerhouse roster from Florida in the semi-finals of the Babe Ruth Tournament. Not even when his mother was laid to rest. She was deeply missed. He wasn't one to show emotion, still holding onto the childhood myth about crying boys and their lack of masculinity, which of course he learned was categorically false. Moreover, it was tough to sob with parents who illustrated superhuman strength. Candace, a fighter to the very last breath, and Dale, a man who picked himself up by the bootstraps when life became insufferable.

"A broken man is a dangerous one." Words from his grandfather that stuck like glue.

Today's weeping was a buildup of sadness, anger, and cheer. Bryce started the car; the time read 2:22 p.m. Tom Petty's "Free Fallin'" picked up where it left off. The lyrics to the song were sure to bring about more tears, but it was a favorite. He opened the sunroof shade slide, cleared the passenger seat of the sunflower's plastic wrapping, and tossed it to the back. Catching his immediate eye was a crumbled gold condom wrapper hidden in the corner, a memento of his wild birthday evening. A smirk crossed his face, the tears ceased. He put on his seatbelt and blew his mother a kiss. "I love you," he whispered, driving off. "Thank you for everything."

21

———

I'M READY

Omari had a resurgence of energy even if it were old matters spearheading his current writing binge. Each day, he constructed new songs, tweaked old ones, and worked on breath control and a series of flows, proving his dedication to the craft. There wasn't a great deal of movement in getting his music into the hands of the movers and shakers of the industry, but he hadn't given up hope.

He browsed through a collection of old rap magazines, inhaling a strong weed, thinking of Shauna, whose Houdini act more than solidified her guilt. Next, he turned his eye to his backpack, where inside was a loaded Glock 19. Privately, he knew keeping the weapon at Brixx's house could put him in hot water, but he needed to take matters into his own hands with the latest brushes of drama.

His rap group didn't have a radio single or a single mention on the countless hip hop blog sites. Just buzz among their circle and a rising YouTube channel. Hip hop was a young person's game, filled with ultra-competitive hungry artists everywhere. The group's age ranged from twenty to twenty-four, perfectly suited for the core demographic of today's listeners and proof there was still time to make waves. But the clock was ticking. With the omission of sports, there wasn't another profession offering a laissez-faire attitude that included lavish living, world travel, and women. It didn't matter how he got there as long as he was a part of it. Even if it meant a false portrayal. Plenty of notable acts followed this formula for a chance of success, why not him? The thought of becoming a larger-than-life story was Omari's motivator.

He texted Bryce over an hour ago, asking if there was any progress with the friend who previously worked at BET. She was their hopeful foot in the door if all else failed. Like clockwork, his phone rang, except it wasn't his brother. The call came from a private number, the second such call of the day. Private calls were sent to voicemail, but this time he promptly answered and muted the call. At the other end, there was light breathing and background laughter from what sounded like a sitcom laugh track. Unexpectedly, silence fell, and the call dropped. Could it have been Shauna calling from a blocked number or an accidental pocket dial? More questions, hardly any answers.

Brixx grew hungry after he finished schmoozing with one of his lady friends. "I wish they'd hurry up with the car so I can run and grab something to eat."

"You smoking?" Omari asked him, offering his blunt.

"Nah, I need food," he replied, removing his Chicago Bulls cap to scratch his freshly faded hair. In the meantime, they listened to a collection of original beats produced by an acquaintance from their audio school.

"This sounds like some ole Mario Brothers shit," Brixx joked.

"I think we should do what my bro suggested."

"What?"

"Grab twenty of the most memorable produced rap songs and recreate our own sound. We can add it to what we already have."

"Didn't G-Unit do that with mixtapes?"

"Nah. They were rapping over radio-dominant singles at the time. We'd embrace old and new by picking songs from each decade. Out of those twenty beats, we'd select about ten. It'll show versatility."

"You might be onto something. I just can't see me rapping over a Kool Moe Dee beat. We need to set some boundaries."

"I wouldn't go that far either. Just '90s and 2000s."

It was Bryce's brainchild, but Omari's mind was worth its weight in gold. He was the brains of the group; all he wanted was to be great. Outside of health, his self-esteem was at an all-time high.

There were many inspiring stories like theirs, serving as confirmation that they too could reach the mountain top. Rome wasn't built in a day, but the foundation to assemble one of hip hop's rising young conglomerates was hardening—if only he could put a stop to his unscrupulous behavior.

[Omari's cell phone rings]

"Sup, big bro."

What's good with you?

"Nothing. Yo, did you just call a few minutes ago from a blocked number?"

No. Why would I block my number?

"True."

I'm driving, so I figured I'd call instead of texting. Are you at work?

"Nah, I finished at three today. I'm at Brixx's."

Oh, okay. As far as ole girl goes, I'm gonna reach out to her tonight. I don't know what her deal is. She texts then disappears. Is there anything you want me to tell her?

"Tell her she'd better hop aboard the train before we leave her ass in the dust."

"Word." Brixx countered.

You wouldn't be talking like that if you saw her pics. Her booty is bigger than y'all rap career.

"Aye, Brixx, he said she's dragging a wagon."

"Tell him to hurry up and smash, then."

Y'all need to relax. How have you been feeling healthwise?

"I'm cool."

Have you thought about working full-time? That way you'd qualify for health insurance.

"Nah. That'll leave me no time to focus on music."

What's more important? The music will always be here.

"I'll look into it. Switching topics, I was just telling Brixx of the idea you had about rhyming over old classics."

What did he say?

"He's down."

Good.

"I think we're about ready to perform now. It's to the point where we've memorized each other's songs. If one of us happens to slip up on stage, the other can pick up the slack."

Good. Keep working. Try to perfect everything. Leave no stone unturned. While I'm at it, tell Brixx he doesn't need to include an ad-lib after each bar. I was listening to one of your songs the other day. It clutters the sound.

"I told him the same thing. Yo, you heard?" Omari asked Brixx, with Bryce now on speakerphone.

"What?"

Your ad-libs, Brixx. I need you to slow down.

"I'm doing too much?"

Yeah. Less is more. Everything else is solid. I can help y'all with the production search but try to grab a few DJ Premier tracks. I'd also look into Pete Rock, RZA, Large Professor... hold on a sec, I've got another call.

[Bryce takes call]

"Hey... how are you feeling? You know I feel terrible about this. That was never my intent. How are you even able to crack jokes right now? I'm ready for the number when you are. Repeat the last four digits. Two, six, zero, seven... okay cool. I'll transfer it now. It's the least I can do. Should hit your account in a few days. Can I call you right back? Of course, I still care about you. Okay. Gimme a second..."

[Bryce returns to Omari]

"Hey, O., let me finish this call. I'll hit y'all back if I hear anything else."

Is that the BET chick?

"No."

⌒

The guys flipped through more hip hop magazines on the hunt for chart-topping songs and underground favorites.

"We should turn this into a 'Best of' series," Brixx added. "T.S.U. Presents: The Best of the '90s and 2000s. Then we record the entire process and upload everything to the channel."

"Dope idea. Yo, we've definitely gotta do 'Quiet Storm,'" Omari referred to the classic Mobb Deep record.

"Queens," Brixx yelled. "My borough doesn't get enough love."

"Do you have the software that strips the vocals from the song in case we can't download the instrumentals?"

"That's an easy fix."

Being captured in a room of music and ideas turned Omari's prior dark mood into a radiance of light—like a harvest moon above still waters. His worries weren't lost, just set aside until the snare drums stopped, a hush settled in, and reality set in. If he could live inside a recording booth, he would. A pen and pad were his true friends, always there by his side, a refuge from the cold world and wicked forces near and far. His phone rang once more; it was another private number. One of these forces wanted his undivided attention.

22

—

CLOSING TIME

Bryce called on Dale for tips on how to eliminate the forceful smell of skunk that had nested on his BMW interior. It all happened the night before, after he was stuck at a traffic light with the wet carcass underneath. The timing couldn't have been worse; he was off to meet Alyssa for their much-anticipated happy hour date.

"You said to mix vinegar, water, dishwashing liquid, and spray it where?"

The tedious task of squirting the car's undercarriage would have to wait until the weekend. Bryce drove the rest of the way with the windows down, taking in the early autumn air, wondering how to approach Alyssa. Should he offer a warm hug or stick to their friendly fist bump? Should he pour on flattery or take things slowly? How would he deviate the conversation from fitness goals to personal life? If he got overtime pay for all this overthinking, he could've purchased a new vehicle with a glorious new car smell, just to ease his worries.

Why was he overanalyzing everything? He had gone on a multitude of dates, what was the big deal?

Alyssa was.

He pulled into the Ale House parking lot. The beautiful

brunette's fresh color blowout caught his eye from a distance as Alyssa stood by the main entrance amid a lively arriving crowd. She wore magenta pink work scrubs and a pair of black Nikes. A purse hung from her shoulder. He immediately rolled up the tinted windows as a cover to examine the location. It didn't make sense for his nerves to be on edge. By now, they had seen each other a handful of times and texted faithfully. He was in the driver's seat with a clear path to her heart if he wanted it. The only thing left was to overcome a growing insecurity about their racial backgrounds. He took a few deep breaths, popped a mint, and checked himself in the rearview mirror to make sure his face was clear of any substances. He exited the car to a band of people walking toward the hangout.

"Hey," she hollered out, smiling broadly. Confusion struck. Bryce offered a fist bump while she leaned in for a hug.

"Let's do both," he suggested, to her delight.

"How are you?"

"Good, and you?"

"Awesome."

"Don't mind my new skunk fragrance if you happen to smell anything. It just hit the market," he bantered.

"Skunk?"

"Long story. I promise I'll explain later."

"You look nice," she continued. "Clearly, I'm underdressed."

"Thank you. I'm still in my work clothes. You look amazing. I'm feelin' the hairstyle."

"Thank you." Alyssa smiled, holding onto the tips of her hair. "I'm so friggin' annoyed, though. I scheduled an appointment about two weeks ago and the lady who does my hair still squeezed in another appointment ahead of mine."

"Well, at least you got it done."

"I know, but it cut into my gym plans. Yesterday was supposed to be leg day. I had to walk the dog *twice* just to feel good about myself."

[Bryce laughs]

"It's not funny. I can't work out again until Sunday and that's a big maybe."

"I can work out for you. I don't mind two-a-days."

Bryce followed her inside where the strumming guitars of Hole's "Malibu" sounded above a raucous crowd. It was their first time at the tavern. As usual, Bryce read the room. He had never been so eager to conduct a head count of the number of minorities in attendance. A phrase Dale commonly verbalized was to "see and don't see"—a telling reminder to observe a situation without allowing the drawbacks to prevail. This was America. Being racially outnumbered came with the territory. He learned first-hand on the baseball diamond as a kid and presently in the corporate world. Yet it always made him wonder how other groups blended in so effortlessly, even in spaces where they were outnumbered, while Blacks were made to feel out of place.

The tavern's marginally diverse crowd was agreeable, but he was still at a disadvantage. Walking in with a smashing beauty could easily draw the attention of probable jealous men consumed by alcohol. Frankly, there weren't many looking to ruffle the feathers of a physical specimen such as Bryce, who could decimate you intellectually and pulverize you with a sharp right hand, but he remained on notice.

"I can't believe this song came out during my senior year in college. Feels like it was only yesterday," he smiled, nodding his head to the melody.

"You're seriously able to remember *that* far back? I can barely remember what I ate for dinner last night," Alyssa replied. "Oh, I hear they have weekly beer pongs here."

[hostess approaches]

"Hi guys. Are you okay with sitting at the bar or would you rather wait for table seating?"

Alyssa observed the wood panel-designed structure, finding the barstools. "How long is the wait?"

"I'd say another twenty to thirty minutes."

"Is there a drink minimum to sit there?" Bryce continued.

"No, you guys are fine."

"What do you think?" he asked Alyssa.

"Let's do it," she replied enthusiastically.

Bryce quietly twittered at his own warped sense of humor, thinking the music would stop and drinking glasses would shatter as they walked through the tavern. Excluding a mix of normal stares, the customers paid them no mind.

He gave Alyssa a full body overview from behind. She managed to dazzle even in a scrub set. The congenial spirits sat at the side of the bar, out of the presence of the hovering televisions set to the lone college football game of the evening. She sipped a lime margarita cocktail, recounting their first meeting at the optometrist office.

"I was joking with one of the girls on the job. I was like, 'Did you see our handsome new patient?'"

"Cut it out," he replied, turning up a Heineken bottle, locked into Alyssa's hazel green eyes.

"I swear. She was like, 'Um, yeah, he's gorgeous.'"

"I don't think I've ever been called gorgeous before."

"Probably unknowingly. You're some serious eye candy. Anyway, she's a lot older, but she was crushing on you heavily. I'm like, 'Um, hello, aren't you married?'"

"So, you guys analyze patients on company time?" he laughed.

"Only the cute ones," she disclosed. "We don't get many, which is why you were the hot topic that week."

The conversation turned personal. His prayers had been answered. During a friendly fun-fact game, Bryce learned the origin of Alyssa's middle name—Sophia—named after her grandmother. When it was his turn to share an unknown piece, she faced him crossing her legs and resting her chin on her hand.

"Okay, so sticking with the middle name theme, my middle name is Aaron. I was named after Hank Aaron."

"I've heard of him. Doesn't he have the most home runs or something?"

"Very impressive. He had the record for many years until Barry Bonds passed him. Do you know who Bonds is?"

"Um, he sounds familiar, but not really," Alyssa giggled.

"No worries. So, the theme on my dad's side was to name all of us after Black baseball legends. I'm Aaron—my dad usually calls me 'BAT' for short."

"BAT?"

"Bryce Aaron Taylor."

"Oh wow. That's so neat."

"Thanks. He almost named me 'Jackson' but my mom didn't like it."

"Who was Jackson?"

"Great follow-up question. Now you're just showing off."

[Alyssa bashfully laughs]

"So, Jackson would've been for Reggie Jackson. One of my father's favorites."

"I think I like Aaron better. I love the whole 'BAT' nickname. It goes in accordance with everything."

"Agreed. I don't know how easy it would've been calling me 'BJT.' How would you even pronounce that?"

Alyssa chortled with glee. "I know, right? *BA-JIT,*" she attempted.

"Exactly. All right, so next is my dad, the oldest of his siblings. His name is Dale, but friends and family call him Jackie."

"That's an easy one. Jackie Robinson."

"Uh-huh. His middle name is Robinson. Dale Robinson Taylor—the man with two last names. Then there's my uncle Willie, the second oldest. His actual first name is William-Gibson. The man with two first names."

Alyssa gave a bewildered look. "William-Gibson? That's like royalty."

"Hey, that's all my grandfather's doing. He took this naming thing seriously. Meanwhile, his name was Bill," he laughed. "Anyway, Uncle Willie has always been 'Uncle Gibby' to me. I'm gonna tell you a quick story. Promise me right now you won't laugh."

"Pinky swear."

"So, I was an exceptional reader as a child. We had encyclopedias everywhere, sometimes I'd even read the dictionary. True story. Anyway, for some reason I struggled with pronouncing my W's. I was three or four years old. Instead of Uncle Willie, I'd call him Uncle Gibby and the name just stuck."

"Aw, that is so cute. Okay, so, explain the other letters. How did the L's in his name turn into B's?" she giggled.

"What happened to the pinky swear?"

Alyssa covered her mouth. "Okay, okay. Let me try again."

"I'm just playing. So, your question is a good one. Let me go back in time and ask my three-year-old self."

[Alyssa chuckles]

"Here's the crazy part. No one ever corrected me."

"Well, Gibby could be short for Gibson, I guess."

"That's probably why."

"I'm sitting here trying to imagine you as a child. Can you say 'Willie' but in your best little kid voice?" Alyssa teased.

"Um, no."

"Please? Wait, was your uncle like the golden child?"

"Not really, but he did play in the Minor Leagues for a brief period. He's named after *Willie* Mays and Josh Gibson. See, I said it perfectly.

"That wasn't in a child's voice."

"I think my grandfather merged two of his favorite players for my uncle because he knew he wouldn't have any more boys."

"I'm fascinated by your family tree. There needs to be a documentary on this."

"I know. I've only told one other person the origins of our names so that should tell you something." Bryce winked, to which Alyssa gently squeezed his kneecap. He covered his hand over hers and a deep stare ensued. "Last would be my Aunt Paige, the baby of the bunch. She was named after Satchel Paige. By the look on your face, I'm assuming you don't know who that is."

"I'm sorry. I suck at baseball."

"This was before our time. He was a pitcher who started out in the Negro Leagues."

"That's awesome. You're a whole baseball encyclopedia. This is amazing."

"It was the glue that kept the men in the family together. You don't even wanna know about the card collection."

"Why not? Tell me."

"We'll have plenty of time for that."

"Did you ever play?"

Bryce scratched his beard. This was part of his story that had always been the most agonizing to share.

"I did. Started out in Little League around eight years old and played until college. I was scouted by a few Major League teams in high school but elected to go to a D1 school on a scholarship. Almost immediately I suffered a severe shoulder injury and ruptured my Achilles heel while tracking a ball in the outfield."

"Aw..."

"Yup. I struggled to regain my form and had to immediately think of a plan B."

"Bryce, that's terrible. I'm so sorry," she empathized, rubbing the side of his arm as a show of support. He took a deep breath before proceeding. "It's all good. I wouldn't have become a gym nut if not for the injuries. Are you bored yet?"

"Are you kidding? I love hearing the backstories of others. I hope I didn't dampen the mood."

"We're good. I look at it like this, life is one big book, right? That was just one of many chapters. When one chapter is complete, you turn the page."

"That is so true. You have such a great perspective."

Over the next half hour, Bryce found out about Alyssa's childhood summers visiting Action Park, her high school soccer team winning state championships in consecutive years, and how a shared rock song favorite was really about crystal meth addiction. More astounding to learn was her father's fatal heart attack when she was eleven years old. Ironically, their deceased parents died the same year.

[Bruce Springsteen's "Hungry Heart" plays in the background]

"Of course, they'd play Bruce Springsteen tonight," Alyssa exasperatingly expressed.

"Jersey's own."

"My dad was extremely critical of his music, according to my mom."

"Really? This is one of my favorite songs."

"He was a Billy Joel guy. Of course, I had to follow."

Alyssa voiced frustration about having to move back home with her widowed mother and younger sister after a seesaw relationship with an ex-boyfriend ended. She explained how he had betrayed her trust, became verbally abusive, and neglected to pay his share of bills, leaving them without electricity and nearly evicted from their apartment. In fact, she temporarily lived out of a hotel room just to remove herself from the hairy situation. Sheer embarrassment was the only thing keeping her from informing her loved ones. One day, she broke down to an old colleague, who provided shelter until she found enough courage to clue her family in.

"I stayed with her for about six months. She was so sweet and kind. I never thought I'd be in a situation like that. It just sucks, cuz I used to stick up for this guy even when my mom and sister saw warning signs. I *knew* he was a prick, but I thought by being a good influence I could... how do I say this... not change him, but tweak a few of his prickish ways."

"That's understandable. People change people," Bryce acknowledged.

"Right. But at the time I didn't realize people need to grow tired of themselves to make changes. He was such an arrogant ass who thought he could do no wrong. I guess I can chalk it up to being in my twenties and gullible."

"I get it. Such a deadly mix. How's the old saying go? Youth is wasted on the young?"

"It's true. Anyway, the good thing is my sister is moving out. She's getting a place with her fiancé so that'll free up some space. For the past few years, I've been crammed in the basement with the dog. The basement is huge, but it gets super cold. I've been saving up for a condo or a ranch home, so hopefully that'll manifest soon."

Bryce could detect pain in her eyes. She was too much of a light to have been sheathed in darkness. He wanted to hold her in his arms and make her heart flutter by asking if she would allow him to love her. It would have been an impulsive move, but that was the type of guy he was. Besides, it was better than extending an invitation to his home. An exorbitant amount of momentum had already been gained for him to waste it on a sexual urge. Whatever was happening tonight was much more.

"Do you still want to play 'fun fact', or shall we switch it up?"
"Let's do a couple more. I've got one." She put on her glasses, directing him to her cell phone wallpaper. "Remember I told you how much I loved tigers?"

"That's a great pic."
"Thanks. I have it tatted on my ribcage. I would show you, but…"
"I'm sure I'll see it one day…"
"I love your confidence."
"Oh, I didn't mean it like that…"
"Mm-hmm, you sure 'bout that?"
"I take it I'm not a good liar."
"But wait, there was more to the animal thing. I'm in the process of adopting an elephant," she shockingly announced.
"An elephant? I would've never guessed."
"Yup." Alyssa sorted through her photo gallery. "His name is

Briscoe. Isn't he adorable? I was thinking about working at an elephant sanctuary with my sister out in Thailand. This was long before she got engaged. I don't know what it is, but I positively love elephants."

"Cute guy. I don't think I've ever put those two words together."

[Alyssa laughs]

"Oh, and did you know yesterday was National Elephant Appreciation Day?"

"Really? Who comes up with this crap?"

"I know, right? People actually get paid to come up with these things. Well, that was my fun fact. Your turn."

"How can I beat that? All right, well, maybe you'll like this one..."

"What?"

"I'm ambidextrous."

"No way."

"Are you?" Bryce asked, thinking they shared yet another thing in common.

"No, but that's so cool. How'd that happen, did you break your arm or something?"

"Close. I fractured my right wrist—wore a cast for about two months and kinda taught myself how to use my left hand. Then..." Bryce paused mid-sentence, shaking his head.

"What's wrong?"

"I was just going to say since I'm someone who lives for chal-lenges, I thought what would be better than to learn how to operate both hands?"

"I love it."

"It's okay. You can call me a goof if you want to."

"No way. I'm completely blown away at how much we have in common."

"My father was already teaching me how to bat left-handed before the injury."

"Oh, like a switch-hitter?" she asked to his surprise.

"You're certainly earning your share of points tonight."

"I had to make up for not knowing who those baseball players were."

Bryce smiled. "Anyway, he thought I'd be more valuable as a switch hitter so I kinda had a head start doing left-handed things. From there, I'd practice my signature using my left hand and just about anything else."

"Your dad was so invested in you. That's amazing."

"I can't complain. Great guy and even better parent. I can 'fun fact' all night if you want."

"So can I."

He continued. "Did I ever tell you I used to watch the Weather Channel just for the jazz music?"

"That's hilarious."

"Tell me about it. They had some jams though. I'd keep it on for hours while cleaning up the house."

"I don't think I can top that. Let me think. Oh, here's something. I can name every state capital."

"Really?"

"Uh-huh. So, back in fifth grade, I was part of a school contest. I got all the way to the finals and choked. I couldn't name the capital of Montana."

"Isn't it Billings?"

"No. I thought it was Anaconda. I can't remember why I chose that but turns out it's Helena."

"Aw man. I would've gotten smoked."

"I still have nightmares about it," she laughed. "Okay, I have something for you Mister Movie-Guy. Name one movie you *have* to watch each summer."

"Oh, that's easy. *The Sandlot*. I don't care how old I am. It takes me down memory lane to my childhood."

"I love that movie. I used to watch it with my brother."

"Did he play ball?"

"Well, he did for a short while..." she paused, flipping her hair sensuously. "He's actually gay, so the whole athletic thing disappeared."

"Oh. Okay. Well, there are plenty of gays in sports. No judgment."

"Yeah, one day he went from playing every sport imaginable to suddenly showing an interest in cosmetology. I love him to death but at first, I was like, 'Um... Michael, what's happening?'"

[light laughter]

"He runs a hair salon in the city." Alyssa added.

"Nice. Hey, he's still family at the end of the day. What about you?"

"What, am I gay?" Alyssa laughed.

"No, silly. Name your must-watch summer flick."

"Wet Hot American Summer."

"Damn. You didn't hesitate for one second."

"Oh my gosh, I love that movie. Have you seen it?"

"No. Is that some type of porn?"

"No. You have to watch it. If you like *The Office,* I think you'd appreciate it."

[Bryce's cell phone rings]

Tasha's unsuspecting call was immediately sent to voicemail. Nothing was going to rain on his parade—not even the vicious curves of a woman he had the hots for. He didn't owe Alyssa an explanation but proceeded to give one anyway, alleging the call came from his brother. Guilt crept in like a thief in the night.

He weighed in on what Tasha's phone call was about. She should've been resting for her overnight shift at the nursing home. He sent a quick message as Alyssa placed an order for French onion soup.

> Hey. I'm out with friends. Reception is bad here. I'll call you later.

It was halfway true.

"Are you going to eat anything?" Alyssa asked.

Bryce had an appetite for the meal seated before him, standing at about five feet six inches with neatly parted hair, pink bow-shaped lips, and a radiant smile.

"I should. I was thinking about picking up a chicken cheesesteak on the way home. In no way am I implying that we leave now. Don't even think about it."

"I was about to say, are you sick of me already?"

"Heck no. Do you know how long I've waited for this? We're gonna talk 'til we're both blue in the face."

"I'm so down, but I wouldn't want you to starve yourself. You're more than welcome to try my soup."

"I'm not much of a soup guy, but I'm usually willing to try anything once. This quesadilla looks delicious," he pointed at the menu.

Enough small talk. It was time to break the ice. As the legendary hockey hall of famer Wayne Gretzky said: "You miss one hundred percent of the shots you don't take." Surprisingly, it was Alyssa's sharp tongue that chipped away first.

"So, what's a handsome guy like you doing single?"

"Who, little ole me?"

"Little? You're like a friggin' giant compared to me. What are you, six-six?"

"Six-four. So, you're gonna put me on the spot?"

"Absolutely. C'mon, it'll be fun."

"Trust me, I've got a well-thought-out answer for you. I just wouldn't know where to begin."

He waited a long time for this and delivered it fittingly. So much so that Alyssa's broiling soup turned into a quick freeze. She was attracted to how well he verbalized himself. It was the first time she heard a man speak so fervently about his likes, dislikes, desires, and expectations. Through their conversation, Bryce endorsed Kristen without signifying regret, admitting to the role he played in their abrupt finish. In the same breath, he revealed his reason for remaining single and incredibly denounced his womanizing ways. Saving the best for last, he finally came clean about his feelings.

"I can't believe how much I'm blushing right now," she acknowledged. "I'm at a loss for words."

"You asked for it."

"I did. Thank you for that. You're so sweet. Did it just get hot in here or is it just me?" she asked, fanning herself.

"Definitely you." He whistled, using two fingers to his mouth. "Okay, I said a mouthful. I'm putting the spotlight back on you. Before you get started, let me ask this, what, if anything, are you looking for?"

[Bryce's cell phone vibrates]

Sexy Neighbor: Whatever.

Fri 7:32 p.m.

"Well just for the record, I've been celibate for three years. In no way am I insinuating that this is your intention, but I made a promise to myself that I wouldn't sleep with anyone unless I was in a committed relationship. I'm not into the whole fuck buddy thing. At the same token, I've learned not to jump into relationships either. I'd much rather take my time and get to know the person."

"Absolutely. I wouldn't have it any other way."

"I'll be perfectly honest with you; I think you're super-hot. You seem like a great guy. I really enjoy how easy it is to talk to you."

"I appreciate that. By the way, Black men don't blush, but nice try."

"You're smart, funny, the conversations are light-hearted... we have quite a few things in common, there's good synergy here. It's like we've known each other for years."

"I feel a 'but' coming on..."

"Nope. No buts. I can't believe I'm about to tell you this but... remember when you asked to exchange numbers? It was the second time we chatted in front of the gym."

"How could I forget?"

"So, I was dying for you to ask. At first, I was like, 'Hmm, maybe I'm not his type.'"

Bryce looked at her like she had three heads. His jaw dropped down to his quesadilla.

"What's wrong?" she asked him.

"Do you know how much I beat myself up that night?"

"No way."

"*Yes* way. I thought about it on the ride home that evening and the following morning on my commute to work." He shook his head. "I felt like such an amateur."

"Oh my God. I thought it was me. Like maybe I had bad breath or something. I even told my sister afterward."

"That's crazy. I'm flattered though," Bryce replied, using prayer hands. "Well, since I've opened up a can of worms, I can honestly say I've been drawn to you since the first time we met, but I thought it would've been distasteful hollering at you at the workplace."

"I wish the old men who come to the office thought that way."

"Well, you were fair game once we bumped into each other at the gym."

"All I can say is thank God I switched gyms."

The burning question remained. Would Alyssa be receptive to exploring a relationship with someone outside of her ethnicity? She was warmhearted and easy-going, someone who appeared unfettered by dating trends and antiquated societal rules. It was safe to assume she was all in, however it was a subject worth discussing.

"I'd be remiss not to ask this. Let's say one day, we woke up and decided to give a relationship a try, how would your family respond to the whole interracial thing?"

[The Outfield's "Your Love" plays in the background]

She rotated the straw in her glass, beaming at his question. "For starters, my mom would adore you. I'm not just saying that to say it. She absolutely would. I think you and my brother will get along. He's the oldest so he's still very protective but in a chill way. Um, my sister Danielle would bug me to death to double-date. She's always trying to get me back into the dating pool for that reason alone."

"Terrible."

"I know, right? They're sports addicts so don't be surprised if they start buggin' you to go to a few games. Hypothetically speaking, of course."

"Yes. All hypotheticals."

"As far as the interracial thing, I've *mainly* dated Black and Latin men. My ex was Colombian. That was about three years of my life I'll never get back. The guy before him was Trinidadian."

"Interesting."

"Honestly, I haven't dated a White guy in a long time. Come to think of it, I haven't dated many people at all. What a sheltered life I've lived," she chuckled. "I'm a relationship or bust kinda gal. I guess based on my past, you can say I have a preference, but I'm simply into *good* people. Treat me with respect and we'll go a long way. But these guys today, man. They show themselves as one way and then it's like a switch goes off and they turn into complete assholes."

"My father always says there's a person you *want to be*, a person you want to be *viewed as,* and then there's the person *you are.*"

"Ooh, I love that. Can I steal it?"

"He might charge you."

"Sometimes I think I'm gonna grow into an old lady with cats."

Not if he could help it.

Alyssa's admission took him by surprise, but she was equally amazed to learn that even with Bryce's magnetic personality and charming looks, he never dated outside of Black and Latin. For Bryce, it was back to square one. Another woman holding out until the "right situation" came along. The difference was Alyssa wasn't a cock tease.

He left a generous tip to the bartender, and together they marched through the standing crowd. Their conversation extended into the parking lot as if the almost three-hour chat at the tavern wasn't enough. She removed her glasses and exposed her face more. The look in her eye was that of a person trying to fight off a burning attraction while also signaling Bryce to make a move. He was conflicted, stuttering over words. Somewhere Porky Pig smiled, and his incoherence was likely causing Candace to roll in her grave. She taught him better.

"Don't look at me like that."

"Like what?" she playfully contested.

He offered a hug and observantly pecked Alyssa on the cheek. Her gold necklace caught hold of the button of his polo shirt, which made things awkward.

"Looks like you're stuck with me," she discerned.

He struggled momentarily to untangle her jewelry. It was their longest face-to-face encounter yet. One could only imagine the outcome if he mistakenly went in for the kiss. He was a gambling man, but the stakes were too high to take the risk. At least the cheek kiss would make up for their topsy-turvy embrace at the start of the evening.

He wanted to honor her wishes and take things slowly now that their feelings were on the table. The question remained: How long could the nymphomaniac keep up the act with a rapid dry spell approaching and hypersexual women at his feet?

"This was great, Bryce. I enjoyed every minute."

"Agreed. We've gotta do it again sometime," he replied, grabbing hold of her hand. "Not to be a pain but text me once you've made it home."

"I will. Are you *always* this sweet?"

He watched Alyssa pull off before giving Tasha a call. Maybe she took the night off and had finally come around. After their steamy summer, she had to have wanted it as much as he did. The phone rang incessantly until the automated voicemail began. He waited a few minutes before placing another call. This time it went directly to voicemail without an explanatory text to follow. Third time being the charm, he was greeted with the automated voicemail after two rings. Tasha had given him a dose of his own medicine. The blow to his ego led to his next mission, reaching out to another contact who seemed ready to put out.

Tell your job to stop changing your mail route. The text read.

Almost immediately, Joy replied.

23

———

WARNING

Omari had hit rock bottom, pleasuring himself to the scores of young women on the internet gyrating to the latest hip hop dance tracks in the skimpiest of clothing. He wiped himself down and stared into the bathroom mirror, marginally ashamed. At only twenty-two years old, he was reduced to the ratchetness of YouTube as a means of enjoyment in fear of contaminating others. His cry for sex was set off by the swift broken box spring sounds penetrating the kitchen ceiling as he prepared a snack. Brixx's parents probably thought he was immersed in music to catch wind of their hanky-panky. They thought wrong.

"Zeus, get down," Omari instructed the house pet.

He was back in the basement, finishing a turkey and cheese sandwich. A catnap was probable after a long day of uninspired writing and recording. In another hour, Brixx would be home from work, fully wired after downing two Red Bulls in preparation for their all-nighter. Omari could regroup then. In the meantime, he grabbed a bed sheet, laid it across the surface of the futon, and plopped onto his back. He set his phone alarm for thirty minutes and listened to "Dreams & Visions", his now completed song reflecting a young man in dire straits.

Had dreams, had visions, made a couple of bad decisions
Bounced back, spit raps, tried to stay out of prison
Did that, young and Black, (why aren't u proud?)
Cuz I slipped up, no rubber stuck with a child
Lost and confused, I'm going backwards my dude
I'm slacking, my dude, this can't be happening, my dude
That's me talking to God, He knew of my plans
But right now, He ain't hearing it, He gave me the hand...
Aw damn, outta luck, unemployed, no bucks
Girlfriend's getting fat, life really starts to suck
Why me, this is bullshit, I didn't deserve this
(I haven't been to church in years) I'm thinking He did this on
purpose
Stressed out, can't lie, contemplated suicide
Shorty looked me in the eye, saw a man who lost his pride
Didn't care, she was having this baby
I'm thinkin' maybe she'll miscarry since she's not having an a-b-o-r-
t-i-o-n, life's a test
We had one before, how I get back in this mess?
Not ready for fatherhood, I don't want a family
Only want money for self, NOT for a Nanny
Chill, this can't be, I'm talking to my Grammy
She's the only one who really understands me
Mom's disappointed, Pop's a bit confused
His dad just passed, how's he gonna handle this news?
Asked God to take me then, but I kept waking up
How am I gonna tell my friends? Phone calls I start to duck
Felt trap, no hope, back to totin' L's
Damage my brain cells if all else fails
But then I realized I was brain-dead based on my actions
Got caught up in a moment of passion
All of this happened for a reason
'Lessons of Life,' a book I suggest you start reading
If you plan on keeping your sanity, your dreams alive
Then you'll wrap up before gettin' in between them thighs

Now two dilemmas face me
Will I care about this baby? And do I really care about this lady?
Girlfriend, baby-mom, don't know what to call her
Do I stick around for our son or daughter?
If not, I'm a deadbeat, but you don't know my story
I wanted to go on Maury to hear him say "You're not the father!"
Now I don't wanna be bothered... that wasn't the case
Cuz when I look at my son... I see my face...

Omari dozed off before the song's completion, his phone planted on his chest. The gutsy verse quickly became a favorite. He hoped to attract an older demographic by paying homage to hip hop's greatest storytellers. As Bryce often reminded him, a young songwriter who didn't glorify the decimation of the Black community was the cream of the crop. Those within his circle were convinced that Omari could secure a record deal on the spot if the heartrending verse was performed at the open mic invitation.

A startling buzz to his chest jolted him from a light sleep. He struggled to lift his head—his consciousness was in a tug of war with a lifeless body. The only light in the basement was that of the Pro Tools software exhibited on the computer screen. The steady buzzing continued. The reverberation of the phone jammed his chest, producing a burning twinge. He yelled out at the top of his lungs to awaken an unresponsive body. His screams were ignored. The short sample of sleep paralysis could've been a result of bad weed. Whatever it was, he was scared stiff.

What seemed everlasting was only carried on for a few minutes. His frantic eyes opened, examining the room where Zeus rested comfortably in the center of the floor. Omari looked at his iPhone—the time read 11:50 p.m. Brixx's shift was almost over. There were two missed calls minutes apart, one from a private number, the other unknown. Neither left a voicemail. Such bizarre timing for anyone to play phone games. He turned on the recessed lights now showing signs of life. His phone rang again. It was a private call.

"Who the fuck is this? Hello?"

"What'chu doing, Pop?"

Reading one of these class action settlement letters I got in the mail. Would you believe I won a whopping nine dollars and forty-one cents?

"God is good."

All the time.

"That's enough money to raid the dollar menu at McDonald's. Are you all set for the trip?"

Terri's packed. I've got to get started. My back flared up on me the other day and...

"Get started? Aren't y'all leaving on Sunday?"

Aye, why don't you come over and lend your old man a hand then.

"Oh, now you wanna pull out the 'old man' victim card. I'm about to head out. Hire some help with that nine-dollar settlement money."

That's what I thought.

"I still can't believe y'all been married five years already. Where is the time going?"

I can't believe it either. That boy almost made it the world's fastest divorce. Don't tell her I said that.

[laughter]

"You've got to tell me how New Orleans is. We've been floating around a few places for our end-of-the-year trip."

Terri's been out there with her sister before, and your Aunt Paige went out there a few years ago. I'm not much of a New Orleans guy but she sold me on the food choices.

Well, happy anniversary. I'll shoot Terri a text in a little while. Oh, I meant to ask you, what's your take on Steve Jobs?"

Wasn't that a shame? How old was he? He couldn't have been older than me.

"I'm checking now... uh, says here he was only fifty-six."

Wow. See? That's why I tell you, BAT, life is short. I know the man was ill, but when the Lord comes calling, that's that.

"I hear you. I wonder how this will affect the price of Apple stock."

Well, if it's cheap, I'd say it's probably time to gobble that up.

"Let me see... looks like it's close to twelve dollars a share. You're right, I should hop on that."

[text alert]

> I Think I Might Wife Her: What do you call a running chicken?
>
> Fri 7:32 p.m.

"All right, Pop, let me get ready. I'll holla at y'all before Sunday."

What'chu about to do?

"Heading over to a friend's house for movie night. Oh, and don't make too much of this but I think I'm getting close to settling down."

Good. Have you been in communication with that Kristen girl?

"I haven't. Pop, there are millions of other women roaming the Earth."

Yes, but you ain't gonna find many as solid as her.

"I beg to differ. I think the person I'm considering might give Kristen a run for her money."

All right, well, as long as she makes you happy.

Bryce pulled up to Joy's Edison, New Jersey home where he immediately scoped out the scene. The house was sizable for a single woman. A white Mercedes-Benz and a red Ford Explorer sat in the driveway. They hadn't spoken much since she jotted her number on a piece of paper, but things would significantly ramp up as he connivingly moved pieces on his personal dating chessboard.

Joy informed him of her stance on motherhood. Family was the most important part of her life, and in a wily way, she viewed the male anatomy a distant second. Of her four children, the oldest was the only one not to have a relationship with the biological father. Mom was all he knew—he was labeled as "the overprotector." Once again, Bryce found himself in an undesirable position all for the thrill of seduction.

A running chicken?? Hmm... I'm thinking.

His visit to Joy's was seen as payback to Tasha—a woman who dared to value herself rather than become a pawn in his game. He didn't have the patience to deal with someone substandard when there were others milling around who could serve as suitable replacements. The idea that he hadn't spent time with Joy was irrelevant. All that mattered was their mutual attraction, and her assertive side excited him.

Ok, I give up...

Bryce turned off the car engine and let Joy know of his arrival. A hand was seen shifting the living room curtain. There were no guarantees about tonight, but he came prepared, hoping to entice her with a certified panty-dropper newly scented cologne.

The petite mail carrier greeted him at the front door as he entered the dark home.

"Ma, who's here?" a deep unseen voice asked. It was her oldest son.

"Mind your business," she answered, hurrying Bryce into the first-floor bedroom. More footsteps raced along the top of the stairs. They weren't going to be alone.

"That better not be *Jersey Shore*. Please don't tell me."

"This is my guilty pleasure," she laughed, covering her mouth.

One of the straps to her white tank top fell from her shoulder—her nipples peeked through the loungewear. He sat at the foot of the bed and handed her a bootlegged version of the movie *Contagion,* a film about a contagious virus effectuating a global pandemic.

"You want something to drink?"

"I'll have water."

Joy reached for her robe. Before she momentarily departed, he caught a glimpse of her curves from the corner of his eye. It was his first time observing her pint-sized body outside of that monotone work uniform, and she looked amazing. Suddenly, there was an urge to bury his face in between her legs.

[Bryce's cell phone vibrates]

I Think I Might Wife Her: Fast food :)

Fri 8:03 p.m.

"My little one is so damn nosy," Joy announced, returning with a water bottle. "She's like, 'Mommy, is somebody here? Can I see them?'"

"That's cute," he replied, fighting to hide the disappointment. He sat against the headboard of her king-size bed. She proceeded to explain the characters and scenes of a mind-numbing fourth-season episode. The longer he glanced at her the more he appreciated her beauty. She came off timid as evident by the constant mouth covering but somewhere in the depths of her core lived an untamed beast. One would think she had to be, in raising three boys.

"Has anyone ever told you how much you resemble Keke Wyatt?"

"All day, every day..."

"Y'all *must* be related. What's your background?"

"Uh, Black..."

"And what else?"

"Y'all kill me with that. Just cuz I'm light-skinned doesn't mean I'm mixed."

"Don't let me find your family tree. I know there's a 'Bob' or 'Beth' somewhere," he joked.

She playfully slapped his chest before proceeding. "Damn, what you got under there, a body armor suit? You almost broke my nail." She rubbed her hand against his pecs a second time to stimulate a rise. "No, you *didn't* just flex your pec muscle. Do it again," she demanded.

"Don't start. Not with your kids wide awake."

"Please. I'm not thinking about them. They know the routine. Don't bother Mommy unless there's an emergency. Most nights, I'm in my room resting up for the next day, and they're going about their business. They just wanna know who's here."

They continued watching the nauseating reality show. Joy's head rested comfortably on his chest and her hand settled across his stomach. The more jokes Bryce cracked the more she covered her mouth. He would soon find out why. Through all of her natural beauty, there was a distinguishable gap between her incisors, about as wide as a football goal post. It wouldn't take away from the attraction—especially with her hand advancing to his midsection.

"I can't believe I'm watching this nonsense. What about the movie?"

She snuggled up closer. "We've got time unless you're tired. Can I just watch this last episode?"

[hard knocks on the bedroom door]

"Ma, whose car is that in the driveway?" the familiar deep voice asked through the door.

"Didn't I tell you to mind your business, Dae'Quan?"

"I'm just asking a question."

"And I gave you an answer. Mind your business. You ain't down here any other time."

"What about me, Mom, can I know?" another voice inquired.

Things weren't looking good.

"That's one of the twins. These kids are gonna be the death of me."

She wasn't the only one.

"I'll be right back. And don't turn off the show either..." Joy slammed the bedroom door. Bryce sat still as a statue. The forecast for their evening appeared stormy. What in the world had he gotten himself into?

Tonight's visit was about adding another body count to his résumé, but what sense would it make to stick around with her pesky meddling kids running roughshod? He could've had a little fun if it weren't for their obtrusive ways. Suddenly, he felt like a captured villain in the old *Scooby-Doo* cartoon.

> Fast food?? I should've gotten that one.
> Loving this...

"I'm sorry about that," Joy replied upon her return. Bryce placed his phone face down onto the nightstand.

"All good. Not that it's a big deal, but I thought you said your oldest was spending the night at his friend's."

"Yeah, so, about that. He hurt his ankle during football practice and can't put any pressure on his right foot."

"Yikes."

"I told him he should rest instead of rushing to leave. He asked if I could drive him over there before you got here but I told him no, so he caught a little attitude."

"Oh. Are those your vehicles in the driveway?"

"The truck is his, but it needs repair. Do you know this kid had the nerve to ask if he could drive *my* car with his bad ankle?"

"Hilarious."

"I had eye surgery about a year ago and needed to be driven around for a week. Ever since then he thinks my car is his."

"Teenage entitlement. Good luck."

"Don't I know. You're like the first guy I've met without kids. I'm still blown away by that."

"I'm a rarity. The last of a dying breed. Guys like me should be celebrated. We should have our own national holiday."

"With all that junk down there, I'm surprised you ain't knock anyone up," Joy replied, referencing the explicit photos she requested weeks back. "Let me find out if you play for the other team."

"Here we go. So, just because I'm childless, that's what you automatically assume? What if I'm just a responsible adult? Better yet, what if I don't want kids?"

"Hmpfh... please."

"If you don't get your little narrow-minded behind outta here," he teased. "What do you call women without children?"

[Bryce sniffs the air]

"You smell that?"

"Smell what?"

"Smells like a double standard cuz you *know* you wouldn't have the same feeling."

"Anyway."

"I rest my case."

"Women can have pregnancy complications."

"And men can have infertility issues. You wanna keep playing? I've got time today."

[light laughter]

"Switching topics, do you think I should introduce myself to your son just to smooth things over?"

"He'll be alright. I'm allowed to have company. I run this house, not him."

Joy's plan to talk Bryce into horseplay crashed and burned when her black stallion drifted off during the opening scene. He awakened in a blur, fully clothed with the television volume loud. He was completely aroused in a spoon position, struggling to recall if they had sex. Joy was half-naked. The fact that his clothes were on concluded they had not.

Crossing his mind was the idea that he might've missed

making a good first impression. A lot was riding on tonight, his reputation for one.

He thought about waking her up to the magical ride of cunnilingus. It was how he awakened Kristen from a slumber when he was in the mood. She loved it and it usually had her walking on air. A performance of such was usually best reserved for someone he had history with. A hint of upstairs movement paused the thought when one of Joy's children raced down the stairs to the kitchen. It was only one in the morning, but the night was officially a dud. He departed Joy's home, surprisingly unannoyed. Even as Dae'Quan peered at the top of the staircase, talking to friends over his gaming headset. *I should've followed through and ate her out just to spite him,* he reflected.

Bryce habitually circled his deficiencies with each encounter. Tonight was about exuding patience—something he battled against Tasha. In hindsight, the night wasn't half bad. He was granted access to Joy's home without spending a dime. Uncommon in the dating world. Secondly, she made passes at him all night long. As far as he was concerned, one foot was in the door, the other not quite in the grave.

～

SATURDAY EVENING

Unfortunately for Omari, a "sinus infection" caused him to miss the outstanding talent show performances at the famous BB King's Blues Club & Grill. Hopefully, another opportunity would present itself down the line. In the meantime, after months of stimulating texts and scheduling conflicts, Bryce and Yvonne finally got together. After the event, they wandered the streets of midtown Manhattan in search of a Halal food truck.

It was a crisp fall evening; hoodie season—Bryce's favorite. He reverted to his low haircut, dressed up in a light army-green flight jacket, white hoodie, and sky-blue jeans. Yvonne wore a tawny brown waist-length jacket, matching knee-high boots, and dark blue denim. She was a plus-size woman, and he found her more than appealing. Most men did.

The pictures on her dating profile focused on her pretty face, the selfies and steamy video clips targeted her seductive side and private areas. Yvonne's breasts could've had their own zip code; the same could be said about her backside. One of her hobbies was applying make-up. She was superb at it. Her face looked professionally done; the matte red lipstick and smokey eye really complemented her brown skin tone.

Bryce swallowed his pride as they walked arm-in-arm through the crowded city blocks. This was only a leverage move to propel Omari's music career. Otherwise, it was laughable to expect him to emotionally attach himself to someone who willingly put him off for six months. Okay, so maybe a micro-fraction of thought was given to curing his sex itch. How could he not? Just hours before, he rewatched a video of Yvonne inserting a sex toy into her innermost sacred area, gushing onto The Fontainebleau hotel bed sheets. The image would live in his head rent-free.

They arrived at the West 47th Street parking garage where Bryce retrieved his car. Though she arrived by subway, he graciously offered to drop her off at her Downtown Brooklyn home.

"I appreciate it," he announced to the valet attendant, handing over a generous tip. Blaring from the radio was René & Angela's "I'll Be Good." Yvonne sat comfortably in the passenger seat, admiring the car's cleanliness and sweet-scented smell.

"You can *still* smell the new car scent. How long have you had it?"

"I bought it at the end of last year, so almost a year now."

"I like it. I remember stalking your page once and finding a pic where you were standing in front of it at a parking lot."

"Oh, yeah? Just once?"

"I swear. You had sunglasses on with your arms folded. I was like, 'Mmm, look at all that chocolate.'"

"That's funny. That was my main pic for a while. I'm just glad the car smells better. I drove for the better part of two weeks with the smell of skunk. It was crazy. What's the matter? Why are you looking at me like that?"

"Like what?"

"You're giving me the googly eyes."

"I'm just admiring your handsomeness. Do you always drive that way?"

"How am I driving?"

"Like you're deep in thought. Look at you all smooth with one hand on the wheel. You have no idea what that does to me," she shuddered.

"Cut it out."

"Did you not expect me to look at you? I *finally* get to see you in person."

"That's on you. You were the one too busy for me."

"You know that wasn't on purpose. I was away on assignment every other week and then I had to set up a production crew for these summer music festivals. Don't get me wrong, I love my job, but I couldn't even get time to myself."

"Except for the time you went to South Beach…"

"Oh, well, nothing was getting in the way of that," she giggled. "It was bikini season, so…"

"Speaking of admiring, let's talk about those videos. I don't take being teased kindly. You're starting trouble."

"How? I told you I'm a very sexual person."

"I see that. No judgment. So am I. I'm just saying first we were talking about horoscope signs and the next thing I know you're sticking a baseball bat inside your girl.'"

"A baseball bat? You're being extra," Yvonne laughed. "I had to spice things up a bit and show you what you're dealing with."

"Noted. Between that and your voice, I'd say you have quite a future ahead of you. If you ever decide to switch careers, let me know. I can be your agent."

"Uh, no. I worked too hard for my degree to go that route, but..."

"Don't knock it 'til you try it. It could be a side hustle. Where'd you go to school again?"

"SUNY Albany. I was gonna say you can be more than my agent if I decided to."

"Oh, so you wanna mix business with pleasure."

"Is there something wrong with that?"

"That's not really my thing."

"I can make it your thing," Yvonne suggested, grabbing onto his crotch.

"See what I mean? You've got the porn dialogue down pat. I'm telling you, I see dollar signs."

Yvonne wouldn't let go of her grip. Bryce's erection grew. He was driving above the speed limit on the FDR when she unbuckled her seatbelt, put her box braided hairstyle in a bun, and unzipped his pants. Of all his sexual adventures—which once included sex on the shoulder of the Garden State Parkway during a heavy rainstorm—driving while receiving oral wasn't one of them. She inhaled him and proceeded with felicitous slurping sounds. God help them if he were to crash.

He considered parking along the overpass on South St. as they approached entry to the Brooklyn Bridge, but the adrenaline kept his foot on the gas. Unthinkably, he never ejaculated from oral sex. He was too busy striving for immorality in the minds of his partners to even allow them fifteen minutes of fame. The sensation of Yvonne's luscious lips and the anxiety of a potential car accident factored in his woeful streak continuing. She removed his succulence. Their eyes met at once.

"What's wrong, Daddy, you didn't like it?"

"I loved it. You ain't feel the car swerve?"

"So, come for me," she demanded, biting the corner of her lip. "You had this big dick energy the other day. I told you it was on when I saw you." Her tongue emerged for another taste as he placed his right hand over her head. The night lights of the Brooklyn Bridge glowed through the windshield.

~

"Make a left here," she instructed, as they pulled up to her Brooklyn Heights neighborhood in one piece. Still sexually charged, Yvonne gathered herself. The look in her eye suggested a call for Bryce to come upstairs but he was unprepared. Omari's eleventh-hour cancellation being one of the reasons. Bryce fully anticipated the three of them grouped together for the evening and neglected to bring protection. Whatever the case, she was a woman on a mission.

"Are you gonna let me finish the job or are you scared?"

"Do I look scared? I'm just concerned about parking. It's gonna take forever to find a spot. Also, where's the closest drug store? I didn't bring any condoms."

"We're good on that. I've got a drawer full." The comment wouldn't upset him. Yvonne was a single woman free to do whatever she pleased. Better to be safe than sorry.

"How do you know which type of condoms I use?"

"You're a 'gold member.' It's obvious. I only mess with your types anyway."

"A gold member? Who am I, Austin Powers?" he laughed. "I feel exclusive. Please, tell me more."

"You know *exactly* what I'm talking about."

She was confident, brash, almost intimidating in a way. They were a sexual match made in heaven. Bryce sat double-parked on the narrow street with his hazard lights flashing as he motioned a van behind to go around. She grabbed her belongings. "At least come upstairs and eat your food," she offered, leaning inside the passenger window. It was ten-thirty. Enough time to warm up his chicken and rice platter, fool around, and startle the neighbors of the six-storied apartment. Conversely, apprehension struck after surveying a text.

> I Think I Might Wife Her: You're probably
> asleep… missed hearing your voice (even
> though we chatted yesterday lol). If I'm being
> weird tell me. I meant to send you these pics
> earlier. Aren't they beautiful? Gonna take
> Bailey for a quick walk then call it a night.
>
> Sat 10:03 p.m.

Guilt swarmed over him like a colony of angry bees. He needed to think fast.

"Give me a hug just in case I can't find parking. I'll circle the neighborhood and see if anything pops up. If not, let's schedule a rain check ASAP."

"Mm-hmm."

"I'm serious. You think I wanna go home like *this?*" he exclaimed, looking down at the expanding bulge in his slim-fit jeans.

"You don't have to."

He exited the car for a warm exaggerated hug. Yvonne playfully reached for his groin. "I'm telling you now if I come upstairs, we're not falling asleep 'til morning. Just so you know, I like my eggs scrambled—coffee with a little half and half, and two teaspoons of sugar," he whispered to her amusement. She entered her building in an unhurried manner. The search for a parking spot was on.

Bryce lapped around the area, settling for a parking space on Clark Street—less than ten minutes from her apartment. Rather than exit the vehicle, he played the waiting game—stiff as a board. A smile formed as he re-read Alyssa's heartwarming text which included a series of fall foliage pictures captured at the park. He looked out the window toward the moon in its Waning Gibbous phase, scratching alongside his jawline to relax a charged mind. A deep breath followed.

So far, no luck. What's your building number just in case?

He connected the auxiliary cord to his iPod. The opening song was set to Grand Puba's "I Like It (I Wanna Be Where You Are)" sampling the sound and melodies of the same song title by R&B group DeBarge and Cal Tjader's "Never My Love." His thumb hovered over the play button.

Ms. Aquarius: 744. She's waiting…

[picture message]

Sat 11:02 p.m.

Yvonne sent a picture of her pastel pink French tip fingernails opening the curtains to "She," her clitoris. The sexy image couldn't drive away a bad conscience. He pressed play on the iPod, checked his blind spot, and sped off into the night hoping "She" and Omari would understand.

24

—

I GO TO EXTREMES

"Who does he think it is?"

"No idea. They won't leave a message. It's been happening for weeks. The other day he mentioned there was someone in the background breathing heavily."

"And the person wouldn't speak?"

"Nope."

"That's so creepy."

"He said there was another time when a loud television played in the background. The person was watching a movie or something, but he heard one of the characters say, 'I'll eff him up myself' and that's when the call ended."

"Seems like they intentionally called to let him hear that line. Hmm... *I'll eff him up myself...*"

"Well, the character used the *actual* expletive word. I'm just paraphrasing. Omari is flabbergasted though."

"I can imagine. It's a bit unsettling..." Priscilla paused, folding her elbows on the kitchen island, squinting her eyes at Bryce, who was preparing a tuna sandwich.

"P., chill out."

"What am I doing?"

"You're trying to figure out the line and what movie it's attached to. I'm not dumb."

Priscilla couldn't control her laughter. "Stop acting like you know me so well."

"I do, that's the problem."

"I was just trying to help. That's a little nerve-wracking, isn't it? Why doesn't he change his number? Does he have one of those stalker-type exes?"

"That's a good question. From the looks of it, I'd say someone is messing with him."

"What if it's someone with the wrong number. Omari doesn't come off like a person who'd have a beef."

"I agree, but you never know with this kid. Well, young man."

"Ooh, *young man?* Shots fired. I thought you hated that term."

"I'm just saying. He likes to play both sides. He's extremely bright but won't let go of this street persona. I get he grew up in the Bronx and lived in Irvington for a minute... yada, yada. All of that is cute, but you ain't an actual street dude. You *lived* in the hood."

Week Seven of the fast-moving NFL season saw Bryce and Priscilla's teams sitting atop their respective divisions on a well-deserved Bye Week. They continued to recap a chain of events on a lazy Sunday afternoon.

"How's his health situation?"

"That's another thing," Bryce continued, in between chews of a tasty lunch. "This dude is so concerned about adding to his body count."

"Ain't *that* the pot calling the kettle black, Mister King-Ding-a-Ling? Aren't you banging your neighbor?"

"You're funny. And, no, I'm not. We'll get into that in a minute. Like I was saying, he was adding to his body count, walking around with herpes *and* HPV."

"Wait, he's got two viruses? Gosh. Poor guy," Priscilla empathized.

"Yes. I had a heart-to-heart with him at the clinic. This isn't a contest. Nobody cares about your body count. *Life* has the most body count. You ain't beating that."

"Life?"

"Yes. Life screws everyone at some point. Sometimes without Vaseline."

"Ooh, I'm stealing that."

"I'm getting frustrated because he tends to be hardheaded."

"Weren't we all?"

"No. I was a saint. I was too busy *staying* busy. Cutting neighbors' grass for side money, working at the video store, playing sports, reading books. When I got older, I started traveling with friends. Look how old I was when I lost my mom. I could've easily spiraled out of control."

"It's a different time though, Bryce. Besides, his dad isn't around."

"I get it. That's another thing. He has no idea how much I vouch for him to *my* dad."

"Well, let's hope for the best. I think we should drive out there and sit in on one of his sessions. Or we can take him out to lunch the next time he comes down. That way we can all vibe out."

[Lizzy coos at Priscilla]

"The one o'clock games this week are hot garbage. Jets-Chargers might be the most compelling one."

Priscilla voiced her displeasure. "The Jets? Ugh."

"I guess we can flip back and forth between that and the Skins-Panthers," Bryce imagined.

"So, tell me what happened with the neighbor? What was her name again? Wasn't it Joanna?"

"Tasha..."

"That's right. Where did I get Joanna from?"

"No clue. There's not much to discuss. We had fun. It was good while it lasted."

"Look at my face," she pointed out. "I smell caa-caa. Who are you fooling?"

"I'm serious. It kinda fizzled out."

"You're telling me *nothing* happened?"

"Yup. She's cool, but I'm also thirty-four, not fourteen. Too much kissing, not enough..." Bryce motioned a form of intimacy thrusting his hips in place of using foul language.

"Not enough... fuckin'?"

"I was thinking more along the lines of... I don't know, rhymes with 'kitchen.'"

"Fiction? Oh, my goodness just say it... wait, don't tell me yet."

Bryce exhaled. "I'm thrusting my hips. Use context clues. Too much kissing not enough... rhymes with 'kitchen.'"

"*Mission?* Like missionary?"

He rotated his hand acting out the phrase. "You're getting warm. Who wrote *Great Expectations*?"

"Wait... I'm thinking."

"Maybe you're more familiar with *Oliver Twist*."

"Charles Dickens?"

"Bingo."

"Too much kissing, not enough *Charles Dickens?*"

"Game over. I'm done."

Priscilla exploded with laughter. "Wait, now I'm completely lost."

"I was trying to rhyme his last name with 'kissing.' Too much kissing not enough..."

"Dickens... Dicken... dickin'?"

"Thank you."

Bryce reached for his phone to shoot Alyssa a quick message when her personalized text chime sounded. It was a picture message of a homemade pumpkin spice beverage.

> We are definitely in sync.

> I was JUST texting you to say hello.

I Think I Might Wife Her: Really? Lol I was
hesitant at first. I knew the games would be
coming on, but I was hoping you'd see it
before they started. I'm super proud of myself.
The latte came out really well.

Sun 12:18 p.m.

"P., have I told you that I'm leaning toward getting back into a serious relationship?"

~

Omari was adrift in a sea of uncertainty. The anal itch and cluster of blistery sores was intolerable. Pride prevented him from refilling a prescription of Acyclovir; fear was the motive for walking around with a loaded handgun stuffed in his backpack. He was leaving Brixx's on his way to his aunt's. The treacherous long subway ride was another setting for inspired writing.

The subway was the cosmos of life, a place where all walks of society gathered in a boundless space, traveling along a journey. He cautiously eyed the patrolling police officers at the Jamaica-Van Wyck station. Granted he was a small fish in an ocean of killer whales and sharks, but with his current streak of bad luck even a vigorous sneeze could tip them off. Thankfully, he made it through the turnstile and onto the platform as an idle E-train awaited.

He carefully removed his rap notebook to craft more lines for a new song titled "Train of Thought." The symbolism was freakish.

> Put on my Yankees cap, pen & pad at my reach
> Lace up my sneaks, it's time I hit the streets
> On the train, people watching like I'm packing a pistol
> A man in girl's clothing staring like it's ME with the issues

I'm try'na blow up before the year 20-12
So, I'm locked in the booth instead of a prison cell

Blowing off the talent show had nothing to do with a mild sinus infection. Instead, Omari had some personal business to attend to. Shauna. She was the real subject matter as he staked out her house that Saturday evening, slouched in the passenger's side of Brixx's family car.

There she was walking along the sidewalk in search of her keys with nowhere to run, nowhere to hide. Omari took matters into his own hands, bursting out of the car nearly causing Shauna a mental meltdown. *Omari Harris* didn't have a rap sheet, but "H2O," his alter ego, fired his weapon plenty in the pages of his rap notebook. It took everything in his will not to revert to that ruthless monster with his gun tucked in his pants and Brixx none the wiser.

HPV was considered small-time compared to the other infection triggering his emotions, and since she was the first to rob him of his health, all he could think about was payback. There was a violent shouting match in front of her house. Shauna kneeled before him, gripping his leg, begging for forgiveness as Omari mortifyingly kicked at her, threatening to take her life. When he wouldn't accept her plea, she leaped to her feet, asking that he finish the job.

"You wanna fuckin' kill me? Go ahead, Omari, do it. Kill me!" she begged, pounding his chest with explosive closed fists. Shauna wasn't calling his bluff. She was dead inside. A stunned Brixx watched from the car, sensing their tiff was deeper than the alleged cheating story he received. Thankfully, the chippy neighbor and his family were out of town.

Shauna's request to be taken out of her misery threw him for a loop. Omari wasn't a murderer, no matter how much "H2O" wanted to wipe her from the face of the earth. When they made their way upstairs, she claimed not to have known about the infection before their New Year's Eve rendezvous and didn't know how to break the news once it was discovered. That was only half of it. By the time she was diagnosed—mid-spring, around the time Omari conducted his own self-inspection—she was hit with another jaw-dropper: Shauna was six weeks pregnant. The double-whammy was the cause of her now-infamous cryptic voicemail greeting.

She blamed her disappearance on stress. Imagine being unknowingly tainted by an ex and left to carry the burden that you've now ruined another person's life. At the same time expecting a child with one of two men who state they want nothing to do with parenthood. The crushing stories were unbearable, leading to an inescapable bout of depression. Shauna was rushed to the emergency room on several occasions, once for exhaustion, the other for a probable suicide attempt. The revelation brought about empathy from Omari, and together they wept. When cooler heads prevailed, he sent Brixx off and spent the rest of the night holding Shauna in his arms, declaring they would pull through. For good measure, he promised to support her and the child. There was a chance he didn't mean the latter, but with a barrage of doubt and an overflow of tears, he reckoned she needed all the encouragement she could get.

~

"Auntie, I'm here," Omari yelled, honoring her announcement rule upon entering the home. The house was quiet, the perfect time to unpack and place his backpack onto the top shelf in the closet of the spare bedroom—out of reach of his cousins. He was in town until his work schedule resumed midweek, which enabled Shauna to fit into his plans in between taking his cousins trick or treating.

Aunt Ramona wanted to share some disheartening news and figured it was better done in person. Omari had news of his own.

It was time to come clean regarding his health. She was the only blood relative he felt comfortable sharing his story with.

There were vast differences between his aunt and mother. For one, she was on the same wavelength—an unambiguous woman who coped with a whole slew of problems beyond teenage pregnancy. During the extremities of single parenthood, she battled alcoholism, causing her to lose custody of her firstborn to the system. Her firstborn was now a parent of her own. On top of that, Ramona wasn't all too fond of Omari's mother. The women were from opposite sides of the tracks, and when Terri dated Omar, Ramona often accused her of being pretentious toward their side of the family. In fairness, Terri had every right. She was involved with an abusive dishonorable man who abandoned her and their only child. Sadly, Ramona never saw it that way.

[text alert]

> Auntie: We'll be back. Running around with the kids looking for last minute costumes.
>
> Sun 3:28 p.m.

Fear was the only reason Omari's health was up for discussion. His body was going through the motions, he didn't have the answers and wondered how his aunt would respond. Moreover, what was happening in her world that required a face-to-face conversation? Was she dealing with a health crisis of her own? Left in a state of limbo, he turned on one of his songs and powered up the PlayStation for a game of *Call of Duty*.

25

———

THE SECOND TIME AROUND

A strong gust swept across the supermarket parking lot; the leaves rustled along the ground. Bryce exchanged pleasantries with an older shopper who was returning her cart to the cart corral. "Be safe," he advised. Tonight's dish was cod fish, mashed potatoes, and creamed spinach, a heavier than usual grub for a work night, but the last meal he prepared before the upcoming Thanksgiving holiday. The thought of Mrs. Terri's sweet potato pie, Dale's delicious stuffing, and an abundance of food carrying him for the weeks ahead generated excitement. Plus, his San Francisco 49ers were scheduled to play in primetime on Thursday's three-game football lineup.

Bryce paced along the tedious speed bumps leading to his home when Tasha's car came into view. She backed out of the driveway without regard to any possible passing vehicle or pedestrian behind, speeding off in the opposite direction. A recent text inquiry about her availability over the extended holiday break went unanswered—now on day two. It was possible she never received the message but the troubling thought that she elected to ignore it left him exhausted.

Their past summer was entertaining, leading to Bryce's renewed energy toward starting a possible relationship. Just not under her terms. This recent approach to touch base reeked of desperation. As existing neighbors, he felt they were better off reconciling than sustaining this sudden tension between them. To no longer speak seemed utterly ridiculous. They had gone about life long before either knew of the other's existence, but that was before lips touched, feelings magnified, and her boys referred to him as Mr. Bryce.

Bryce's frustration with Tasha was due to a lack of understanding. She had two kids from separate men, and in all likelihood, the last boyfriend didn't have to work as hard to get the goods. Why did he have to, then? There was only so much kissing and dry humping a grown man could take. In his eyes, the preservation train had long left the station. But he would be a fool to waste their progress. What was one more try?

He imagined being able to patch things up by saying sweet nothings in her ear, and before long, give her the most mind-blowing sex she'd ever experienced. All the while keeping Alyssa in close distance. Of all the available options, he had the most history with Tasha. She was closest to providing him with "something" that ordinarily came easily. That "something" Julissa routinely offered and insanely risked her marriage over. "Something" a random beauty at a nightclub presented with no strings attached.

[text alert]

It was Joy responding to Bryce's request for a meet-up at his place.

> Mail Lady: I gave you the pussy and you fumbled it lol. You were scared. It's okay.

> Mon 7:11 p.m.

Of all the women in Bryce's circle, he held Alyssa to a higher standard. How could he ever ignore her emergence? Their growing bond wasn't coincidental. Nothing in life was. She was placed in his life with a purpose. They recently broke a sweat as workout partners and agreed to a second date. Their future was hopeful if he could remove Tasha from his system. Unfortunately, his conscience wouldn't let him live if he didn't at least *try* to make amends.

> Hey. Not sure if u got my text the other day. Just wanted to know of ur holiday plans and whether they could include me. Maybe we can hang out before or after. Let me know.

He could be as stubborn as a mule.

[camera flash sound]

Bryce hadn't logged into his Facebook account in a while. The novelty of the social media platform wore off, but tonight's dish looked too good not to share with others. He conducted grace and uploaded the picture before placing the fork in his mouth. Within minutes, friends, family, and colleagues applauded his efforts. He spent dinner scrolling through his feed, reading, and responding to a wave of messages. There were friend requests from former teammates new to the platform and one from Yvonne sent months ago. First, he needed to address Joy's text.

> True, u did hand it to me. But did it ever occur that maybe I didn't wanna "sneak" with ur kids in the house? Ur son knocked on the door like he was SWAT lol.

The "lol" was to signify that he was unbothered by her son's actions. Secretly, it aggravated him to no end.

[Gucci calling]

"Yo."

What's good, kinfolk?

"Chillin', eating dinner. What's up with you?"

Can't call it. I was trying to see which clubs were hopping in Vegas.

"We're less than a month away."

No doubt. I'm already packed.

"Did you pack four days worth of velour suits?"

Five, just in case you wanted to be like me one night. You know I got you.

"Nice rebuttal. Yo, I swear, these women are something else."

Who?

"Hold on, let me take you off speaker. So, this one broad I'm talking to swears I'm scared, all because I ain't smash the other night. It's the *first* thing they say when you don't give into them."

I'm sure there was a good reason. Was she on the rag or something?

"Chick had about twenty kids in the house."

Oh, hell nah.

"You know my rule of thumb. She's texting me now, talking about how I fumbled the kitty. How'd I fumble when your house looked like *The Brady Bunch*?"

Oh, I see, she tried to get cute with the little football reference. Tell her that her kids intercepted the puss.

"Exactly. That's not even the main part, though. Her oldest son came knocking on the door like the cops. Talking 'bout, 'Ma, who's in the room?'"

Word? I would've been like, 'Me, punk. I'm about to blow your mom's back out. Now scram.'

[laughter]

"She doesn't know any better. I'm gonna let her live, but somehow, she found a way to spin this on me."

That's what they do. Meanwhile, her son's over there cockblocking, playing bodyguard. Listen, Playboy, she wanted a thug that night. You were supposed to tap into your inner Tupac and beat it up.

"I thought about it, but her kids were all over the place."

Yo, I meant to ask you about that fine thang in the pic from your birthday. The one standing next to Priscilla.

"Who, Celeste?"

Is that her name?

"Yessir. She's bad, right?"

I need to find me one of those. Are her parents beavers? Cuz damnnnn...

"She's single too."

Ole girl is thicker than a cold bowl of grits. Hook me up, Playboy.

"Well, according to her, she doesn't do the side chick thing anymore."

I don't either. I'd leave my old lady for that.

[Gucci proceeds to sing Usher's "You Make Me Wanna..."]

"Dawg, I needed that laugh."

What's the name of the dating site where you meet some of these women? My homie is back on the market. He says it's hard as hell out here. That man can't get a date on a tombstone.

"He ain't lying. It's rough finding compatibility. Is he willing to come out of pocket? I pay monthly membership fees for the legit ones."

I'll have to ask.

"There are a ton of baddies on the free sites but it's a crapshoot. A lot of them play games. I can send you the links now." Bryce moved the cell away from his ear to a group of texts.

Mail Lady: It's okay to admit you were scared lol. And sometimes you've got to improvise when there are kids at home. We could've turned up the volume, I could've buried my face in the pillow, and you could've handled business. The opportunities were there.

Mon 7:33 p.m.

I Think I Might Wife Her: Sorry I took so long to respond. I went to get my nails and eyebrows done with my sis and then my mom had us running around like a chicken with its head cut off.

How was your ride back home?

What does a house wear? No cheating.

Mon 7:34 p.m.

Still no response from Tasha, but Alyssa's text gave rise to a smile.

"Guc, let me hit you right back. I'll send you some of the links now."

Bryce proceeded to text Joy.

You really think I'm scared huh? You better ask about me lol. It's cool though. See for yourself when the time comes. I don't have those same distractions at my spot, so if ur able to swing by, let me know. Imagine me, a grown man, being "scared" of something that's been thrown at me since...

The last sentence was quickly deleted to avoid any pushback. He proceeded to message Alyssa.

All good. Send me a pic when u have a moment ;)

I think I actually know the answer to that one. Is it "clothes-sure," like a house closure?

I Think I Might Wife Her: So close. It's "a dress." Get it? (address). But that was a good try.

Mon 7:40 p.m.

I Think I Might Wife Her: [picture message]

Mon 7:41 p.m.

> Mail Lady: Yup. S-C-A-R-E-D. Poor baby. It's okay lol. Since we're in the holiday season the mail deliveries are gonna pick up, but I'll see about coming over if I get some time.
>
> Mon 7:44 p.m.

SATURDAY, DECEMBER 3

Love was in the air. What else could explain the movie whiz's bold move to see *In Time*, starring former boy band extraordinaire Justin Timberlake? Bryce glowed at the performance, sitting across from Alyssa at an Indian restaurant, sharing a large plate of chicken tikka masala and chai drink. The introduction to the widely popular Indian dish was just one of many hopeful milestones between them.

[text alert]

> Pop: Thank you for the birthday wishes, son.
>
> Sat 5:50 p.m.

Alyssa was giddy from the moment she arrived, and tonight was the unveiling of an impressive wardrobe. She was slightly tanned, wearing soft glam makeup. Her hair was parted down the middle and neatly layered. Her usual hazel eyes gave off a hint of green. A gold stud ring on her left nostril matched a thin gold necklace. She wore a black top with a plunging neckline. Her blue jeans were ripped—just like her body—as proven by the forearm veins.

Amongst light flirting and witty remarks, their conversation took on a more serious tone. They opened about the impact of losing a parent, life aspirations, the controversial looming "end of the world" prophecy, and a list of desirable vacations when Bryce revealed he was leaving for Las Vegas in the coming weeks. Oftentimes their eyes locked, creating a trickle of sexual tension. He fought earnestly not to shift their banter into something tasteless. By the looks of her hellacious stares, that was exactly what she wanted. It was Alyssa who after their last date made an inferred suggestion that she needed to apply her adjustable shower head to her private area to cure a sexual urge. Instead of indulging in an X-rated spinoff, Bryce laughed it off, but the thought was tantalizing.

Saying goodbye came easier at the conclusion of tonight's date. The setting was dark, the parking lot deserted, and a sizzling kiss could've diverted their attention from the late autumn chill. Alternatively, Bryce played it cool, gesturing for her hand. Their arms swayed impulsively like two lovebirds. He charmed her with a slow side kiss, landing as close to the corner of her mouth as possible. An extended hug followed. With one whiff, he captured the scent of her hair, a mixture of coconut water, honey, and aloe vera gel. The warmth of his nostrils and prickling beard sent a chill down her spine. Alyssa's bummed-out look indicated she wanted more. Had they passionately kissed, it would've kissed his current options goodbye, and in all probability hurried sex. His warm embraces were like the cherry on top to *most* women. Only Tasha would escape. Under no circumstances could he allow Alyssa's celibacy streak to end in vain.

After parting ways with Alyssa, Bryce delivered a powerful prayer asking the Lord to provide her with understanding. By no means was he rejecting her—after all, it was at Alyssa's request they moved along slowly. If this were a test, then undoubtedly, he passed with flying colors.

26

—

WAKING UP IN VEGAS

There was no talking Gucci out of bringing his waist-length snow white mink bomber jacket to the desert where temperatures were expected to climb to the mid-sixties. The mink was immediately laid across the lounge chair inside the spacious two-bedroom suite, soon after they arrived at the luxurious Cosmopolitan hotel. It was the gang's first getaway outside of a bowling alley or Atlantic City casino, and he was all but ready to show out. As expected, Lorenzo wouldn't make the trip but vowed to make it up to the guys as talk of a summer retreat was already underway.

❧

Bryce gave a big stretch and stifled a yawn, still feeling a bit groggy after their late-night flight into McCarron airport. He waited for the guys at the Overlook Grill skimming the breakfast menu, humming along to the chorus of "Kokomo" by The Beach Boys. A small group produced double-takes in passing. Maybe it was his sleek check-stretch Burberry shirt, gaudy gold watch, or black fisherman hat hiding half of his face that was drawing attention. Either way, he offered a tight-lipped smile in return.

Following breakfast, the guys planned to take a trek through the iconic Strip before spending the rest of the afternoon at the casinos. They heard stories about Las Vegas—Bryce even read a collection of books documenting the infamous "Rat Pack" and old mobsters who frequented the town, but there was nothing like being there.

"I told you his punk ass wouldn't come," Junior clued them on Lorenzo's absence.

Bryce countered. "Well, to his credit, it's the holidays. He's the only one with little ones. Plus, he's been out here more times than I can count."

"It's all gravy, baby," Gucci responded. "Let him play Santa. I'll be out here messing with the ho, ho, hoes."

"Yo, Guc, it says here that it's supposed to be forty degrees tonight. You bustin' out the mink?"

"I've been tracking the forecast like stock, Playboy. When you *stay* ready you ain't got to *get* ready. Aye Junior, hurry up with the gotdamn syrup. My waffles got goosebumps."

"Hopefully, it ain't too dead out here. Fish says we should be good, but my gut was telling me all along to book the trip for next week. That's when it's usually live," Bryce continued.

"Isn't New Year's week more expensive?" Junior asked.

"It is, but it might've been worth it."

"Shit. Don't matter to me. As long as I see women, we all winning," Gucci said.

"*Women* and *winning* don't rhyme, my boy," Bryce jested.

They traded more jabs until Gucci started chatting up their young server about the top nightspots on the Strip. The server gave them a breakdown of where to find the most success. The pointers earned him high praise and would almost certainly garner a handsome tip.

"Okay, gentlemen. I'm gonna leave the check right here. There's no rush whatsoever. If you need anything else, just give me a holler. It was a pleasure to serve you all."

Bryce carried cash—five hundred dollars to be exact—but

placed his platinum American Express card inside the check holder.

"Damn. Don't do 'em like that, Playboy. You pulled out the big boy."

"Nah, that's the Black card," Bryce replied. "I ain't on that level… yet."

"My man said *yet*. Damn. I'm trying to be like *you* when I get older," Gucci replied.

"You're older than me now."

"That ain't the point."

[laughter]

"Let me see what it says—member since *ninety-three,*" Junior squinted.

"This fool said ninety-three. You think I've been carrying an AMEX card since I was sixteen? It says two thousand and three."

"Ole blind bitch," Gucci burst out.

"Blind or dyslexic," Bryce replied. "Don't one of y'all have the Gold card?"

"Not me. We have the business card with Chase. Junior got a couple of cards."

"Yeah, I keep a few just for financial breathing room."

"But your cards don't get the panties wet like *this* mothafucka here," Gucci pointed to the check holder.

"Are your panties wet, bro? Do I need to call Mom?"

"Man, fuck this guy," Gucci protested. "Good lookin' out, Playboy. Drinks are on me later."

"Of course they are, since you know I'm not a heavy drinker," Bryce replied, giving him the side eye.

Tourists congregated for photos next to some of the famous landmarks on the Strip. There was a Michael Jackson street performer in a Saint Nick outfit demonstrating funky dance moves, a living statue spray-painted in festive colors, psychic readers, and a group of sexy female handbillers dishing out fliers for personal entertainment.

"Guc, take a pic of me standing here. Wait 'til the water rises,"

Bryce instructed, referring to the beautiful waterfront of the Bellagio fountain.

"Ain't it on a timer? We could be standing here all day."

"I think you're right. Snap me anyway. I'm gonna send this to P."

Las Vegas Boulevard was quite active for a late morning in December. They continued walking along when Bryce opened the floor on a noteworthy topic, seeking the opinions of the guys.

"Fellas, this time next year, it's a wrap. Let's enjoy ourselves while we can."

"You believe in that nonsense?"

"What y'all babbling about?" Gucci asked.

"He's talking about that end of the world bullshit," Junior continued.

"Oh, word? Playboy, you think we're done?"

"I can't call it. They say it's the end of the Mayan calendar. If you study the history of human civilization, there are a multitude of calendars. Why is there so much talk about it now? Where there's smoke, there's usually fire."

"Man, ain't nothin' gonna happen. It's all fear mongering," Junior snapped.

"I don't think anything will pop off organically. It'll be man-made. I can get deep with this but y'all fools ain't ready for Bible talk."

"Yo, save Jesus talk for Jersey," Junior added. "We can't be out here in Sin City talkin' 'bout God."

"Look at Guc. He's nervous," Bryce shouted enthusiastically.

"Uh-huh. Shittin' bricks."

"Guc, you good? Are you wondering if you can wear a mink in heaven?"

"His ass better hope he makes it," Junior replied.

"I'm great. I ain't with all this nerd shit. Y'all having an A & B conversation so I saw my way out the door."

"This joker said, 'A & B conversation.' I ain't hear that since the third grade," Junior replied.

"I wouldn't be surprised if they did something just to give the impression of an end-of-time scenario," Bryce continued.

"You mean like a false flag?" Gucci asked, stumping the guys.

"How the fuck you know what a false flag is?" Junior asked.

[laughter]

"It'll be some type of fake war or global pandemic. I don't trust the government as far as I can throw them. They're sitting around moving pieces on a chessboard. We've seen it time and time again. Instead of us bonding and utilizing our power as a people, we fold..."

"Like a mothafuckin' lawn chair," Gucci finished.

The guys mingled with a mix of upper-class students at a nearby Starbucks who were in town for a second time this year from the University of California, Berkeley. The party of four was down-to-earth, making way for friendly chit chat. Bryce, the youngest of his group, did most of the talking.

The conversation started after the guys inquired about the whereabouts of the famous neon "Welcome to Las Vegas" billboard. The women offered to assist, delighted to come across "chill guys" as they so stirringly described, awed by their accents and east coast swagger. The young ladies stayed at the well-known Flamingo Hotel & Casino, spilling wild pool party stories from their recent summer visit. Gucci wouldn't say much but listened with enlarged eyes. Bryce compared the events to some of the happenings he witnessed during his college days, sparing full detail to avoid aging himself. The lone brown skinned girl of the bunch spoke Valley Girl like the others. She had smooth, impeccable skin, the prettiest teeth, and the hots for Junior, giggling at his every word, even the non-funny ones. The ladies insisted that both groups party together before their departure in a few days.

"All right, so one last time, you said the billboard is at the southern point of the Strip?" Bryce asked the tall blue-eyed blonde, who wore a half-up French braid crown.

"Yeah... like, we can all walk together if you want."

"That's entirely up to y'all," Bryce replied, turning to the others.

"Oh, totally," her Samoan-descent friend chimed in. "If you guys weren't like super cool, I'd be like, 'Um, McKenzie, what are you doing?'" she laughed. "Wait, we've got to ask Megan first." She pointed. "She's the responsible one of the group." All eyes turned to their quiet friend, seeking approval.

"Don't put it all on me."

"Aye, Megan, baby girl, the ball is in your court—don't let your boys down," Gucci blurted out.

"I'm fine with it, but, like, don't leave it up to me."

"I'm sorry, did she say your name was McKenzie?" Bryce cut in, asking the tall blue-eyed blonde.

"Uh-huh," she nodded enthusiastically.

"McKenzie, I *know* you play some type of sport. The suspense is killing me."

"I was gonna say the same thing," Junior furthered.

"I do. Me and Maya are on the volleyball team."

"I knew it. My athletic senses were tingling. I'm Bryce." He offered his hand. "So, you all have names starting with 'M?'"

"I don't," the brown skinned girl replied.

"What's your name?"

"Jordan."

"You *had* to be the fuck up," Junior mocked, shaking his head.

"Oh my gosh, that's so mean," McKenzie reacted.

"Jordan?" Bryce continued, "That's an easy fix. We can call you MJ. You know who that is, right?"

"She'd better. She's wearing his sneakers," Junior added.

"He makes sneakers, doesn't he?" Jordan asked, with a quizzical look on her face.

"She just tarnished the man's entire legacy. Gotdamn." Junior implied, visibly disappointed.

～

After a much-needed nap, Bryce awakened in the king-size bed of his studio suite to the vociferous talking heads of ESPN. Sadly, the sun had already crossed over to the other side of the luxury resort, leaving trails of purple and orange in the sky. He stepped onto the private terrace, staring deep into the mountain backdrop overlooking the Strip, helping himself to a sequence of pictures. Despite missing the sunset, the view was still a thing of beauty. He spent the next hour catching up with Priscilla while Gucci and Junior dilly dallied at the casino. In a few hours, the guys would head over to Caesars Palace and try their luck with a recommended nightclub, known for great bottle service, large crowds, and their big-time DJs.

So, what are you about to do now?

"Probably grab a bite to eat and see what these clowns are up to. I'm not the biggest gambler aside from placing a few sports bets."

What? You're the biggest gambler I know, Mister I-Bang-Married-Women."

"Another nickname? You couldn't help yourself, huh? And I only banged one. Thank you."

[Priscilla laughs hysterically]

"As I was saying, I'm not the biggest gambler but I usually have a little success at the roulette table."

What's wrong with your voice? You sound like... who's that singer with the deep voice from back in the day?

"Who, Barry White?"

Yes. Is this supposed to be your sexy Vegas voice?

"I just woke up, doofus..."

See? Instead of watching something festive, now I'm in the mood to watch Casino.

"That reminds me. We need to watch *Contagion* when I get back."

Con-who?

"*Contagion*. Omari brought some DVDs to the house a few

months ago. The name grabbed me. I read the plot, watched it, and never got past the first scene."

Let me get this straight, the movie was so bad that now you wanna suck me in? I thought we were friends.

"No."

We're not?

"I'm talking about the movie. It's a long story. I'll explain once I'm back in cold snowy Jersey instead of my *luxury suite overlooking the Strip... with mountains and palm trees in the backdrop.*"

Ooh, I see what you did there. Not cool.

"Did you get my pics from earlier?" Bryce asked.

I did and I'm super jealous. We'll talk about why I didn't receive an invite when you get back.

"It was a guys' trip. We planned it months, maybe years ago."

So, what? I could've drawn a mustache on my face, sagged my pants, hid my hair under a cap and been like yo, yo, what's crackin'?

"Is that how you perceive us? You think that's how men speak?"

Anyway, behave yourself, mister. Don't get too carried away.

"Always. I have a budget set for the casinos, and I'll probably have a drink or two tonight. Might as well try to experience Vegas while I'm here."

Don't come back talkin' about how an Elvis impersonator acting as an ordained minister ushered you into marriage.

"You watch way too many movies."

～

THURSDAY, DECEMBER 22 - 8:10 A.M.

Thinking about you :)

It was a twinge of guilt bringing on such an emotion, but it was too early to send Alyssa the heartfelt text. Too soon in their kinship and ill-timed in nature. She was likely headed to work or already there and wouldn't see it until break. Bryce typed the thoughtful words again—this time saving it as a draft message. It was sure to make her day whenever he decided to press send.

Sunlight radiated through the sliding glass door. He must've been in a coma to not have closed the curtains or turned off the television the night before. Bryce never experienced a blow job quite like the one he encountered just hours ago, when a stranger made his dreams come true. The bulge in his red boxer briefs indicated his manhood craved more.

His intent was to experience Las Vegas and all its luster while still being composed. That plan was short-lived once the drinks kicked in. He lay motionless, gathering what he could remember about the previous night. It was a blessing to not end up in a drunken stupor like Junior, who found himself nearly coming to blows with a famous entourage. Bryce's buzz was light compared to the drunkard's. Just enough to talk a fine young lady into joining him in his hotel suite.

Of the hundreds of women on the scene, Kaylani was unquestionably one of the most dashing partygoers there. A cross between Lauren London of the comedy-drama film *ATL* and Nicole "Hoopz" Alexander from the reality dating show *Flavor of Love*—caramel-complected, dainty, and confident. The septum piercing added a bit of sass; the tips of her long curly black weave kissed her miniature breast. He hadn't seen anyone pull off fishnet stockings with knee-high stiletto boots and high-waisted shorts quite like she had. She was dressed like a woman on the prowl, and the sleaze look reeled him.

They spent time talking over loud music. Kaylani was well-spoken even through condensed deliberate replies. The part-time student, Hooters restaurant server, and "boss bitch," as she expressively labeled herself, stayed at The Venetian Resort by way of Orlando, Florida—though she was originally from New Jersey—to Bryce's surprise. Through their exchange, she praised his physique, refusing to believe he worked in corporate. Bryce was far from wealthy, but it was his aura that usually contributed to the gratifying scent of celebrity.

Admittedly, Bryce quietly celebrated when Lorenzo bailed on the trip. Of course, being joined by his long-time friend would've been nice but it also meant sharing a two-bedroom luxury suite and being talked out of having a good time. Once Lorenzo turned down the offer, it opened the door for the presence of a fine lady to take his place, just as the bachelor envisioned a stay in Las Vegas should go.

Bryce and Kaylani walked at a distance upon entering the glossy Cosmopolitan lobby. His experience with Julissa kept him guarded. Kaylani was a total stranger. You never knew if a jealous ex-boyfriend lurked in the shadows. Inside, she sat at the foot of the bed, where she took a hard look at him. It was then that Bryce noticed her almond-shaped eyes and crystal blue contacts, which he foolishly believed were her natural color. The liquor might've eased some of the anxiety, but it impaired his judgment. He remembered fetching a kiss and Kaylani showing apprehension. The combination of her full-sized lips and erotic eyes had him in a daze. His deviant behavior was uncharacteristic, but what was there to lose?

His morning wood expanded the more he gave thought to what happened next—unforeseen back-to-back ejaculations after Kaylani took a hold of his manhood and snatched his soul. Had Bryce not just awakened from a blissful hibernation, he would've been perfectly content joining his mother in the heavens and missing out on the perceived end of the world, now only a year away. What a way to leave Earth: *Man found dead in his hotel room, no signs of foul play. Woman in question claims to have only given him fellatio.* Such a headline would've imploded the internet and possibly caused thousands of men to arrive at her front door with their pants down to their ankles. He struggled to remember the time she left the room. No chance he could allow her to leave town without an encore—and then it struck—they hadn't exchanged numbers.

Your generosity saves lives. A monthly donation of nineteen dollars can go a long way.

Bryce scoffed at the charitable commercial, rising out of bed like a bat out of hell. Instantly, the room began to spin. He collected himself, put on his black tank top, and inspected the suite. Everything appeared normal until he noticed his chic wallet opened on top of the wet bar. It was next to a wine glass with a napkin underneath. He would never expose such a personal item in a hotel room, proving last night's victor was the triple shots of vodka. He grabbed his wallet, wondering if he had been fleeced. Thankfully, his identification was intact, providing a temporary sense of relief. However, it wouldn't erase the thought of stolen identity. Kaylani could've jotted his credit card information, taken a screenshot, or stored it in her memory. He opened the bill section to find himself short of a hundred dollars in addition to the C-note spent at the casino. Multiple recounts wouldn't make a difference. He had been robbed—like former Vice President Al Gore following the 2000 presidential election.

There was blue ink printed on the napkin:

(862) 555-1710 Text only (pls nothing inappropriate).

I'll be here for a few days. Hope we can hook up again.

Why would she only take a single bill and not run off with my wallet? Maybe she didn't want to be blatant, he gathered. More than that, who commits theft and leaves their phone number? The whole idea of "Hey, I just robbed you, but text me so we can meet up later" didn't make sense. He shook his head in disbelief, trying to retrace his steps. A long hot shower and a cup of coffee would do the trick.

Your generosity saves lives. A monthly donation of nineteen dollars can go a long way.

He searched for the remote control and muted the television, growing frustrated at the "Save the Children" charity commercial eating up the early morning time slot. Strangely the mystery of possibly being robbed excited him. It didn't hurt that a good-looking person committed it. He was still alive, and at least he had been greatly rewarded.

Glass half full.

He walked around the suite with the towel wrapped around his waist, having washed off the thrills of last night. Junior was probably still hungover, but Gucci was sure to be up, gambling his life away, so he gave him a call.

[slot machine sounds]

What up?

"You're at it early."

Early bird gets the worm. I've been hollering at one of the servers. She's got a prosthetic leg and all, but shit, that ass is talking to me.

"Yo, if you smash a chick with a fake leg, I'll personally hand over my life savings."

Don't tempt me. I told you about the midget I took down back in the day. Fattest ass I'd ever seen.

"Small person."

[Gucci laughs]

Is that what they call them now? Shit, fuck around and you'll have a big fat zero in your bank account. If you're pokin', I'm strokin'.

"Yo, crazy story. Tell me why I got robbed."

Robbed? How the fuck that happen?

"Did you see the chick I was talking to before Junior started wildin' out last night?"

I saw you with someone after we took shots, but I was doing my own thing. There were too many fine ladies in that piece for me to be concentrating on y'all.

"It had to be her. I'm short a hundred dollars."

Damn. You sure? It's funny because I was about to call you and ask if you hit that, and then I got wrapped up in conversation down here. Wait 'til I tell you how Junior fucked up my whole situation last night. Finish your story first.

"I mean, it's possible that I misplaced the money, but when I woke up my wallet was open. I *never* do that."

Damn. Maybe you left the wallet open. Your ass was buzzed. I remember that part. You only had what, two or three shots?

"I'm not a seasoned vet like y'all. Most of last night was a blur. I've been backtracking since I got up. This is crazy. Anyway, what happened with you?"

There were a few joints giving me the eye last night. So, after Junior passed out, I brought one to the room, and we started smashing in the bathroom. Junior wakes up and starts banging on the door, saying he needs to come in there. Next thing you know, this mothafucka throws up all over the gotdamn floor.

"Bruh..."

Yo, you should've seen the steam coming outta my ears. Anyway, I couldn't nut after that, so I sent shorty on her way. I went to the casino afterward and found a nice redbone. Agreed to go to her spot and took her down.

"Gucci, the hoe slayer."

Put that on a T-shirt. Yo, come to think of it, you probably fucked a worker.

"What'chu mean?" Bryce, now confused, questioned.

They were all over that joint last night. You said you were missing a hundo? That's how much the second bitch charged just for head, and she wanted me to wear a rubber. I was like, "Oh hell nah, baby, save that for the lames." I had to tap, though. Her ass was bigger than the National Debt. We were walking in the hallway, and she started bouncing that thang in my face. I was like, "Is butt-cheek one word or do you want me to spread it apart for you?" You would've liked her, too. Oh, I ain't even tell you how the first bitch asked me to smash with my mink on before Junior interrupted. Yo, you there? Playboy?

And there it was. The conversation triggered his absent-minded self. Kaylani had insidiously cautioned that she was an escort prior to their arrival at the hotel. "I'm working, baby," as she had tellingly disclosed when he inquired why someone so attractive would be at the club alone. The seductive stares are what led him to approach her in the first place. Now the whole "boss bitch" thing made sense. This was Las Vegas, where the tired slogan held true: What happens here *stays* here. It wasn't like he planned on bringing her home to meet the family.

"I'm here. Yo, I think you're right. She might've been a worker. It's all coming back to me now."

Like a Celine Dion song.

"Yeah. I'm gonna get a quick workout at the fitness center. What time you wanna do breakfast?"

"Dawg, what happened last night?"

"I don't even know. I was good for a minute, but then I kept noticing these dudes staring at a distance. I'm like, 'All of these fine ass women and y'all wanna stare over here at a bunch of men?' I don't even remember the rest."

"That's because you were wasted. Your dumbass passed out while I was clappin' and slappin' some cheeks in the bathroom. Then you wanna wake up and vomit all over the gotdamn place."

"Can I get another water, please?" Junior asked the server.

"All I remember was watching you throw a roundhouse and stumbling to the floor," Bryce demonstrated in slow motion, as his black 49ers cap fell onto the table. "Then I heard a few people yelling 'WorldStar.'"

"They're lucky I ain't connect. I would've knocked their asses into next week."

"I overheard someone afterward saying those dudes were with Floyd Mayweather's team."

"I don't give a fuck *who* they were with. I'm from *Nork*."

"Brick City, baby," Gucci blurted, reading the menu.

"So, it's *Nork* and not New-ark. Got it. I've been lied to my whole life," Bryce sarcastically replied.

"That's how the fuck we say it. You ain't from there. Stay yo ass in the boonies."

"Gladly," Bryce laughed. "You don't have to tell me twice. And the last I checked, you were out in the sticks with me."

[laughter]

"Playboy got fucked up last night and thought someone robbed him," Gucci announced.

"You're lying. You don't even drink like that."

"I know. I'm a lightweight compared to y'all."

"What happened, though?"

"I wouldn't say I was drunk. More like 'feeling good.' I was talking to this one *bad* joint and eventually took her to the room. Yo... I ain't *ever* get top like that before. Good Lord. She was mean with it, but, like passionate at the same time." Bryce revealed, wearing a confused expression.

"She gave you that sloppy-toppy-look-you-in-the-eye head? Who she sound like, Guc?" Junior asked, referring to an old flame.

"My future wife."

[Gucci sings chorus to SWV's "Weak"]

[group laughter]

"All I know is, I woke up with a Kool-Aid smile and my toes were curled."

"Oh, you had a soul snatcher? This fool got head from the Undertaker," Junior shouted, rapidly backslapping Gucci's shoulder. "You ain't get her number?"

"Nope. I'm not even sure where she's staying."

That was Bryce's only-child syndrome in full effect. He had Kaylani's information tucked away, like a squirrel hiding nuts, and there wasn't a snowball chance in hell he'd share it. Not until he experienced another round.

The guys recapped their encounter with the lively college girls at Starbucks.

"Ole brown skinned girl was huntin'," Bryce ribbed.

"Shit, they all were," Junior replied.

"I'm looking at you the whole time, wondering when you were gonna get her number."

"Nah, she was too young and small. Bitch was like five feet. I liked the... the tall tanned one with the long hair," Junior stuttered, attempting to recall Maya, the Samoan-descent woman.

"She was cute, too. Guc, ain't know what to do. Dawg, I've never seen you that quiet around women in my life," Bryce laughed.

"Those girls were still teething. I need my women seasoned."

Bryce pulled out his phone ready to make Alyssa's day.

> Thinking about you :)

Meanwhile, Kaylani replied to his earlier question.

> (862) 555-1710: Yes, you were conscious lol. I wrote my number down before you walked me to the door.
>
> Thurs 12:06 p.m.

"So, what do y'all wanna do today?" Bryce asked the guys, relieved by the text.

~

> (862) 555-1710: In the cab now. Which floor are you on again?
>
> Thurs 8:10 p.m.

The high-powered orgasm from last night left Bryce lusting for seconds. After a long day of loafing around the casino to the earnings of six hundred dollars, it was time to treat himself once more. Showered and sobered up, he lay down, flicking through the channels. It was easy to become annoyed at the thought that he hadn't released through penetration since his birthday weekend but at least he showed restraint. Tonight, not so much.

He removed three hundred dollars from his wallet—the discussed amount for full-service from the upscale worker—along with two gold condom wrappers from his designer fanny pack. Without blinking an eye, he stuffed his wallet back into the pouch to avoid another mishap. The television was on, and the room light was dim. His stomach produced a maddening growl. The anxiety was unusual. Conceivably, it was the thrill of doing something taboo, but prostitution had gone on since Biblical times. He downed a bottle of room-temperature water when three gentle knocks surfaced. Inhale, exhale. He marched to the door and squinted through the peephole where Kaylani adjusted her hair. She looked even better than before.

"Sup, lady..."

Kaylani smiled and replied with a soft "hi" as she strutted through the doorway, partly pigeon-toed. She wore black boots, a hooded mid-length black trench coat and carried a black-metallic handbag. She smelled like a mix of exotic weed and strawberry fragrance lotion. To cure his jitters, he attempted a self-deprecating joke regarding his previous night's actions. Kaylani laughed inwardly.

"So, what do you *really* do?" she asked with an unnatural pitch, her face expressive.

"I'm in corporate. You *still* don't believe me?"

"No."

"You do know that not all of us rap or play sports."

Kaylani sucked her teeth at the comment. "I didn't say that, but I know you must be doing well for yourself. I mean, look at your room."

Bryce was drawn to her lilting, nasal voice—soft and measured. He watched Kaylani closely as she sashayed through the suite.

"You ain't doing too bad yourself, traveling state to state. You said you live out in Orlando, right? How the heck you end up being neighbors with Mickey Mouse?"

"It's a long story," she laughed. "But I love it there."

He was captivated by her face, particularly her seductive gaze. It was as if she was anxious to get fucked. Par for the course from a sex worker.

"Can I get a kiss?" he asked.

"You asked for a kiss last night."

"And I don't recall you giving me one. Are you gonna make me beg?"

"You don't have to beg, baby. Do you have my donation?"

He redirected Kaylani to the nightstand where the money was halfway tucked under the room service phone. They stood toe to toe and shared a quick peck. She thanked him with a suggestive moan.

There was a stigma attached to kissing women in this controversial line of work but gone were the days of dilapidated hookers infested with VD. Through research, he learned the vast majority kept themselves in better health than the average woman. They had to. It was an integral part of growing and sustaining a long-term clientele. Bryce plopped onto the center of the bed and waited with bated breath. Kaylani couldn't look away from the bright lights of the replica Eiffel Tower.

"You wanna sit out on the balcony?" he asked her.

"As long as it's not too cold."

"Why don't you come take care of me first?"

She removed her trench coat, blowing him away with a sexy lace garter belt lingerie set. Kaylani was shaped like a track star—wiry and toned—with just the right amount of cushion behind. There was a queen of diamonds tattoo on the inner half of her deltoid muscle. On her stomach was a glittery naval piercing. She hopped onto the bed, positioned herself onto her stomach and pulled Bryce's pants down, rubbing his erection against her jawbone. Her fingernails were long and colorful, her grip was soft, her mouth watered.

After another amazing head-clinic, Bryce motioned Kaylani to the sliding door. Sex on the balcony overlooking the Gambling Capital of the World was what dreams were made of. He anxiously grabbed the condoms from the nightstand, picked up a white thermal top from the lounge chair and raced behind. She pressed her hands against the glass in a surrendering gesture. Bryce clenched her waist with one hand and caressed her breast from the exterior with the other. They reached for the latch and unlocked the door to a chilly desert air. He sat slouched on the cushioned bench to unroll the condom as Kaylani prepared to sit in a reverse cowgirl position. He elected to slide her G-string to the side as there were too many straps to unfasten on the lingerie set. She immediately grabbed hold of his excitement to insert him. The light tension produced simultaneous moans. Their pace picked up—her yelps increased. Soon, they rose to their feet, facing the city's glare. Kaylani rested her arms against the railing as Bryce plowed from behind, his hand fixed against the upper half of her throat. John 8:7 repeated in his head. Viva Las Vegas.

∾

SATURDAY, DECEMBER 24

Bryce gave the city one last stare before the pilot positioned the plane in line on the runway. A window seat with no one seated next to him, six hundred dollars richer, and a four-month sex drought dead and buried. Priscilla would be proud to see he hadn't returned with a "Happily Married" tattoo centered on his forehead. Las Vegas treated him kindly.

He placed his mystery-thriller Stephen King novel down and retrieved his phone. Based on the weeks of silence, it was safe to assume Tasha had moved on to greener pastures. Maybe Joy would take him up on an offer to make dinner on New Year's Eve.

At this point, he was only trying to keep his options alive before moving onto a new chapter.

She was effervescent, buoyant, and enjoyed cloudy days. *[pilot reviews airline's seat belt policy to passengers]*

~

Bryce's enjoyment of sex was just a euphemism for "sex addict," but he hadn't always been this way. Sex became a pastime of sorts, catalyzed by feelings of discontentment for the pool of women who came after Kristen and the lone one who came before.

The statute of limitation would unarguably apply to his tenth-grade English teacher Ms. Blake—a strawberry-blonde-haired woman who benevolently looked after him following Candace's death. It was possible she felt bad and wished to keep one of her top students from derailment. She couldn't imagine the pain he was in. Ms. Blake was one of the youngest teachers on staff. She was gregarious, relatable, and a great listener to go with a chic colorful style of dress. In retrospect, maybe she intended on giving the boys in class a peek at her bra strap and cleavage line from time to time.

Bryce made light of her physical contact—whether a quick hello shoulder tap or the incidental brushing of his hand when she squeezed in between desks. He quietly enjoyed the feeling of her firm ass against his fingers and intentionally left his hand at the edge. Ms. Blake laughed hardest at his wit and shared more off-the-wall conversations with Bryce than any student. She sought him out as an unofficial teacher assistant in the classroom and for off-ground projects as head of a community-educator program. That's where it all began.

Beyond doubt, she felt a connection, but after paying close attention, Bryce couldn't shake off the thought that she had eyes for him. The idea was astounding but he got his answer soon enough after a small group of scholars returned from a field trip. As the pair unloaded items at the back of the school bus, the sexual tension escalated after an unforeseen intimate kiss shared between them. It was Bryce who dared her.

Ms. Blake's yearlong intense stares and underhanded compliments jump-started their relationship, leading to after-school meetups underneath the track and field bleachers, where they'd make out for the better part of his junior year. Suspicion grew on the day before spring break when she openly placed her hand against his cheek in a secluded area of the hallway, catching the quick eye of a student. Bryce scrambled to do damage control. A little white lie kept word from spreading and Ms. Blake out of a heap of trouble. He couldn't afford to lose her. She was the perfect distraction, his part-time baseball videographer, and a great school reference for college applications.

It took some time before he discarded her perfume-scented handwritten letter passed along on graduation day. Inscribed at the bottom of the paper were the letters "K.I.T.," a heart image and her phone number listed underneath "Evelyn," her forename in red ink. In the letter, she thanked him for his trustworthiness and kindness. Ms. Blake was in a vulnerable place, too.

The young divorcee was a Colorado transplant far away from family, working with a staff where the women envied her, and the men questioned whether she rightfully belonged. Some even accused the school of nepotism, claiming she only got the job due to a relative being on the board. She was ostracized by her peers and as a result bonded with the students. Many of the boys liked her, the jocks in particu-lar, but Bryce's distinct maturation earned him points even if she was nearly twice his age. It wouldn't make her actions right, but these were the facts.

After Bryce lost his virginity, he expressed remorse with the belief that he had become disobedient to God. Pre-marital sex was a big deal despite many of his friends having already experienced intercourse, and it was Ms. Blake who comforted him first. Although writing letters to one another had become a common theme once he entered college, Bryce's emotional outburst wouldn't come courtesy of a ballpoint pen. Instead, it was directly in front of his former high school teacher—as she lay naked beside him in an air-conditioned hotel room during summer break, miles from home.

He was nineteen years old, well above the age of legal consent, but in his heart, he knew he had done wrong. Her hand rested on his bare chest as she attempted to talk him off the ledge. She carefully deduced it as consenting adults having an overdue moment, but it wouldn't stop him from questioning their act as two spiritually grounded people. To stabilize him, Ms. Blake performed fellatio. Receiving oral sex was like ingesting a prescription drug to numb the pain. He never imagined their interaction being the cause of a sexual awakening that would last for years to come, but it explained plenty.

[ladies and gentlemen, please prepare for takeoff]
Flight 988 picked up its pace, and before long, they ascended above the runway. He looked through the window where the City of Sin was now beneath them. They were up in the clouds— symbolic of the gang's short stay in America's Playground.

27

—

LOST IN EMOTION

Omari was saddened to learn about his father's bout with stage four stomach cancer during his last visit to Aunt Ramona's days before Halloween. The heartrending story affected him in such a way that he delayed sharing his own crippling health crisis until his next visit before Thanksgiving. He also learned of his father's failed attempts to reach out. Presumably, he was the person behind the unending private calls. It was a case of an overflow of emotions during a time of year when smiles were brightest, and holiday cheer was spread about.

In preparation for Kwanzaa, he spent Christmas week in the Bronx with his family while making the commute to work. It enabled more drop-ins to Shauna who was less than two months away from delivery. Her recent cries for his touch put him in good spirits but the extended visits led to an inevitable rift with Brixx who questioned his musical commitment. Little did he know that Omari would consider a full-time move to his old borough once Shauna had given birth.

~

As expected, Aunt Ramona handled Omari's STD revelation like a pro when he confided in her on Thanksgiving morning. There were no signs of panic, she had been through trials and tribulations plenty. Unthinkably, she saw his dilemma as fixable, almost weightless in comparison to the load she carried through the years. She gathered her resources to provide him with immediate medical attention but not before giving him some real talk—the kind he had tried to evade months before. Omari was like a third son. As much as she loved his father, she didn't want to see her nephew follow in his footsteps.

His aunt embraced the holistic-ancestral lifestyle where oftentimes candles, incense sticks, and oils were burned through the home to help remove bad energy. She advised that he pay closer attention to his body and avoid endangering others. By not protecting his temple, Omari was putting himself at risk of welcoming incoming soul ties that could have major consequences. He soaked up the information, hoping to turn the page on an ugly chapter, yet it was unreasonable to reach the end of his story without obtaining more dirt on Shauna's ex.

Unconcerned about who fathered Shauna's unborn child, the only thing that mattered to Omari was the virus spreader. Who was it? Shauna opened on the *who, when* and *why* during another tearful testimony. All that was missing was *where*. When asked, Omari got nothing other than "at his house." Through a little carelessness of her own, he found his answer on her laptop. Shauna had a bad habit of forgetting to log out of her Facebook account. Maybe it shouldn't have been seen as a bad habit at all.

He was on the hunt for answers. In her inbox lay the gold mine. Months of messages stored between Shauna and Dante, the culprit—a flashy fraudulent Harlem tough guy with average looks and a head size only a mother could love. Omari wrestled with trying to contain his excitement as Shauna rested beside him. In one of the messages was Dante's address posted as a refresher for Shauna's eyes only, sent on the alleged day of their encounter. Omari took pictures of Dante's photos, studying them as if they were notes for an upcoming exam. A trip to Harlem was inarguably in the works and he would be accompanied by his firearm in case of a run-in.

[Omari reflects on Black Friday morning, 2011]

There was a fury beyond words when exiting the 145th Street and St. Nicholas subway station. Walking on unfamiliar grounds with a concealed weapon could even make a scaredy cat feel superior. Omari had become a master of the stakeout. There was an immediate future in detective work if he ever wanted one. Thankfully for his sake, it wouldn't get that far.

It wasn't supposed to be *this* easy. He wasn't supposed to have slipped through the main entrance door of the apartment building so effortlessly. Perhaps the landlord should've prioritized fixing the front entrance lock, especially during this time of year when robbery numbers spiked. Omari was in pursuit of apartment 5B, hoping to present Dante with his date with doom. He sat on the stairs, listening to the sounds emerging from the apartment units on the fifth floor. There were pots and pans clanging, excessive dog barking, and then continued silence. He removed his fully charged phone to entertain himself when suddenly a door unlocked, causing him to have a case of the jitters. It was the home adjacent to 5B. He made an about-face, pretending to walk up the stairwell. His reaction was striking, proving he wasn't ready for a confrontation to this extent.

For the next hour, Omari gave innumerable thoughts to expediting the oncoming war. In one ear, he concentrated on apartment noise, in the other, he listened to "Kick in the Door" by The Notorious B.I.G. At last, it clicked. He needed to make a move or risk being in the stairwell all day. With all his might, he pounced on the door like a drug raid, adding a violent back kick. His fresh Nike Air Max squeaked along the floor like a rec center pickup game as he fled down the staircase. His plan to terrorize the apartment unit had gone accordingly. He hid behind the stairwell of the main floor until the oncoming activity ceased—then he struck again. The cat and mouse game rivaled that of a *Tom and Jerry* episode.

A bum ankle hindered his usual fleet-footedness when he elected to leap over several steps in an attempt to defy the laws of gravity in his escape. Seeing that the elevator had an active camera, it spelled the end of his attack. It was important that he left without getting caught, in hopes of another stand-off.

Striking terror into someone's home was beyond him. It was an immoral act done to rattle Dante. Unfortunately, it would involve family members who had nothing to do with his beef. They were seen as collateral damage. Omari ran the shower water, feeling terribly about what he had done. His guilt trip was quickly annulled once the steam from the shower incited the burning fissures in the crease of his inner thigh and buttocks. Dante was lucky to be alive.

He questioned himself wondering why he hadn't finished the job that Black Friday morning. He also wondered if he was captured entering and exiting on the building's main entrance camera. If he had only waited a little longer for Dante to leave the home, there wouldn't have been a nagging ankle sprain—just Dante's blood splattered on the waxed floor.

Unbeknownst to him was Dante's apartment's frontal view where the alleged culprit stood terrified watching his antagonist through the window staggering along the street. Dante was without a clue as to why his home had been terrorized, and now he was on high alert.

SATURDAY, DECEMBER 31

Did you ever catch those Christmas games?

"Nah. You know I don't mess with the NBA. I was hoping the lockout lasted for the rest of the season," Bryce answered Lorenzo, as they shared an enthusiastic phone conversation.

Oh, hell nah. I was losing my mind over here.

[laughter]

Anyway, Kobe dropped twenty-eight and we still lost to the damn Bulls.

"Oh, wow. Honestly, I haven't watched a full season since they left NBC. There was something about watching the *NBA on NBC* when we were coming up."

True. Whenever that theme music came on you knew what time it was.

[Lorenzo hums the tune]

"Did you know John Tesh composed that?"

That's the dude from Entertainment Tonight, ain't it?

"Yup."

Get the fuck outta here. He was a musician this entire time?

"I swear. Look it up."

That's crazy. Anyway, what'chu about to get into?

"Nothing much. Probably just relax. I'm still recovering from Vegas."

I bet.

"I'll probably start to cook in a little while. I'm supposed to be having company later."

Ringing in the new year in style.

"Nah, this is regular stuff. "

[children playing in the background]

"Oh, tell Daija and the girls I said Happy New Year."

Bryce gave a quick glance at his cell phone at the call's conclusion, awaiting Joy's response to her dinner preference. It was only mid-afternoon, and she was likely finishing at the post office hub, but he wanted to get a head start.

With his New Year's Eve partying days long behind, he typically spent the early part of the day at the bowling alley or at home, binge watching movies until church service—capping off the night transfixed in an enjoyable book with scented candles and a square meal amid a little John Coltrane. After taking an interest in ancient civilizations and world history, it was unclear if January 1 was even the official start of the new year. He saw it as a contrived holiday likely developed by an unknown elitist group to further an agenda. In fact, March was the first month of the new year, according to the old Roman ten-month calendar, in addition to a thirteen-month calendar concept circulating during olden times. March signified the arrival of spring, a welcoming shift in weather and nature. A true reason to celebrate, unlike the bitterly cold and lifeless month of January.

It was a time for reflection. Life was "good." Professionally Bryce never felt better, physically he was in the best shape of his life. His family and friends were healthy and thriving. Sadly, it was only Omari scratching and crawling for dear life. His brother's struggles were just one of two pet projects preventing him from accomplishing an almost perfect year. The other, goes without saying, involved his affairs. If woman was intended for man, where was his Eve?

He played the dating game the best way he knew how. Selfishly. There wasn't a better way to go about it unless you were gluten for punishment. How could he ever appease a fling if she didn't meet his best interest? This was *his* life, he was in control, and he had Ms. Blake to thank for the narcissistic attitude.

The ravishing former English teacher indirectly gave him a hard lesson on life and its cyclical stages. This all occurred when he believed they should carry out a relationship after their hotel encounter. She taught him that there were seasons where people entered and exited. Every beginning ends; each ending starts a new beginning. Rather than play the blame game or drown in his own sorrows, Bryce used their experience as a teachable lesson. In addition, it coincided with his spiritual learnings. God wouldn't intentionally inflict harm on one of His children without there being an educational moment. Even if it came at the expense of one's innocence. If not for Ms. Blake's exploitation—a course of indecency and tough love—maybe Bryce grows into a glorified simp, one who loves hard and gets taken advantage of. It wasn't an implausible thought considering his mother wasn't here to guide him on the inner workings of women.

Through Bryce's earlier encounters, he learned how to stabilize his emotions, giving most the impression that he didn't care. All things considered; it was an act. Underneath was a magnificent guy. A lover, fighter, protector, an edgier version of Dale with a heart of gold like his mother. Kristen and Julissa knew it, as did Ms. Blake, his first love, who only withdrew to protect him and her career. In truth, she created a monster.

In a perfect world, Bryce and Julissa would've become husband and wife. It's who he had the longest history with. Former high school classmates reunited through Facebook. The ending to their precious love story. If she wanted out of her doleful marriage as she led him to believe, she would've rationalized enduring nine months of turbulence without explanation, and they would've figured it out. Instead, there was the abortion hanging over Bryce's head. As a show of goodness, he transferred half of the abortion payment to Julissa's bank account. That phone call, now a few months old, was still fresh in his memory. She never asked him for the payment, but it was the least he could do. His generosity spelled the end of their mischief with the script ending exactly how it began—complicated.

How's the lentil soup coming along? Make sure you save me a bowl. Can't believe you've talked me into eating soup, he messaged Alyssa.

Alyssa was the person Bryce came closest to wanting to settle down with in a long time. Her soul matched her physical beauty.

She was everything he hoped for and more. Love didn't have a face, skin tone, or body type. It was a feeling—an action—which he hadn't sampled much. However, standing in the way was his intemperate sex addiction. It was critical that tonight he proved Joy wrong. He couldn't live with the "scared" claim when all he did was show respect and decency at her home that evening. How ridiculously tone deaf could she be? Bryce shined brightest when the pressure was on. She would find out in a few hours.

Once that challenge was conquered, another one neared. Could he remove his desire to be on every woman's radar and become a better version of himself? Since entering the dating market, Bryce slept with more women than some would in an entire lifetime. It would take plenty of prayer and obedience to prevent his obsession from blocking his blessings.

He conclusively made the dinner decision for tonight, removing the boneless chicken breasts from the refrigerator and placing them next to the breadcrumbs on the counter. Chicken parmesan and angel hair pasta. No chance Joy would resist.

Outside looked bright but a dramatic drop in the temperature was expected by nightfall. These were the times he wished for a significant other to cozy up with, listening to the crackling fire of a fireplace. It was imperative that one was included by the time he purchased his next home.

An assessment of the past year helped put things in their proper perspective but there was one other area that needed closure. Since the unanswered email to Dominique, he hadn't given much thought to Kristen. It seemed like eons since he last worried about when she would respond. It was a wonder if the women were even friends at this point. He walked toward the dining area where his laptop sat, figuring some quick detective work wouldn't do much harm. He and Omari would make quite the duo.

By the looks of things, Kristen was still unfound on the growing number of social media platforms, and Bryce had the passing thought of paying a monthly membership fee for the release of her current phone number and home address. Figuring that might've been taking things too far, he surmised that a more descriptive search in the web browser would generate greater results. He typed in *Kristen Davis Savannah State University* her alma mater to the outcome of marginal detail. Another attempt was *Kristen Davis Central New Jersey.* Nothing. He inserted *Kristen Davis kinesiology & dance major Georgia.* Instead of scrolling through the news links he clicked onto images, searching rows of pictures. After a tireless review, the third time proved to be successful. Why hadn't he thought of this before? There she was featured on the cover of a children's dance instructor magazine. She wore a natural hairstyle, bringing him back to when he used to randomly play in her hair. And that smile—boy oh boy that smile. She looked like she just hit the lotto. Kristen's dreams manifested, and Bryce was incredibly proud to see it, but it wasn't enough. He clicked on the link underneath her picture and paused. Suddenly, butterflies took shape. The same butterflies that erupted when he first laid eyes on her.

Kristen Clark
Hip Hop, Afro Fusion, Modern Dance Teacher
Founder & CEO of KayDee's Dance & Arts Center

Kristen Clark, a Georgia native and Cum Laude graduate with a degree in kinesiology & dance is passionate about empowering others through art. She went on to participate in and create choreography for performance groups while at Savannah State University. Kristen also worked as an Assistant Director at a dance school in New York City where she helped choreograph the moves of some of hip hop's top talents. Her dream of running her own studio finally came true in the summer of 2008 when she founded KayDee's Dance & Arts Center. The objective: To build relationships with children through dance. The art was used as a form of bonding with her family when she was a child and she hopes to pass the tradition onto her two girls, Ava, 3 and Kennedy, 1, whom she shares with her biggest supporter, Andre, her husband.

Kristen *Clark? Andre? Husband?* The blow to the gut was equivalent to June 3, 1991, at approximately 1:48 p.m. Upon completion, he got his answer. Kristen was alive, well, and happily married. A hard pill to swallow but well deserved.

> I Think I Might Wife Her: [picture message]
>
> Already on it. My mom was like, 'Who are you making an extra bowl for?' lol. It came out nice and thick.
>
> Sat 4:34 p.m.

Alyssa's text came right on time, softening the striking blow to the gut.

It is said to be an Italian tradition dating back to ancient Rome when gifting lentils or eating lentil soup shortly after midnight brought good luck and prosperity for the new year. At this point in their friendship, Bryce was more than certain Alyssa would agree to meet him at a neutral site to personally hand-deliver the dish. Unfortunately, it would have to wait as he was busy playing chef. Speaking of which, he gave Joy a quick call. She should've been off work and gearing up to arrive. Since his return from Las Vegas, she had playfully taunted him about their next encounter. He snickered at her most recent text:

> Mail Lady: I'm gonna get there after work. So,
> when I'm there I need you to feed me and
> fuck me. Don't waste my time lol. My oldest is
> heading out that night so I'll need to be back
> for the kids before he leaves. Anyway, I'm
> getting ready for bed. Have a good night.
>
> Thurs 8:34 p.m.

The phone rang several times before going to voicemail. He waited a minute before placing another call. This time there were no rings, just an automated message. She was probably getting ready—no need to get himself into a stew.

> FYI I'm making chicken parm. Tried calling
> twice. Let me know when ur on the way.
>
> Sat 5:30 p.m.

[John Coltrane's "I'm Old Fashioned" plays in the background]
Dinner was ready and waiting on the stove. Bryce worked up a sweat performing last-minute cleaning before a date with the shower. The lights in the bathroom were off, candles lit, the air misty. Running hot water from the oversized showerhead never felt so good. He used the moment to count his blessings. Clean, hot water was a gift that should've been granted to all and yet there were millions in the world still living without it. He couldn't imagine not doing something as natural as cleaning his body. Contrary to his earlier beliefs, life wasn't "good," it was great.

His phone usually sat on the bedroom nightstand during shower time. Today it was on top of the bathroom sink with the ringer at maximum volume. He dried off and viewed the home screen. Time was racing and yet no call, voicemail, or text from Joy.

Lizzy sat in total darkness in a loaf position in the center of the bed. The earlier sunlight was no more. Daylight Saving Time could be such a killjoy. He got dressed, added a few pumps of a new Burberry Brit cologne, and headed downstairs to a lengthy conversation with Dan about the ongoing baseball free agency signings. Following that, a call with Priscilla where he helped himself to a small plate of food listening to her gloat about her recent savings account achievement. Hopefully there was still enough time for Joy's appearance. She hadn't a clue what she was missing out on with tonight's dish.

8:15 P.M.

He poured himself a dribble of red wine, staring out the kitchen window at Tasha. She was on the go again, off to celebrate the new year with people—or perhaps a special someone—who would appreciate her time. He pressed the talk icon and then Joy's number. Voicemail. The writing was on the wall. Joy's unwillingness to check in proved she didn't care about their planned dinner. She stood him up.

The brand of Stella Rose tasted sweet going down, now overtaken by bitterness. Bryce's evening turned into a cataclysmic failure. If something had gone terribly wrong, what harm would a text have done? Rather than wait to find out, he blocked her number. She would never get a second chance to humiliate him. He stored the food in the refrigerator, grabbed his wine glass, and whispered a short prayer thanking the Lord for today's divine awakening. Maybe tonight wasn't a loss but a triumphant victory in disguise. Glass half full. He watched *The Twilight Zone* marathon until it was time to conduct a New Year's Eve countdown of his own—one to bedtime.

28

UNDENIABLE

The mad rush of the holidays and Alyssa's extended work hours limited their brushes at the gym. Excluding the New Year's Day drop off of the lentil soup, they hadn't spent much time together since the movie date. With the holidays in the rearview mirror, Bryce wanted to put an end to his seesaw dating run and bet all his chips on her.

Family and friends were usually put on notice during the NFL Wild Card weekend. If the 49ers were playing and it wasn't an emergency, all calls should wait until halftime. If your life were in jeopardy... call 911. Fortunately, his gridiron favorites wrapped up their division weeks ago, enabling a first-round bye and providing him with a little weekend wiggle room.

Alyssa's birthday was in a couple of days, and for a while he was thinking of a way to surprise her. When it came to commemorating loved ones, he took pride in doing something memorable. It wasn't quite love between them yet, but "Aly" had reached nickname status. A small deed to a major development. He learned about Alyssa's love for musicals months back, but it was right before his darling thirteen-win San Francisco 49ers officially clinched the NFC West when he decided on her gift. He asked that she carve out some time on her birthday weekend before going online to search for the best seat in the house. Tickets to a Broadway matinee wasn't earth-shattering news. She had already seen *West Side Story* with her mother and most recently *The Lion King* with her sister, but it was where they were seated that leaped out: fourth row at the famous Majestic Theatre. Any closer, and they could've joined the cast of *The Phantom of the Opera* on stage. Moreover, it was the event planned afterward that could potentially earn him a VIP section in the bowels of her heart.

Bryce raved about the phenomenal performance, most notably the falling chandelier which had the audience in a stir. Alyssa displayed mixed emotions, recounting the dynamic developments of the love story with a tear in her eye. He comforted her by wrapping his arms around her waist resting his chin above her pom-pom beanie hat as they waited to cross onto Eighth Avenue. She laughed at herself for becoming an emotional wreck, even going as far as apologizing. There was nothing to be sorry about. The emotional outburst validated her giant-sized heart.

The pedestrian walking signal flashed; Bryce offered his hand and Alyssa accepted. They crossed the busy street to a café for cups of hot cocoa. Soon, the sun would fade into dusk setting the scene for his romantic presentation—which he promised would be waiting for her when they got "home."

"I knew a kid *so big* he could only play 'seek.'" Bryce's dad-joke attempt lifted Alyssa's spirit, but he needed a little more practice before quitting his day job.

Walking along to the sights and sounds of the city was always pleasurable to him. They weren't too far from his Bryant Park office building which he hoped to show, but they were pressed for time. Engrossed in thought, he made a quick call to an unidentified contact as they crossed over to the 42nd Street-Port Authority subway station. His face went from pleasant to expressionless. Alyssa waited off to the side, sipping her hot beverage.

"Is everything okay?"

"All good." He replied wearing a snide smirk. "I was making sure the guy at the parking garage had the car warmed up before we got there."

They waited on the subway platform for an arriving express train. Anticipation filled the air. Alyssa put on a good face but hated surprises. The suspense made her nervous. The headlights of an approaching northbound A-train meant they were at the finality of his revelation.

The next stop is: 59th Street– Columbus Circle. Stand clear of the closing doors, please.

"Wait, we're going uptown? Didn't we park near the Holland?" she replied, referring to the Holland Tunnel which made for an easier escape out of Manhattan.

"Damn. You're right. We'll get off at the next stop and turn around."

"What would you do without me?" Bryce didn't know the answer to that question and at this juncture, he didn't want to find out.

He stood against the subway door as the train raced through the tunnel. Alyssa glowed standing in front of him, looking glam in her red lipstick and hooded winter coat. Her soft waves dropped from underneath the beanie cap. He was lost in her multicolored eyes. No one should look *this* good.

She stuck out her tongue to break up the monotony. Her unwillingness to look away was telling. He saw it as a courageous gesture that made him want to kiss her on the spot. Patience. As he looked around, shockingly, they were the only interracial duo on board–even in a city as diverse as New York. But that wouldn't matter. What mattered was their destination.

This is: 59th Street–Columbus Circle.

He grabbed her hand darting through the crowd of onboarding passengers moving rapidly along the stairs. There was a downtown A-train waiting on the other side of the platform. He had no intention of connecting to it, but his acting was worthy of an Oscar.

"Bryce," Alyssa howled.

"Yes, ma'am."

"What is happening?"

"Just play along, Aly."

> Ok. We're here. Crossing into Central Park now.

(212) 555-4112: Ok my friend. We're waiting. I'm wearing a red coat.

Sat 4:42 p.m.

They were back in the cold.

"I need you to close your eyes," Bryce instructed. Alyssa complied but couldn't wipe the smile off her face. They walked along 59th Street and Central Park when her eyebrows rose, and her nose twitched. "Are you taking me to a friggin' barn?" she asked, thrown off by the smell of horse manure.

[taxi horn blares]

"Close."

For added security, he covered her eyes with his gloved hand and waved off the insistent coachmen standing along the sidewalk finally spotting the man of the hour. A short stout guy in a top hat and red coat patting a chestnut brown stallion.

"Felix?"

"Aye, my friend." The men embraced. Felix's firm handshake nearly ripped Bryce's arm out of the socket.

"Is *this* birthday girl?" Felix asked, using improper English with an unrecognizable accent.

"That's her. Aly, you can open your eyes now."

"Oh. Nice to meet you," she giggled, looking positively googly-eyed at Bryce and the horse.

"Beau-ti-ful. You guys ready for fun?"

"Oh my gosh, Bryce." She blushed.

Felix helped Alyssa board the horse carriage. "Thank goodness I wore combat boots instead of heels."

"Okay, my friends. Copper and I will take you on nice tour of park. Sit back and enjoy ride. If *enny* questions, please, ask. Okay?" Alyssa snuggled next to Bryce, adding in a tight arm lock before briefly placing her head onto his shoulder.

"You're so sweet. So, this is why you kept asking me not to plan anything. When did you arrange this?"

"I'm not giving away my secrets."

Premium seats at the Majestic Theatre and a romantic horse carriage ride through Central Park, for a pair who hadn't quite established themselves, might've been a stretch for some, but this was Bryce's bent knee moment. His way of asking for her hand.

～

MONDAY, JANUARY 16

A Midnight Jasmine scented candle drifted through the darkened living room where Alyssa rested comfortably across his sofa. They just finished watching *The 40-Year-Old Virgin* through unapologetic tears of laughter. Following their fairytale date and hours into her birthday, Bryce avoided the standard conversation which usually precedes confirmation of a relationship. Instead, he surprised her with six unexpected words during his commute that morning: *Thinking about you... let's do this.* Her rapid reply of "You must be psychic" all but sealed the deal. They agreed to take their respective lunch breaks at the same time, where a discussion arose about trust. Bryce owned up to his last sexual encounter with Julissa while conveniently excluding the one-night stand with Jazmin or the most recent meet-up with Kaylani. Two women he was sure to never see again. Without reservation Alyssa admitted to feeling safe with the certainty Bryce had her best interest at heart. Her admission brought him immense pleasure.

"Is this real?" she asked, looking up at him.

"As real as reality television," he laughed, playfully covering her face with strands of hair to resemble Cousin Itt from *The Addams Family*. "Yes. It's real." She brushed her hair to the side staring at him in amazement. "You make me feel... I dunno. It's hard to explain."

"Well, hopefully it's *good*."

"Of course. And no, I'm not just saying this because I'm feeling mushy."

"Well, you unequivocally deserve to feel good. I feel the same way."

"Aw. By the way, you have such gorgeous teeth."

"You're trying your hardest to make me blush, aren't you? Your teeth look way better."

She gave another delayed look. "Open your mouth. No way. They're not as white as yours..."

"That's racist," Bryce snickered.

"Can you believe after all this time we'd be sitting here in your living room?"

"Absolutely."

Alyssa rose up. "Absolutely? Okay, Nostradamus. So, you knew we'd end up here ten months later?"

"Has it been ten months since the eye appointment? Honestly, if I told you what I was *really* thinking that whole time you'd think I was psycho."

"No, I wouldn't."

"You were on my mind—a lot. Sometimes too much. I spoke about you to my closest friends. Just wait 'til you meet them. They'll tell you personally."

"I'd be lying if I told you differently. I used to catch myself staring at you whenever we'd bump into each other at the gym. I'd have my cap on thinking I could get away with hiding my eyes. One time you..."

"One time I caught you."

"I was just about to say that. I was like, 'Damn, busted.'"

"I could sense your stares."

"No, you couldn't." She patted his chest. An enormous difference from Tasha's stinging body blows.

"I think I smirked the first time."

"You did," Alyssa agreed.

"I knew you were special the moment I paused my music to strike up convo," he continued. "It was the first time I saw you leaving the locker room. I *never* do that."

"What did I do?" she chuckled.

"Look too damn good. My eyes nearly popped out of my head."

"Really?"

"Yes, really. I think I was listening to Pearl Jam or something and then..."

"Pearl Jam? Oh my God, that's one of my favorite groups. I didn't know you liked them."

"Why is that? Is it because..."

She rose up once more. "Don't start."

"I was gonna say is it because I look more like a Third Eye Blind kinda guy?"

[laughter]

"Do you remember which Pearl Jam song?"

"'Even Flow.'"

"That's so cool. I'm dying to see them in concert."

Bryce licked his lips. "I see you tried your hardest not to look good tonight. Nice try."

"I look like crap. My sweats have holes in them," she laughed. "I got home, showered, and threw something on. Nobody should be looking that deep anyway."

"C'mere..."

He helped reposition Alyssa into a straddling pose on his lap. She shifted her hair and folded her lips going from forthright and direct to shy and demure. Bryce grabbed her by the chin and moved in. Her lips were butter soft. Their passion was slow and steady, just like their pursuit. His massive hands ran across her chiseled back, prompting light moans from her mouth. It had been a long while since she last felt a man's touch. She slipped in a little tongue, and he returned the favor. His light tug on her bottom lip afterward made her tremble with excitement.

She moved away from his mouth, sweeping her hair to the right with a sexually arousing look in her eye. Behind Alyssa's left ear was a miniature tattoo. One of which he couldn't make out. He marked her outer neck with his tongue—a key sensual spot. Finally, after years of being the main character, Bryce allowed for his own erogenous zone to be discovered when she navigated her tongue around his right earlobe, sending him into a state of lust.

It was eight forty-five—a work night. Their fiery lovemaking ceased. Alyssa sat on top of him in a sports bra and sweatpants having removed her tank top and joining it with his sweatshirt on the carpet. She seemed embarrassed, trying to explain how long it had been since she felt this good. He pressed his finger against her dripping mouth to quiet the noise. She kissed his finger, inching closer to his face. They couldn't keep their hands off each other. He laid her flat on her back, planted light kisses on her stomach and caressed the outside of her sports bra before pulling down her sweatpants. Alyssa was without underwear as if she anticipated the moment. She was clean-shaven with a small butterfly tattoo appearing on her groin. The tattoo placement gave off a rebellious side. At least it wasn't the name of an ex-lover. He helped himself with a sample. Her scent was that of fresh-cut roses. She tilted her head back; her eyes rolled in the same direction. Within minutes, he proudly watched her soul levitate from her body, floating toward serenity.

They finally found themselves in his bedroom because she insisted. Otherwise, he was content with ending their evening on the sofa with her cries of joy settled on his mustache. She wanted to "feel him" —her words. He was delighted to have been chosen as the person to end her inspiring celibacy run. The irony that it would occur on Dr. Martin Luther King's observed birthday.

The bedroom setting was constructed hours ahead of her arrival. Fresh bed sheets and a slow-burning, sweet-smelling candle. The only thing missing was a soundtrack. He thought about playing Pearl Jam for laughs and giggles, but the mood didn't call for that. They would have plenty of time to goof off now that they were officially an item. Instead, he settled for an independent rock band known for their acoustic guitar-inspired love songs.

The director in him wouldn't die. "Bachelor Bryce" was dead but even the new and improved version needed to administer the bed sequence. Alyssa was tense below and he wanted to take his time. Developing good in-bed chemistry was key to withstanding a long-term relationship. She mounted him while removing her sports bra. Soon their bare skin met and then their mouths. The make-out intensified. The contrasts of their skin tones looked like a work of art. Alyssa was leaky-faucet wet, and his erection knocked at her door. He gripped her backside to synchronize with her motions. In time, the floodgates opened.

He interrupted their performance to grab a condom from inside the nearby nightstand. Sitting upright he scooched her closer, propped her knees and grasped her trapezoid muscles through the way of her armpits. "Hold onto the headboard," he advised. At last, he was in. Alyssa let out a sharp shrill—her body was stimulated. "Don't rush. Take your time, baby," he whispered, intentionally placing his mouth against her earlobe. The lead female singer of the independent rock band serenaded the couple through the harmonic chorus as they kissed passionately through slow penetrating thrusts. Alyssa gripped the headboard and transferred her hair from one side to the other. Bryce turned his attention toward her nipples and applied light sucks shifting his hand down her back. "How does it feel?" he whispered. She was too discombobulated to give a comprehensible response. He targeted her trachea and neck with his dripping mouth. Without removing himself he shifted his weight on top of her, falling methodically onto the bed. Their mouths salivated as they looked each other in the eye. Alyssa lifted her head for another kiss; her moans increased with each lunge; her nails dug deeper into his flesh.

"Oh my God... you feel so good."

He heard that part loud and clear.

29

—

MY SACRIFICE

Priscilla couldn't help herself. The taste of victory was too sweet not to rub it in. Bryce would hear about the Giants' Super Bowl victory against the New England Patriots from now until the end of time, which according to the Mayan Calendar, was ten months away.

It was Bryce who dished it first two weeks prior when he declared his 49ers would beat her Giants in their epic NFC Championship game showdown—only to find himself numb on his living room sofa as Priscilla's deafening screams of joy ricocheted the walls. He was so upset about the 49ers shocking overtime loss that he called in sick to work the next morning. It took some bribing, but Bryce finally agreed to join Priscilla at her sister's house to watch Super Bowl XLVI, keeping distracted by e-filing Omari's taxes. There was no way he could subject himself to more Eli Manning heroics. That was like kicking at a corpse.

On his long solo drive back from VCU's Homecoming Weekend, Priscilla urged him to cross over to Big Blue's winning tradition. "There's still room on the wagon," she offered. It was much too late for that. Bryce had been a 49ers fan all his life. Super Bowl XIX was the first big game he could recall watching as a third grader, falling in love with Joe

Montana and the hard-hitting Ronnie Lott. Once Jerry Rice became a prominent member of the high-powered West Coast Offense, it all but solidified his allegiance to the "red and gold." Bryce trusted coach Bill Walsh and their winning tradition enough to dismiss his hometown Washington Redskins—much to Dale's dissatisfaction. Becoming a Niners fan also helped him offset the losing ways of the Baltimore Orioles as his gridiron heroes would go on to win four Super Bowls through the '80s and mid-'90s.

Bryce finally gave Priscilla the scoop on Alyssa, who was ecstatic to learn he put his single days behind him. However, the excitement didn't come without a stern warning. She would only be onboard if he promised not to allow it to interfere with their personal friendship, which he assured was well protected. In fact, his friendship with Priscilla was one of the first heart-to-heart conversations he shared with Alyssa, who admitted to not being the jealous type.

The talk switched to Omari. Priscilla listened in disbelief, unable to make sense of his courageous decision to become an acting father.

"B., does he know what he's getting himself into? A person has to really love someone unconditionally to take on such a role."

"I've talked to him. There's not much I can do, P. He's his own man. I'm sure a lot of this has to do with his upbringing and not having his dad around."

"I get that. I mean, I didn't have my father either, but... I mean... he's still so young. Why not have the same energy for your *own* life rather than put all your chips on a chick who ruined your health and a baby that isn't his?"

"I understand. All we can do is continue to encourage him. Maybe he sees something we don't see?"

Inspired by his conversation with Priscilla, Bryce decided to pull over to a rest stop for a restroom break and a quick check-in with his brother. Shauna was expected to give birth at any moment.

MONDAY, FEBRUARY 13

> Big Bro: When u get a chance, read
> Philippians 4:4-9. Keep me posted on
> Shauna.
>
> Sun 5:13 p.m.

The time stamp showed Sunday, but it was only a few short hours ago when Omari opened the message. He arrived at the hospital to a relieved girlfriend, who looked at him with weary eyes. Her grandmother sat beside her. Omari planted a kiss on Shauna's forehead and positioned himself at the foot of the bed. She had just given birth to a healthy boy who took the name of Omari's favorite rapper and Shauna's last name: Cameron Bomani Pierce —six pounds, fourteen ounces. He wouldn't expect anyone to understand his decision or implicit attitude on the subject matter. In his mind there was a deeper meaning to why they were together.

Their commitment was twofold, and Shauna was his safest bet under the circumstances. Who in their right mind would risk compromising their health by dealing with his medical condition? The other thought was Cameron. Every child deserved the chance to be raised by two parents. Since the newborn's biological father didn't want the responsibility, Omari was presented with the opportunity to become the father he longed for. Cameron was his new lease on life, a shot at pressing the reset button and giving love a chance. Not the usual thoughts of a now twenty-three-year-old, but he had an unusual way of thinking.

Shauna's excitement grew for the setup of Cameron's room, in which her uncle was constructing last-minute furniture in time for their arrival. Omari took a picture of the newborn sending a group message to friends. Shauna was convinced her new bundle of joy shared a strong resemblance, raising an interesting question: How would Omari handle Cameron's transformation once Dante or the mystery gentleman's genes kicked in? He jotted a few thoughts in his rap notebook recognizing Cameron was born the day before Valentine's Day. What a momentous story that could've been had he arrived twenty-four hours later—an unwanted child introduced to the world on a day of love.

Omari pointed out a series of congratulatory replies from the group message before Shauna shamelessly announced that she would never put her body through the torturous pain of a pregnancy again. Unforeseen was a call from an unknown number which happened only days before. When answered, the caller immediately hung up. Directing the calls to voicemail was of no use either. Omari stepped out into the hallway.

"Hello?"

[inaudible sound]

"Hello?"

No response. He had a grimace for a face upon his return to the room.

"You look annoyed. What's wrong?" Shauna asked.

"I don't know. I've been getting these strange calls from an unknown number. Sometimes four or five times a day. When I answer, nobody says a word."

"Telemarketers, maybe? Or it could simply be an accidental butt dial."

"Whoever that mothafucka is must have a wide ass cuz it happens all day long."

"Omari! Stop cussin' in front of the baby."

His father admittedly hid behind a private number in his earlier efforts to reach out. It was done out of fear and not knowing what to say after years of silence. That was no longer the case. These were the actions of someone trying to get his attention, but who? It could've been a telemarketer as Shauna suggested or just some dope who hadn't grasped the rudimentary concept of how to reciprocate a phone greeting. Either way, with a new year came change. Undoubtedly Omari was off to a tremendous start, but it was time to consider a new phone number.

Shauna's grandmother watched Cameron through the glass window as he rested in the nearby newborn nursery. Meanwhile, Shauna closed her eyes with Omari next to her. He skimmed through Philippians 4:4-9. The verse emphasized the Lord's presence—to remove fear and present all requests to Him through prayer. Ordinarily, Bible language was seen as foreign, and he shamefully ignored most of Bryce's reading recommendations. Not today. He thanked him in a follow-up text asking that he keep his sickly father in his prayers and, for good measure, help improve his own prayer life. His request wouldn't come without a counteroffer.

> Big Bro: Deal. But I need u to get back to making music and start talking to ur mom. She loves u bro…
>
> Mon, 4:41 p.m.

"Babe, we should take a light run through the park trail."

It was Presidents' Day morning, and Alyssa's Mazda CX-5 had been parked in Bryce's driveway since early Saturday evening. He was preparing to whip up breakfast and analyze the plot of *Safe House,* an action-thriller they'd seen the night before, starring Denzel Washington and Ryan Reynolds.

"Don't you wanna eat something first? I'm sure we've already burned *thousands* of calories," Bryce hinted, creating laughter between them. "I don't know where all this energy is coming from. Is the gym open today?"

"I think it closes early but we have one on the complex."

"Oh. I completely forgot."

"Let's eat something light, hit the trail and then I'll make something fancy when we get back."

Alyssa settled for fruit while Bryce scarfed two strawberry-banana flavored yogurts. He stirred pancake batter and eggs to dish up when they returned. It was seven thirty, the sky had its usual assortment of colors, the sun looked like a tangerine, and the air was painfully cold. They elected to go to the woodsy hiking trail less than five miles from the house, the first visit for either of them. She put on a pair of high-waist purple leggings and one of Bryce's oversized sweatshirts. Meanwhile he shuffled through the drawers for a long-sleeved shirt to wear underneath his graphite grey VCU Rams hoodie. When it came to the cold, Bryce didn't take chances. He came upon the infamous "The Man, The Legend" T-shirt during his search. Alyssa's sense of humor was surely able to handle the obscenity.

"Aly, look…"

Alyssa belly laughed. "Do you actually wear that outside?"

"I've worn it a time or two but mainly around the house. Would you mind throwing it in the trash behind you?"

"Don't throw it away. You can wear it to the gym. Wait, that's probably not a good idea."

"Uh, yeah, great observation."

"Let me wear it. I can plaster a 'W' and 'O' to spell out 'woman.' It'll be cute."

"Nobody needs to know about *your* legend." Bryce smirked, rubbing Alyssa repeatedly along the inner thigh. "Stop it," she gushed, pecking him on the lips. She balled up the shirt and dumped it in the trash at his request.

This felt right. Like they belonged. Alyssa matched his kind-heartedness, playful side, and wit. She was smart and simple with an acquired taste no different than his. Most importantly when they were at the courting stage, she made him feel like a priority, starting his morning with warm messages and ending the day with check-ins. Bryce wasn't the needy type but a show of concern from a friend or loved one was one of his love languages. It was the little things.

They discarded skin color and found prosperity even if he had reservations about meeting her family. His angst was a result of America's grisly racial history and social differences which had cultivated division for generations. Bryce worked hard to fight through false narratives painted by misanthropists, who used savvy tactics to unfairly taint the minds of a population. Despite having a college degree, an honorable career, and high-class socioeconomic status, he was still viewed as a Black man first—where the biased depictions were vastly widespread. Secondly, there were still families who condemned and banished relatives for partnering with a person of color. *Stick to your own kind,* the uncharitable words uttered through history usually kept those tempted to crossover left to their fantasies. In the spirit of Presidents' Day—in this great nation of stolen land—Bryce and Alyssa walked out of the house hand in hand having robbed the other's heart. They were unwaveringly optimistic about embarking on life's most polarizing moments, and nothing would stand in the way of that.

30

WIDE AWAKE

"Hey man, I know we ain't hit it off before, but..."

"Try starting off with a little humility. How about, 'Good afternoon, sorry to disturb you,'" Shauna rehearsed.

[faint baby cry in the background]

"I'm not kissing that fat motha... sorry, I'm not kissing his ass."

"You're not kissing his ass, Omari, you're proving to be the bigger person. Think of it as taking the high road. There's less traffic up there."

"You're asking for a lot. That man threatened my life."

Omari was preparing to patch things up with Shauna's downstairs neighbor. If he was going to become a permanent fixture in her home and around the neighborhood, it was important to clean up the mess from last summer. Shauna only crossed paths with the neighbor once since returning from the hospital, a quick hello wave as she was downstairs retrieving the mail.

"Good afternoon, sorry to disturb you and your family. I just wanted to remind you that you're a fat piece of shit."

"Omari," Shauna yelled.

"I'm joking. Look, you startled Cam."

The infant squiggled on the receiving blanket; his eyes wandered the room. Omari sat on the bed and placed his finger inside of Cameron's tiny palm which he latched onto for added comfort.

"Aw, that's so cute," Shauna relished.

"That's my little man. I love this kid. All right, I'm gonna head down there and see what's up."

"Omari don't do anything stupid. I'm serious. And take off the du-rag, please."

"You want me to put on a three-piece suit while I'm at it?"

"Yes. Go clean yourself up," she joked, to which he playfully chased her around in a pair of Timberland boots across the hardwood floor. Shauna screeched at his insistent tickling.

[neighbor below bangs on the ceiling]

"Shhh, you can't be running around in those heavy ass shoes."

[Omari's phone rings]

"Yo," he answered, panting heavily.

Whoa, am I interrupting something? Y'all making a sex video?

"How'd you know?" He replied to Brixx.

Fam, what's good? I feel like I haven't seen you in years. You ain't fuckin' with this rap shit anymore?

"Says who? I'm still writing. Just trying to get some personal stuff in order. Working on getting a car. Tired of taking public transportation."

I feel you. DP and Ford were asking about you the other day.

"What did they say?"

They were like, 'Does he still wanna rap?'

"Don pops up every few months and nobody says a word. I take a little break and suddenly our breakup is as bad as Roc-a-fella's."

Nah, he was just like, 'Where's O.?' I was like, 'Ask him.' By the way, he came at you hard on a track the other day. I ain't gon lie, it was fire.

"Who, me? Did he bump his head or somethin'? Tell Don he's light work. I'll light that ass up."

That's between y'all. All I know is he smoked you on that track, son.

"Yeah, all right."

Yo, what's up with your brother's friend?

"Who?"

The BET chick. I feel like she gassed us.

"Oh. I think that's a wash. He hasn't mentioned anything about her. Remember I was telling him to smash that, thinking it would speed things up?"

You think he did?

"I don't know. He said something about how he used to hit her up and she'd take weeks to reply."

That's cuz he ain't holding it down right. Tell her to come holla. Watch how fast we'll get a deal.

[hard knocks on the door]

"Let me hit you back…"

No doubt. Real quick, did you get the letter about the graduation date?

"They probably sent it to my bro's crib. That's where most of my mail goes."

Oh, all right. Holla at me later then.

Omari walked back into the bedroom where Shauna was feeding Cameron with a concerned look.

[second set of door knocks]

"Were you expecting anyone?"

"No."

"Do you want me to answer?"

"You're gonna have to. I'm feeding the baby," Shauna whispered. "Look through the peephole first." Omari walked over to his bag, grabbed his handgun, and craftily slid it into the back of his pants out of Shauna's eyeshot. He tiptoed toward the door, looked through the peephole, and gestured downward with his finger. It was the downstairs neighbor.

"I'm not gonna let them hold us hostage like this," he whispered, standing in the bedroom. "It's the middle of the day. He's lucky Cam sleeps through the night but what happens if he starts crying one night? Are they gonna bang on the ceiling?”

“I know. Just go and see what he wants.”

“Your uncle is the landlord, but this fat ass walks around thinking he owns the property.”

[Omari slowly unlocks the door]

“He was only seventeen...” Pete Johnston informed.

“That’s terrible. He had so much life to live,” Jenna replied.

“I know.”

“What’s the shooter’s name, *Zimmerman?*” Roy asked. “But doesn’t he look Hispanic?” Zoë grabbed his phone as she and Bryce inspected the photo.

“Maybe his dad is Caucasian,” Bryce suggested.

“Isn’t there a saying, ‘You are what your father is’?” Roy asked.

“Then that would make you a Goober.”

[laughter]

“Way to make light of the situation, Zo.”

“I’m not even talking about the shooting but if we were to use that logic then it would explain a few things, mister.”

“Okay, so, that makes you White since Bob Ross is your dad.”

“Blah, blah...”

“Um, guys, hello. Two Caucasians at the table,” Pete waved, reminding the group.

“On a serious note, I understand crime happens every day, but this one definitely hits home,” Bryce explained. “Trayvon could’ve easily been me, my brother, or you, Roy. Now we’ll never get the full story.”

“I know,” Jenna empathized. “This world is going to hell in a handbasket. Did you know gay marriage was just legalized in another state?”

“Where now?” Pete inquired.

"Maryland, I think? Don't quote me."

"Smooth, ain't that your hometown? What's up with that?"

"I didn't know you were from there," Jenna announced.

"Maryland was home for five years. I'm originally from New York. Roy's just being Roy."

[Roy orders from the menu]

"I'm not opposed to people of the same sex being in love and wanting to marry, it's just tough trying to explain it when you have kids. Especially a son who claims he has three girlfriends," Zoë informed.

"I couldn't imagine having kids in this day and age," Jenna added. "It's not even a thought. I feel terrible about this."

"I'm with you. I have tons of nieces and nephews. I would imagine trying to explain the birds and bees is a tall order nowadays," Pete added.

"Listen, I grew up in church, so you guys know where most people stand on this topic," Bryce said. "I haven't given gay marriage much thought, but I'm a contrarian by nature and so I find the backlash interesting."

"How so?" Jenna asked.

"The idea that love has no boundaries *except* for when it involves homosexuals."

[light laughter]

"That concept of thinking is peculiar, but what do I know?" He shrugged. "I don't make the rules."

[Jenna orders from the menu]

"Isn't it crazy how often we see this girl now?" Zoë pointed at the nearby table.

"Maybe she works around here," Bryce replied.

"I love her style of dress. Maybe I need to play for the other team," she joked.

"You can pull it off," Roy baited. "Who are you talking about?"

"The one over in the corner. She's so pretty. She dresses like one of those old-school actresses but with a splash of today's fashion."

"You're right. She's got a chic elegant style. Smooth, isn't that the same girl you almost leaped over the tables to speak to?" Bryce looked back in the direction of the woman. He was right, it was her and she was insanely gorgeous.

"This guy *seriously* exaggerates. Zo, was I leaping?"

"You kinda were…"

"Don't listen to these fools. I didn't even budge."

Bryce didn't have time for Roy's witty repartee. Instead, he texted his current love interest who was no slouch in the looks department.

Hey Babe. What time were you coming over tonight? He texted Alyssa.

"I'm gonna go over there and tell her that she has a couple of admirers." Zoë left the table to chat with the mystery woman. Meanwhile, Pete chuckled to himself.

"What's so funny?" Jenna asked him.

"Oh nothing. I can have a perverse sense of humor at times."

"Spill it," Roy insisted.

"I was just thinking what if Zoë walked over there and the girl had a deep voice. All her beauty and grace only to sound like the guy from *Green Mile.*"

"Michael Clarke Duncan?" Roy tittered.

"Wouldn't that be something?" Jenna asked in amazement.

"No," Roy shot back. "This is New York City. Expect the unexpected."

"One might conjecture that's the writer in you," Bryce declared of Pete.

"You're a writer? What type of writing?" Roy inquired.

"I am. I've written a few screenplays. My buddies and I wrote a TV pilot a few years after college. It was a comedy that we tried to pitch to the major networks. But then reality television bit us in the ass."

"What the heck are you doing at Hudson Investors?"

"Welp... I needed to pay bills somehow."

Zoë returned to the table dumbstruck. She looked up from her cell phone. Her mouth opened but words hadn't formed.

"Dude, what's the matter with you?" Roy asked. Bryce locked eyes with the mystery woman thinking something had gone terribly wrong. She smiled back, sipping her beverage, removing strands of hair from her face.

"Well, that was interesting. Anthony just texted me that AJ had a fight in school and suffered a severe meltdown. He's heading over there to pick him up."

"Aw, poor guy," Jenna conveyed.

"Boys being boys," added Roy. "I thought something happened with the lady over there."

"I did too," Bryce indicated.

"Oh. No. She was super cool. My poor baby, though. It must've been that bully he was telling me about. Ugh."

"Sorry to hear that, Zoë," Pete pitied.

"What did the lady say after you complimented her?" Roy asked, trying to switch subjects.

"Thirsty much?" Bryce called out. "You've got a little drool in the corner of your mouth there."

"I mean, boys fight all the time. What's the surprise here? AJ will be fine. Do you know how many fights I had at his age? I was just curious about what the woman said."

"I told her she was gorgeous, and how we admired her style. Then Anthony started texting. He said the school tried calling me, but I don't have any missed calls."

"We get that. Now finish telling the story about the lady."

[Jenna laughs]

"Eww, Milk Dud get a hold of yourself. All she said was 'thank you.' She's Brazilian so there was a slight language barrier. She had the squeakiest voice though. It was so cute."

Pete's eyes grew three sizes. "Shucks, I was close," he announced, snapping his fingers.

"What do you mean?" Zoë asked.

"I'll explain later."

"Yeah, it was Mickey Mouse squeaky. Oh, and Bryce, she recognized us." Zoë used her best broken English accent to mimic the woman. "She was like, 'I work near library. I remember you and tall guy. I see you walk together. He play sport?'"

"What did you say?"

"I told her no; you're one of us."

"Aw, sorry about that, Bryce," Jenna empathized sarcastically.

"Aye, Smooth, go holla at her. You speak a little Spanish."

"They speak Portuguese, Einstein," Zoë advised.

"I'm happily involved," Bryce alerted. "Thanks anyway."

The fashionista made eye contact with the group and offered a friendly wave goodbye as she prepared to leave. Meanwhile, about every guy at the eatery watched her walk confidently to the exit. Boys being boys.

～

"Yeah bro, she's on her way to the house now. We're about to meal prep. I've got to give it to her, she's a great girl," Bryce informed Dan.

I'm proud of you, dawg. That's a big move.

"It wasn't easy. You know I was holding onto bachelorhood with my fingertips."

I hear that.

"It was time to hang up the jersey. All of the signs seemed to point that way."

Sixty-nine might be the first number of its kind to hang from the rafters.

[Bryce laughs]

"I don't recall ever wearing that number. You know I'm gonna have to search to see if sixty-nine is retired."

It would have to be a football player. Maybe an offensive lineman. By the way, is she a baseball fan? I'm looking at the O's schedule now.

"She played a smidgen of softball…"

My bad. You mentioned that the last time you came down.

"Yeah. I think she'd be on board. I was thinking about getting tickets to the Yanks—O's when they come up at the end of April."

That'll be nice. As usual, the O's are on the road on the Fourth of July. When's the last time they had a home series during that holiday?

"Good question."

Maybe we can shoot for the Tigers series on the thirteenth if y'all come down.

"Let's hope they aren't mathematically eliminated by then."

A final task awaited following the call with Dan, one that would spell the end of Bryce's former bachelor world as we know it. He logged onto a handful of dating sites and glanced over a few stimulative messages. Next, he hovered the cursor over "delete account," closed his eyes ever so slightly and with a click of the mouse the accounts were deleted. It was one small step for man, one giant leap for mankind.

The last step was his phone contacts, which were filled with more numbers than the old Yellow Pages. It was necessary to remove the bulk of female acquaintances if he genuinely wanted to put the past behind him. For a moment he calculated why one contact was more favorable to keep than the other. Perhaps the person offered more than sexual favors like Yvonne or even Porsha, a person in management with whom he worked in proximity. Their names were safe for now. He struggled to remove Julissa's name despite not having spoken to her since the transfer of funds. He wasn't trying to hold onto his one-time flame but there was the inescapable guilt that had him in a chokehold. As for the rest, their names were immediately expunged one by one.

Meal preps were typically scheduled for Sundays but Alyssa's prior family obligation halted plans until tonight. She arrived at the door wearing two long braided pigtails and a low-fitting beige cap with "Point Pleasant, NJ" embroidered on the front. Bryce planted a wet kiss on her lips, gushing over her appearance while retrieving the grocery bags. The chic baseball cap appearance was it. Simple, effective, and usually had him in a frenzy whenever they'd cross paths at the gym. She learned more about its magnetic pull as they prepared dinner.

They spent time in the kitchen discussing vacation bucket lists and activities they hoped to explore. She expressed interest in traveling to Seattle for the Museum of Pop Culture and Cherokee, North Carolina for its scenic hiking trails. Meanwhile, Bryce added sunny San Diego and Arizona to the list. Mutually, they agreed on the idea of visiting the Androscoggin River in Turner, Maine for its spectacular autumn foliage display. But first things first—frequent visits down the Shore to Alyssa's family summer home for those early morning sunrise jogs and romantic strolls under the moonlight. The anticipation of it all was invigorating.

Through the grace of God there were no fisticuffs between Omari and Shauna's downstairs neighbor Carlos, who came in peace. What precipitated his visit was the belief that Shauna's safety was in danger, her startling cries, as Omari tickled her, resembling the scream queens of the all-time great horror films.

Carlos acted as the house watchdog and his antennas were up. It started after he noticed a few unrecognizable faces loitering out front. Shauna apologized for the confusion and thanked him for the concern. Omari did the same and used the opportunity as a peace offering. The gentlemen proceeded to the front of the house engaged in a chirpy conversation. Carlos offered high praise for Omari's gutsy decision to support Cameron and extended himself if they were ever in need. Their growing tension was seemingly put to rest. Next, Omari walked to a nearby bodega—his weapon still in tow—picking up his favorite: a turkey and cheese with lettuce, tomato, onion, mustard, and light mayo on a Kaiser roll. He called his father who was scheduled for more tests the next morning. Their conversation was brief and thorough, but it saddened him to hear how fatigued he sounded. Nonetheless, they discussed audio school and floated around the idea of reconnecting soon. Their once irreparable relationship showed much promise. It was a testament to Omari whose personal growth was apparent. Two significant figures in his life were given second chances, and he made good with a neighbor he once envisioned gunning down. His transformation wouldn't go unnoticed.

31

STATUS SYMBOL

Bryce was calm and collected through the twenty-minute drive to Alyssa's until he pulled up to her quiet Middletown Township neighborhood and rapidly became a bundle of nerves. The sight of her mom overseeding the front lawn certainly didn't help. It was his second visit to their home, the first since dropping Alyssa off following the romantic birthday weekend evening where he sat in the car and watched until she entered the doorway. Today was a different story.

Her mom had tickets for a one-day bus tour to Washington D.C. which included a visit to the Smithsonian Museum and the famous cherry blossoms. Their introduction came as a surprise. Bryce never met the parents of a significant other and wasn't expecting to meet Alyssa's mom in only three months. He only received the invitation after her mother's girlfriend couldn't make the trip. This was her way of laying the first stone.

"So, this is the handsome guy who's stolen my daughter's heart? We do hugs around here," she motioned. "Ooh, such a gorgeous *young man.*"

Ugh.

"Ma, can you stop? Sorry, Babe."

"Don't apologize," Bryce replied, pecking Alyssa on the lips.

"Nice to meet you, Ms. Nicoletti. I'm Bryce. I'm sure you already knew that."

"Whaaa, Al? He is." Alyssa's mother stressed. "I knew your name, honey. You're all she talks about. And please, call me Lauren."

"No way. I could never call you by your first name. How about Ms. Lauren?"

"Gosh. That has such an elderly sound to it. I don't like it. I'm still somewhat hip, right Al? I said, right Al?"

[Alyssa laughs in the background]

"I don't friggin' know."

"You guys are hilarious."

"Oh, suddenly I'm not cool anymore. You see how she treats her mother?"

"You're *very* cool," Bryce added, earning major brownie points. "I see where Alyssa gets her looks." Lauren reveled in the moment.

"Babe, please don't get her going."

"Al, he's a gentleman. Leave him alone."

Lauren was a debonair woman in her mid-fifties who could certainly turn heads. She was short and slender; her salt and pepper hair was as long as Alyssa's.

They arrived in D.C. a little before eleven-thirty. The weather was comfortable for the first week of April but there was a slight chill in the air. Bryce wore a light jacket and his Orioles cap as he ordinarily would when coming back to the DMV area while Alyssa wore a black New Jersey Devils cap—her father's favorite hockey team—over a braided ponytail, a black graphic tee, ripped black jeans, and red Converse sneakers. They held hands while the tour director instructed the large group.

At lunch, Lauren provided more context on the difficulties of raising three children without her husband. She blamed herself for her son's alternate lifestyle and explained the reason she wouldn't remarry. Lauren was equally astonished to learn of Bryce's own loss. The revelation gave her much hope regarding the couple's future with their unfortunate commonality being the glue. She continued to endorse how good they looked together, even predicting the beauty of their future children. The talk of starting a family was illogical, they had only been dating a few months, but she wouldn't mean any harm.

After an amazing exhibition, the rest of the afternoon was spent taking pictures. Bryce snapped a beautiful photo of Alyssa standing in a pathway underneath the cherry blossom trees and in the same location, Lauren got a shot of them face to face with Alyssa's leg bent at the knee behind her. Bryce immediately asked for the picture to upload to his Facebook page. The contrasting colors of the photo were too good to pass up.

They were entirely exhausted by the conclusion of the trip, but Alyssa wasn't going to turn down an opportunity to spend the night at Bryce's. He made her feel good in ways she had never experienced. They picked up two Caesar salads on the way to the house and recapped the day seated at the dining room table. Lizzy hadn't quite warmed up to Alyssa but fetched for a rub anyway before darting off. Bryce anxiously waited to address Yvonne's quizzical Facebook status. It all started after he uploaded the picture of him and Alyssa.

Yvonne J.
They run off and get a Becky when they can't handle a REAL woman.
44 Likes 18 Comments
1 hour ago

Without question, it was a direct shot at him, leading to a high volume of engagement. The first person to openly object to his new relationship wasn't a White bigot as he imagined. Instead, it was a person identifying as the same ethnicity as him.

Yvonne's mindless claim was ill-informed and untrue. Of all the times Bryce extended himself, she waited until now to play Punxsutawney Phil and come out of her hole. This was a clear case of sour grapes, or she had a natural disdain for interracial couples. Eager to find out, he excused himself from the table.

That's how you feel? He texted. Almost immediately, Yvonne replied.

Ms. Aquarius: Lol. You couldn't handle a real woman with a career huh?

Sat 9:28 p.m.

That's what u do, run off to Facebook? Lol. What makes you think I couldn't handle you? And what makes u think she's not a "real woman?" How many times did I try to connect with u only for you to blow me off?

Ms. Aquarius: I reiterate. You couldn't handle a real woman.

A strong, BLACK woman with a career.

Sat 9:30 p.m.

You aren't the only person with a "career" lol. Don't flatter yourself. Why are u throwing shade? People make time.

Ms. Aquarius: You could've just been a man and told me you wanted to move on.

Sat 9:33 p.m.

You actually needed to hear the words out of my mouth? How would that have been accomplished when we barely spoke? Anyway, I see where this is going. You're mad… it's cool.

Ms. Aquarius: Never mad, honey. Just admit, you couldn't handle a real woman. You're a little boy. You need mommy to make you a bottle? Lol. I'm not a babysitter. I told you what I was looking for in the beginning and you pretended to be down. If you wanted someone to be under you all day you should've said something.

Sat 9:34 p.m.

Bryce needed a moment to take in the "mommy" dig. Yvonne had no idea he had lost his mother. It was a bit inconsiderate, but he wouldn't hold her to the comment.

Interesting take. A "little boy" who's older than you… with a career, own crib, car… college graduate… self-sufficient… I can go on if you'd like.

Ms. Aquarius: That should tell you something. All of these "accomplishments" and you still can't handle a REAL woman bwahahaha. Don't make me laugh.

Sat 9:37 p.m.

Whatever you say…

Again, we're going in circles. You wanted a FWB arrangement, I told you I was down and the next thing you know I'm chasing you down over something I get on the regular. I'm not your guy. Sorry, I don't chase.

Ms. Aquarius: Have fun with your little Becky friend.

Sat 9:38 p.m.

Is that all you got? Childish name calling? Good luck finding a sucker who's willing to wait around for you. If you're mad that I'm in a relationship with a White woman just say that. Other than that, I really don't know what this is about. You want a FWB but don't make time for the 'benefits' part lol. Again, I'm not the one. No hard feelings. Peace.

Ms. Aquarius: Boy bye... lose my number.

Sat 9:40 p.m.

[Bryce deletes Yvonne from contacts]
What did she want from him?

Beyond doubt Yvonne was a repressed agitator with an axe to grind. Every woman Bryce ever involved himself with thrived professionally. He intentionally sought these types. Yvonne's vendetta was more about who he elected to be with and not the career talk she tried to disguise it as. Her behavior was truly asinine. It was time he moved on.

"Jesus, are you okay?" Alyssa asked. "I thought you fell asleep on the toilet or something." Bryce laughed before sharing another passionate kiss. "Couldn't be better. I didn't realize how junky my bedroom was. It was bothering the heck outta me. How's the salad?"

"I'm stuffed. I just wanna hop in the shower, throw on a big T-shirt and..."

"Watch last week's episode of *Curb Your Enthusiasm* on the DVR?"

"Well, we can do that too," she laughed.

"Do you think your mom likes me?"

"What? She friggin' loves you. See for yourself."

I friggin' love him, the text read.

"Wow. Verbatim."

"Yup. I'm like, 'Mom you're doing too much.' You literally *just* met."

"Hey, you've gotta trust a mom's intuition. Maybe one day you're in that same situation as a parent."

"Yeah right. Oh, let me warn you, she's gonna try to get you to help with projects around the house, especially at our Shore home. She does it with my brother-in-law and he's a skinny guy."

"Fine by me," Bryce shrugged.

"She's like, 'Does he like the beach?' I'm like, 'Who's dating him, you, or me?'" Bryce laughed before shooting Omari a quick text.

FYI, the music exec is out. Waste of time...

32

—

THE FINAL COUNTDOWN

had to let go and let God was Terri's way of describing her rocky relationship with her son. It stirred up emotions but got the message across without delving into her personal life with friends. She was strong-willed, but Dale recognized her mood shift ever since Bryce informed them of Omar's reemergence. It wasn't Bryce's story to tell but he brought it up as proof that all things were possible through Christ—Philippians 4:13. In truth, Terri prayed for her son's moment of appeasement with his father. It was part of her duty as a Christian woman. Her time with Omari would come because their names were in the prayers of others. That's just how prayer life worked.

The graduates at the audio school were only allowed to have two guests, and Omari longed for Bryce and Aunt Ramona as the invitees. Once informed, as a show of gratitude, Bryce asked Terri to go in his place. It was Terri who carried and nurtured Omari for nine months, tended to his every need, and kept a roof over his head. All Bryce ever did was act as a mentor. No small order but it paled in comparison. With the idea of giving up his spot as a guest, Bryce envisioned a long-awaited reunion between mother and son with Mother's Day around the corner. A beautiful ending to a rocky relationship. Sadly, Omari hadn't warmed up to the idea, forcing Terri to take the graduation ceremony snub in stride.

How hard would it have been for him to let go of the resentment toward his mother? He was obviously still blinded by the act of being kicked out, unwisely ignoring his actions that caused it. Omari had no clue of the hurt Terri was dealing with in making such a decision. He wasn't present when Dale first hinted at having regret for remarrying and the acute grief that followed. Or the time she overheard Dale tell someone over the phone how he should've stayed single. That was only at the preliminary stage of their marriage. The proverbial honeymoon. The idea that Terri's insubordinate son was the primary source of their discord led her to conduct a private meeting with Bryce—who confessed to being the person on the other end of that heartbreaking phone call with Dale. Bryce was more practical with his takes on life, illustrating a stoic attitude through his own sorrows. All things considered, he was Terri's last and *only* hope. He did more than pay for Omari's school and mentor him; he salvaged an entire family, earning the right to share the spotlight with the new audio school graduate.

～

SATURDAY, JUNE 16

It was Father's Day weekend. Bryce's first stop was the barbershop where his father arrived beforehand for his regular hot towel treatment and beard pruning. 'G's Stay Fresh' was Bryce's favorite place for trims until Omari became his in-house barber. Since the recent graduate was spending more time across the George Washington Bridge, Bryce reacquainted himself with the disorderly group of funnymen who persecuted him regularly for his disloyalty.

"Who's this tall, fake ass sex symbol entering my shop? Fuckin' Teddy Pendergrass-lookin' ass. Did you make an appointment?"

"Fam, you have no grounds to speak to me like that. Not with a name like Sebastian. I wanna speak to your manager."

[the two men embrace]

"G.'s on a call..."

Bryce walked quietly over to Germichael, the owner of the shop, to give a fist bump.

Hi. Yes, my name is Germichael... that's G, as in gentrification, E, as in extraordinary, R, as in rumbustiousness, Michael. That's M, as in micromanagement, I, as in institutionalize...

"Yo, something is seriously wrong with this dude," Bryce announced to one of the newer barbers who was prepping hair clippers. "Bash, did you hear G.?"

"What did he say?" Sebastian replied.

"He's over there spelling out his name. That joker said, 'G as in gentrification.'"

[laughter]

"Aye, BAT, grab my cell outta my pocket, please," Dale asked.

"How are you supposed to see your phone if Sebastian's about to shave you?"

"He ain't shaving my eyes, is he?"

Bryce's cell vibrated. It was Priscilla.

P-Nut: Be there in 5.

Sat 10:14 a.m.

Alyssa scheduled a self-care day and planned to meet up with her best friend, making way for Bryce to play catch-up with Priscilla. It wasn't often you found women hanging around a crude environment filled with men's locker room humor, but Priscilla was seen as one of the guys. She could hold her own on the sarcasm end and was protected largely in part because of the owner's relationship with Dale.

"Oh, I thought game three was tonight. It's tomorrow," Dale informed the guys, holding his cell to his face. "OKC ain't winning a damn thing. You know the league's gonna find a way for LeBron to win."

Germichael jumped in. "They lost to the Mavs last season."

"And that's exactly why the Heat are gonna win *this* season. The NBA loves a good storyline. They couldn't let LeBron win last year after they'd just formed the Big Three. It would've raised too many eyebrows. This season is his comeback story. Pay attention."

"Pop, you sound like a hater," Sebastian added.

"Big hate," Germichael finished.

"See, this is part of the reason I only watch college basketball," Bryce furthered. "I can't get behind the NBA and its blatant favoritism. They don't even try to hide it. You had that ref come out a few years back and admit to fixing the games. That was it for me. Ruins the integrity of the sport."

"Oh, what's his name... Tim something..." Germichael replied.

"Donaghy."

"That's him."

Bryce added, "Dude came out and was like, 'Yes, I'm guilty, I bet on games and purposely blew calls' and yet everybody kept watching. The league should have gone under."

"Too many sheep," Germichael declared.

"Do y'all remember that Lakers playoff series against the Kings? I forgot the year. I was at my man's house yelling at the television like, 'Yo, you don't see this? Why aren't they calling fouls against LA? He's a Lakers fan and even he was in shock. They didn't want Sacramento in the finals. No one can convince me otherwise," Bryce replied irritably.

"That was the team with C-Webb and dem boys..."

Dale chimed in. "Funny story. I sent Bryce to a basketball camp one summer. BAT, how old were you, thirteen?"

"Maybe fifteen... it was after Mom passed."

"Yes, it was a summer camp held by one of those boys on the Nets..."

"Kenny Anderson."

"That's him. When I tell you Bryce hated basketball, I mean, he absolutely *hated* it."

"Why'd you put him in a camp then?" Sebastian asked.

Bryce jumped in. "I had a growth spurt the previous summer. My gym teacher pulled me aside, handed me a camp flyer, and asked me to consider switching sports. I was playing baseball and running track. His exact words were, 'Aye, Carl Lewis, brothas don't play baseball.'"

[laughter]

"Nah, that wasn't funny," Bryce laughed irritably. "I let him plant that seed in my head. I figured it wouldn't hurt to work on my game in case the other sports didn't pan out. As soon as I got there, I was like nope."

"What also sparked interest was the 'Dream Team,'" Dale said.

"Oh yeah. I got hyped after we found out they were teaming MJ with Bird and Magic for the Olympics. I'm telling you; I was a basketball nut."

"Who was your team?" Germichael asked.

"I rooted for the Nets, but I became a fan of Orlando once they got Shaq."

"The Nets and Orlando? The Nets were trash though," Sebastian responded.

"For real. How were you not a Knicks fan or at least the Bulls?" Germichael questioned.

"Probably because we went to a few Nets games when I was a kid, and I got attached. If you can remember, Orlando and the Hornets were the flavors of the month back then. They were fairly new to the league. Every kid had a Hornets Starter Jacket or Shaq jersey."

"True," Germichael replied. "Teal was the official '90s color."

"I hated the Knicks. I didn't like their style of play. I only liked the flashy teams. When Chuck Daly got to the Nets, he let Anderson and Derrick Coleman run the floor. But Shaq and Penny? Those boys had a different energy…"

[Priscilla enters the shop]

"Hey, y'all…"

"Morning, beautiful," Germichael flirted.

"Aye Priscilla don't start with your Giants talk," Dale warned.

"I didn't do anything… yet." She walked over to Bryce who was seated in Germichael's barber's chair. They shared a half-hug before Dale continued. "You already did enough by wearing that T-shirt." A reference to her "Giants Super Bowl XLVI Champs" gear.

"You'll hate what's on my license plate," she laughed. Priscilla immediately switched subjects, turning to Bryce. "Dude, I think you're onto something with this end of the world thing."

"Why, what happened?"

"So, on my way here I noticed the birds were flying low to the ground. It looked like they were taking nosedives into the car. I was freaking out. Don't they have wings? Why aren't they soaring through the sky?"

"I've been telling you something is off."

"Y'all buying into that BS?" Germichael said, applying a black nylon cape over Bryce. "Nothing's gonna happen."

"Not organically. My theory is they'll create some type of event."

"I taught you better than that, BAT."

"Look." Bryce directed everyone to Dale. "He's about to recite Matthew 24:36. I can see the words forming on the tip of his tongue."

[laughter]

"You already know. Don't let me get biblical up in this joint."

"I'm just saying, there's something to it. They made a movie about 2012 and the conversation about the Mayan calendar picked up afterward. Why? There have always been doomsday dates. Why weren't their movies made about those years? Better yet, why didn't we hear about the end of the Mayan Calendar in the other decades?"

"Probably because they never thought we'd reach the two thousands," Germichael replied.

At that instant, Bryce stared a hole through Priscilla. "P., don't even think about it."

"What?" she bellowed with laughter. "You swear you know me."

"What are y'all talking about?" Germichael asked.

"You can't say *two thousands* around this one or she'll bust out the Juvenile song. You know the line he says before 'Back That Thang Up' comes on."

"I wasn't even thinking about that." Priscilla grinned.

"Sure."

"So, what do you think will happen with the Mayan calendar?"

"Germichael, don't let BAT get in your head. Open your Bible," Dale replied.

"I'm curious. Do you think we'll get hit by a meteor or something?"

[hair trimmer buzzing]

"I couldn't tell you," Bryce answered. "If I had to take a guess, I'd say it'll be some type of manmade situation. Maybe a world-wide virus or something. Maybe nothing happens at all. What do I know? Y'all need to see the movie *Contagion* though."

"Yes," Priscilla co-signed.

"I've heard about that joint," Germichael replied.

"It doesn't deal with end of the world stuff but it's a definite eye-opener."

"They've made movies like that before. Y'all don't remember *Outbreak?*"

"You're right. There was *12 Monkeys* and... P., what's the other one?" Bryce snapped his fingers.

"*28 Days Later?*"

"That's it."

"B. might be onto something," Sebastian added. "Think about how many deaths have happened this year alone. We're only in June."

"People die every day, bro," Germichael replied.

"Yeah, but it's getting outta control. Whitney Houston, Don Cornelius... all these legendary figures... gone."

"That has nothing to do with the price of tea in China."

The topic of viruses must've awakened Omari's senses; he unexpectedly texted Bryce asking for a favor. He would also inquire about changing his phone number since their accounts were linked through a family plan. The unidentified calls were constant, and now, he began to receive odd texts from an unrecognizable number—doubtful if the two were related. Clearly, it was a distressing point in time.

~

SUNDAY, JUNE 17

Their sunrise jog was completed. Bryce and Alyssa showered together, ate a snazzy breakfast, and ventured out on errands before visiting Dale and Terri. Today would be their first pop-in as a couple.

Father's Day was presumably rough for Alyssa. As time moved forward, the memory of her dad had become hazy. Still, she tried to envision how different life would be with him here. According to Ms. Lauren, Vincenzo, or "Vinny" as he was known to family and friends, was a ray of light. Each day was met with laughter, and he repeatedly told his family how much he loved them—unless of course they interrupted him during a Yankees telecast.

Alyssa used an old picture of her dad at her fourth-grade dance recital as wallpaper on her phone. In the photo he knelt to her side, wearing his signature aviator sunglasses. His smile was as wide as the Grand Canyon. The proud Italian American was slim with perfectly quaffed hair, a lustrous smile, and a pleasing singing voice. Bryce learned of Vincenzo's unusual, yet fascinating musical range. He was a Led Zeppelin diehard who also enjoyed the imaginative storytelling talents of hip hop artist Slick Rick, suggesting they would've gotten along just fine.

The first order of business was the Farmers Market to grab fresh produce for their weekly meal prep. Since Alyssa opted to drive, she shuffled through a playlist choosing a feel-good pop song. Bryce's eyes popped out of his fancy gold frames. "Aly, I'm not listening to Hannah Montana. I love you and all, but..." he paused at the Freudian slip. Alyssa grinned at him like a Cheshire cat and proceeded to turn down the volume to Miley Cyrus's "Party in the U.S.A."

"Baby... did you just say the 'L-word'?"

There was no escaping it, but he'd try anyway.

"What, *listening?*"

"And what did you say after that?"

"I can't remember."

"Seriously?"

"Busted."

"Don't sound so disappointed."

"I'm not. I said it more as a figure of speech, but I'll own it. I'd be lying if I said there wasn't some truth to it."

"Aw. You're literally blushing—look at you."

"I don't blush. And don't try to change the subject either. This is about you trying to torture my precious ears. Miley Cyrus? What did I do to deserve that?" Alyssa motioned forward to grab his face. They shared a kiss waiting at a red light. "I love you too."

The cat was out of the bag. There was no turning back. He didn't want to.

Alyssa selected another song favorite that Bryce could fully get behind: Third Eye Blind's "Never Let You Go."

The couple loaded up on chicken breast, sweet potatoes, brown rice, and vegetables which would serve as tonight's dinner. Upon their return, Alyssa changed into something more appropriate before the anticipated visit to Dale's. She had a choice of two outfits lying on the sectional sofa—ripped acid-washed jeans and a royal blue top or a floral sundress and sandals. She removed her oversized vintage Nirvana top and biker shorts, sneaking into the kitchen without notice where Bryce stood rinsing off the chicken. She positioned her arms underneath his and nibbled on his right earlobe signaling that she was in the mood. She was assertive but in a reserved way. Bryce made a swift turn, to the sight of her trotting away in a black Calvin Klein racerback sports bra and matching thong. He caught her in the foyer and spun her around. Their bodies and lips pressed together at once. With brute strength, he carried her to the nearby powder room where they continued their embrace sitting atop the toilet seat cover. Soon after, their genitalia joined with Alyssa's face pressed into his collarbone and the lower half of her body moving feverishly.

"Now it's *my* turn to play DJ," Bryce announced, shuffling through a song playlist. Ahead was Tasha and her two boys who just missed the couple exiting the house. He was certain she was wise to what was going on, but a small part wished that she would've seen them walk out.

Petty? He would agree.

She yelled at her boys with knitted brows, watching them take off on their skateboards. How quickly time had flown. This time last year they were preparing for their first movie date. These days, Tasha could barely stand sight of him... until now, when she glanced over at Bryce's driveway after detecting motion. What could she be thinking with Alyssa's SUV parked there almost exclusively? It was possible she didn't care. Bryce pulled off without even looking her way.

[OutKast's "Southernplayalisticadillacmuzik" plays in the background]

"Baby, do you think I have too much makeup on? Be honest."

"Nah, you look great, and I *love* the wet and wavy hairstyle," Bryce mocked. "Did you catch the reference?"

"Ha-ha."

She wanted to make a strong first impression and worried about Dale's reaction. "You have nothing to worry about. He's super chill. He's gonna talk your ear off."

"I don't know why I'm so friggin' nervous."

"I kinda felt the same way before meeting your mom. All I can say is relax. You'll be fine."

"Okay, okay..." Alyssa sighed.

"He'll use a little of what I've shared and create dialogue. That's how he operates. If he detects nervousness, he'll throw in a few jokes. Trust me. You're gonna see a lot of our similarities."

"I hope you told him good things."

"Nope. I told him you're a slut-whore. And just wait 'til I tell him you broke my toilet seat."

"You were the one sitting on top of it," Alyssa hurled back, slapping his shoulder.

"I was, but your added weight was the icing on the cake. And I wasn't the one moving at a hundred miles an hour," he laughed.

"Oh, so now I'm a *fat* slut-whore who breaks toilet seats. What a nice way to talk to your girl."

"Hey, I never technically called you fat. You're putting words in my mouth," he laughed. Bryce took a more peaceful approach caressing her chin. "Breathe, baby. Woosah," he urged. "I don't care about the toilet seat. I'll get another."

"Don't try to butter me up," she replied, shifting her head away playfully. They joined hands; Bryce kissed the surface of her skin.

"Get ready. They're over by that cul-de-sac."

"There's my future daughter-in-law," Dale shouted as the couple pulled up to the home. Bryce turned to his beaming girlfriend. "See? That didn't take long, now, did it?"

Terri and Alyssa hugged, exchanging compliments on the other's dress choice. Meanwhile, Bryce handed Dale his Father's

Day card. He was sure to get a kick out of what was inside—tickets to the Baseball Hall of Fame Museum.

"This is from me and Alyssa. She picked out the card."

"Alyssa, I *knew* you were a good one. I don't care how badly Bryce spoke about you."

"Nice try, Pop. I already hipped her to your dry sense of humor."

"Oh, you did, huh?"

"Yessir. Try not to open the card 'til we get to the restaurant."

"Copy."

They carried out their traditional father-son handshake, much to Alyssa's delight.

"Did you hear about Rodney King?" Dale asked him.

"No, what happened?"

Terri jumped in. "They found him dead at the bottom of his swimming pool this morning."

Bryce's jaw dropped and his eyes widened. "Are you serious?"

"That's terrible," Alyssa exclaimed.

Lunch reservations were scheduled at a waterfront seafood restaurant in nearby Perth Amboy, but first Dale wanted to give Alyssa a quick tour of their home, specifically the inside of his garage. She stood in amazement, gushing over younger photos of Bryce while admiring Dale's massive sports memorabilia collection and historic photos.

"Alyssa, do you like sports?" Terri asked.

"I do. I'm not an avid watcher, but I did play soccer in school. I've gone to a couple of hockey games with my sister and brother-in-law. Bryce just took me to my first baseball game... oh, and I've gone to a football game with my co-workers."

"As you can see, I'm a big football fan," Dale inserted. "How'd you like that experience?"

"Not much at all. It was so cold that day, and the game was sloppy."

"Really? Who was playing?"

"The Jets."

"Well, that explains it..."

[group laughter]

"I took her to see the O's at Yankee Stadium back in April. We nearly froze to death. They've got to start the season closer to May. I shouldn't be wearing a beanie, scarf and mittens at a baseball game."

"Oh no," Terri burst out laughing.

"We're gonna drive down to Maryland next month and catch a game with Dan and his wife."

"Yes, I can't wait," Alyssa responded. "I love road trips."

"That should be nice," Terri replied.

"Who are they playing?" Dale asked. Suddenly his phone sounded. It was a text from a name he hadn't seen in years. If he didn't believe the world was months away from ending, he was sure to become a believer now.

> Terri's Son: It's Omari... Happy Father's Day.
> Thank you for raising Bryce.
>
> Sun 2:03 p.m.

Dale, a healthy brown skinned man, appeared ghostly.

"Pop, what's wrong? You look like you just finished watching a Redskins game."

"Well, this is strange..."

33

—

MY OWN WORST ENEMY

THREE MONTHS BEFORE DOOMSDAY

September had arrived. It was back to crowds of yellow school buses jamming the roads and the start of a new NFL season where the 49ers were already off to a sizzling start. Soon the weather would cool off, the days would shorten, and the fate of the world would be determined.

Summer raced along and the beach visits with Alyssa were plentiful. She received a stamp of approval from friends. Only Gucci had yet to meet her due to conflicting schedules. For Bryce's thirty-fifth birthday, there would be no Party Yacht Cruise. Instead, Alyssa treated him to a spa day and dinner at a spiffy restaurant that included a nice cigar lounge. Through their eight-month journey, Bryce learned to put aside his pre-existing paranoia amid the scattered stares—primarily from elderly Caucasians who hadn't caught up with the times. Such disapproval came with the territory. As he learned firsthand with Yvonne, there was no escaping petty people with opinions. Trying to convince complete strangers of his decision to date Alyssa wouldn't be easy, but his love life wasn't up for debate. He was happier than a pig in mud. Their linking up wasn't about proving a point. They had simply fallen into each other's laps because sometimes love had a funny way of working.

They were in their own world when traveling about. Even through the sprinkle of flattering gazes. Bryce had never been undressed by the eyes of so many women while in the presence of another. Not even when walking with Priscilla or Zoë, undoubtedly two of the prettiest women breathing. Then again, he wasn't seen holding hands or publicly making out with them either. When the stares heightened toward him and Alyssa, he gripped her hand tightly. With love came a responsibility to protect. Alyssa was a big girl but under no circumstances would he allow someone to go out of their way to intimidate his lady.

Their day started early—about three forty-five in the morning, thanks to Alyssa's sexual voracity. She had the resurgence of a Phoenix even after climaxing just hours before. The early birds scheduled a light jog and spent the rest of the afternoon on an apple farm. Alyssa's spontaneity matched his exploratory trait and today was just one of many new adventures they hoped to explore. Their next quest was only weeks away—a scheduled weekend of fun in a rented-out cozy log cabin near the Androscoggin River.

Nightfall was upon him. The sky cracked, thunder roared, an indication of tempestuous weather ahead. With Alyssa at home, it was time to decompress and soak up the sounds of nature. Bryce was showered and stretched out on his sofa, ready to dive into the autobiography of Shirley Chisholm. First, he needed to configure an efficient lineup for his struggling fantasy football team in time for Sunday's games.

[cell phone vibrates]

H2O: Name your top 5 all-time rappers.

Sat 7:55 p.m.

> LL Cool J
>
> Nas
>
> Pac
>
> Redman
>
> Kool G. Rap/Jay-Z

Bryce placed the phone down in anticipation of their ensuing debate. Omari was sure to be fired up that the list wouldn't include his rap favorite, Cam'ron.

[cell phone vibrates]

As expected, his little brother replied quickly... or so he thought.

> (862) 555-1710: Now visiting NJ. Offering special monthly rates through October. Call or click the link for more info.
>
> Sat 7:57 p.m.

It was Kaylani. What a surprise. Bryce sat up from a slouched position, thinking of a good reply until inevitably experiencing a flashback of their Las Vegas episode. The enemy was doubtlessly hard at work trying to disrupt his joy with Alyssa.

> I'm surprised you remembered me...

> (862) 555-1710: I'm sorry. This was a group text to my NJ clients. You would have to refresh my memory.
>
> Sat 8:02 p.m.

> Oh. I'm the dude who stayed at the Cosmos in Vegas. Remember u thought I was an athlete lol.

(862) 555-1710: Oh, I remember lol how are you?

Sat 8:04 p.m.

Can't complain. And you?

Bryce found himself in a peculiar situation. How does one engage in conversation with an escort without mentioning sex? It was like talking to a Financial Advisor withholding financial information. He wouldn't be able to take their dialogue far, not if he truly turned the page.

Vegas still pops up in my mind...

Evidently the pages were glued together.

(862) 555-1710: Good times. We should link up again soon.

Sat 9:11 p.m.

She was a businesswoman—what was she supposed to say?

As long as we can find another balcony view lol.

(862) 555-1710: To be honest I'm surprised to hear from you.

Sat 9:12 p.m.

He tried talking himself out of entertaining her, but Kaylani's latest remark was a headscratcher.

Surprised? Why?

(862) 555-1710: Because some guys have remorse after it hits them.

Sat 9:25 p.m.

Remorse? Now YOU'RE gonna have to refresh MY memory lol. Why would there be any remorse if I've already seen you twice?

(862) 555-1710: Because it was Vegas. Nobody cares lol. It's when they go home to their wife and kids.

Sat 9:26 p.m.

She was speaking in riddles, and it drove him ballistic.

I'm not married so you're gonna have to help me out. My bad for not understanding. You said you were surprised to hear from me because u thought I'd have remorse, but I saw u twice. Where would the remorse come in? I know I was tipsy and all, but did something happen?

(862) 555-1710: lol. I'm guessing you don't remember our conversation at the club and on the ride back to the hotel?

Sat 9:31 p.m.

Sadly, I don't. What did I say?

He started to reflect on that indistinguishable joyride back to The Cosmopolitan.

(862) 555-1710: I always ask new clients if they're open-minded beforehand. You asked me what I meant. After I explained, I gave you my rates and then we hopped in the cab.

Sat 9:34 p.m.

Oh. Did we have a threesome or something? I'm drawing a blank.

(862) 555-1710: [picture message] I'm transgender, baby. A unicorn. I come with a lil something extra.

Sat 9:38 p.m.

From the looks of it, getting hitched to a stripper at a seedy chapel in Las Vegas didn't sound so bad.

Bryce lay on his sofa, momentarily dead to the world. The feeling was equal to that of a stoner after the buzz set in. The room was spinning at the speed of a pinwheel. He was calm but hadn't blinked for over two minutes. Kaylani had to have pulled his leg. Even if he were as drunk as a sailor there was no way he would've missed the signs. Not him. Oh, what a tangled web he'd weave.

There were signs of life. Bryce's eyes circled the room, finding the portrait of his mother who would've told him to lean on the Lord in times of unrest. He proceeded to ask aloud, "What *really* happened on that December night?" God was the only person he'd ever have to answer to but the reaction of Dale or his closest friends—if news ever broke—made him self-conscious. Admittedly, Kaylani's fellatio was the best he ever had. It wasn't even debatable. Still, he could hear Gucci's voice from a mile away saying something incendiary. *Playboy, you went from being a straight-A student to no longer being straight.* Something along those lines.

His confession regarding her oral skills wouldn't determine his sexual orientation. Bryce liked women. There was no need to shout it from the mountain top. Kaylani's whole demeanor screamed 'woman' from top to bottom. It is what attracted him in the first place. She was submissive and built like many who came before her. The argument could even be made that Tasha's aggressive nature or Alyssa's toned physique made them *appear* more masculine. Kaylani's sexual identity wasn't the issue. If this was who she identified as, who was he to judge? Bryce was a lover of most people as evident by his girlfriend and an array of friends and acquaintances. His concern regarding Kaylani was their second night when a sober version of himself penetrated her on the balcony. What now?

[Bryce examines Kaylani's picture message]

Instinctively, his eyes traveled down to her midsection. There wasn't a bulge or anything in the scantily clad picture implicating her claim. She could've easily been the lead lady in a music video. My goodness. Thinking back to their romps, he found no evidence there either. Not even when his hand was across her throat facing the city glare. He never removed her patent leather G-string that evening out of sheer laziness. What reason would he have to suspect Kaylani to share the same XY chromosome combination when she had a face that could grace the cover of *Vogue*?

> So, do you still have a penis or...

He strayed from asking the insensitive text in favor of something more suitable.

> Since you seem to have a better memory of night one, was there anything more that happened? For the record I'm 100% straight. I can't imagine I would've allowed anything more.

Based on the payment agreement, it was safe to assume

nothing more transpired. However, he sat on pins and needles until Kaylani finally responded—the next day.

(862) 555-1710: No. You only paid for head.

Sun 10:17 a.m.

A sense of relief came over him.

Throughout their scattered conversation in the days to follow, Bryce learned many of Kaylani's clients were heterosexual men—some married. Even a trace of prominent pro athletes whom she bumped into while working as a Hooters server. The revelation was indeed surprising but wouldn't make him feel any better.

It would've been too easy to point a finger when there was plenty of blame to go around, starting with Ms. Blake, the person responsible for amplifying his teenage sexual desires. He would be remiss not to include himself in the equation. Becoming impaired in an uncontrolled environment—in *Las Vegas* of all places—was beyond him. As his psychology professor once explained: "True growth only begins when a person can address and correct their own behaviors." On that night at the club, he was enticed by the depiction of a woman, but no one forced him to approach her. That was his choice. Bryce's messy ordeal immediately changed the landscape of his homophobia toward Roy.

They were in a much better space following his thirty-fourth birthday celebration, but it shouldn't have taken that long after five years of working together. He only stayed away because of a baseless rumor and innuendo. Now that his own truth had been disclosed, how would he feel if the shoe were on the other foot? Having said that, he needed to come to grips with what happened in Las Vegas and pull himself together. Prayer was the only way he knew how.

~

Omari never replied to Bryce's top five all-time rappers list. He was busy recording a track in the basement studio—until he was distracted by another phone call from an unknown person. After he'd initially inquired about a phone number change, Omari bailed on the idea. It was the only number he owned, and he didn't want to go through the hassle of informing others of a switch. After a war of words with an old flame, it was time to reconsider.

The mystery of who was behind the cryptic phone calls and text messages was greater than any whodunit in American television history, yet he was drawing closer to finding an answer. Tonight's mystery started with an unrecognizable number and a text displaying three question marks followed by a phone call from a blocked ID. The raw lyrics to 50 Cent's "Many Men" played on the voicemail. Oddly, the song's volume elevated on a particular line raising his eyebrow. About twenty minutes later, he received an unusual text from Shameika—a former acquaintance listed in his contacts—asking "Was it him?" Omari excused himself to Brixx's backyard to address the matter.

What exactly was she referring to and could she have been the person responsible for the other calls?

A shouting match led Brixx out back where Omari paced the grass with his fists balled. He was covered in sweat, bearing a resemblance to a swimmer who had just taken part in a two-hundred-meter freestyle Olympic swim. There was rage in his eyes and his face wore a menacing grin. Brixx had never seen his friend like this, urging him to end the call. Omari was justifiably bothered by Shameika's threats but wouldn't specify her fighting words.

She was confused as to why her health had declined. Shameika had only been active with one other person in recent years, a boyfriend who was coming home from Rikers Island with a new lease on life after serving a five-year bid. Omari's repeated reply of "I don't know" wouldn't cut it. Not with the enraged ex-felon on her heels. She was asymptomatic for a brief period when unexpectedly she suffered severe abdominal pain and lymph node swelling around the groin. The effects brought about a visit to her physician and soon the inevitable.

Shameika was the only person to come forth from the group of women Omari encountered through a dating service while unknowingly infected. The same dating service where he was exposed to genital herpes. He wore protection at the time of their hook-up at her Astoria, Queens apartment. She wouldn't have had it any other way. He was supposed to be her sexual place-holder with her boyfriend's initial release date still in the air. The idea that she took precautions and still contracted an STD blew her cover as being faithful and put her lover at risk. Despite an attraction to bad boys, they always protected her health.

34

———

IT'S THE END OF THE WORLD

Hurricane Sandy slammed into the eastern seaboard, destroying much of New York City and New Jersey, including the Shore points, with record flooding and sweeping power outages. The event put a damper on Alyssa's spirits after she and Bryce returned from an exhilarating trip to Maine just two weeks before. Her family's Shore home took a major hit, and they were looking at a great deal of repair work down the road. The house had been a staple in her family for many years, passed down by her grandparents, who at one time owned a real estate brokerage.

Subsequently, an unexpected nor'easter hit the region. There was something about snowfall on the East Coast—only days after Halloween—that didn't sit well. The traditional charm of autumn was no more. With a recent string of natural disasters thrashing unusual parts of the map—including the earthquake from a year ago—it was clear Mother Nature was in a bad mood. That or it was a sign of the end. The prologue to the book of Revelation. Something.

~

For Omari, his world was already in shambles long before the talks of doomsday. The amount of self-sabotage was incriminating, however 2012 turned into a come-up. He took the year by the horns, turning lemons into a pitcher of lemonade. From there he graduated from audio school and obtained his security officer license—after resigning from his car lot position—now working overnight security at a midtown office. The idea was to provide Cameron with around-the-clock coverage since Shauna worked during the day. The new role awarded him health benefits, a significant bump in pay and a decrease in visits to Brixx's basement studio.

With sacrifice comes great reward.

His pen stayed active, as the certified night owl continued to create music working the graveyard shift. Rap music was life, but for now, his primary focus was to rehabilitate his own life and evolve as a person. As engineered by Aunt Ramona, Omari made up with his ill father to the tune of speaking multiple times a week. Omar was proud to hear of his son's recent accomplishments and with his health in steep decline, sought their reunion. Lastly, the unexpected warm greeting text to Dale on Father's Day —though the relationship with his mother was still problematic. The only glitch left was Omari's poor health.

For every itch, bout with pain, or ingested antibiotic, he was reminded of his slip-up. It was unclear who the responsible party was in spreading herpes and he didn't want the headache of interrogating a list of names. Unfortunately, the STDs were something he and Shauna would have to live with until further notice. On the other hand, Shameika wanted answers. She deserved them. Just as he did when he blew up Shauna's phone like a pesky car insurance salesperson offering an extended warranty.

In Shameika's latest call, she asked to meet up at a neutral site to smooth things over, claiming her emotions had gotten the best of her. Omari wasn't buying it. Her sudden plea wasn't long after she called him every effeminate name in the book while issuing a warning about her gangbanging cousins inflicting physical harm to him if found. Omari called her bluff through the heated exchange and announced the home address of Brixx and Shauna, practically begging them to show up whenever he was around. Violence wasn't the answer but sometimes it could act as a quick solution.

He understood Shameika's anger and felt terrible about the possibility of having wrecked multiple innocent lives. Still, he wasn't ready to come clean. But as was the case with Carlos, his antennas were up. Threats weren't to be taken lightly. The only difference this time? He was empty-handed, having ditched his firearm. This, after Shauna voiced concern about it being in the home where a child actively roamed. Omari had a god complex while in possession of a gun. Admittedly, it made him feel like the Terminator. Now he felt naked without it.

~

TUESDAY, NOVEMBER 6

Baby, watch out for deer if you're driving to the gym tonight.

"Is it crazy out there?" Bryce whispered to Alyssa, in an effort to not distract the resting passengers on board during the bus ride home.

They're all over the friggin' back roads. I see a bunch walking along the grass over by me.

"Must be mating season. All right. I'll keep an eye out for them. I'm gonna take a nap. I should be home in another forty-five minutes."

Okay. Be careful. Do you want me to bring over some pasta salad? You can take it for lunch tomorrow since we didn't prep.

"That sounds good. I'll think about it and let you know once I get off the bus."

Okay. I love you.

"I love you too."

He looked at their recent text thread, chuckling at his reply to the question of 'What's the most shocking thing you've ever done?' "The What Game" was an activity played by Alyssa and her colleagues to pass the time between patients.

I drove through a school bus stop sign when I was super late for an appointment.

The other answer floating through his head could've jeopardized their budding romance.

Strangely, there weren't many passengers on board this evening. Maybe they received notice not to show up to work in the event of something dramatic. What *else* could go wrong with 'Doomsday December 21' only a month and a half away?

The sky was pitch black and the roads never looked so empty. Daylight Saving Time was only two days ago, could it be that everyone was still adjusting to the time change? Possibly. Bryce stared out the window at the fluorescent lights of the Lincoln Tunnel as the melodious chorus from "MoneyGrabber" by Fitz and the Tantrums played in his head. The fast-growing radio single pumped through the bowling alley speakers over the past weekend where Bryce and Alyssa paired against her sister and fiancé. Alyssa hadn't bowled much but it wouldn't take long for the "pull-up queen" to get into a rhythm. If they were to ever have children, the young athletes of tomorrow had better watch out.

Bryce and Alyssa were approaching a year together and with Danielle's wedding slated for next June, they were certain conversation would evolve on their own matrimony date. Even at thirty-two years old, Alyssa refused to work off a biological clock. She never dreamt of a fancy white dress, much less a wedding. Her father wasn't here to send her off to the groom and marriage wasn't her end-all-be-all. It was a nice thought, but she was just as content with becoming a pet parent with a man who swept her off her feet. Then again, she'd never been with a guy like Bryce, meaning that opinion could change over time.

Just months before, the happy couple looked in on a few open houses courtesy of Daija to get a feel for a housing market that was starting to show signs of life. Alyssa fell in love with Dan and

Amina's Maryland home at first visit and wouldn't rule out a future out-of-state move since Danielle planned to live close to their mother. As the feelings between them soared, they were intrigued by the idea of coming home to one another. Alternatively, Bryce considered giving Alyssa a spare key now that Omari was permanently fixed in the Bronx. It was a small step in becoming familiar with the other's in-house habits before their next big relationship leap.

Bryce's eyes were shut. Donell Jones's "Where I Wanna Be" sounded as good now as it did back in the fall of 1999 when he labeled it 'perfection.' A long day of conducting interviews and crunching numbers wore him out. Maybe going home to a bowl of his girl's pasta salad and a movie was just what the doctor ordered. The more he saw Alyssa the more it lessened the impact of Kaylani's bombshell.

[text notification chime]

He scrambled to find his phone, hoping the loud sound wouldn't disrupt the driver. Surely, the handful of people on board—half of whom dozed off—wouldn't mind, but he wanted to honor the large sign plastered in big bold lettering above the windshield: *PLEASE PLACE CELL PHONES ON VIBRATE.*

With weary eyes he glanced at the brightly lit screen.

La Gatita: Don't forget to vote. Obama baby!

Tues 7:44 p.m.

Election Day. That could've explained the scant lines at the Port Authority Bus Terminal and bare highway on the drive home. Bryce soured on politics. Presidential voting was about as useless as drinking alcohol-free beer. However, it was nice to see Julissa didn't harbor any ill feelings after twenty years of cordiality. To avoid the trap of heading down memory lane he offered a suitable response.

Democracy is hypocrisy.

He immediately changed her contact nickname to her actual full married name, placed the phone back into his carry-on bag, and prepared for departure.

~

FRIDAY, DECEMBER 14

Nobody said life was fair. One of the most challenging aspects of the human experience was time. The adage "time flies when you're having fun" hurts because that is what truth does. It can sting like a bee. Good times aren't everlasting. They won't carry on. Instead, they become memories that with age can fade into obscurity. To make up for it, we find ourselves in constant need to create new experiences, because life is not measured by time, it is measured by moments. Events that will produce temporary fulfillment until that window closes.

What about those dreaded mistakes that can't be erased which serve as great learning tools? Some of our past errors unexpectedly haunt us, causing inevitable regret, yet we are told not to live with regret, to leave the past behind. Is it *even* humanly possible not to think about the "what ifs" knowing that it could've changed the trajectory of your entire life? God doesn't make mistakes, but humans certainly do. And some of us have paid dearly for our past miscues.

We are reminded how our time on earth is a blessing, good, bad, or indifferent. Genesis 12 provides further context. What we choose to do with the allotted time is a part of God's free will. Many will seek Him through limitless prayer, entering His house every Sunday morning to praise and worship Him. Others remain spiritually inclined, acknowledging signals throughout their daily travels. And then, there are those who wish to take a walk on the wild side. What is life if you aren't *living* it? Words that applied to Omar Sadiq Harris, Omari's father, who sadly wouldn't make it because time wasn't on his side.

~

The trip dates were already set. Aunt Ramona and her boys would leave for Kissimmee, Florida at the start of winter recess and stay for a week while Omari planned to leave on the first day of Kwanzaa into the New Year. He spoke to his father often for the better part of a year now. They had years of catching up between them and were looking forward to the time spent.

Omari was still in his work uniform washing out Cameron's bottles when Aunt Ramona's somber news hit. *He didn't make it,* the text read. One could only hope that his soul would. Omari turned off the kitchen faucet and looked toward the ceiling. Deep down, he felt this day coming. He heard it in his father's weakened voice with each conversation, their last being at the end of November when he first informed him of his upcoming travel plans. That was only two weeks ago. Far too long to not have checked back with him. Now he wished he had called more. Omar was a shell of his former self. The bravado was gone, and his lively energy was zapped. However, confirmation of his son, sister, and nephews' pending visit gave him *temporary* life. That is what life is. Temporary.

The recollection of their last conversation put a hard lump in Omari's throat, but the tears wouldn't fall. Their lack of a sound relationship was the cause of sadness, but there was no room for weeping with Cameron eyeballing his every move, waiting to be playfully body-slammed onto the sofa. Shauna offered her condolences, insisting she call out of work to allow him time to grieve. Omari encouraged her to move on with her day. It is what he had to do going forward. Besides, he could use the welcomed distraction of babysitting. Now a funeral loomed, sure to be loaded with siblings he never met and relatives who hadn't laid eyes on him since he was a child.

One of Omari's first phone calls about the grave news was to Bryce; a man Omar grew to admire. The idea of someone stepping in to rescue his son from a slippery slope once brought him to tears. Another telltale sign that Omar was ill. He never showed so much emotion before. In their only conversation, on an evening when Bryce drove up with Priscilla to listen in on a CashFlow session, Omar thanked him for his generosity, asking that he join Omari on the flight to Florida once a date was set up. If only to look him in the eye, shake his hand, and *maybe* sneak in a game of bowling. Flattered by the offer, Bryce respectfully declined, specifying the importance of Omar's coming together with his estranged son. He would propose a visit in the foreseeable future. Unfortunately, that meeting will never occur.

Omari then spoke to Kim, his father's long-time girlfriend who indicated how his father didn't *just* turn his life around. It was a work in progress that started several years ago after they got baptized and gave themselves to the Lord. The days of Omar chasing skirts—impregnating randoms and child abandonment—were long gone. Despite Omar's imprudence, he was quite selective with whom he shared children with—usually cultivated beauties with the natural ability to nurture. The types who craved a sprinkle of spice in their lives. The ladies were drawn to him and his brightly colored Sergio Tacchini tracksuits like a snake to a charmer. Omar loved the idea of spreading his seed but was unenthused about settling down. Street life circa 1980s and '90s was where the action was, and it was too intoxicating to sit at home acting like "father of the year" with an abundance of money to be made. He traveled up and down the interstate selling kilos, breaking bread, and sending lump sums to the mothers of his children hoping it would keep them quiet. Kim wasn't at all moved by the flash or cash. She only wished to open his eyes to child abandonment, having been a victim herself. They wouldn't share children together, but she was credited for Omar's recent peace offerings to more than half of his eight children before taking his final breath. Better late than never.

35

CIRCLE OF LIFE

At last, the moment arrived. Doomsday. Bryce kissed Alyssa on her arm, fell to one knee and thanked the Lord for another day. His limbs were still intact and so was the world, at least for now. He gave more thanks for having the stamina of a long-distance runner after last night's explosive role-playing theme titled "Armageddon." Alyssa gave him something to remember her by in case the planet was blasted by a series of meteors. Soon, she would awaken and drop him off at LaGuardia Airport, where he planned to connect with Omari, Ramona, and her kids for their eleven o'clock flight for Saturday's funeral.

There was something eerie about the 2012 phenomenon comparable to the Y2K abnormality. Bryce wouldn't buy into the hype then because it was impossible to think human civilization rested in the hands of a computer's inability to recognize the year 2000. Even so, what was the big deal? Humans operated fine before the advent of computers. However, as New Year's Eve 1999 approached, he found himself caught up in the brouhaha. Fast forward to today and it was almost identical.

He began watching various TV programs midway through the year. Shows packed with over-sensationalized theories from deep-voiced, over-the-top narrators, who advised viewers on proper survival techniques in case of an apocalyptic event. In some cases, anxiety was at an all-time high. As a sunset enthusiast and firm believer of UFOs Bryce always kept his eyes to the sky. Now it was more frequent. He was in search of Nibiru, the rumored planet predicted to collide with or pass Earth. What a spectacle to perhaps find a mysterious planet closing in on our atmosphere becoming as visible as the moon and sun.

The end of the Mayan calendar was never intended to signify doomsday. The Maya culture believed it to be the end of a cycle and the start of a new age. A resetting of sorts like the old Nintendo gaming system. The correlation to the lives of Bryce Taylor and Omari Harris couldn't be more noticeable.

~

[Radiohead's "Let Down" plays in the background]

Alyssa pulled into Terminal C, put the car in park, put on her hazard lights, and shared a long kiss with Bryce. By all the emotions, you would think he was leaving for a six-month Mission's Retreat to the Fiji Islands. This wasn't goodbye. He was only going to Florida, but it was the first weekend they had spent apart in quite some time. A light saliva was transferred to his mouth during their exchange. She removed it with her finger before caressing his smooth skin and playing in his beard with freshly manicured nails. They prayed for the others' safety and kissed again until he exited the SUV to retrieve his carry-on luggage from the trunk.

"Bye, Babe. Text me when you land."

"I will." He blew a kiss and followed a crowd of travelers toward the revolving glass door.

"Wait, come back," Alyssa yelled through the passenger

window, honking for added insurance. Bryce hurried to the vehicle.

"How the heck did you get in the passenger seat so fast?"

"You forgot something." She wanted another kiss for the road.

"Well played," he smiled. "I love you."

"I love you too. Make sure you grab something to eat."

"I will... if you ever let me get inside."

"Okay, I'm leaving."

Bryce checked in and frittered away time searching for something to eat. There was a breakfast bar serving appetizing pastries and fruits. He settled for a warm flaky croissant and a small coffee. Seated beside him was a young family and an older married couple discussing the recent Sandy Hook Elementary School shootings. He hadn't paid much attention to the tragic news story with all the hoopla surrounding doomsday and his playoff-bound San Francisco 49ers but decided to scroll through the news articles on his phone. He shook his head in between taking careful sips of piping hot coffee, deeply touched by the incident.

Shortly after, he walked to the gate and sat in a remote area among the other Delta flight passengers. Priscilla sent a text wishing him a safe trip. Minutes later, Dale offered encouraging words from Isaiah 41:10. It is what he always did to settle his own nerves when his son traveled. Bryce replied to the messages and returned to the home screen staring at his phone's wallpaper. It was an amazing photo of him and Alyssa on a balmy summer afternoon at the beach. Their glowing smiles provided warmth to help cope with the airport chill.

Alyssa was near perfect in his eyes, and it was the happiest he had been in any relationship. At this time last year, he was arriving in Las Vegas. Today, he was processing how madly in love he was. Further proof that God was a romantic. But there was something hanging over him. Something which needed addressing. Something Alyssa didn't factor into. The issue was with himself and the bottomless hole he dug. The lust demon hadn't escaped. His obsession with casual sex prohibited him from loving unconditionally. He *wanted* to believe he was faithful. His relationship with Kristen was proof. Despite their breakup, he was one hundred percent faithful. He'd also been on his best behavior with Alyssa once they made it official. But Bryce categorically loved the idea of having options. *The Matrix* grew to become one of his favorite films. Red pill/blue pill.

Life was about making choices. Some harder than the others. The idea of taking the occasional calculated risk excited him. It was an outlandish brain exercise that prohibited him from replicating the same mundane acts again and again. Think Bill Murray's *Groundhog Day*. At times, Bryce put himself through unnecessary scenarios just to obtain knowledge on the subject. It gave him the ability to share some incredible stories. Experience was proven to be man's greatest teacher, and Bryce was an amazing storyteller. Taking risks was part of why he wore his hair in locs through college in a state synonymous with its sinister history and exploitation of Black people. It is why he agreed to mentor Omari or break down the interracial dating barrier and risk losing his beloved identity with Black women. The need to make unfavorable choices and defy the odds kept his soul alive.

Today, Bryce was at a crossroads, a spiritual one. Yet under God's free will, he was at liberty to go in any direction he chose.

> Good morning. I'll be in Florida til Sunday. How far are u from Kissimmee? Maybe we can link up.

He conducted a brief search of his own before sending the text. Orlando was only thirty-five minutes away. He looked out the window to observe a plane take to the air as he gathered his thoughts. A long exhale emerged from his lips, creating a light condensation on the glass window. Finally, he pressed send.

Only God could sensibly judge him.

∼

MONDAY, DECEMBER 31

Omari was thankful for Officer Thompson. Most of the young security officers were. The retired NYPD police officer agreed to swap shifts with him and another member on staff, meaning the seasoned guard wouldn't lie in his own bed until late Tuesday afternoon. Overnight double duty tours were never fun, but he would rather be the recipient of a hefty paycheck than sit home and watch *The Honeymooners.*

Officer Thompson arrived at the site about thirty minutes early with the MTA operating on a holiday schedule. His promptness would allow Omari to make it home to Shauna and the baby in time for the New Year festivities.

[elevator ring]

Omari made his way back to the lobby after changing into street clothes. The idea of being spotted on public transportation in a security uniform—even at night—made him uneasy. The men conversed for a few minutes before Officer Thompson checked in on his well-being. It was their first conversation since his return from his father's overemotional funeral.

"All right, man, good talk. Happy New Year." Omari waved, hurrying to the revolving glass doors. "I'll try to relieve you early on Wednesday."

"*Try?* Don't play with me. Your ass better be here ten thirty sharp," Officer Thompson teased. "Oh, and stop giving all these women the job number. Somebody asked for you when you were out."

"Who?"

"I forgot the name. I jotted it down on a post-it and left it at the desk. I'm guessing somebody moved it. I gave her your work schedule so she could stop annoying me," he laughed.

"Ten-four."

"Aah, you're getting good at this. Excellent job," Officer Thompson applauded. "Happy New Year. Don't get too drunk, you hear?"

"Nah, I'm good. I'm not really a drinker."

Today, Omari learned all about working the second shift in a busy office building. The afternoons were a different animal compared to overnights, where he was used to dilly-dallying under less watchful eyes and writing music on the company's dime. He spent half of the shift answering calls and aiding building personnel before he'd attend to his rap notebook. He was working on a song dedicated to his father and hoped to finish writing it on the long ride home.

The workday went without incident though he experienced his own round of mystery. This time, a baffling text and an unusual call to the job phone line. Under normal circumstances, he would've written it off as a random wrong number except the caller waited until he answered with the company's standard greeting before hanging up. It could've been coincidental but minutes later he received two head-scratching texts. "I know where you work" and "We need to talk." That was the final straw. A new phone number was necessary, adding it to a lengthy list of priorities set for the upcoming year.

[party horn sounded]

The night sky was foggy, the streets were energetic, and the city lights gleamed. Omari spoke to Shauna on the short walk to Times Square where he bumped into a mob of people heading to the subway. The countdown to the new year was underway.

The guy never came to fix the lock downstairs.

"Did he ever call and say why?"

My uncle called and told me that he had an emergency or something.

"Oh. Is your uncle back?"

No, he's still in St. Kitts. That's why he reached out to the guy. He won't be back until the middle of January.

[Cameron yells in the background]

You wanna speak to Daddy? Huh, BoBo?

"What's up Cammy-Cam? Are you being nice to Mommy?"

You should see him. He's looking around the room for you. "You can't find him? Huh? Where is he?"

[Shauna applies a zerbert to Cameron's stomach]

"Try to keep him awake 'til I get there."

Awake? I'm trying to tire his ass out so I can smoke.

"How much bud do we have left?"

There's enough but we're running low on dutches.

"Okay. I'll pick some up on the way. I'm at the subway. See y'all in a bit."

He walked through the dingy subway concourse seeing the best and worst of the Big Apple. One thing was certain: the city was alive like never before. He approached a standing room only express train, occupying a space by the doors. It is where he stood for the duration of the train ride.

Excuse me, Ladies and Gentlemen...

A foul-smelling panhandler requested the attention of the passengers as the train moved along. Trapped inside a subway car without police presence and a possible loose cannon was usually nerve-wracking but the homeless man gave a tearful speech. His cries were met with blank stares while many on board navigated through their electronic devices. Omari listened intently. Was it plausible the vagabond was nothing more than a failed actor who made a living conning commuters? Sure. The internet was flooded with videos of such scenarios where con men and women returned to their fancy penthouse apartments with loads of cash after a day of deceiving the public. However, this gentleman genuinely looked to have fallen on tough times, and it touched an obvious soft spot. Omari reached into his pocket, pulled out a few singles, and held his breath.

"Thank you, sir," the deeply saddened man replied, pressing his palms together. His hands were as dirty as a mechanic's. Omari exhaled, adjusted his headphones, and continued rehashing the first few lines of the new song.

It's kinda hard to start this song off without getting emotional

You're no longer around just when I started gettin' comfortable
Dialing up those digits hoping to lift your spirit
Now I'm writing lyrics hoping that you'll hear it...

In the blink of an eye, the broad smiles of midtown Manhattan turned into the hardened faces of the Bronx. The distance between the boroughs was a mere eleven miles. At times they felt worlds apart. The worst thing about this trek was transferring from train to bus, especially on nights when the frigid air was unwelcoming. A sharp wind caused Omari's shoulders to shield his neck during the wait. At long last, the bus arrived. He walked to his favorite window seat all the way in the back. Amongst popular belief, the back of the bus signified freedom. He was far away from wandering eyes who could potentially peek at his candor thoughts.

It's kinda hard to start this song off without getting emotional
Shit hit the fan just when I started getting comfortable
Dialing up your digits hoping to lift your spirit
Now I'm writing lyrics hoping that you'll hear it
(They say) Death don't fear it, so I'm tryna remain tearless
With a broken heart and only God can heal it
With time on my side I had to put away the pride
No longer could I deny that I was burning up inside
Angry most of my life–had me feeling betrayed
Upset stomach–y'all kept feeding me grenades
Turned into a ticking time bomb
Didn't feel loved, never found a shoulder to cry on

The bus ride had never gone so fast, but he was delighted to make it back to familiar grounds. It was 11:40 p.m., enough time to run to the store. "Happy New Year" texts poured in from friends and family hoping to get a head start before the satellites jammed. Omari was in the middle of composing a text message of his own when Brixx buzzed in making a last-ditch effort to bait him into attending a New Year's Eve bash at a hole-in-the-wall strip club. The premise: Cheap booze and scores of strippers willing to put out. The last place Omari needed to be. He left the store with a bag of Lay's Barbeque potato chips, a Sprite bottle, and two packs of Dutch Masters' Cigars.

Ahead were the obnoxious honks of an aggravated double-parked driver. A Reggaeton song blared from afar mixed in with a profanity-laced dispute in Spanglish. The uproar produced few stares, but only Omari and a random pedestrian walked toward the fracas.

"Hold on," Omari informed Brixx, sending the now completed text.

My dude, where are you? It's mad loud.

"I'm walking up the block. Even with all the single-family houses we're still sorta in the hood."

Oh. I wouldn't know. I'm in the suburbs.

"The suburbs? We were almost in the middle of a shootout last year," Omari laughed. "Jamaica Ave is right down the street from you."

[Brixx sucks his teeth]

Yo, did one of your old joints get in touch with you at work?

"What'chu mean?"

Somebody named Liz.

"Liz? I haven't spoken to her in a minute. Why'd she call *you?* Oh, probably when I was using your phone at the time."

Probably. She said it was important. I gave her the job number because I know you can't use your cell at work.

"She has my number though."

[Shauna buzzes through on the other line]

"Brixx, hold on... hello?"

Hey. Are you home?

"I'm like a minute away. Why?"

I heard someone walking up the stairs a few minutes ago.

"Hold on a sec. Yo, Brixx, let me call you when I get inside."

All right. One.

"Sorry. You think it was Carlos?"

No, he and his family are out. They left all dressed up about an hour ago.

"Oh. That's strange. Well, I'm at the front of..." A shadowy figure quickly emerged from behind the driver's side of a parked Dodge Charger, turning Omari's attention away from the call. The unidentified person gave a lifeless stare as he walked in the opposite direction, his hands stuffed inside his kangaroo pocket. "Yow-yow," he chanted bizarrely.

Omari? Shauna asked.

"I don't know why this dude was all in my face... anyway, I'm..." Omari turned toward the stairway of the house when another mysterious figure wearing a ski mask and dark clothes bum-rushed him from behind the front door. Omari stared the assailant in the eye and then his mouth opened.

"Oh shit!"

What's wrong?

[gunfire]

Omari's phone and bag of snacks dropped onto the pavement.

[Shauna screams]

Omari? Omari!

The parked vehicle's engine revved; the headlights turned on. The shooter scooped Omari's phone from the ground and hopped in on the passenger side. The car peeled off bypassing the stop sign ahead. The pedestrian who trailed Omari from a distance hurried off in the opposite direction.

Dale and Terri shared a kiss in celebration of the clock striking twelve. She took a sip of wine and placed it on the nightstand.

"All right, enough of this Seacrest fella," Dale said, grabbing the remote control. "I don't know how much more I can take. He ain't no Dick Clark, that's for sure."

"We're losing all the good ones. My goodness," Terri replied.

"I still haven't gotten over Sherman Helmsley's death. That one hurt."

"Seventy-four is a lot of life..."

"Is it? I guess Methuselah didn't get the memo," Dale quipped.

[laughter]

Terri grabbed her Bible to examine the actual age of the biblical patriarch. "It's somewhere in Genesis," Dale continued. She silenced her phone from the ongoing celebratory texts laying eyes on an unexpected one. Her cheeks glowed and her eyes sparkled like Van Gogh's *Starry Night*.

> Son: Happy New Year Mom. Let's talk soon. I love you.
>
> Mon 11:42 p.m.

AUTHOR'S NOTE

Thank you for joining me on this exuberant rollercoaster ride—my second novel and first foray into fictional love stories—following the parallel lives of Bryce Taylor and Omari Harris. *Formidable Affairs* was inspired by real people and true life events, unfolding into an obsessive narrative that became my sanctuary, shielding me from the noise of the world. To every aspiring writer craving an escape: Indulge in daydreams. Grab your laptop (or pen and pad), find a safe space, and allow your mind to be free. *Your* masterpiece awaits you.